P9-DCG-

**Mystery
Award Winner**

Justice at Risk

John Morgan Wilson

Justice at Risk

A Benjamin Justice Mystery

DOUBLEDAY
New York
London
Toronto
Sydney
Auckland

PUBLISHED BY DOUBLEDAY
a division of Random House, Inc.
1540 Broadway, New York, New York 10036

DOUBLEDAY and the portrayal of an anchor with a dolphin are trademarks of
Doubleday, a division of Random House, Inc.

All of the characters in this book are fictitious, and any resemblance to actual persons,
living or dead, is purely coincidental.

Library of Congress Cataloging-in-Publication Data

Wilson, John M., 1945–
Justice at risk: a Benjamin Justice mystery / John Morgan Wilson.
1st ed.
    p.   cm.
I. Title.
PS3573.I456974J8   1999
813'.54—dc21   98–50084
CIP

ISBN 0-385-49116-6
Copyright © 1999 by John Morgan Wilson
All Rights Reserved
Printed in the United States of America
August 1999
First Edition

10 9 8 7 6 5 4 3 2 1

Ingram
7-99
14.23

In Memory of Chris Brownlie

Acknowledgments

As always, I must thank my intrepid agent, Alice Martell, and my sensitive and skillful editor at Doubleday, Judy Kern, for all they have done and continue to do on my behalf.

My gratitude also goes to Dad and Bonnie, for taking so many of my phone calls and questions during the writing on this and that; my aunt and uncle, Betty and Bud Dean, for their golfing acumen and vocabulary skills; to my friend and neighbor, and Sheila Higgins, for her guidance through the world of videotape editing and production, where I have worked myself without quite knowing what I was doing.

Special mention must again be made of the nonprofit AIDS Healthcare Foundation (6255 West Sunset Boulevard, Sixteenth Floor, Los Angeles, CA 90028), which depends on the generosity of donors to continue providing direct medical treatment to thousands of men, women, and children living with HIV and AIDS, regardless of their ability to pay, while keeping overhead and administrative costs to a minimum, and hope alive.

Justice at Risk

Prologue

I'VE HEARD that turning forty is the hardest passage for men. It's such a clear demarcation point in the average male life span—youth gone, middle age looming, physical powers and youthful passion waning, dreams unrealized and starting to feel dishearteningly elusive, while the reality and finality of death begin to insinuate themselves on the consciousness now that the years seem to pass so much more swiftly. Perhaps that's why so many men attempt such desperate transformations as they pass through their forties: dumping mates, leaving families, changing careers, consuming more and more alcohol to numb the fear, as the suffocation of routine and the shock of shattered illusions leave them trembling deep inside where we men keep our private truths so well hidden.

My fortieth year was not like that. Most of my close friends were gone by then, having died suddenly or faded miserably away beginning in the early eighties, many of them well before their fortieth birthdays. This wholesale loss of friends, and the rapid succession of funerals and memorials that followed, is something men and women are supposed to experience piecemeal over several decades as they grow older, with enough healing time in between to allow for genuine grieving when the next death notice comes. Yet more and more in my world, it was the lucky survivors who buried the young, with numbing regularity, as in a long war.

My landlords, Maurice and Fred, together now for almost five decades, were among those who attended selflessly to the dying and the dead. I stood dutifully if more aloofly beside them, saluting the fallen long after my tears were spent, until I lost Jacques, the one who mattered most to me, and the tears came back in a torrent, erupting from somewhere within me I previously had no knowledge of, with such wild force I was left shaken to my soul. My shameful reaction was to write a fictitious series of newspaper articles about a young man dying, cared for by his lover, but changing enough of the cold, harsh facts to create a warm fantasy I foolishly felt I might live with. I wrote with such desperate guilt that many people were moved by the articles, by their strange power, and a great prize was awarded to me that I was later forced to return when my pathetic act of fraud was exposed. After that, I shut myself away, hiding from the plague that had consumed us both in different ways, burying the pain, embracing denial like a sedative, and seriously afraid I would go mad if I attempted to participate in a world that went merrily about its business while so many suffered so horribly and died so young.

Then, after several years, I was turning forty. Why I had survived—uninfected by the virus, no less—was something unanswerable, as impenetrable as the notion of fate. To a generation of men like me, the age of forty was an unexpected threshold, and the possibility of reaching fifty a near miracle. It came upon us like a burst of sunlight illuminating a path in a dark forest where we had become utterly lost, never expecting to emerge. I realize this may sound overly dramatic, needlessly exaggerated, to those who were not directly involved in the plague that swept my particular community. I realize also that many people are simply tired of hearing about it. I cannot help that. It was a terrible, terrible time.

So I turned forty, with life ahead, but without the usual markers behind me. I had no career to change; to even think in those terms was laughable. I had no real family to abandon, only the faint outlines of one, made up of others, like myself, who had no close families in the traditional sense. There was no central relationship in my life; I had made sure of that by falling safely in love with the most improbable partners, or those for whom death was imminent, a guarantee the union would be brief, the loss expected, preordained. I was nearly without possessions, certainly without goals or dreams. The millennium was quickly approaching, with its own inevitable momentum and change, reminding me that forty was merely a number without much meaning in the great scheme of things.

In an odd way, with such a messy life behind me, turning forty felt like the end of a long, troubled childhood, and the brink of a bright adventure. It was a milestone that marked the end of the long crisis, a time for celebration, renewal.

Maurice and Fred wanted to throw a little party—Maurice, of course, never forgot a birthday or an anniversary, and loved nothing better than the gathering of friends. The idea was to invite Harry Brofsky, who had once been my editor at the *Los Angeles Times* and had managed to forgive my journalistic transgressions, even though they had nearly destroyed his own career; Alexandra Templeton, a young reporter at the less respected *Los Angeles Sun,* where Harry now worked as her editor, and with whom I had become friends; and one or two others whom I saw from time to time. Predictably, I begged off, finding arranged social gatherings not just awkward, but almost unbearable.

So Maurice and Fred climbed the old wooden stairs to the small apartment over the garage that I called home, and invited me down to the house for dinner. We celebrated afterward with a delicious sponge cake Maurice had baked that afternoon, frosted white and decorated with colored sprinkles, and festooned with a single tiny candle. Maurice led the way, and we took our plates out to the front porch, where we sat in the swing in the peace of the early autumn evening, looking out on Norma Place as our West Hollywood neighbors passed in the twilight, with the dog and the two cats curled up at our feet or in our laps.

That was how I quietly entered my forties, and began a year in which two men, each improbably beautiful and appealing in his own way, would come into my life and turn it in a profoundly new direction, while the cold shadow of violence returned, darkening my existence as it never had before.

One

A COOL SPRING RAIN fell throughout the afternoon, cleansing the city, and when the skies cleared at dusk, the streets glistened and sparkled in the changing light.

It was a Sunday, early March. I drove to Little Ethiopia with the top down, south along Fairfax Avenue, listening to a tape of *soukous*, Congolese rhumba. It featured the great Zaïrian vocalist Nyboma, and had been a gift from my friend Alexandra Templeton. The music was jubilant and rousing, a hot mix of rhythmic guitars punctuated by brilliant drum passages that sounded Cuban and got my pulse pounding. It suited my mood; for the first time in years, I was feeling reasonably good about things.

The dinner was also on Templeton, who was bringing with her an advance copy of the April issue of *Gentleman's Quarterly. GQ,* as it was better known, had once been a lightweight fashion rag whose most devoted readership was comprised of gay men who liked to ogle the gorgeous male models in the designer clothing spreads. In more recent years, *GQ* had grown considerably in scope and stature, regularly running articles of substance along with the usual Hollywood pop culture claptrap that had come to clutter up so many of the national slicks, but without entirely losing its underlying homosexual sensibility. The April issue carried an article by Templeton, her first major magazine piece, for which she had been paid the astounding sum of $10,000—astounding by my personal standards, at least, and remarkable, I felt, for a youthful reporter like Templeton, who still spent the bulk of her working time covering the crime beat for the *Los Angeles Sun*. But then, Templeton had scored an exclusive, pitching *GQ* a story no one else had, or could get, about an elusive subject the editors apparently felt many readers were eager to fathom. The subject was me.

I crossed Olympic Boulevard into the vintage commercial zone that served as the culinary heart of the Ethiopian community in Los Angeles, which was dominated, like Ethiopia itself, by the Amharas, the Christian peoples of the highlands. Back in the eighties, before I had self-destructed as a reporter, I had written a series for the *Los Angeles Times* on the political conflicts that had torn the motherland apart, causing tens of thousands to flee to Southern California and elsewhere, looking for a better life. Some of the details were coming back to me, a welcome indicator that after nearly a decade of wallowing in alcohol, depression, and self-pity, my brain wasn't a total wasteland.

As I reached the crosswalk that divided the long block, the angular squiggles of the Amharic alphabet shared sign space with lettering in English, and the air was heavily scented by frankincense and myrrh. The neighborhood had been Danish in the nineteen forties, Jewish in the fifties and sixties, then Asian well into the eighties, with the city's first Vietnamese restaurant nestled among a number of Chinese cafes. In the nineties, Ethiopian émigrés ushered in a new ethnic identity by opening a scattering of Amharic-flavored boutiques, restaurants, and one or two espresso bars that served dark, rich coffee brewed in the traditional way from bright green beans imported from their homeland, where *Coffea arabica* was a native plant.

Templeton and I had eaten here on a few occasions in the past year, as our friendship gradually deepened. While I had consumed more of an Ethiopian beer called Orit than was good for me during our last visit, I had apparently not behaved so badly as to rule out a return invitation. The restaurant Templeton had chosen this time was called Addis Ababa, after the Ethiopian capital that had once been one of civilization's great centers of commerce and culture. I found it near the end of the block, occupying a large corner space. I slipped the old Mustang into an available slot and put the top up. A minute later I was stepping into a foyer designed with a thatched roof, where the atmosphere was aromatic with the spicy kitchen smells of ginger and red pepper, cardamom and rue seed, and in the background, flute-like music floated. Within moments, I was welcomed by a dusky-skinned, middle-aged woman wearing an embroidered white cotton dress and flowing shawl, in the Ethiopian tradition. She showed me to a small round table near the back, which turned out to be a large drum covered with goatskin, propped up on a goat's feet and legs, which were anchored to the body of the drum. Templeton, usually a teetotaler, was sipping a glass of *t'ej,* the Ethiopian honey wine distilled from the *gesho* herb that I had amply sampled on one of our earlier dinner dates. The hostess asked me if I cared to order the same, or one of several Ethiopian grape wines the restaurant carried. I declined, and asked for coffee. She nodded, smiled, and went to get it.

I sat on a hand-carved wooden chair, resting my elbows on the tanned hide of the deceased goat, and gazed into Templeton's extraordinary face. With her striking bone structure and dark beauty, she might have been an African princess sitting there, although she had recently given up the long braids she had been wearing the day Harry Brofsky introduced us not quite three years ago. Now, her dark hair was cut into a boyish bob, accentuating her large brown eyes and delicate, shapely mouth, and making her look younger than her twenty-seven years.

She regarded me curiously.

"Not drinking tonight?"

"Not for a while, actually."

Her eyes widened.

"When did you quit?"

"I didn't say I quit."

"Oh."

I shrugged.

"It's been a few weeks."

She leaned over to survey my body.

"It shows."

"I've been working out a little."

"You? At the gym?"

"I said I was working out a little, Templeton. I didn't say I'd lost my sanity."

"The gym's not such a bad place, Justice. Who knows? You might meet someone interesting there."

"A remote possibility, I suppose."

She smiled mischievously.

"Afraid of the competition?"

"With what? All those mirrors?"

She laughed, then paused significantly.

"So. *Are* you seeing anyone?"

I shook my head, feeling my fair skin starting to flush, and happy to find the coffee arriving. The hostess set a round tray with three cups on the table. I was surprised to see the third cup. Also on the tray was a small tin saucepan, a *miqhat;* a black clay pot, or *jabana,* rounded at the bottom and resting on a donut-shaped pillow to keep it upright; a tin brazier, filled with glowing charcoal; and a single piece of burning charcoal in a small copper bowl, on top of which rested a lump of myrrh, its pale smoke rising to sweetly scent the air. The hostess filled the bottom of the *miqhat* with green coffee beans, breathed life into the charcoal by waving a woven straw fan, then stirred the beans over the brazier until they were roasted darkly. She brewed the coffee in the *jabana* and when she felt it was ready, began pouring the steaming brown liquid into the small cups.

After filling the second one, she turned to Templeton.

"Will your other friend be joining us soon?"

"He's been delayed. Just pour two for now, please."

The other woman smiled, set the *jabana* back on its pillow, handed each of us a filled cup, and departed again.

Templeton raised her cup to mine, and we toasted.

"Here's to the halfway point in your fortieth year, Benjamin, which seems to have started out quite well." Her eyes swept over me again, looking gratified. "I see that you've even invested in a new wardrobe."

"I used some of the magazine money we earned together last year. The jeans and T-shirts were wearing thin."

"Nice change. Also, the beard. Thick, blond, nicely trimmed. I like it."

"To compensate for the disappearing hair."

She patted the small bald spot on the top of my head.

"Still, a far cry from the grungy Justice I used to know."

I sipped my coffee, but kept my eyes on hers.

"The hostess mentioned a third person."

Templeton attempted a shrug that fell flat under the weight of its insincerity.

"Just a friend."

"Anyone I know?"

"Not really."

"Does this friend have a name?"

"Oree. Oree Joffrien."

"A date?"

"Not exactly."

Whenever Templeton used the words *not exactly*, my radar started looking for mysterious missiles.

"You didn't mention a third person. That's not like you, Templeton. You're usually quite thorough and precise."

"I guess I forgot."

"That's not like you, either."

"You haven't asked about the *GQ* piece." She reached into her big handbag, fumbling for the magazine. "That's the whole purpose for our getting together tonight."

"Is it?"

Our eyes met; hers moved away.

"If you must know, Oree's a professor at UCLA. Anthropology. Very smart, and genuinely sweet, once you get to know him." She laughed uneasily. "Also, quite good-looking. Here it is. The *GQ.*"

She handed it across. Gracing the cover was the face of a pretty young actor who appeared, though in his mid-twenties, to be stuck permanently in mid-puberty, and in need of hormone shots. Apparently, the megastar of the moment. I set the magazine aside.

"Aren't you going to look at it?"

"Later, maybe."

"I figured you'd be crazy with anticipation."

"Not really."

"Are you mad at me, Justice? For writing it?"

"You asked my permission beforehand, which was gracious of you. I didn't ask you not to."

"You didn't exactly give me your blessing, either."

"It wasn't my place to stand in your way, Templeton. You're a journalist, and a grown woman. Readers love to revisit a good scandal. As they say, it's a free country."

"It isn't just a rehash of the Pulitzer scandal, Ben. It goes all the way back to your childhood, then forward, through your relationship with Jacques when he was dying. It puts things in perspective."

"I'm sure you wrote a fine piece, Alex."

"I really appreciate your support."

"Don't mistake it for support."

"You are mad at me."

"Don't mistake ambivalence for anger." I sipped more of the rich, dark coffee. "Now, tell me about this person who's having dinner with us, this Oree fellow, before I begin to suspect I've been set up with a blind date."

Her eyes flickered defensively. She reached across and placed her hand on the magazine.

"You'll read the article and tell me what you think?"

"Quit stalling."

"You're not going to be upset, are you? Even if, just by the slightest coincidence, he turns out to be gay and unattached."

"Damn you, Templeton."

"Promise me you won't be unpleasant."

"I wasn't put on this earth to please people, Templeton, any more than a self-respecting author writes books to please critics."

She sighed heavily, settled back in her chair, picked up her wine, frowned, put it down, selected her coffee instead.

"I met him at a conference of African American journalists."

"I thought you said he was an academic."

"He does some freelance writing on the side. High-level stuff. *Harper's, The American Scholar,* the *New York Times* op-ed page. He's younger than you, only thirty-six, but he can be just as intimidating. Somehow we hit it off right away."

"Let me guess—you were on the rebound."

"I'd just broken up with that point guard from the Lakers."

"The one with the big hands."

If Templeton had been fair-skinned like me, I'm certain her face would have been a raging wildfire.

"Right." She smiled sheepishly. "The big hands."

"So you broke up with the point guard, and ran into this Oree fellow."

"Oree Joffrien. I believe it's French. His father's Creole, from down around New Orleans. Mother's Malaysian. He has an interesting look."

"If he's as cute as Tiger Woods—"

Templeton put up a hand.

"Please don't mention Tiger Woods, Justice. It's a touchy issue with Oree. You know, the Asian thing."

"I'm afraid I don't."

"Certain people make a point of emphasizing that Tiger Woods is half Asian, as if that might be the reason he's so smart and personable. They never do that when it's a black guy who's in trouble. You never hear them say, 'Oh, that murderer has light skin. Must be the white blood in him that made him kill.' Oree says they only question your blackness when you've accomplished something, never the other way around."

"Anything else you need to tell me?"

"When he gets here, try not to drool."

"He's that good-looking?"

"Spectacular would not be overstating it."

"Let me take a wild guess, Templeton. Being on the rebound, which is most of the time, you fell immediately in lust, and you still haven't quite come out of it."

"It wasn't like that, I swear."

"What was it like?"

"I really *liked* him, Justice. We got along so easily. He's interested in politics, social issues, race, all the things that matter to me. He's even a fan of straight-ahead jazz, like me." She laughed awkwardly. "And, well, like you."

I tried to keep my voice from grating.

"Go on."

"We went out a few times. Dinner, a movie, coffee afterward. We became friends very quickly—that should have been a tip-off right away that he wasn't straight." She shrugged, and sighed again. "Not with my luck, anyway."

"He sounds perfect."

She sat forward, brightening.

"He is, Justice! Did I mention that he's quite good-looking? Not that it would matter to you, of course."

"As a matter of fact, you did. Twice."

"I hate it when you get that edge in your voice."

"I hate it when you attempt to engineer my life."

"I think I've done a pretty good job so far. With Harry's help."

I wasn't amused, and didn't pretend to be. I finished my coffee, fixing Templeton with my most malevolent stare. Suddenly, her eyes darted with relief across the restaurant, toward the entrance.

"There he is now!" She raised her long, slim arm, waving a hand. "Oree! Over here!"

Templeton hadn't been exaggerating when she'd used the word *spectacular* to describe Oree Joffrien. He was roughly my height, six feet, maybe an inch taller, with a lean, lanky frame and surprisingly broad shoulders that tapered to a waist so narrow it suggested that his upper body might topple. The attractive frame was draped in a stylish, loose-fitting, dark brown jacket, a brightly patterned tie against an off-white dress shirt, and pleated, tawny-colored slacks that floated slightly as he moved. I figured his soft loafers for Italian, and probably expensive. His motion had the ease and grace of an athlete, reminiscent of the finest runners—those in the long-legged events, like the hurdles, or the four hundred meters.

For all that, it was his remarkable face that riveted my eye: molasses brown, clean-shaven, with piercing dark eyes set at an attractive slant, hinting at the Asian blood I'd been cautioned not to mention. His cheekbones arched dramatically, like his dark brows and oddly pointed ears, toward a smooth-domed head shaved clean. His nose was broad and blunt, and his upper lip voluptuously large, shaped sensually like the double-curved crown of a valentine heart. With his keen, narrow eyes and un-smiling mouth, he looked almost fierce. Not a scowl, exactly; more like a statement of pride, challenging anyone to think otherwise. What some with small minds might call supreme confidence in a white man, and arrogance in a man who was black.

As he made his way in our direction, Templeton leaned across the table and said quickly: "I didn't find out until our third date that he's gay. How was I supposed to know? He's so masculine."

"I thought that stereotype died with Rock Hudson."

She made a quick face, then smiled as we stood to meet Oree Joffrien. The hostess was right behind him, bringing menus. Templeton introduced us and we shook hands—single grip, the old-fashioned way, which seemed to be coming back into style—but he barely looked at me as we sat down. Without being asked, he ordered a bottle of Congolese beer called Ngok'. The menus were handed around, and they kept us busy for a minute or two. Joffrien was apparently well acquainted with the cuisine—it was he, I learned, who had suggested we meet at the Addis Ababa—and Templeton asked him for recommendations.

"Both the *wat'* and the *alich'a* are quite good. They're both spicy beef stews—red peppers in the *wat'*, green peppers in the *alich'a*." Joffrien's voice was deep, rich, and cultured, with a trace of Louisiana bayou country. "I'm told the *kitfo* is also quite good here, though it's beef served raw. If you'd prefer it lightly fried, ask for *lebleb.*"

Templeton made a face at the mention of uncooked beef.

"I'm suddenly feeling veggie."

"You might try the lentil salad then. They season it with chopped shallots, lime, minced ginger root, and serrano chiles. Tasty, and fairly substantial."

She slapped her menu shut.

"You've made up my mind. Justice?"

I closed my menu as well.

"I'll try the beef *t'ibs,*" I said evenly, referring to a braised dish served with a hot red chile paste on the side.

Joffrien raised his eyebrows in understated salute.

"You're the adventurous type."

"Or maybe just independent-minded."

His penetrating eyes settled calmly on mine.

"Admirable, either way."

"To a point," Templeton put in. "Justice has a way of taking things to extremes."

"I got that impression when I read the *GQ* piece."

This time, my eyebrows did the arching, though less pleasantly.

"You've already seen Templeton's article?"

"She faxed me a copy this morning. Thought it might be a good icebreaker when we met this evening." He glanced her way, as calm and composed as a Buddha, but with the trace of an ironic smile softening his formidable face. "That was the way you put it, wasn't it, Alex?"

I shot Templeton a glance sharp enough to slice a cheap steak. She responded with a sheepish look, as the hostess arrived with

Joffrien's beer to take our orders. When that was accomplished, and she was gone, an awkward silence fell over us. Joffrien sipped his beer thoughtfully, stared into the distance a moment, then turned purposefully in my direction.

"Alex tells me you might be looking for a writing assignment."

"I'm always looking for a writing assignment. Given my history, they're not easy to come by."

"It was my impression you were doing fairly well."

"I've managed a few freelance magazine pieces lately. Mostly nonmainstream, publications like *Out* and *Poz*. That's about it."

"You don't sound all that happy about the way it's going."

"I'm grateful for the work."

"The assignments aren't meaty enough?"

"I'm getting strictly color pieces, offbeat features, usually on the seamy side. As if my checkered past enables me to bring something special to tawdry subject matter, but also limits me to it. I'm becoming a journalistic oddity, the reporter tainted by scandal, and I'm not sure I like that. On the other hand, I made my bed, so I have to sleep in it, don't I?"

"Restlessly, it seems."

Joffrien's eyes had never left mine; I felt strangely connected to him, almost against my will.

"I've always been restless. And you? Does academia suit you?"

Instead of answering, he looked up as the hostess returned, accompanied by a slim, handsome waiter with the same dusky skin, who served plates all around, and placed bowls of side dishes in the center of the table. We ate in the traditional way: with our fingers, using swatches of *injera* bread in place of utensils, mopping up the rich, spicy pastes and sauces with the meat and vegetables. During a long silence, I caught Joffrien exchanging a glance with Templeton. A moment later, he spoke offhandedly, without looking up from his food.

"I have a friend, a television producer, who might have a project for you."

I swiped at the red chile paste on my plate, fed the peppery *injera* into my mouth, and chewed, saying nothing. Joffrien pushed his point.

"Have you ever considered working in television?"

"Not for a moment."

"Justice considers television the death knell of civilization."

"My friend, Cecile Chang, does some interesting work. Documentaries mostly, funded by grants. At the moment, she's producing a nine-part series for PBS."

"What's her topic?"

"AIDS." He hesitated, as if to let the word sink in. "From what I read in *GQ*, you might bring something special to the subject—some interesting insights."

"I'm afraid my credibility is suspect."

"Cecile's a maverick. She likes to take chances on people, looks for the alternative viewpoint. When she did a series on prisons, she hired an ex-con to write one of the segments."

"Sounds like an interesting lady."

"I'd be happy to give her a call."

"Thanks, but I don't know the slightest thing about writing a television script."

"Neither did the ex-con. Cecile gave him the guidance he needed. He won a Peabody Award."

"He didn't have to give it back, did he?"

Joffrien grinned, and shook his head.

"No, Ben, he didn't have to give it back."

Templeton leaned forward on her elbows, her hands folded optimistically.

"At least you could talk to her, Benjamin."

"I guess I could do that."

She beamed. Joffrien didn't move a muscle, just kept his reassuring eyes on me, as if giving me whatever time I needed. Accepting kindness, even simple compliments, had never been easy for me; I had grown up tasting love in the form of scraps, handed out on loan, attached to debts and expectations. I believe Joffrien sensed that instinctively; perhaps he'd even read something of it in Templeton's *GQ* profile, and remembered. Whatever the reason, he exuded patience and understanding. I was beginning to see why Templeton had fallen so hard for him so fast.

"I appreciate the offer, Oree."

His voice became warm, his words slow.

"Not at all. Cecile's an old friend."

Templeton clapped her hands.

"Just like the three of us!" Suddenly, she was standing, looking very pleased with the way things had gone. "I hate to be a party pooper, but I'm afraid I'm going to have to leave you two to have dessert without me."

I looked up, perplexed.

"You're leaving already?"

"I've got a shot at a plum assignment. Editorial meeting first thing in the morning. I want to be well prepared."

I stood, worried as much about the check as being left alone with Oree Joffrien. I had no credit card—hadn't for years—and was carrying barely enough cash for a tip.

"It's not that late, Templeton. Stay awhile."

"I've got a ton of notes to go over, Justice. Harry's going to choose a lead reporter to cover the selection process for the new police chief. I think I've got the inside track, and I don't want to blow it."

Joffrien stood and helped her on with her coat.

"From what I hear, with an African American chief suddenly retiring, the old boys' club sees an opportunity to get the first white chief appointed since Daryl Gates."

"That's one of the issues, for sure."

Joffrien's smile turned sly.

"The one no one wants to talk about."

Templeton grinned.

"Maybe the *Sun* will change that."

"We'll keep our fingers crossed for you."

She and Joffrien hugged, and she kissed him on the cheek. When she embraced me, her lips were close to my ear, whispering.

"Don't worry about the check. It was all taken care of in advance."

"You really planned this well, didn't you?"

"Just have a good time, OK?"

She kissed me quickly and left us. Joffrien and I watched her disappear out to the street, where headlights and taillights crisscrossed in the deepening darkness.

Joffrien moved first, retaking his chair, refilling my cup.

"She's full of surprises, isn't she?"

"Templeton? More and more."

When he'd warmed my cup, he refilled his own, and we began to talk. An hour later, I realized that the sole subject of conversation had been me. Joffrien had skillfully steered the discussion back to Templeton's *GQ* piece, my childhood in Buffalo, my unfortunate flirtation with patricide, and the subsequent deaths, to alcohol and drugs respectively, of my mother and sister. It wasn't territory I was eager to reexplore, yet Joffrien had coaxed me through the entire story—including my fast rise in the journalism world after college, straight through to the fabricated *L.A. Times* series that had won me the Pulitzer eight years ago, along with a ruined reputation when I'd been found out. In his steady, mesmerizing way, Joffrien kept me talking until I was speaking falteringly of my relationship with Harry Brofsky, my onetime mentor, who had maneuvered me three years ago into teaming up with Templeton on a reporting assignment.

Joffrien folded his long fingers under his chin, regarding me thoughtfully.

"You survived. You've got friends, your health—a lot to be grateful for."

"I suppose that's true. Harry and Templeton try to remind me of it when I forget."

His smile was comforting, almost paternal.

"Things, as they say, could be worse."

"And what about you, Oree? Happy with the way life has gone?"

His steady gaze shifted, almost imperceptibly.

"All in all, no serious complaints. Though I'm not saying there aren't things I'd change if I could."

"We met more than two hours ago, and I have yet to hear about even one of those things. I know almost nothing about you."

He glanced at his watch, then pushed back his chair, and stood.

"Another time, maybe. Like Templeton, I've got a busy day tomorrow."

As I rose, I told him that Templeton had taken care of the check, something he already knew. We thanked the hostess, and stepped outside, where we stood listening to an outrageous jazz recording coming from a small cafe two doors away. I cocked an ear, as the musician performed a devilish dance up and down the scales with his saxophone.

"That's quite an ax."

"James Carter, if I'm not mistaken."

"You've got a sharper ear than I do, Oree."

"It's a passion of mine."

Another half minute passed, each second ticking pointedly away. The fine jazz continued, but I sensed that neither of us was listening to it quite so keenly now. Finally, I took a deep breath, gathering my courage.

"Maybe we can catch a concert some night. Make an evening of it."

"Sounds like a possibility."

The night sky had clouded over again, and a cold wind gusted along the street, suggesting another storm. Joffrien turned up the collar of his jacket and hugged himself, looking vulnerable for the first time.

"I should have brought a topcoat. I need to be more careful."

I put a hand on his arm, rubbing it warm.

"It's really not that late. Do you have to be on your way?"

He smiled apologetically.

"Everything in its time, Ben. If it's meant to be."

"Fair enough."

We'd exchanged phone numbers inside, and there didn't seem to be a lot more to say. Joffrien prepared his departure.

"I'll call Cecile first thing in the morning. Give her your number. I'm sure she'll be in touch."

"Where did you say you knew her from?"

"I didn't, actually." He was stepping away, on the verge of turning. "Let's talk soon."

Then I was watching him move away in long, loose strides, toward the corner, and around it. A section of newspaper scuttled by me in the gutter, rattling dryly against the curb before being caught in a puddle, where it struggled but finally settled helplessly into the oily rainwater.

From an adjoining neighborhood, I heard the wail of a police siren, reaching across the streets and boundaries, searing the cold night with auditory heat, like a cry of pain from a distant stranger.

Two

T HE NEXT AFTERNOON, I drove to Studio City and a
scheduled appointment with Cecile Chang.

I took the narrow, four-lane road that winds from West Hollywood through leafy Laurel Canyon, passing crumbling cabins
and faded ranch houses once owned by legendary movie stars,
following the flow of traffic up to the crest at Mulholland Drive,
then down into the flatlands of the triangular San Fernando Valley.

Chang's offices were housed in a smallish, older, two-story
building on Ventura Boulevard that looked drab and a bit forlorn
compared to the flashy new business towers rising up a block or
two down the street. The rear of the old building butted up
against a wide alley that separated it from CBS Studio Center,
which had been the home of Republic Studios in the thirties and
forties, when the company was grinding out hundreds of B West-
erns with the likes of John Wayne, Gene Autry, and Roy Rogers
riding the purple sage of the vast back lot. Some of the original
soundstages remained, along with a cluster of quaint bungalows,
but most of the back lot had long ago been sold off and subdi-
vided for freeway ramps and middle-class suburban homes. I
found a parking space on a shady side street, and hiked back to

the business district on the boulevard, where parking was scarce and costly.

The storm of the night before had passed, leaving in its wake a blustery breeze, high clouds, and a postnuclear glare that had me slipping on my dark glasses as I emerged from the protection of oak and eucalyptus trees. The temperature in the Valley is invariably ten degrees warmer than in the rest of the city, and by the time I reached Chang's building, my body was weeping with sweat. A sign out front announced the name of her company: New Image Productions. I pulled open one of the glass double doors and stepped into a modest but pleasant, plant-filled lobby, decorated with framed posters advertising several of Chang's film and television projects, along with a number of commendations and awards, including an Oscar nomination for best feature-length documentary. There was a mustiness about the place that suggested an old building ventilated by windows that actually opened, letting in real air. It felt quaint and hospitable, and oddly refreshing.

A receptionist looked up from behind a moon-shaped counter as I entered. He was a perky young man with lavender spiked hair, an assortment of piercings, fluttery hands, and a lively lisp that hissed like a greenhouse misting hose each time an *s* got involved. He put down a copy of *Details*, took my name, picked up the phone, announced my arrival, and hung up, all in a matter of seconds.

"Cecile's upstairs," he said, hissing madly while he extended his hand to examine his sequined nails, "shooting some footage for a fund-raising video. She'll be down soonish. Plant your tush and stay awhile."

I found a seat, picked up a copy of *Video Review,* and began idly leafing through it. The receptionist glanced over without turning his shoulders, like a diva showing off her good side, and asked me if I cared for a glass of water while I waited. I told him that would be nice.

"I'm afraid it's tap," he said, as he returned with ice cubes and water in a frosty glass. "Our current budget doesn't allow for the bottled kind. No Evian served here!"

"Tap will do just fine."

He responded by tap-dancing his way blithely back to his desk,

stopping midway to perform a full spin and a nifty soft-shoe routine in his retro platforms, which couldn't have been easy.

"My name's Harold, by the way."

"Ben."

"Ooh. Big Ben, maybe?"

"Just Ben, thanks."

"I have a special nickname myself."

"Ah."

"Maybe I'll share it with you sometime. If we become friends."

"I can hardly wait."

I turned back to the magazine.

"Aren't you going to at least guess?"

"Harry?"

"You're getting warm." He wagged a finger at me. "No more
guessing. I'll surprise you when we achieve the proper level of
intimacy, which hopefully will be sooner than later. In the meantime, it's just plain old Harold."

I smiled, and turned some pages. When Harold was seated
again, he sneaked a glance in my direction, got caught, smiled
coyly, then busied himself with the day's mail while humming
"We Shall Survive."

Several minutes later, a woman in a hand-driven wheelchair
appeared in the hallway to my left, coming my way. She was
middle-aged, with bifocals, a pleasant, weary smile, and no legs;
her plaid skirt was pulled down and tucked up under her knees at
the stumps.

"Mr. Justice?"

"That would be me."

I stood.

"I'm Denise, Cecile's assistant. She can see you now."

Harold waved bye-bye with his extremely flexible wrist while
Denise performed a deft one-eighty in the chair. I followed her
back down the hall, around a corner, and all the way to the end of
the next corridor. Along the way, I glimpsed small, cluttered
offices filled with people at work, most of them under thirty,
many in front of video viewing screens. Denise stopped her chair
outside an open door.

"Go right in. She's expecting you."

Before I was through the door, Cecile Chang was standing

behind her desk across the room, then coming around it. Behind her was a window that faced west across a small parking lot in which every space was taken. Her office was roughly twice the size of the others I'd glimpsed; nearly every inch was stacked with videocassettes, scripts, or file drawers, but all of it appeared to be necessary and well organized. On her desk was a PC, surrounded by neat stacks of documents and other papers, and on the credenza behind it, a framed photograph of an Italian-looking woman with short-cropped hair and a cocky grin. An entire wall to my right was devoted to a chart heavily marked in different colors of erasable ink, which accounted for the peculiar chemical odor that permeated the room. Stenciled at the top in bold letters was the title *"AIDS 2000."* Underneath the chart was a long couch that looked sturdy but well used.

"Mr. Justice. Welcome."

Cecile Chang appeared to be Chinese or Korean, as her name suggested, and on the tall side for an Asian woman, in the range of five-six to five-seven, not counting her three-inch classic pumps. She was wispishly slim, with shapely legs and an exquisite face, her dark hair pulled back and done up in an elaborate bun. Her face was carefully made up, including lips blushed in subtle pink and around her dark eyes lines of mascara so fine and understated they might easily have been missed. A delicate bracelet of gold-encrusted jade stones graced one of her slim wrists, matching a pair of oval stone earrings clipped to her delicate lobes. Her business suit was soft gray and well cut, almost elegant, buttoned all the way to her neck, where a dark green silk scarf was loosely knotted. She seemed overdressed for both the work and the weather, but fashion statements were something I'd never pretended to understand.

We shook hands in the middle of the room; hers was soft and slightly moist. She asked me to take a seat facing her across the desk. I put my notebook in one chair, and settled into the other. When she was seated, she folded her pale, fine-boned hands in front of her and spoke with her pointed chin slightly lifted.

"Oree speaks highly of you, Mr. Justice."

"You're aware that he barely knows me."

"I trust his judgment as if it were my own."

"The two of you must be close, then."

"We go back quite a few years."

"To childhood?"

"Not that far. We met in the late eighties, as graduate students at New York University. He was pursuing his doctorate in anthropology. I was finishing my master's in film. We became very good friends."

"It was kind of him to call you on my behalf."

"You're available for work?"

"Between assignments, you might say."

"As you must know, Mr. Justice, writing fact-based television scripts is quite different from writing for print. Among other things, one must learn to write for the ear rather than the eye, for the viewer and listener rather than the reader. It's essential to let the pictures do much of the work while keeping the words to a minimum, all the while paying careful attention to structure, such as scene beats and multiple act breaks. Timing is also important, right down to the split second in many cases."

"Sounds challenging."

"It can be quite frustrating for a prose writer such as yourself, who's accustomed to churning out reams of copy, with only the occasional photo along the way for visual support."

"Maybe I'm the wrong man for the job."

"Not at all, Mr. Justice. I look for the enterprising writer with an interesting background, a different viewpoint—someone who can bring something unique and personal to the work. I'm willing to work with writers new to the medium such as yourself, providing the editorial guidance and production support they need."

"That's very generous."

She smiled.

"There is a downside, of course."

I smiled with equanimity.

"There always is."

"The pay isn't that high, and the workload is intense. This isn't network television and union scale we're talking about. If you decide to sign on, your contract would call for a fee of twelve thousand dollars, paid out in six installments as you complete various drafts and versions of the show, from the script outline to the final off-line edit before your segment goes to on-line."

"I'm afraid those terms mean nothing to me."

She stood, smiling more warmly.

"You won't be expected to learn everything at once." She came around the desk, picked up a pointer, and moved over to the big wall chart. "The six steps in our writing and producing process generally require four months, which includes some downtime here and there, while we review what the writer has done. I should warn you up front that either one of us can terminate the agreement after any one of the six stages, if we sense things aren't working out. It's a safeguard we feel is necessary with untested talent. At the same time, it offers you a way out if you're unhappy for some reason, or if a better opportunity arises."

"Sounds fair enough."

I rose and stood beside her as she pointed up at the chart.

"Each of these columns represents one of the nine episodes in the series New Image is producing for the Public Broadcasting System. It's an ambitious project—probing key issues and examining the scope and impact of AIDS as we enter the new millennium."

"A subject an awful lot of people have grown tired of."

"Exactly why I'm producing it, Mr. Justice."

The tip of her pointer ran across the nine working titles: *AIDS at Home (U.S.)*, *Does the Public Still Care?*, *New Treatments/New Hope*, *The Funding Dilemma*, *Has Prevention Worked?*, *The Bareback Sex Issue*, *The Commercialization of AIDS*, *Fund-Raising Successes and Scandals*, *The Grim Global Picture*. Listed at the top of each column, under the show's working title, were the names of the writer and segment producer. In a few cases, she explained, the writer and producer were the same. The six squares of each column represented the six stages of script development; all but one of the shows were assigned and apparently well under way, with most of the squares checked off.

Her pointer landed on the sixth column.

"I assigned the bareback sex show several weeks ago to Tommy Callahan, an experienced videotape editor who's wanted to move into writing and production. He presented an intelligent proposal on the issue, seemed insightful about it. You're familiar with the term 'riding bareback'?"

"If you're referring to bareback sex, you're talking about people who refuse to use condoms while fucking, despite the risks."

"Our episode examines that, as well as the phenomenon of gay men in general who continue to engage in unsafe sexual activity."

"Statistically, heterosexuals are being infected at a faster rate these days. Especially teenagers. If I'm not mistaken, that's been the case for some time."

She pointed to the first column, then to the fifth.

"We're dealing with that in two other segments, in some detail. Our bareback sex segment gets to the heart of an especially troubling issue within the community where the epidemic has so far had the most devastating impact. It's one of our more sensitive and controversial episodes, and we've fallen behind schedule on it. That's where I hope you'll be able to help out."

"This Callahan—how far along is he?"

She told me that Callahan had taped most of his interviews and gathered together many of the visuals he needed, or assigned camera crews to shoot more footage. But he'd broken down at the writing stage, falling behind schedule.

"After the first draft, it became clear that Tommy's not a skilled enough writer and lacks the journalistic instincts to handle such an assignment. I'd like you to take over the writing of the script, get it into shape, get us back on schedule. He'll continue as the segment producer, working closely with you."

"How does Callahan feel about that?"

"We discussed it last week. Frankly, he seemed relieved to have the writing responsibilities off his back."

She stepped away to search her desktop, found what she was looking for, and handed me a heavy three-ring binder with the title "Bareback Sex" on the front. She told me it was the bible for the episode, with the proposal and general outline up front, and much of the research that was already done organized by categories in the back.

"Also, Tommy's script, plus his notes, dated and in chronological order."

I opened it, quickly leafing through it.

"There's a lot here."

"Take it home, study it, then decide if you'd like to take a shot at it. I'll give you one or two sample scripts as well, from some of our better shows, to give you an idea of the format."

"You haven't even asked to see my resume."

"I know your work, Mr. Justice. From the *Los Angeles Times,* back in the eighties."

"Before you went east to do your graduate work?"

"That's correct."

"You grew up in Los Angeles, then."

She turned toward the credenza, where a faxed copy of Templeton's *GQ* piece lay between the framed photo of the grinning woman and a small crystal vase holding a single white rosebud.

"I've also read Miss Templeton's article in *Gentleman's Quarterly.* In hiring you, Mr. Justice, I feel I know what I'm getting." Almost as an afterthought, she added, "Yes, I grew up in this area."

"Family still here?"

Her smile was fleeting, bittersweet.

"I have no family to speak of, Mr. Justice."

"I guess we share something in common, then."

"Probably more than you realize."

The phone rang. She picked it up, sat, and swiveled, so that her back was to me. Her voice took on a new affection. As she talked, she studied the framed photo, simultaneously leaning over to inhale the aroma from the white rosebud. After making a soft kissy-kiss, she turned to face me again, slipping the phone back into its cradle.

"Please forgive the interruption."

"The woman in the photograph?"

"How did you know?"

"The change in your voice and manner."

Color seeped into her face.

"You don't miss much, do you, Mr. Justice?"

"I try not to."

She reached back for the photo and held it in front of her, gazing at it fondly, not unlike the way a sentimental male executive might regard a photo of his cherished wife.

"Her name's Tiger. We've been together four years."

"Then you must be very happy together."

She looked up, obviously pleased.

"Thank you. We are."

I reached for the picture.

"May I?"

She handed it across, and I studied it more closely.

"I have the feeling I've seen her before."

"Her name is Tiger Palumbo. She's been fairly active in the movement."

"Unless I'm mistaken, she owns the Powder Room."

"A co-owner, actually. With three other women. How did you know?"

"I live in West Hollywood. The Powder Room is an institution—the only woman's bar in the heart of Boy's Town." I handed the photo back. "As I recall, she also held some kick-boxing titles back in the eighties."

Chang laughed.

"You really don't miss much, do you?"

"There weren't too many women in the ring in those days. Tiger got her share of publicity on the sports page, and more than her share of victories inside the ropes."

"She owns a kick-boxing club here in the Valley. That's where you'll find her most days. Nights, she keeps an eye on the Powder Room."

"When does she find time to keep an eye on you?"

"We're both busy people, but it's worked out. We couldn't be more different. Maybe that's why it works. And you, Mr. Justice? Anyone special in your life?"

"Not at the moment."

"Maybe that will change."

"You never know."

She put the photo back in place, then stood and came around the desk again.

"Let me take you down the hall and introduce you to the associate producer you'll be working with. Peter Graff. You'll find him a tremendous help."

"If we both decide I'm right for the job."

"I'm convinced, Mr. Justice. It's really your decision at this point."

She led me back down the hall to an office with a closed door. She knocked, opened it, and ushered me in. I was totally unprepared for what awaited me.

"Peter, I'd like you to meet Benjamin Justice."

I've never been particularly attracted to blonds; more often than not, I find them rather bland and ordinary, possibly because

I have to look at one in the mirror every day. But Peter Graff very nearly took my breath away, he was that stunning. In his early twenties, he was trim and tanned, with a chiseled, angular face that included a square jaw cleft neatly with a dimple only God could have given him. The centerpiece of his flawless face was a pair of blazing blue eyes, set perfectly under thick waves of golden hair that tumbled boyishly across his forehead. As he stood—in shorts, T-shirt, and sandals—I saw a body of average height that was compact but lean, with silky golden hair sprinkled generously along his firmly muscled legs and forearms. If there was anything imperfect about him, I didn't see it.

I was gawking as he shook my hand, feeling ridiculously overwhelmed by his beauty. I heard Cecile Chang in the background, beyond the buzz in my head, explaining to Graff that I would probably be "joining the team," and that he was to assist me in every way possible. Then she was facing me.

"I'll leave you with Peter, Mr. Justice. We're shooting a video for presentation to potential grant donors, and I'm afraid I'm the star. We're using one of the upstairs editing bays for background. I've kept the camera crew waiting longer than I should have."

I came out of my trance and followed her to the door.

"I'm sorry I took so much of your time, Cecile."

"Not at all. I've looked forward to meeting you. You'll want to talk to Tommy Callahan as soon as possible about his script. I'm sure you'll have some questions for him."

Graff spoke just as she started through the door.

"Cecile—"

She hesitated, looking a trifle impatient.

"I haven't heard from Tommy since Wednesday night."

She cocked her head, and her voice quickened.

"That's five days."

Graff nodded, and her voice rose with urgency.

"He agreed to continue as producer. He knows we've fallen behind."

"I've tried calling him." Graff shrugged. "No luck."

"What about his beeper?"

"He's not answering his pages."

"Why didn't you tell me this sooner?"

"You've been so busy with the fund-raising video and your

other shows. I figured he was sick or something. I've been keeping up with the video logging. We're in pretty good shape.''

Her eyes roved our faces, while not quite looking at either of
us. Then, as suddenly as she had tensed up, she relaxed.

''Of course. Why am I even worrying? I'm sure we'll hear from
him soon enough.'' She glanced at her watch. ''Now, I've really
got to get back upstairs to the shoot. In this business, time is
money.''

Then she was gone, and I was left alone with Peter Graff, trying
to figure out where to put my eyes. He offered me a guided tour
of the building. I told him it was an excellent idea.

We'd started down the hallway, toward a stairwell, when I re-
membered that I'd left my notebook in Cecile Chang's office.
Graff offered to get us coffee and meet me back in the same spot.
He turned one way and I turned the other.

I stopped at Denise's desk in the cubicle outside Chang's office, and explained the situation. She told me to go on in, and
turned back to her keyboard, punching keys.

My notebook was where I'd left it, in one of the chairs facing
Chang's desk. As I retrieved it, something out the window caught
my eye.

I saw Chang hurrying across the parking lot to an older white
BMW sedan. She was in such a rush that she fumbled with her car
keys, dropping them before she unlocked the door and slid inside. Then she was looking over her shoulder, backing out, impatiently twisting the wheel, and speeding to the exit that led to
Ventura Boulevard.

I watched her tires spin as she hit the accelerator too hard,
before she raced away into the mid-afternoon traffic, like a
woman on a mission.

Three

THESE ARE the editing bays, Mr. Justice, where the shows are technically pieced together."

"I'll make you a deal, Mr. Graff. If you'll call me Ben—"

Peter Graff grinned: dazzling white teeth, healthy pink gums.

"You won't call me Mr. Graff. It's a deal."

We stuck our heads through the door of a room the size of a large closet, with the lone window sealed off against the sunlight. An electronic control panel stretched nearly the width of the room on the window side, with two video monitors positioned above rows of buttons and dials. Near the door was a small table with another video display monitor sitting atop a machine that resembled a VCR but was more elaborate, with big knobs and lots of calibrations.

"I don't see any editing machines."

The dazzling grin again.

"You mean, like a Moviola?"

"Right, something to cut and splice the film with."

"Mr. Justice—I mean, Ben—that kind of editing went out a couple of decades ago. Today, it's all done electronically."

I suddenly felt forty, times two.

"Oh."

"It's not even linear any longer. It's all digital now."

"I'm afraid I don't know linear from digital."

"Let me see if I can lay it out simply for you."

"Please, the simpler the better."

"As a writer, working with a producer, you select the shots you want to tell your story. Film, videotape, photographs, whatever picture elements you need, within budgetary limitations and clearance constraints. Once those elements are chosen, they're noted in your script in the order you want them, corresponding to the words you've written. Words, or voice-over, on one side, and visual elements on the other."

"That part seems comprehensible."

"The videotape of all the visual elements you think you'll need, including sound bites from taped interviews, is then put through a digitizing process. That enables the videotape editor to assemble them on the computerized AVID composer system—the digital editing system you see here. Even basic special effects, like fades and dissolves, are done from the digital board, electronically. That's called the off-line process. When your show is finished, and meets the requirements of the timing sheet, and Cecile's approval, it goes to on-line, for final technical processing. What they call air quality."

"Whew."

I felt his hand on my shoulder.

"Don't worry. Everyone's very helpful here." His eyes roved the room. "This is where Tommy Callahan taught me the basics of the AVID system. He kind of took me under his wing."

"The guy who's late with his script."

"Right. He's been an editor for almost thirty years. Wanted to get into the production end. He's not the greatest writer, but he was coming along." Graff chewed his lip. "I wonder what's going on with him. There are a lot of details in putting a show together. Normally, he and I talk several times a day. Five days ago, I suddenly stopped hearing from him."

"You sound pretty concerned."

"Maybe I shouldn't tell you this, but Tommy has a drinking problem. I'm worried that he might be off on a binge or something. He's been really good to me. I'd hate to see him get fired."

A young black woman with long hair braided the way Templeton used to wear hers slipped between us, into the room. Woven into the braids were colorful African-style beads. She set a stack of tapes on a side table, all bearing a set of letters and numbers.

"You need the room, Itabari?"

She glanced over at Graff.

"In a few minutes. We're booked from four to midnight. Going on-line Friday, if I can get my ass in gear."

"We'll get out of your way, then."

She smiled and started out.

"You haven't seen Tommy Callahan, have you?"

" 'Fraid I haven't, Peter."

She left us. Graff glanced at his watch, biting his lip again.

"He was doing so good. With his drinking, I mean. Cecile took a chance when she hired him. A lot of people around here were surprised. I hope he's not blowing it."

"Does he live nearby?"

"He's been staying at a motel. Over the hill, on Sunset."

"Maybe we should check up on him."

"My car's in the shop. My girlfriend's picking me up after work. I guess we could do it then."

My mouth spoke words it had no business saying, as if it had a mind of its own.

"I wouldn't mind giving you a lift that way."

"I couldn't do that, Mr. Justice—Ben."

"It's practically on my way home. Your girlfriend could meet us there, if it's not inconvenient. We could even grab a bite together. Lots of great Thai food over that way."

"No, really, I couldn't."

I gazed into his eyes, drinking in their clarity and color, wondering if he had any inkling what he was doing to me.

"Why? You don't accept rides from strangers?"

He laughed, looking embarrassed, and shoved his hands into the pockets of his shorts.

"You're not a stranger, Ben."

"Then you don't have any excuses, do you?"

His eyes met mine with surprising directness.

"I guess not."

We left the editing bay, trotted down the stairs, and he grabbed a knapsack from the room he'd been working in. On the way out, we slipped into a rest room to pee, standing at adjacent urinals, keeping our eyes straight ahead, taking longer than usual before things started flowing. At the sink, we washed up quickly, avoiding each other's eyes in the mirror the way men in rest rooms tend to do.

I have no business doing this. Not having just turned forty. Not having just met someone like Oree Joffrien, where the connection felt so natural, so strong. Graff's a kid, straight at that. Leave him alone, Justice.

We dried our hands on rough paper towels, and Graff asked me if I was ready to go. I told him I was, and followed him out, staring at his muscular calves. I was still staring at them as he pushed open the downstairs door to the parking lot, where we encountered Cecile Chang coming in, tossing a burning cigarette, slightly out of breath. She clutched her handbag under one arm, and when she saw us, she pulled up, startled. Graff was nearly as surprised.

"I thought you were taping upstairs, Cecile. Using one of the editing bays as background."

She indicated the smoldering Capri on the pavement, smiling tightly.

"I needed a quick nicotine fix—stepped out for a moment."

A few strands of dark hair had worked loose from the bun behind her head, and drifted down to the left side of her neck, pasted by a light film of perspiration. As she reached to push them back, her hand brushed her ear, causing her to momentarily pause, then turn away, showing us her other profile as she pushed the renegade hairs back into place. She spoke quickly, finding her breath where she could.

"We're breaking to a new location. Down in the production offices through the afternoon. We'll finish up back in research tonight."

Graff looked confused.

"I thought you completed your setups in research before lunch."

"The morning shots, yes. I want to go back again when everyone's gone for the day, and it's empty and quiet. I thought that would make a nice ending to the presentation. A day in the life of New Image Productions, from beginning to end."

She broke off, looking apologetic.

"But you two don't need to hear all this, do you? I'm sure you both have more important things to do than listen to me natter on about our shooting schedule."

Graff shoved his hands into his pants pockets, his worry showing again.

"Actually, we're on our way to Tommy Callahan's motel. To make sure he's OK."

Her busy hand, still fussing about the side of her face, became still.

"To Tommy's motel? Now?"

"Ben suggested it."

"Peter seemed concerned."

Her glance caromed off Graff to me.

"Of course. Check in on him, by all means. Let me know if he's having any problems."

She turned and hurried on, and we stepped out to the parking lot as the door closed on the clicking of her high heels. By the time we reached the Mustang several blocks away, then found our way back to Ventura Boulevard, it was half past four, with traffic beginning to congeal. We headed east along the boulevard toward the Cahuenga Pass, staying off the freeway to avoid the crush. As we climbed a slight rise, parallel to the freeway, an orange sun flooded the suburban landscape behind us with sharp light, turning my rearview mirror into a flaming sphere. The fireball disappeared as we descended into the heart of Hollywood, slowing to a crawl along Highland Avenue, inching our way past the Hollywood Bowl, the Hollywood Museum, Hollywood Boulevard, the Hollywood Walk of Fame.

By the time Hollywood High School came into view, alerting me to Sunset Boulevard, I had learned a great deal about Peter Graff, who answered all my questions openly and amiably, and seemed utterly without guile or pretense. He told me he was from a mid-sized town in Minnesota, the son of a hardware store owner and a mother who had never held a paying job, but had raised six children along with a passel of pets and the "best summer vegetable garden in the state." I asked him what constituted "mid-sized" in Minnesota, and he put the number at fifteen thousand. He and his girlfriend, Cheryl, both twenty-four, had dated since their senior year in high school, and had begun living together two years ago, after college and against their parents' wishes. Not quite a year ago, they had moved from Minneapolis to Los Angeles, where they had taken an apartment in Venice, right off the beach, hoping to find work making documentaries about "important subjects." Only recently had they agreed to a trial separation, at Peter's urging, to take some time apart and "and gain some real life experience," before making up their minds about their future together.

"I want to know everything about life," Peter said. "The good along with the bad. All of it. So I really know who I am and what I want, before I finally settle down."

The light turned green, and I eased the Mustang into the middle of the intersection, waiting for a break in traffic.

"Just be careful, Peter. Los Angeles has a way of giving some people more experience than they bargained for."

"I may be from a small town in Minnesota, Ben. But that doesn't mean I don't have a clue." He said it matter-of-factly, without rancor, while staring out the windshield at the busy street. "It doesn't mean I don't know how to make conscious choices."

I glanced over at his sharp Nordic profile. The sun had disappeared behind the Art Deco buildings of Hollywood High, leaving a glowing halo in the western sky; the gentle light washed over him, highlighting the fine blond hairs along the slope of his neck. I had the notion that he was deliberately letting me study him, though I sensed no vanity in it. I still wasn't sure he realized just how beautiful he was, and how much power that gave him with a certain kind of man.

He turned his eyes on mine, blue on blue.

"I can take care of myself, OK?"

"OK, Peter."

Our eyes remained fixed as the light turned yellow, then red. The driver behind me blasted her horn. To clear the intersection, I made a fast left onto Sunset Boulevard, and drove a block or two until we reached the Sunset Tiki Motel, where Tommy Callahan had told Graff he was staying. A sign in garish neon advertised single rooms at $29.95 a night, a rate for Los Angeles that put the place squarely in hookerville. As I turned in, we could see a small squadron of both genders doing the stroll along the grubby sidewalk.

I parked in front of the manager's office, a small room that protruded from the corner of the motel's main building in the shape of an island tiki hut, with a security window that looked out on the parking lot. Inside, a wizened, middle-aged Vietnamese man smoked a cigarette and read a newspaper. Graff approached him and spoke to him through a hole in the window, asking about Callahan. The man looked suspiciously from Graff to me, certain, I'm sure, that Graff was a hustler, attempting to turn a quick trick using Callahan's room, without paying extra. Graff turned in my direction, raising his hands in frustration.

I climbed out of the Mustang and joined him.

"He doesn't want to tell me what room Tommy's in. He says he hasn't seen him for a couple of days. Tommy's paid up through Wednesday."

I poked my nose into the hole and asked the manager if he understood English. He said he did.

"We have reason to believe Mr. Callahan may be having problems. We need to check on him."

"I think you try to use his room without pay."

"I'll tell you what, smart guy. We'll put in a call to 911, and get the cops down here to do our checking for us. How does that sound?"

I turned toward a pay phone. Standing next to it was a hooker of indeterminate gender in a tight red dress and matching heels, who waltzed away leering over one shoulder. Before I reached the phone, I heard the manager's voice, calling me back.

"OK, OK! No call police! He in cottage number six. Around the back."

We crossed the parking lot to a row of small bungalows built along the southern boundary of the property, dwarfed by enormous date palms with trunks thicker through the middle than a Russian weight lifter. Sixty or seventy years ago, when those palms were first planted, the cottages had probably been quaint, even attractive. Now, they were as tacky as a late night conversation at a Sunset Strip go-go bar.

Graff knocked on the door of number six. We could hear a TV set droning inside, tuned in to the evening news, and see the muted glow of the screen through the raggedy curtains. A half minute later, Graff knocked again, louder, then called Callahan's first name. I reached past him and tried the handle. The door opened.

There was enough light from the TV set and the fading sunset to show us the room had been turned upside down. I found a switch, and when the light came on, we saw how thoroughly the trashing had been. There wasn't a drawer, door, or piece of luggage that wasn't open, the contents strewn about. The mattress had been upended and sagged awkwardly against a wall, covering a rickety writing desk. Even shoe boxes had been flung into odd corners, as if they'd been searched and discarded.

I looked in the kitchen and bathroom. No Callahan. Then, as I pushed the soiled mattress back onto the bed to look behind it, I saw blood. Not a lot, but enough to indicate someone might have taken a good beating on that bed, maybe even been cut up a little.

"We'd better call the cops after all."

"What do you think happened?"

Graff's voice was anxious, frightened.

Welcome to L.A., Peter.

"Let's not speculate just yet." I handed him some coins. "Why don't you call? I'll look around a little more. You might call Cecile while you're at it."

When he was gone, I stood in the doorway, then systematically moved my eyes around the room, trying not to miss an inch. I touched nothing more, left no new fingerprints beyond those I'd already pressed into the door handle and light switch. There wasn't much in the room except clothes, a few books, and personal items in the bathroom; the books were all gay titles, on the more literate side—James Baldwin, Edmund White, Felice Picano, Michael Cunningham, Dale Peck—but with a smattering of hardcore S&M fantasies among them, along with a few kinky tales by Anne Rice. I was about to move on to the kitchen when I spotted something familiar nestled in the cheap beige carpet near the nightstand. I knelt for a closer look.

It was an oval jade stone, encrusted in gold. An earring, exactly like the ones Cecile Chang had been wearing when I'd first met her earlier that day. I rose, thought for a moment about what I'd discovered, then went to stand on the porch of the old cottage and wait for the police to arrive.

Four

I DIDN'T MENTION seeing Cecile Chang's earring to the cops who answered the call at the Sunset Tiki Motel, or to anyone else.

I figured it was police business now, not mine. My business was getting my life back on track, earning a paycheck, and I didn't need a stranger's errant blood and unknown whereabouts distracting me.

The opportunity I'd been handed by Chang was like a gift from heaven, a dream job for a washed-up reporter like me. Out of nowhere, I suddenly had the chance to turn the corner, maybe develop a new skill and even a refurbished reputation that could lead somewhere. I didn't like admitting the need for that, but I'd hit the big four-zero, and my perspective had shifted. I wanted self-sufficiency again, and nobody's pity. It was as simple as that, and I wasn't going to blow it by sticking my nose where it didn't belong.

That night, after driving Graff back to his Venice apartment, I sat up studying the show bible Chang had given me for the bareback sex segment, reading by a table lamp in the living room of the little house on Norma Place. My elderly landlords, Maurice and Fred, were on a second honeymoon in Europe, financed by an inheritance Maurice had received unexpectedly that fall from

the modest estate of an older sister, who had been his last surviv-
ing relative when she passed. It was Maurice's idea to cruise down
the Rhine with Fred, feeding him cheese and wine and pointing
out the magnificent German castles on the hilltops, before the
water got too low for passage. They would then continue touring
by rented car, until they ended up in France in time to spend
April in Paris, where Maurice intended to have his picture taken
kissing Fred atop the Eiffel Tower—something he had wanted to
do, he'd told me, for more than forty years.

For another month, possibly longer, I was to stay in their house
instead of my usual place in the small apartment over the garage
out back and care for the pets. It felt unusual, living in homey
comfort, a place with a sense of permanence, after so many years
without an anchor. As I sank into the deep couch with the two
cats beside me and the dog nearby on the braided carpet, my
slippered feet propped up on the divan, I had to concede that it
didn't feel half bad. There would be some who would say I was
going soft, losing my edge, selling out to the conforming notion
that there was no place like hearth and home. But I'd sown my
wild oats, taken my walk on the wild side, been as much a liber-
tine as any of them; I'd also seen and experienced my share of
heartbreak and senseless death along the way, and I'd had
enough. Now I was ready for something different, more careful
choices, something—something I couldn't quite put my finger
on, couldn't quite name, but that I wanted nonetheless.

That notion—making careful choices, leading a safer, saner
life—was at the heart of the bareback sex issue I'd just been hired
to write about. On one side were those men who proclaimed
bareback sex with multiple partners to be an individual right in a
free society and a bold stand against puritan forces determined to
oppress gay sexuality. On the other side were those who felt
strongly that in the age of a deadly virus like AIDS, unprotected
sex with multiple partners was irresponsible beyond description,
destructive not just to individuals but to an entire community,
particularly the young, who had so much to lose but were often
without the foresight to see it. That was the basic schism, at least
as I understood it, with countless related issues to be considered.
How I was going to explore it, tell the story, remained to be
worked out.

I sipped coffee in the lamplight, studying the sample scripts

Chang had given me to get an idea how such things were put together and what specifically would be expected of me, line by line, page by page. Then I leafed through the three-ring binder, making notes along the way. Most of the research was already in place and meticulously organized by Peter Graff. Tommy Callahan had assembled an impressive list of visual elements to illustrate the piece. Yet, as I read the first draft Callahan had written, it wasn't difficult to see why Chang had been so desperate to bring in someone with a stronger writing background—Callahan's structure was awkward and unwieldy, his writing rhythms ragged and unpolished, his wordcraft barely serviceable.

By dawn, as the birds began to make their noise outside and the animals around me began to stir, I had a reasonably clear vision of how I wanted to tell the story, and what my viewpoint was. I caught a few hours sleep, then called Chang at ten sharp and accepted the job. We spoke only briefly about the trashed room Graff and I had discovered at the Sunset Tiki Motel and the mysterious absence of Tommy Callahan. Not surprisingly, she said she hoped Callahan would be found safe and sound. I concurred, and neither of us spoke on the subject beyond that.

During the next three days, as my contract was prepared, I worked diligently on my outline, using the sample scripts as a guide for format and structure. The script outline proved to be considerably different from the general outline of the material in the segment bible, and thoroughly frustrating, as Chang had warned me. I soon realized, as I tried to fit everything I wanted to cover into a single hour of air time—less several minutes for the opening titles, host's introduction and closing, and end credits— that in television, you had to leave out much more than you put in. I typed up my outline on the new PC Maurice had installed in the den just before his departure for Europe, a purchase he'd explained away with some nonsense about a memoir he'd always wanted to write. He might as well have said it with a wink because we both knew the truth. He was hoping I'd begin using it in his absence, hurrying along my return to the writing game, which is exactly how things were turning out.

On Thursday afternoon, just seventy-two hours after I'd first shaken hands with Cecile Chang, I was back in her office, handing in my outline. I'd spoken briefly to Peter Graff beforehand, and there was still no word about Callahan's whereabouts. Graff was clearly troubled by it, but I kept my focus on my new writing assignment, determined not to be derailed by my feelings for Graff, or by the chance discovery of a stray earring on a tacky motel room floor.

Chang shut the door, asked Denise to hold her calls, and took fifteen minutes looking over my outline and asking me questions. She had a few comments about the structure and pacing that made sense, warning me in particular to avoid going off on tangents, but otherwise, she told me, it looked sound. The important thing, she said, was to get started on a first draft as soon as possible, and to plan on lots of revisions.

"That's it? I'm now a working television writer?"

She smiled.

"That's it, Ben. Welcome aboard."

"I've always heard things move quickly in television."

"You've seen nothing yet. The pace tends to accelerate exponentially. With all the money that's tied up in production, staying on schedule is crucial. Which brings us to the next step. Your deadlines."

She handed across a sheet of paper detailing exactly when each draft was to be completed, handed in, returned for revision, and so on, all the way to the final off-line edit.

"Given the time we've already lost, we're looking at three months at the outside. That may seem like a long time now, but after you've spent a couple hundred hours viewing and selecting footage and sound bites, you'll see it differently." She stood and escorted me to the door. "Denise has your contract. Please look it over. If you have any questions, just call. By the way, Peter has confirmed your first interview—Oree Joffrien."

"Oree?"

"I thought it would be good if you cut your teeth interviewing Oree, since the two of you are already acquainted."

"Sounds reasonable."

"To be honest, I offered this segment to Oree first, when it became clear Tommy Callahan was in over his head. Oree has a related book in the works, which should be out by the time our series airs on PBS in the fall, so he was an obvious choice. Unfortunately, he's got too much on his plate at the moment, and turned me down. But he recommended you."

"For which I'm more than a little grateful."

"If you get the kind of quality sound bites from Oree that I believe you can, you may not have to interview more than one or two others to round out those we've already done. You'll find him as articulate as he is knowledgeable, and he should look good on camera."

"He's an attractive man."

"He caught your eye, then?"

"More than just my eye."

She looked bemused, maybe a little pleased.

"You'll be seeing him again tomorrow, just after lunch. The taping is set in his office at UCLA. Peter has all the details."

Suddenly, my stomach was fluttering.

"We're taping tomorrow? That's pretty fast."

"Peter's good with a camera crew. He'll lead you through it."

"He's barely out of college."

"You'd be surprised how many bright young people there are at entry level in this business who know their way around. They're the underpaid workhorses we producers depend on—tomorrow's producers. Just to be safe, I'd like to see a list of interview questions first thing in the morning, to make sure you're on the right track."

We faced each other at the door, and I thanked her again for the opportunity she'd given me. I noticed she was wearing a different set of jewelry today, floating opals rather than jade. I kept my mouth shut on the subject, which wasn't easy.

"It's mutual, Ben. It's not easy finding writers with your experience willing to work for what we pay. Especially on such short notice."

Her hand was on the door, hurrying me along.

"It doesn't look like I'll be able to talk to Callahan about the material before I start writing. Given the signs of violence in his motel room."

"No." Her smile was rigid, appropriately sad. "No, I suppose we have to move forward without Tommy, don't we?"

Five

WITH THE EXCEPTION of a quick drug fix, or a trip to Disneyland, there may be no faster way to leave the real world behind than to take a stroll on a lovely spring day across a university campus, as I did early Friday afternoon on my way to interview Oree Joffrien.

I parked in Lot Three, on UCLA's northern boundary near Sunset Boulevard, and wound my way through the fantastic shapes and myriad concepts of the Franklin D. Murphy Sculpture Garden toward the heart of the campus. After a season of generous rains, the grounds were as green as I'd ever seen them, and the jacarandas were full and fluttery with lavender blossoms; squirrels were everywhere, scampering across the lush lawns and up and down the trees, which were thick with foliage, while the edges of the landscape were bunched with ferns and *Agapanthus*—Lily of the Nile—about to bloom like purple fireworks exploding. Hundreds of students in summery clothes made their way to lunch, or to their next class, their faces ranging from deeply studious to blissfully carefree, but all of them basking in the last blush of youthful freedom before facing the reality of having to earn a living and pay their way in the world, or else try to survive on its desolate fringes, as I had done in recent years. A decade or more had passed since my last visit here, when I'd

appeared as a guest lecturer in an evening class offered by the
UCLA Extension Writers' Program, at a time when my career was
in its final ascent before the big crash. The only change I could
see was more Asian students than ever, and fewer students with
dark skin—a sign that the affirmative action programs of another
era had been dismantled, and, for those beginning life with less,
harsh reality was becoming that much harsher.

Joffrien's office was on the third floor of Haines Hall, one of
about forty Italian Romanesque buildings in red brick and terra-
cotta designed in the 1920s, part of a cluster set on a hilltop in
the manner of a northern Italian village, overlooking the picturesque slopes of the western campus. Inside Haines, I passed endless and confusing room numbers, along with bulletin boards and
display cases devoted to the subject of anthropology, which told
me I'd at least found the right department. Posted on a wall was a
dictionary definition someone had photocopied and blown up to
poster size.

> **an thro pol o gy**, *n*. **1.** the science dealing with
> the origins, physical and cultural development,
> racial characteristics, and social customs and
> beliefs of the human race. **2.** the study of man's
> similarity to and difference from other animals.
> **3.** the science of man and his works. **4.** the study
> of the nature and essence of man (also known as
> **philosophical anthropology**).

As I neared Joffrien's office, I met him coming out. Graff was
right behind him, and I shook hands with both of them, feeling
lumpy and nondescript between two such gorgeous men, who
couldn't have looked more different or appealed to me in such
different ways. Graff and his camera crew had decided Joffrien's
office was too small for comfortable shooting, and had relocated
their equipment to one of the open-air loggias of nearby Royce
Hall, where the arches and shadows seemed suitable for the serious subject matter at hand.

Graff led the way, not wasting a moment.

"They're already setting up the lighting. We should be ready to tape in about fifteen minutes."

He led us out of Haines to a concrete and brick pathway that was one of several crisscrossing Dickson Plaza, where students sauntered along the walkways or napped on the broad lawns in between. It struck me that Graff would not have been out of place among them, perhaps as a tanned and golden member of the swim or water polo teams, yet he led the way to our taping with the confidence of someone far removed in time and experience from the peaceful isolation of a university never-never land.

I recognized Royce Hall the moment I saw it. Renovated and retrofitted since the devastating Northridge earthquake of ninety-three, the stately domed structure, inspired by a number of northern Italian cathedrals, was probably the most filmed college building in the country. There was some irony in Graff's choice for our backdrop: We'd be discussing a topic the patriarchs of the Catholic church would no doubt consider unholy, something to be locked away in the deep vaults of denial, like the subject of priests who engage in pedophilia, or seduce the devout who come to them for counsel, or simply depend on booze to get them through their night's despair. Yet, disregarding its churchliness, the building's solid stonework and architectural stature seemed ideal for our needs, and the choice left me more impressed than ever with Graff's maturity.

The camera and lights were set up in a corner of the broad loggia on the building's southern side, with two chairs facing each other. The camera was behind and just to the left of one of the chairs. Graff asked Joffrien to take the other one, a position that allowed him to be framed nicely in the background by a brick arch, with muted light beyond. Graff fussed about Joffrien, straightening his collar and tie, while the lighting man took numerous measurements with a meter near Joffrien's face, making allowances, I was told, for the extra absorption of light that was a natural consequence of Joffrien's darker skin. Graff then placed me in the chair nearest the camera, and I felt his hands on my arms and shoulders as he adjusted my body to keep me just outside the camera's lens.

"Be sure not to lean to the left, Ben, or you'll be in frame. Mr. Joffrien, try to maintain eye contact with Ben, and talk to him as if you're having a normal conversation. Be as animated and spontaneous as you want. Gesture with your hands, if it feels comfortable. Just don't move from your basic sitting position, or we'll lose you in the frame and have to refocus."

Graff knelt, with both hands resting on my thigh.

"Remember to ask your questions in a way that elicits open-ended responses—a complete answer, rather than just a yes or no."

"Gotcha."

I took a deep breath, feeling almost as if I were the one facing the camera. Graff must have picked up on it, because his voice became more soothing, reassuring.

"Don't worry about how you sound. Your questions will be edited out. We'll only use Mr. Joffrien's responses. The important thing is to listen carefully, and lead him naturally into the next question without interrupting a good sound bite."

"Got it, boss."

He grinned, squeezed my leg, then went to check the microphone clipped to Joffrien's shirt, just below camera range.

"If you can, Mr. Joffrien, try to begin each answer by restating the question in some way, so we get a complete sound bite."

Joffrien smiled, as calm and composed as the night I'd first met him.

"I've done this a few times, Peter. I know the procedure."

"I guess we're ready then." Graff took his place behind the camera. "Whenever you are, Ben."

I glanced at the notebook in my lap, and my list of questions, then took a deep breath.

"Anytime, guys."

The tape rolled, then immediately was stopped as the sound man picked up the buzz of an overhead plane in his earphones. A minute later, as it passed and we were about to start again, a car alarm began blaring in nearby Lot Five. When it finally stopped, we resumed. I asked my first question, which was actually a request.

"Explain for us, if you will, what is meant by 'riding bareback,' or 'bareback sex.' "

Before Joffrien opened his mouth to reply, Graff interrupted.

"I'm sorry, Ben. Have him give us his name and his exact title, slowly spelling out his first and last names. For logging and research purposes. You always do that at the beginning of an interview."

Joffrien complied, without my saying a word. Nearly half an hour had passed since I first sat down in my chair, and the interview had yet to get under way. I was beginning to feel like the least important person on the shoot.

"We're rolling, Ben."

I cleared my throat and started again.

"Please explain what is meant by 'riding bareback,' or 'bareback sex.' "

"The term 'riding bareback,' or 'bareback sex,' refers to the activity of people who are apparently willing to put themselves in danger of becoming infected with HIV, or infecting or reinfecting others, by engaging in high-risk sexual intercourse without using condoms."

"Is this strictly a homosexual problem?" I stopped. "I'm sorry, that sets up a yes or no answer, doesn't it."

"It's all right," Peter said. "Keep going."

I repeated the question, and Joffrien responded.

"Although many people, both straight and gay, are obviously having unprotected sex, there is one group of gay males in particular who deliberately, almost defiantly, continue to engage in unprotected anal intercourse, regardless of the risk. Gay writers and others originally coined the term 'riding bareback' or 'bareback sex,' to describe this phenomenon within a small gay subculture, which has generated a great deal of controversy in the midst of the continuing AIDS epidemic."

"Knowing how many have died of AIDS, and how horrible a disease it is, why would anyone willingly engage in bareback sex?"

"Why anyone would willingly put themselves at risk in this way is a complex question. It cuts through a number of issues the gay community has been facing in the 1990s, and even earlier. These include a sense of doom on the part of many gay men, low self-esteem, questions of consensuality and responsibility in sexual coupling, the fiercely held belief by some that sexuality must remain as natural and unfettered an experience as possible, no matter what the consequences, and so on. There are also questions about the impact of drugs on sexual activity, the unique commercialization of sex and sex-and-drug activity that simply does not exist in any other subculture in quite the same way. Also, the issue of enslavement to the so-called muscle culture, which puts such high value on youth and looks, and seems to devalue the old or less attractive. All of these issues come out of a deeper matrix of medical, political, and spiritual questions that are currently the subject of heated debate within the gay community and among AIDS activists and others.''

I left my list of questions for the moment.

"Is that how you personally see the issue, Oree? Or were you speaking as an academic and social observer?''

"I was speaking analytically, as an academic. Personally, as a part of the queer community, I view bareback sex at this point in our history as either murder or suicide. I see it as a grotesque symptom of a subculture within a subculture twisted by society's oppression, but also by its own self-hatred and sexual compulsion. These traits are not exclusive to gay men by any means, but given the context of the AIDS crisis, they take on a darker meaning, at least in my view.''

"Yet, with the advances in treatment, AIDS is no longer considered the automatic death sentence it once was.''

"The epidemic isn't over, it's just that the color has changed. People are still dying, especially those who can't afford treatment, or whom education and prevention have not reached. The African American and Hispanic communities are being decimated by this disease while a lot of gay men, mostly Caucasian, argue the pros and cons of slipping on a condom. In the meantime, the plague is exploding in third world countries, beyond all previous expectations. Knowing that, to deliberately expose another to HIV infection borders on evil, and to turn one's back on the continuing catastrophe is almost as bad. I see it as callous, elitist, even racist.''

Joffrien paused, then smiled.

"Is that what you were looking for?''

"That'll do nicely, thank you.''

As I continued to move down my list of questions, sometimes jumping ahead if it felt right, or revisiting a question I felt needed more exploration, time seemed to stand still, and for the most part, I forgot the camera that was looking over my shoulder. Joffrien and I discussed the new sexual conservatism espoused by a vocal segment of the gay community, the moral issue of sex clubs and commercial sex-and-drugs events, such as the gay circuit parties that brought together thousands of gay men in a celebration of sensuality, the importance of the erotic impulse to gay self-identity, and on and on. From time to time, Peter Graff interrupted because of more audio interference, or when lighting or camera adjustments were needed, or the camera operator needed to change tapes. Several times, he broke in with a suggestion for reframing a question, or to ask Joffrien to repeat himself, emphasizing some aspect of his response, or articulating it more clearly. Once, as his throat grew dry, Joffrien asked for a glass of water, which Graff had ready for him. Then, after two hours that felt more like two minutes, we were finished.

Graff had manipulated everything behind the camera with an unobtrusive touch. Joffrien had given me a stream of quotable material that might provide me with the narrative thread I felt I needed for the piece. Together, they had pulled me through my first interview, and I felt closer to both of them for the experience. Yet, in my gut, I knew whom I would have preferred to be with when the day was done: the knowledgeable professor, the jazz lover, the seasoned gay man close to my own age, my intellectual superior, perhaps, who might challenge me in that respect, but with whom I felt so at ease, with a special kinship that seemed deep and real.

As I gazed across at him, doing my best to thank him with my eyes, I felt Graff's fingers busy at my shirt front, as he unclipped my microphone.

"That was great, Ben."

I turned my attention to his earnest face.

"You're not just saying that to make me feel better?"

"Trust me, you handled it like a pro."

Joffrien stood as the sound man unclipped his mike.

"He's right, Ben. It went very smoothly." He stepped over to us, extending his hand. "Congratulations."

We shook hands as Graff turned away to answer a call on his cell phone. I suddenly realized I was no longer a virgin in my new field, that I had my first interview under my belt. It wasn't as exciting as the first time I'd seen my byline on a newspaper article two decades earlier, at the age of twenty, but it would do.

Joffrien and I talked about the taping for a minute, until I was able to nudge the conversation toward the subject of dinner. I was about to ask him if I could buy him a good meal as a way of showing my appreciation, when we heard Graff cry out nearby.

"Oh God, no!"

I turned to see Graff holding his phone at his side, his shoulders slumping, eyes downcast.

"What is it, Peter?"

His eyes teared up as he looked over.

"They found Tommy. He's dead."

"Tommy Callahan?"

Graff nodded, and he looked away. I took the phone from him, and found Cecile Chang still on the line. She told me that she'd just been contacted by a homicide detective from the sheriff's department. He'd informed her that Callahan's body had been discovered that morning in a shallow grave in the Angeles National Forest, just north of the city, which fell under the sheriff's jurisdiction. Callahan hadn't just been murdered, she said; he'd been tortured, and had died a slow death. I asked her if she'd told Graff all that. She said she had, as delicately as possible.

I glanced at him as he stared at the ground, fighting his tears. He no longer looked the part of the commanding associate producer. He looked more like a lost little boy.

"I think Peter needs a shoulder at the moment."

I told Chang I'd be in touch, and heard her click off. I didn't know how to shut off a cell phone—I'd never used one—so I handed it to Joffrien and asked him to take care of it. Then I turned back to Graff, who looked up at me.

"Tommy was always really nice to me. He was the first real friend I made out here."

"I know, Peter. It's tough."

"I've never lost anyone I've been close to, not even my grandparents. I've never even been to a funeral."

"You'll get through it, Peter."

"You've lost friends?"

"Most of them, actually."

I stepped closer, and opened my arms. He fell slowly against my chest, and I wrapped my arms around him, telling him it was all right to let out whatever he was feeling. It wasn't necessary: He was already weeping quietly against my shoulder, digging his fingers into my back as he clutched me tighter, while I tried to ignore how indescribably good it felt having his body so close to mine, and how much shame that caused me, given the circumstances.

Six

W^{HERE'S HARRY?"}

"I stood looking over Templeton's shoulder as she pecked away at her keyboard in her reporter's pod at the *Los Angeles Sun*. She kept punching keys, barely glancing up.

"How'd you get in?"

"I'm dating the security guard."

"Dominick? Give me a break."

"You think I'm too old for him, now that I've hit forty?"

"He's not gay."

"How do you know?"

"He's got a wife, six kids, two girlfriends."

"Probably overcompensating."

"So how *did* you get in, Justice?"

"Dominick wasn't at his station. I waltzed right by. Came up in the elevator."

"Not good."

"Sneaking in?"

"Lack of security. It means they're stretching everybody as thin as they can. Another sign the *Sun* is on the financial skids."

"It's been on the skids as long as I can remember."

"This time it's serious."

"So where's Harry?"

"In a closed-door meeting with Roger Lawson, trying to figure a way to save the paper."

"Roger Lawson—the weasel management brought in last year to trim fat?"

"He prefers the term managing editor."

"From what I hear, he's management's hatchet man."

"He's been behaving that way, putting the screws to Harry."

"This sounds serious, Templeton."

She glanced up, rolled her eyes.

"I just said that, Justice."

"So what are you working on?"

"Trying to work on, while you keep bothering me with meaningless chatter." She flipped some pages in her notebook, found what she was looking for, deleted a few lines from the screen, resumed writing. "It's a piece on the selection of the new police chief. Front page, Sunday edition."

"You got the assignment you wanted."

"Correct."

"Congratulations."

"Same to you. For the TV gig."

"You heard."

"Oree called. It's nice to know somebody cares enough to let me know what's going on in your life."

"Sorry. I've had a full schedule. Learning a new trade and all."

"So why aren't you at home working on your script? Or out chasing people with a camera. That's what Mike Wallace would be doing."

"I have a favor to ask."

"Bad time, Justice. This story's industrial strength. I see it heating up as a black-white thing. Could be explosive."

"Are you sure you can be objective?"

"Screw you, Justice! You're telling me some lily-white reporter is going to be any more—"

She broke off, glanced up, saw my grin.

"Gotcha, Templeton."

"Very cute." She swiveled in her chair to face me. "Now that you've completely destroyed my concentration, what is it you want?"

"There's this kid at the production company, Peter Graff. Not a kid exactly. Two years out of college. A friend of his turned up dead this morning. He's pretty broken up about it. Wants to know more about what happened.''

''I thought you made a New Year's resolution not to get involved in anyone else's troubles until sometime well into the next century.''

''That's why I'm here. I was hoping you'd take it off my hands.''

''Sorry. Not with my workload.''

''He's drop dead gorgeous, Templeton. Smart, sensitive, hardworking.''

''Straight?''

I nodded.

''This might be the one.''

''Now look who's playing Cupid.''

''Don't tell me you're not a little bit lonely out there in Santa Monica in that big condo of yours. Now that the Laker with the big hands is gone.''

''Let's not go there, shall we?''

''Maybe you could just give Peter a call. Fax him a copy of the police report in a day or two, when the dicks have something down on paper.''

''Talk to Harry, Justice.'' She spun in her chair, facing her computer screen again. ''I really have to get this piece finished.''

I'd forgotten just how tough Templeton could be, now that she was a few years into the reporter's trade. A lot of that toughening came from Harry, some from me. An occupational hazard. I forgave her.

''You told me Harry's in a meeting.''

''I think it's ending.''

She nodded at a computer message at the top of her screen: *I'm free if you need me. How's the page one coming?*

She erased his message, hit the command for a clean memo of her own, addressed it to *Brofsky H,* and typed in: *Making progress. Sending Justice your way. Please keep him out of my hair.* She punched the send button, and the message disappeared.

I did the same, heading for Harry Brofsky's office, where Roger Lawson blocked the doorway, with his sizable butt filling most of it. Lawson was a big guy, a couple of inches over six feet, with a husky body that had probably never had much muscle on it. He wore his brown hair long, tied back in a ponytail, a throwback to his younger, more adventurous days, even though everybody knew he'd sold out to management years ago, become a numbers cruncher and a yes man on his way up the corporate ladder, scared shitless of those above him, and taking it out on those below. That said, I'd given several years of my life to the *Los Angeles Times,* and you can't get any more establishment than the good, gray *L.A. Times.* Maybe that was why I resented Lawson so much; maybe I saw a piece of myself in him that I didn't like.

I waited wordlessly until he lumbered off, his shirttail flopping out of his pants, which hung loosely around his sloppy gut. He was the kind of guy who tried hard to walk and talk tough, but every time I saw him, I saw the kind of big, soft high school kid who'd always been third string on the football team, and spent the rest of his life trying to make up for it.

"You and Roger Lawson getting chummy?"

Harry looked up from poring over a stack of budget statements. He smiled grimly, and motioned me silently to take a chair, which in Harry's world translated roughly as *take a chair and shut up until I'm ready to talk.*

I did, and used the time to study him. I didn't like what I saw: He was haggard, his skin pallid and bloodless. The empty cigarette packs in the wastecan told me he was probably smoking more than ever, and I thought I detected a tremor in his hand as he jotted notes in the margin of the document under his scrutiny. He was a shade past sixty but looked older. A hell of a lot older, with too many hard years behind him, some of which I'd given him.

He finally shoved the printouts aside in frustration, pushed his bifocals higher on his nose, placed his elbows on his desk, and ran his hands through his hair, which had gone nearly white sometime in the past year without my realizing it. When he looked up, his eyes were rheumy and red with fatigue.

"How the hell am I supposed to let another dozen reporters go and still put out a paper?"

"That bad, huh?"

"Worse. I talked that bastard Lawson *down* to a dozen." His eyes made a quick survey of the small room: plaques and awards on one wall, favorite front pages framed and laminated on another. A lifetime of achievement, which guaranteed you nothing when you were sixty years old in a business that was downsizing everywhere you looked, trying to survive the onslaught of the electronic media. "Christ, there's nothing sadder than watching an old daily go down in flames."

He reached instinctively to his breast pocket for a cigarette, an old habit from the days when smokers were allowed to light up inside. He sighed wearily, stared at his desk.

"Take it easy, Harry. Things'll turn around. They always have."

"Look who's handing out optimism. You get a job or something?"

I nodded.

"Not publicity, I hope."

"Television."

He made a small *hrummph.*

"Just as bad."

"Maybe not. It's a documentary series for PBS."

"Mating rituals of South American butterflies?"

"I'm glad to see you've still got your sense of humor."

"So what brings you down to the *Sun,* Benjamin? To watch it permanently set?"

"Park rangers found a d.b. this morning, up in the Angeles National Forest. Mutilation job. I was hoping you might have a reporter on it."

"You knew the victim?"

"Friend of a friend."

"Irish guy? Early fifties?"

"Thomas Callahan, yeah."

"I saw the story come across the wire. We're running a short item in the morning edition. Southland briefs, page two."

"That's it?"

"A dead body in the Angeles forest isn't big news, Ben. Those mountains have been used as a dumping ground for inconvenient corpses longer than you've been alive."

I stood.

"Templeton didn't want to help me, either."

"I didn't say I wouldn't help you. Sit down."

I sat.

"I said I don't have anything on it besides what ran on the wire." He looked at me sideways. "You think it's worth looking into?"

"Callahan was a videotape editor with a drinking problem. He was writing and co-producing a segment for the PBS series that I inherited. His first writing-producing job. Disappeared mysteriously from a hot pillow joint in Hollywood. I think he was gay, maybe with a taste for sadomasochism. That's about all I know."

"I'll have Templeton keep an eye on it."

"She's got her hands full."

"With the cuts I'm about to make, her hands'll be dragging down around her ankles. One more murder shouldn't make all that much difference." Harry tried to smile, didn't quite get there. "She's come along real well, Ben. Two or three more years, and I could have rounded her into shape. The way I did you, before you went and fucked everything up."

His eyes twinkled a little through their puffiness, and the grin finally showed up on his sagging face. We'd both come a long way to get to this point, where we could smile about what I'd done to both our careers. Harry, in particular, had gone the extra distance. I was damned grateful for it. Someday, I'd have to tell him that.

"I'd offer to buy you dinner at the Mandarin Deli, Harry, but I have a feeling you're going to be working late."

He stood. I did the same.

"Yeah, I got more meetings." He came around his desk, and surprised me by putting an arm around my shoulders as he walked me to the door. "This wasn't the way I saw it all ending, Ben. Petering out with a whimper, instead of going out with a bang."

"Is it that definite—the *Sun* folding?"

"The guys upstairs are trying to round up investors, find a buyer. Pull in another loan if they can, but that's a real long shot."

"Maybe something good'll happen."

"Yeah, maybe."

"Get some rest, Harry."

"I'll do that." The smile was long gone. "Right after I call in twelve reporters and tell them they don't have jobs anymore."

Seven

AT SUNDOWN, I walked Fred's golden retriever, Maggie, around the Norma Triangle, turning down her favorite streets where the smells were strongest. She shuffled along slowly, with a slight limp, and it took us a while. As I meandered along patiently beside her, I tried not to see Harry in her tired gait.

Back at the house, I brought in the day's mail, fed the cats, then logged a three-mile hike up into the hills above Sunset Boulevard, which I finished off with a hundred sit-ups, fifty push-ups, and a chicken-and-bean burrito from Taco Taco down on the corner. After a nap and a shower, I called Oree Joffrien, hoping to score a dinner date sometime in the next week. He was out, and I left a message on his voice mail, thanking him again for giving me such a valuable interview earlier in the day, and asking him to call, no matter how late.

Then I settled into the living room couch with the television on and the volume low, to make another pass through the research material for my show, making notes about the gaps I felt needed filling. It was sometime after ten when the chimes rang. I opened the door to find Peter Graff standing on the welcome mat, dressed in deck shoes, faded jeans, and a Minnesota Twins T-shirt, his hands pushed into his pants pockets.

"Peter. What a nice surprise. Come in."

"It's not too late?"

"Not at all."

He stepped past me, and faced me in the middle of the living room.

"What's on your mind?"

He shoved his hands deeper into his pockets so that his arms were fully extended, and the knobs of his shoulders raised a little. Then his eyes came up, slowly, until they found mine. His voice was quiet, sad.

"I just wondered if you'd learned anything more about Tommy."

"I talked to a couple of friends at the *Sun*. They said they'd call if anything significant turned up."

"A detective got in touch with me. From the sheriff's department. Asked me some questions."

"I imagine I'll be hearing from him, too, since I was with you when we found Callahan's motel room trashed." The rims of his eyes were red. "How are you doing?"

His shoulders rose briefly, before sagging again.

"I'm OK."

"Sit down. Let's talk."

We sat on the couch with a yard of upholstery between us. Maggie came over to get her head scratched, and Graff obliged. He ruffled the fur between her ears, then up under her chin the way she liked it, as she lifted her head and closed her eyes. Maggie had belonged to a young man named Danny Romero, someone close to Graff's age, until Fred had inherited her the previous year as Danny was dying; he'd left me his pickup truck, which still sat unused in the garage, and a beautiful table he'd made by hand that I kept upstairs in the apartment, overlooking the yard.

Maggie seemed to take to Graff, and settled down on the floor by his feet, her big golden head on her paws. He rubbed her with the rubber toe of his shoe as he talked.

"This detective asked me a lot of questions about Tommy. What he was like, who his friends were. What kind of relationship we had."

"What did you tell him?"

"That I'd met Tommy when Cecile hired him a few months

ago. That he had a drinking problem he was trying to control, and this was like a second chance for him, late in his life. I told him Tommy seemed to be a loner, not much social life." Graff's eyes shifted awkwardly. "I mentioned that Tommy was, you know, gay. I figured they'd find out sooner or later, anyway."

"It's not like he was burying bodies in the backyard, Peter. He just liked guys."

"Yeah, I guess you're right."

"When did you first find out Callahan was queer?"

"Couple months ago. After we became friends."

"Did it surprise you?"

"A little, I guess. Maybe I should have seen it coming, I don't know."

He stretched his arm across the back of the couch. His hand was strong and well veined, and his forearm heavily burnished with blond hairs that glowed in the lamplight like strands of fine silk.

"How close did you and Callahan get?"

His eyes were on the move again.

"Pretty good friends, like I told you before."

"That covers a lot of ground."

"His friendship was important to me. Losing him hurts."

"I can see that."

He didn't say anything, just stared down at Maggie, who rolled on her side while Peter rubbed her chest.

"At what point in your friendship did he try to seduce you, Peter?"

His blue eyes flashed.

"What makes you think he did that?"

"It would take an awfully strong-willed gay man not to try to get your clothes off."

"Are you saying that all gay men—"

"I'm saying that you're a young man of extraordinary beauty, whether you realize it or not. If you happened to be female, instead of male, most straight men would be looking at you pretty much the same way. It's a problem men tend to have, objectifying those we find desirable."

His eyes steadied, landing on mine, staying there.

"Is that how you look at me?"

"My guess is you already know the answer to that one."

When his eyes moved again, it was nervously, like blue neon flickering.

"You still haven't told me if Callahan tried to get you into bed."

"One night, in the editing bay, he said he wanted to kiss me. He asked me if it was OK."

"And what did you say?"

"I asked him why. He said he really liked me. I told him I'd never done anything with a guy, no sex or anything, you know, except when I was a lot younger, fooling around, like most guys do."

"And after that?"

"I said if he really wanted to, I didn't mind. That I was open to new things, as long as he didn't expect something more. He said that was all he wanted, just to kiss me, that he'd been thinking about it for a while. So we tried it."

"How did it go?"

"We never really kissed. Somebody came in, one of the video library guys. He almost caught us. After he left, I told Tommy I was tired and wanted go home."

"Alone?"

"To be with Cheryl. My girlfriend."

"When was that?"

"Last Wednesday. It was the last time I saw Tommy." He swallowed hard, looked away. "The last time I'll ever see him."

"Did you tell the cop about your relationship with Callahan?"

"Not about the kissing stuff. I told him we worked late that night. He asked me if I was gay. I told him no, that I had a girlfriend. That was about it."

He asked me if he could use the bathroom. I pointed to the hallway and told him to take a left. While he was gone, I tried to absorb the extent of his innocence, which wasn't easy. All around me, in the musty, kitsch-filled living room, walls were covered with framed photos of friends Maurice and Fred had lost over the years; most of the faces were male, on the shy side of fifty, men who had passed in the last two decades. Jacques's face was among them, a man who had packed a lifetime of emotional and physical experience into his twenty-nine years, before the virus had claimed him. Graff seemed like someone from another planet.

When he came back, it looked as if he'd blown his nose and

washed his face. I'd turned up the volume on the television set to hear the eleven o'clock news. One of the promos mentioned a mutilated body discovered that morning in a shallow grave in the Angeles National Forest.

"You may not want to see this, Peter."

"No, I'm OK with it. I figure it's going to get worse, anyway. As more information comes out."

Toward the end of the show, after using the sensational torture angle as a teaser before two commercial breaks, the "news team," as the Eyewitless News readers referred to themselves, covered Callahan's murder in about twenty seconds. The only video they had was footage of a group of detectives and criminalists on a mountain roadside, clustered around a body covered by a coroner's blanket—not enough to warrant even half a minute.

I glanced with sympathy in Peter's direction.

"You'd think they could give the poor guy more than twenty seconds."

"Without pictures, you don't get on the air. That's the way it works."

The brief segment didn't tell us any more than we already knew, and I did some channel surfing with the remote control to see if we could find more complete coverage elsewhere. We didn't. As I clicked through the channels, we landed on a late night syndicated show called *On Patrol*. Graff reached for my hand, holding it on the remote, stopping the clicker.

"Tommy worked on this show almost fifteen years ago."

"That's a coincidence, coming on right after the report of his death."

"Not really. *On Patrol* is on five nights a week in reruns. It's so popular, the station runs it twice, in the afternoon and again late a night. A new episode airs each week, on Sundays, opposite *60 Minutes*. It's pretty hard to miss."

"Somebody's getting rich from it."

"The executive producer. That's the one who always cleans up when the show goes into reruns. No more production costs, just syndication fees rolling in from a couple of hundred stations around the country."

I'd seen the show before. As Graff said, it was hard to miss. It was one of those so-called "reality" shows, with a camera operator riding along with the cops in their patrol cars and chasing after them as they ran down suspects. It looked like a lot of similar documentary-style shows glutting the airwaves, only maybe more exciting and better edited. I said as much to Graff.

"This was the original," he said, "the show that started that whole reality trend. It was a breakthrough when it first went on the air. A really simple concept—a good camera guy following cops in action, and some sharp video editors to stitch it together. No actors or narrator to pay, no script, not much in the way of production costs. With almost fifteen years' worth of shows, it's got to be a gold mine in syndication."

"You seem to know a lot about it."

He shrugged it off.

"Everybody in the business knows about *On Patrol*. It's a TV landmark."

"And Callahan was one of the original editors?"

"That's what he told me. Said he hooked up with them the first year, lasted into the second season."

"Did he say why he left?"

"He didn't talk about that." Graff was standing. "I should get going. Thanks for letting me stop by. I guess you figured out I needed to talk to somebody."

"What about Cheryl?"

"Yeah, she's good about it. But, I don't know, I just wanted to talk to you, I guess. You've been really good to me. The way Tommy was."

"Time heals, Peter."

"Yeah, I've heard that."

I found myself saying something to him I'd said to Oree Joffrien only a few evenings before. Even as I spoke the words, I felt foolish doing it.

"You have to go so soon?"

"I really should."

"It's Friday. No work tomorrow."

His hands were back in his pants pockets, finding the bottoms.

"I've got to move in the morning. Cheryl's going back to Minnesota, to a teaching job. I can't afford to keep the apartment on my own, not with what I make." He laughed, and moved toward the door. "L.A. prices, they're insane."

"You have a new place?"

"Not yet. I'll probably take a cheap motel for a few days, till I find something I can afford."

He opened the door. One of the cats darted in, heading for the kitchen. Maggie trotted out to pee on the front lawn. My mind was moving at lightning speed, in a furious tug-of-war with itself.

"Listen, Peter—"

He stopped on the front steps, bathed in the overhead porch light.

"There's an empty apartment out back above the garage. My place, actually. I won't be using it until Maurice and Fred get back from Europe in a few weeks. My landlords."

"I couldn't do that."

"Why not?"

"I don't know, I—"

"Then it's settled. The place is yours, at least for a week or two."

"You sure?"

"It'll give you some time to find a place, get some money together. It'll be convenient while we're working on the show."

"They won't mind, Maurice and Fred?"

I shook my head, and he glanced around the yard.

"I could help out around here. Cut the grass, pull some weeds, things like that."

"You noticed I've been neglecting it."

He flashed a smile. God, he was good to look at.

"OK. I'll take you up on it. Just until I find another place."

"You need help moving?"

He turned his eyes toward his vintage Volkswagen at the curb.

"Actually, I could use a little help. A bigger car. Can't get too much into the bug."

"There's a pickup truck in the garage. Doesn't get much use. What time?"

"Noon, I guess."

"Noon it is."

"You've really been terrific, Ben. I mean it."

He laid a hand on my arm, left it there a moment, then shuffled down the steps and the front walk, stopping along the way to say good night to Maggie. I watched him climb into the VW, heard it sputter as the engine caught, and stood on the porch as it putted off down the street, thinking about the line I'd just crossed.

Inside, the phone rang. I dashed in and grabbed it in the kitchen. It was Oree Joffrien returning my call.

Eight

PETER GRAFF and his girlfriend lived on one of the narrow walk-through streets that run perpendicular to the beach in Venice, lined on either side by quaint cottages and aging apartment houses filled with surfers, artists, graying hippies, and monied yuppies eager to rub up against bohemia and pretend they're part of the counterculture, as long as they don't have to give up their new BMWs and five-hundred-dollar cappuccino machines.

Peter's place was on the north side, across Windward Avenue, in the heart of the action that had turned the funky little beachside community into one of Southern California's busiest tourist attractions. I arrived at half past ten, in time to find a parking spot on a nearby side street before the masses of weekend visitors swarmed in from every direction like buzzards descending on fresh roadkill. I pared away some time strolling Ocean Front Walk, where the vendors and sidewalk entertainers were busy setting up, and the morning breeze was brisk and salty. The Mystery Annex of Small World Books was open, and I bought their last copy of Walter Mosley's *Gone Fishin'*, then turned south along the broad walkway toward the basketball scene. Out on the courts, the pickup regulars made their showtime moves and dissed each other as they sprinted up and down the warm asphalt wearing down the soles of their hundred-dollar air shoes. Nearby, the narcissistic Muscle Beach boys pumped iron in the open-air weight-lifting arena, displaying their grotesquely developed bodies to passing gawkers while lithe gymnasts swung on the high rings a hundred feet away, performing graceful flips before landing in the sand feet first. I dodged some speeding in-line skaters, weaved through a flock of half-naked surfers, bought a corn dog, and turned in the direction of Peter's apartment.

He and his girlfriend shared a one-bedroom unit in a single-story duplex, a modest wood frame with a narrow porch and two doors, one on either side of the short front steps. I'd walked Peter as far as the front gate on Monday night, after driving him home from the Sunset Tiki Motel; I hadn't gone in, though I'd glimpsed his girlfriend's silhouette through a window, as she waited up for him. I pushed open the gate to a small yard covered in concrete and littered with cheap lawn furniture corroded by salt air, and draped with faded beach towels. The door I wanted was on the left, with a number that ended in a half. It was open, but the screen was latched from the inside, where the theme music from *Titanic* was being played. I rapped my knuckles on the warped frame, and a few seconds later Cheryl appeared, pulling a robe closed while tying the sash at her waist. An easy smile creased her pleasant face.

"You must be Mr. Justice."

"I am."

"You're early."

"Should I go away and come back?"

"Oh, no. Please, come in."

She unlatched the screen and pushed it open, and I brushed past her into a small anteroom, where I faced her for a better look. She was on the short side, conventionally pretty, with warm brown eyes and an open, friendly face. Her hair, light brown and cut neatly, fell in soft curls, just hiding her ears. Around her neck, on a delicate chain, hung a small silver crucifix that lay atop a cluster of freckles on her upper chest. Despite her bulky terrycloth robe, I could see that she was narrow-waisted and small-breasted, with slim legs that tapered to tiny bare feet.

"It's really nice of you to help Pete out like this, Mr. Justice."

"Not at all. I take it you're Cheryl?"

She threw out her hands, palms up.

"I'm sorry, I forgot to introduce myself. Yes, I'm Cheryl."

We stepped into a tiny living room filled with sealed boxes, a few pieces of luggage, and not much furniture. What there was looked thrift shop purchased.

"As you can see, we don't have a lot. Can I get you some coffee?"

"Maybe later, thanks."

"Pete tells me you're a journalist. He said you're very well known out here."

"Is that how he put it?"

"Pretty much. He said you used to write for the *Los Angeles Times,* and that you've done some magazine work. And now you're moving into television."

"He's very generous to put it that way."

"He probably mentioned that I'm going back to Minnesota to teach."

"He also said something about a trial separation."

She pulled her robe a little tighter around her.

"That's part of it. We both felt—well, mostly Pete—he felt he needed more time. To find himself, to become a more complete person, before he made a final commitment in terms of our relationship."

"How do you feel about that?"

"Honestly? I'd hoped we might be married by now. Pete's the only person I've ever been involved with, the best person I know. He's my whole life, really. I guess that's not a very modern way to be, a woman whose identity is so tied up with one man. Maybe that's part of the reason Pete needs to be away from me for a while."

"It must be hard leaving him here."

"I respect what he's trying to do. He feels it's important to change, to grow. I think that's the main reason he wanted to come out here in the first place." She did her best to reinforce the smile. "If he needs more time—well, I'll just have to wait, won't I?"

"He's lucky to have someone so understanding."

She widened her eyes, along with her falsely bright smile, and bobbed her head from side to side like a metronome.

"I'm doing my best."

There was a clatter on the porch, and we turned to see Peter leaning a wet surfboard against the wall. Then he was coming into the house, while I tried to keep my eyes above his neck.

"Ben, you're early."

"A little."

"I wanted to catch some waves one last time before I headed inland."

"I can see that."

I used the moment to steal a better look at him. He was wearing a bright red thermal wet suit that extended down not quite to his knees, with a healthy bulge midway between his hips, where things had been kept warm. He'd unzipped the top, freed his arms, and peeled the rubber suit down to his waist, exposing a finely muscled torso that was glistening wet from a quick shower on the beach. His nipples were still taut from the cold water, and a lovely web of soft golden hair spread lightly across his upper chest and into a narrowing trail down his rippled belly, which still heaved from his run up the sand. My eyes retraced their steps to his face before I spoke again.

"Cheryl and I have been getting acquainted."

He crossed the small room and kissed her on the cheek. When she spoke, it was without much sincerity, and the tightness in her voice gave away a little more of the pain she had to be feeling.

"How was the surf, honey?"

"A little blown out. I got a few good rides." He put an arm around her, pulled her close. Then, tenderly: "How are you doing?"

"I'm OK."

He kept his arm around her, but glanced my way.

"Let me jump in the shower and pull on some clothes, and we can get my stuff loaded up."

When he was behind the closed bathroom door, I asked her if she had met Tommy Callahan before he disappeared. Her curls bounced as she shook her head.

"Pete talked to me about him. Told me how Mr. Callahan had taken him under his wing, given up his personal time teaching Pete about the new editing systems."

"He had a crush on Peter. Were you aware of that?"

She turned away, rummaging through a box.

"Let me show you something, Mr. Justice." She handed me a

framed, wallet-sized photo. "This is Pete when he was seventeen, the year we met. I transferred that spring to his high school. We started dating late that summer, just before our senior year. He was generally considered the cutest boy in school, the most popular. You can see why from the picture."

I studied it a moment, handed it back, and she tucked it away, still talking.

"With most people, you assume they'll gradually lose their looks as they grow older. Sometimes, when you run into people you knew in high school, it's almost shocking how much they've changed in just a few years. With Pete, it was just the opposite—he grew into this incredibly beautiful man. The amazing thing is, he seems almost totally unaware of how attractive he is, the effect he has on certain people."

"Yes, I've noticed."

"When we're out, photographers stop him, wanting to know if he'll pose for pictures. People offer him modeling jobs all the time, promising all kinds of money. He just gets embarrassed, has trouble relating to it. So it didn't surprise me when Pete told me how Mr. Callahan felt. I'm accustomed to seeing the way some men look at him."

"What about Peter? Was he upset? Or has this kind of thing happened to him before?"

"Pete doesn't have any conflicts about his sexuality, Mr. Justice. Curiosity, maybe. Pete's curious about everything, it's one of the things I love about him. But he's a heterosexual man, I can assure you of that, if that's what you're asking."

"Actually, it wasn't."

For the first time, her smile faded, and her face lost its sweetness.

"No, he wasn't upset by the way Mr. Callahan felt."

The bathroom door opened and Peter appeared, wearing a pair of cutoffs but still toweling dry. As he joined us, Cheryl took the towel from him and used it to wipe away the dampness on his chest and arms, as routinely as one might scratch an itch.

"My plane leaves at three, Pete. I should get to the airport early. You know how busy it is on weekends."

"I'll drive you, honey. If Ben doesn't mind driving a load of my stuff back to the apartment without me."

"No. You go with him. I'll catch the shuttle."

"You sure?"

She touched his lips with two fingers, while her eyes roved his face.

"The sooner I get used to being without you, the better it will be." She stretched up and kissed him on the lips. "I'd better get dressed. It's almost noon."

Her eyes and fingers lingered on his face, and I wished I'd had the foresight to leave them alone for a while. I was about to excuse myself when she turned my way, trying to find the smile she'd lost in the last few minutes.

Her words were simple, her voice steady.

"Take good care of him, Mr. Justice."

Nine

L ATE SUNDAY MORNING, Templeton swung by the house in her freshly waxed Infiniti, draped in a casual weekend outfit from Saks that would have qualified for the pages of *Vogue*.

You can travel in style when you're the only child of a money-bags lawyer who sets you up in a half-million-dollar condo with an ocean view, puts a new car in the garage every other year on your birthday, and slips a platinum credit card into your Christmas stocking, lest you forget that you're Daddy's favorite little girl.

Templeton was, which made it all the more amazing that she was still grinding away on the crime beat at the *Sun*, determined to work her way up in the trade and become the best reporter in the business. Not the best female reporter. Not the best African American reporter. The best reporter, period.

We were meeting for brunch, and this time the meal was on me, in honor of the high-profile assignment Templeton had landed as the lead reporter on the developing police chief story and her initial front-page article in that morning's *Sun*. We called Oree Joffrien to see if he could join us, but he was on his way to speak at a symposium at USC and asked for a rain check. When we tried Harry, his machine told us he was downtown at the newspaper, catching up on his work, which caused Templeton to frown, and me to fret aloud about Harry's deteriorating health.

We were in the kitchen, near the window, with the two cats rubbing around our ankles. It was nearly eleven, and Templeton was getting hungry.

"I guess it's just the two of us, Justice."

That's when she spotted Peter Graff in the backyard, rough-housing with Maggie, who was romping on the grass, getting in touch with her inner puppy.

"Who is *that?*"

After helping Graff move in the previous afternoon, I'd done my best to put him in the back of my mind, preferring to keep my radar pointed at Oree Joffrien. But there he was, right in my own backyard, freshly showered and shaved, looking like a young Robert Redford, though somehow more golden.

"That's Peter. The guy I tried to tell you about Friday afternoon when I dropped by the *Sun* and you didn't have any time for me."

"The one whose friend they found in the mountains?"

I nodded. She stared out the window, her jaw hanging.

"He's adorable."

"That's what I tried to tell you Friday afternoon."

"What's he doing in your backyard?"

"Playing with the dog."

"Yes, I can see that." She gave me a look. "Justice?"

"He's staying in the apartment until Fred and Maurice get back."

"Well, isn't *that* convenient."

"It's temporary, Templeton. Until he finds a place of his own. By the way, as far as I can tell, he's homosexually challenged."

"Straight? And that good-looking? Hard to believe."

She was staring out the window again. I noticed that her upper lip was slightly moist.

"Shouldn't we invite him to join us, Ben?" She looked over, her eyes soft, her voice syrupy. "It would be the polite thing to do, don't you think?"

Graff accepted our invitation, and the three of us sauntered down to Santa Monica Boulevard, swung left, and headed toward Boy Meets Grill. I hadn't seen so many heads turn along the boulevard since a dark-haired, doe-eyed actor named Esai Morales had ridden through with a bunch of his Hollywood pals on their Harleys. As we passed the sidewalk tables outside

Rimbaud's, where the brunch champagne was flowing among the older crowd, there were the usual murmurs and low whistles. By the time we'd passed A Different Light and reached Boy Meets Grill, we'd left several cases of whiplash in our wake.

All three of us got high on caffeine, passing on the complimentary bubbly, while Templeton interviewed Peter with a reporter's relentless curiosity and the savvy of an experienced single woman closing in on her prey. When Graff excused himself to use the rest room, I warned Templeton that she was in danger of scaring him off.

"You think I'm overdoing it?"

"You haven't let up on him since we left the house."

"You're right. I'm being a complete fool. It's just that—"

"He's totally delectable, in every imaginable way."

"He must have some flaws, Justice."

"Let me know when you find one."

"Someone should put him in the movies."

"Yeah, playing Jesus."

"I suddenly feel like I'm fourteen again. I haven't felt this flustered since my first Michael Jackson concert."

"Exactly my reaction the first time I met him. Completely disorienting."

She paused with a forkful of eggs Benedict poised in midair, offering me an ironic version of a happy face.

"Isn't it nice when we see eye to eye on something, Justice?"

"How about getting me a copy of the police report on Tommy Callahan's murder? Maybe the autopsy as well. You think we can see eye to eye on that?"

"I guess I could find some time. Since you're giving Peter to me."

"Sorry, Templeton, you have to earn him."

She looked up, across the room.

"Here he comes. What should we be talking about?"

"How about your new assignment at the *Sun*?"

Graff took his seat, and placed his napkin back in his lap.

"The people in here are really friendly."

Templeton and I exchanged a glance, and worked hard not to laugh.

"Alex and I were just discussing her new assignment." I dug

into my Belgian waffle. "You might fill Peter in, since he's something of a newcomer to the city."

In a nutshell, Templeton laid out the evolving story: After two successive police chiefs who were African American, it appeared that Los Angeles might once again have its first white chief since the notorious Daryl Gates. Gates, a public figure of unsurpassed arrogance and insensitivity to social issues and minority groups, had presided over the Los Angeles Police Department from 1978 to 1992, a period when crime and racial tensions in the city grew to an all-time high, along with complaints against the department for racism, misogyny, homophobia, and brutality. Gates's tumultuous reign culminated in the videotaped beating of African American Rodney King in 1991 and the full-scale rioting that swept the city after the acquittal of the four white officers criminally charged in the King incident by an all-white jury in suburban Simi Valley. After Gates's forced resignation, a new charter amendment established a maximum of two five-year terms for the police chief, who came under the scrutiny and supervision of the five-member Board of Police Commissioners. Due to deaths and resignations on the board, and new appointments by the current mayor, the board was now predominantly white and largely conservative. The most recent chief had unexpectedly resigned for health reasons. Pressure was building for the appointment of a Caucasian chief from among the LAPD's so-called "rank and file"—comprised primarily of white male veteran officers—who were concerned that too many recruits were being drawn from among minority applicants, reversing the hiring patterns of the Gates regime, while promotions were going less often to white officers.

"There are several veteran officers in the running," Templeton told us, "all of them well qualified, with the requisite experience and credentials. A mix of races, even a Jewish candidate, which is unusual. But the selection process has become politically charged, and the feeling seems to be that Taylor Fairchild is the front-runner for the job. He started his climb to power during the Gates era and is currently the assistant chief."

I put down my fork, getting interested.

"A Gates crony?"

"From what I understand."

"Eager to turn back the clock?"

"That remains to be seen. But there's definitely plenty of controversy swirling around him."

Graff wiped his mouth with his napkin, looking confused.

"Why are people so upset? I mean, if he's risen so high through the ranks during three different administrations, he must be pretty good at what he does."

"I know that he's a devout Christian," Templeton said, "which has caused concern in some quarters. His mother is Rose Fairchild, one of the wealthiest women in the country."

"You're saying a Christian shouldn't be police chief? Or somebody who happens to be rich?"

Templeton smiled benignly.

"I'm not saying that at all, Peter. I was raised a Baptist myself, and my father earns a bundle. If I'm not mistaken, the last two chiefs, who were black, were both Christian and regular churchgoers."

"But you just said—"

"I said there's concern in certain quarters, apparently because Fairchild is rather rigid in his religious convictions, which lean toward fundamentalism. He's also very close to his mother, who reportedly funnels millions of dollars into fundamentalist right-wing causes, while keeping it quiet. Some people question whether a man with such strict religious beliefs and extremist political connections can run the day-to-day operations of the police department in the most culturally diverse city in the world with an open and flexible mind. The issue isn't religion or money so much as tolerance."

I smiled weakly.

"Or the lack thereof."

Peter glanced at me, offering a small shrug.

"I guess I can see where that would be a problem."

"Not here in West Hollywood, thank God."

"Not directly," Templeton said. "But anyone who takes over the LAPD inevitably has a profound impact on the entire region. The chief commands more than nine thousand sworn officers, the second largest police force in the country. His annual budget exceeds a billion dollars. It's a very powerful position. Some people feel Fairchild wants to use the chief's position as a stepping-stone to higher public office. It wouldn't be the first time."

I raised my eyebrows.

"Sounds like a meaty assignment for a reporter with some *chutzpah.*"

"Does it make you wistful for the old days, Justice?"

"Not at all. To my utter amazement, I'm a documentary writer now, getting a new start." I glanced across at Peter. "With an ace associate producer to show me the way. Right, Peter?"

He turned an endearing shade of crimson, and stared at a sprig of parsley on his otherwise empty plate.

"I'll do my best."

Templeton fixed him with her lively dark eyes.

"I hope Ben leaves you enough time for a social life, Peter. You know the old adage about all work and no play."

We all smiled, while the busboy warmed our coffees and cleared away our empty plates.

Ten

O N MONDAY MORNING, I arrived at New Image Productions to find three boxes of labeled videocassettes waiting
for me in the office I was to share with Peter Graff.

Graff detailed the drill.

"These are all three-quarter-inch dubs that you can view on
your VCR at home if you'd like. The master tapes are all in the
library on beta, which is half inch. Each tape is numbered. For
example, Joffrien-1. That would be the first reel from the Oree
Joffrien interview.

"When you view the tapes, you'll see a time code burned in
along the bottom, which tells you where you are within the tape,
broken down by hour, minute, second, and split second. When
you find a sound bite or section of footage you think you might
use in your show, make a note of the tape number, along with the
general beginning and end time, so we can find the bite later for
transfer and digitizing purposes."

I scanned the three boxes, calculating roughly a hundred
videocassettes.

"I have a feeling I'm going to be watching a lot of television."

He laughed.

"Viewing and selecting footage is a big part of the job. Could I
make a suggestion?"

"Of course."

"Look first at what Tommy already selected. He wasn't too good at the writing part, but he had a great visual sense. You may find that a lot of what he's already picked out is stuff you can use. Then you can start going through the rest of the tapes to see what else you might want, or make a wish list of things you feel you still need."

"So I don't just sit down and write the script first?"

"I don't want to tell you how to work, Ben. You know a lot more about writing than me."

"Peter, help me out here."

"If it were me, I think I'd want to get a pretty good idea of what kind of visuals were available, or within our budget range, before I started writing. I think that's what most of the writers do."

There was a knock at the door. It was Denise, Chang's assistant.

"Cecile wonders if you could stop by her office for a moment."

"Both of us?"

She nodded, backed her wheelchair up, turned, and we followed her to the end of the hall. Chang sat on the edge of her desk, propped up on slim legs and high heels. Her face was solemn, almost ashen.

Sitting on the couch was a heavyset woman with messy blond hair that showed dark roots, and golden brown eyes that were moist and jumpy. She was wearing pale lavender warm-ups that looked as though they might be from K Mart, and a pair of walking shoes that needed washing. As we entered, she put her hands on her big thighs and heaved her body up, then tugged her warm-up top down around her broad hips.

Chang slipped off her desk and joined us.

"This is Melissa Zeigler. Miss Zeigler, Benjamin Justice, Peter Graff."

Graff and I waited out a brief silence, while Chang grew uncharacteristically uneasy.

"I suppose I should just say it straightaway—there's been another murder."

"Connected to Tommy Callahan's death?"

"Possibly. Melissa and the victim were engaged to be married. Melissa has some information—well, I'll let her tell it. She came here asking to talk with anyone who knew Tommy."

"That would be Peter, not me."

"I thought you might be able to speak with her, Ben. Since you and Peter went together to the motel last Friday. We never did go into any details about what you might have found there."

"Just a tossed room, Cecile, and some blood on a mattress."

Her eyes never left my face.

"Nothing more than that? Nothing—out of the ordinary?"

"I didn't see anything. Did you, Peter?"

"No, just what Ben said. Like we told the police."

Chang smiled sympathetically.

"I told Melissa we'd do our best to answer her questions. She feels strongly that there's a connection between Tommy's murder and the death of her fiancé."

I asked Melissa Zeigler what she thought that connection might be.

"Indirect, through Byron. My fiancé, Byron Mittelman. He and Mr. Callahan worked together once." She blinked back sudden tears, got control of herself. "Byron was found shot to death Sunday morning, a week ago."

"Do you mind if I ask how?"

"His brother found him. We were all going to temple together."

"No—I meant, how had he been shot?"

She grimaced.

"What the detectives called execution-style."

"A single bullet to the head?"

"Yes!"

She blurted out the word, then the tears came in a rush. Graff led her back to the couch, urging her to sit. Chang went to her desk and came back with a box of tissues. Zeigler took one, while I stood looking on, feeling like a jerk.

"I'm sorry for being so blunt, Miss Zeigler. I was a crime reporter once. It can harden you. I guess I'd forgotten how much."

She dabbed at her eyes.

"Yes, I know your background, Mr. Justice. I recognized your name when Miss Chang mentioned it. She confirmed it for me."

She blew her nose, and Chang held out a wastecan for the used tissue.

"I'm a social worker, Mr. Justice. You wrote a series for the *Times* in the late eighties on nursing home abuses. It got some regulations changed, made a difference for a lot of people." She smiled, still sniffling. "I haven't forgotten it."

"Forgive me, but I'm not sure how I can help you now."

"I'm not really sure myself. I'm searching for anything, anyone who might have some answers. The police don't seem to be doing anything. I guess I'm feeling a bit desperate."

Her words came at us rapid-fire, as her voice wound tighter and tighter. I asked Peter to get her some water. While he was gone, I sat at the other end of the sofa, while Chang leaned on the edge of her desk again, arms folded across her chest.

"Why don't you start as far back as possible, Melissa, when Tommy and Byron worked together."

"It was fourteen, fifteen years ago. On that show, *On Patrol*—the one about police officers. Cinema verité Byron called it. He doesn't like the term reality show, except for the ones that use actors and reenactments. Anyway, Byron was a cameraman on the show the first year, and Mr. Callahan was one of the editors. Mr. Callahan was fired during the show's second season, and Byron lost touch with him. Then, the week before last, Thursday I think, Mr. Callahan called Byron, warning him that he might be in danger."

"Byron told you this?"

She nodded.

"All these years had gone by, and suddenly Callahan called him out of the blue. Byron was really upset by that call. He tried to pretend he wasn't, but I could tell. I finally made him sit down and tell me what was going on."

Graff returned, handed her a glass of water, and took one of the chairs next to Chang's desk. Zeigler sipped some water and went on.

"Byron told me that during that first season, while he was out riding with an officer from the Hollywood division, he videotaped two other officers beating up a transvestite on a side street. Byron remembered the incident very clearly. He still had a lot of guilt about it—about what happened later."

"Did he give you any details?"

"He said the incident took place in an alley off Hollywood Boulevard, near the old Egyptian Theater. The two officers who were beating up the cross-dresser were in an undercover car, which was parked nearby. Byron even remembered the date. April fourteenth, his mother's birthday. He said that when the patrol car he was riding in turned into the alley, the other two officers had this man on the ground, kicking him. Byron said one of the cops was in a frenzy, like an attacking shark. Laughing, cursing, calling the man terrible names. Just kicking the hell out of this poor man.''

"And the officer Byron was riding with stopped it?''

"Yes, immediately. He told the other two cops to back off, and they did. Byron said the man on the ground was hysterical, begging them not to arrest him. He told them he was married, not a prostitute. That he dressed and made up as a woman in secret, and his family didn't know.''

"Byron recorded all this with his camera?''

"Most of it, until the third officer, the one who intervened, told him to stop taping. He sent the other two cops away and called for an ambulance. Byron said the victim was very badly beaten. Basically, this third cop saved this poor guy's life.''

"What happened to the videotape?''

"It was never shown on the air. Byron told me the police departments all have the right of final approval over each show's content. The footage was locked away with other sensitive incidents that had been taped in different cities. You know, police officers harassing suspects, using foul language, racist behavior, that type of thing. Anything that cast the police in a negative light. Byron was young, it was his first good job in TV. So he went back to work and kept quiet about it.''

"That's why he felt so guilty.''

"Yes. Because he hadn't done anything to get those two bad cops off the street.''

"Where does Tommy Callahan fit in, Melissa?''

"He was fired about a year later, apparently for excessive drinking. Byron said he was furious about losing his job. He felt they should have given him another chance, the way they do executives who have drinking or drug problems. Before he left, he got into the vault where the outtakes were kept and stole the reel Byron had shot of the transvestite beating, along with some of the other censored material.

"Apparently, he kept it all these years, waiting for the right time to use it to his advantage. When he called Byron not quite two weeks ago, he said he'd been in contact with one of the cops who did the beating, trying to make some kind of deal. I don't know what happened exactly, but Callahan was afraid for his life. He reminded Byron that he was the only eyewitness to the incident, except for the other officers involved. And, of course, the victim."

"Let me see if I have this right, Melissa. Two cops in an undercover car trapped a transvestite in an alley and beat the hell out of him. A third cop intervened, and Byron, your fiancé, caught it all on tape. Callahan stole that tape, and fifteen years later tried to use it to pry some cash out of one of the cops who were involved. Only it backfired, and he got scared and tried to warn Byron to watch his back."

"Yes, that's pretty much what happened."

"Do you know where Callahan was calling from?"

"A motel in Hollywood. That's all he said."

"What happened after that?"

"Byron heard a struggle at the other end of the phone. There was some kind of commotion, and he heard Mr. Callahan crying out. Then the line went dead. Byron told me about it on Saturday. He was killed that night or early the next morning, after we'd gone to the movies and he'd dropped me off at my apartment."

"They broke into his place?"

"No." Her chin trembled, and she wrung her hands. "No, they ambushed him outside his apartment. In the carport. That's where his brother found him."

"You read about Tommy Callahan's murder in the paper?"

"I saw it on the news. It seemed obvious to me that Byron and Mr. Callahan had been murdered by the same people."

"There's more than a murder a day in Los Angeles, Melissa. Murders happen for all kinds of reasons."

"Then why was Byron shot just once in the head like that? Nothing was stolen. He's never been in any kind of trouble. He was just a sweet, hardworking man who wanted to get married and raise a family."

She buried her face in her hands and began weeping again. Peter carried the box of tissues over, set it beside her on the couch, and went back to his chair, looking shell-shocked.

"Did you tell all this to the police, Melissa?"

She nodded and blotted her face with another tissue.

"Yes, just the way I've explained it to you. They took notes and seemed to act as if it was important. But since I first talked with them, another detective has taken over the case, and I haven't heard another word about it. Sergeant Felix Montego, that's his name. The original detectives told me Montego is handling Byron's case, and also the Callahan murder, so there's obviously a link. I've tried calling Montego, but I think he's avoiding me."

"I'm not surprised. It's a volatile story."

"I don't know what to do. To be honest, I'm a little scared myself."

Cecile Chang slipped off the desk, came to the couch, and sat on the arm.

"You're going through a terrible experience, Melissa. You should be grieving, and instead you have all these other matters troubling you." She laid a comforting hand on Zeigler's shoulder. "Maybe the thing to do is to let things lie for a bit. Until you've had a chance to let your emotions settle and begin to get some closure."

Chang turned, casting her eyes over me, on their way to Graff.

"Maybe that's the best thing for all of us. To let the police handle it for now, in their own way. By their very nature, police investigations can be slow, painstaking procedures. Isn't that true, Mr. Justice?"

"So can police cover-ups."

"All I'm saying is, the police may be doing more than we're aware of. Will you grant me that much?"

"It's a possibility, I guess."

She returned her attention to Melissa Zeigler.

"Perhaps it would be wise if you let them proceed in their methodical way for now, and not let your concern for your fiancé cause your emotions to run wild."

Zeigler folded her elbows into her lap, then clasped her hands, rubbing the palms together. She looked exhausted, spent.

"It's all so confusing. There are so many questions that need to be answered. So many questions . . ."

Eleven

AFTER MY MEETING with Melissa Zeigler, and the unsettling new twist in the Tommy Callahan case, I returned to the office I shared with Peter Graff to view tapes.

I sat in a hard steel folding chair for an hour or two, looking at footage of circuit parties, gay bathhouses, and sex clubs, and two or three interviews Callahan had conducted, stopping, rewinding, fast forwarding, and noting reel numbers and time codes when certain snippets caught my interest. But as hard as I tried, I couldn't keep my mind on my work. Finally, when Graff was out of the room, I called Templeton at the *Sun*.

"Make it quick, Justice. I'm on deadline."

I told her that in addition to the police and autopsy reports on the Callahan murder, I needed similar documents involving a murder victim named Byron Mittelman and anything she could find on an incident of police brutality going back fifteen years to April 14.

"I should be able to get you the recent reports, Justice. But the one from fifteen years back, that could take some time. More than I've got at the moment."

"It may lead to something interesting for a smart reporter I know who's always on the make for a good story."

The tone in her voice became more attentive.

"What's going on?"

"Find me what I need, and if there's something there I'll talk to you about it."

"How about if I turn you over to Katie Nakamura? She can dig for the old report while I round up the new ones."

"You think she's got the time?"

"Katie got her two-week notice. With only two years on staff, she was one of the first to go."

"Tough break. She's an ace. Nice kid, too."

"It's eating Harry up inside. So, yes, Katie's got some time on her hands. Harry won't bitch if she does a favor for you."

Templeton transferred me to Nakamura, a graduate of Northwestern who had done an internship at the *Sun,* then a year of database research in the *Sun*'s library, and had spent the last year as a news reporter, following in Templeton's footsteps.

When she came on the line, I told her I was sorry to hear she'd lost her job.

"I'll survive, Mr. Justice. I know my way around the Internet pretty well. I'm not worried."

"The Internet. The wave of the future."

"I'm afraid the future is now, Mr. Justice."

"I'm afraid you're right, Katie."

I told her what I was looking for: any kind of police or ambulance report dated fifteen years ago on the night of April 14, in the proximity of the Egyptian Theater on Hollywood Boulevard. I suggested she look for a male victim, though he might be identified as wearing women's clothes.

"That's all you can tell me, Mr. Justice? No names?"

"I wish I had more."

"I'll see what I can find."

After that, I called Oree Joffrien at UCLA. This time, I managed to catch him in, and asked if he had plans for dinner. He suggested a Mose Allison concert first, at a small club on Vine Street in Hollywood. I managed to get home, feed the animals, get in a hike and a shower, and meet him at the club just as the first show was starting. Allison, the king of white cool in the world of jazz, was in top form, running through his standards and a few tunes I hadn't heard in his inimitable, laid-back style. He was especially good on "Seventh Son" and "Parchman Farm," and had the crowd hollering for more when his set ended at half past nine.

Oree and I stood at the rail separating the bar from the supper club, a great place to catch the show, and I should have been having a swell time, but I wasn't. For the first time since I'd stopped drinking cold turkey a couple of months before, I was hearing the clatter of ice cubes in liquor glasses and the pop of wine and champagne bottles being opened; after a while, I realized I was paying as much attention to that distinctive cocktail music as I was to the crooner and his combo out on the floor. When we finally moved with the crowd out into the blinking neon night, I felt a sense of safety and relief, and tried to redirect my attention to the alluring man beside me.

We ate nearby at Chan Dara, the cozy little restaurant just off Sunset Boulevard that had helped start the Thai craze in L.A. back in the seventies. Our table was tucked into the little window nook in the side room, where we could look out at the drunks, hustlers, and homeless people shuffling between Sunset and Hollywood boulevards, looking for a handout or just a place to get out of the cold for the night. It wasn't the most romantic setting one might hope for, but in this part of town it would have to do. We started by sharing a bowl of Tom Kah Kai, a spicy soup of chicken cooked with Thai herbs in coconut milk, then gorged on peppery Beef Panang and thick Pad Thai noodles, washing it all down with tall glasses of sweet Thai iced tea. The conversation was just as rich and varied and went down just as smoothly, without the awkward silences that plague so many first dates.

Toward the end of dinner, I found myself asking Oree about his friendship with Cecile Chang.

"Why so curious about Cecile, Ben?"

"She's your good friend. I work for her. Is there a problem?"

He studied me a moment, his eyes thoughtful.

"No problem." He sipped some of the creamy tea. "We met by accident, really. We were both deep in the closet at the time, and damned miserable about it. One night I got up my courage and attended a meeting of the Gay Students' Union. This was the late eighties. The subject was coming out in the age of AIDS, something like that." He smiled a little, shaking his head. "I sneaked in with my collar turned up and a cap pulled low over my ears, and took a seat as far in the back as I could. I felt like a nigger crawling to the back of the bus, if you want to know the truth.''

"Cecile attended the same meeting?''

"She arrived just before it started. Took a seat near me. During a break, we started talking. Maybe because she was female, and that made me more comfortable.'' His smile widened. "We've never stopped talking, really, even when I came west, and she stayed behind, making her mark in the documentary field.''

"When was that?''

"I joined the faculty at UCLA in ninety-two, three years after getting my Ph.D. Four years ago, Cecile came to L.A. to be with Tiger.''

"They met in New York?''

"They hooked up on an all-lesbian cruise, up in Alaska. Tiger's the first woman Cecile's ever been in love with, from what she tells me. And if I know Cecile, there won't be another.''

"She seems to know what she wants, and how to get things done.''

"No question about that.''

"In a roundabout way, she brought us together.''

I reached across the table, laid my hand over his. He allowed my hand to stay for a polite moment, then withdrew his own.

"She also brought you together with Peter Graff.''

"Peter and I work together, that's all.''

"My eyes deceive me, then.''

"He's hard not to look at, Oree.''

"For some, maybe.''

"You're telling me you don't find Peter Graff attractive?''

"Not my type at all. Too young, too pretty. I like a man with some years on him, who's a little rough around the edges.''

"Do I happen to fit the profile?''

"Very nicely, as a matter of fact.''

"The feeling's mutual, in case you hadn't noticed.''

"You seem to have a wide range in tastes.''

"They narrow pretty quickly for the right man.''

"I don't believe in moving too quickly myself. Not in matters of the heart.''

"Been hurt once too often?''

"I have my reasons.''

"I'm all ears.''

"It's late, Ben."

"Not really."

"Yes, really, it is."

"I think this is where we said goodbye the last time."

"Different time, different place, Ben."

"But not the right time yet."

"It's been a nice evening. We should do it again. Keep getting to know each other, little by little."

"Do you mean that, Oree? Or are you just being polite?"

"You'll have to be patient, Ben. You'll have to be willing to let things develop. I can't be hurried. I won't be."

"I've never been the patient type."

"Maybe it's time you gave it a try."

I drove home along Santa Monica Boulevard mulling that last minute before we paid the check and said good night, with a brief hug but nothing more. I was still mulling it as I pulled into the driveway on Norma Place. It was a few minutes after eleven, and I could see Peter Graff up in the apartment, practicing Tai Chi movements under the bare bulb. I turned out the headlights and sat watching him for several minutes, deciding whether to go up and say hello before I finally climbed out and went into the house instead.

I took notes during the final minutes of that night's rerun of *On Patrol.* The name I was looking for in the end credits was that of the executive producer. It turned out to be Jacob Kosterman, which I jotted down. But during the crawl, which I'd learned was the correct term for the rolling credits, I saw another man mentioned, whose name also went into my notebook. His title was technical consultant. The name was Taylor Fairchild.

Twelve

AN UNSEASONABLE warm front hit the Southland, and the route through Laurel Canyon on Tuesday morning was a journey through speckled sunlight and steamy air infused with earthy fragrances rising from the damp wooded hillsides.

My belly was filled with a good breakfast and plenty of coffee from Duke's up on the Sunset Strip, where I'd eaten at a long table that included a heavy metal band at one end and two uniformed deputies at the other, and the usual odd assortment in between. I had the top down and the radio on to 88.1 on the FM band, and I twisted the wheel through the winding canyon to a nifty Art Pepper rendition of "Patricia," his mellow sax providing a perfect punctuation to the pleasant rhythms of the morning. I wondered if Oree Joffrien might be listening to the same tune at that moment, and, with any luck, thinking about me the way I was thinking about him.

I smiled at the thought, and was still smiling when I pulled into the small parking lot at New Image Productions. When I arrived a few minutes later for a scheduled appointment with Cecile Chang to sign the final contract I'd approved I found a note taped to her office door: *All meetings canceled Tuesday while I finish cutting the grants video upstairs. Apologies. Please reschedule with Denise.*

Denise, I learned, had called in sick with the flu, and wasn't expected back for another day or two. Meanwhile, I was close to being flat broke—Mose Allison and dinner with Oree had pretty much tapped out my checking account—and I needed a paycheck sooner rather than later. At the very least, it seemed to me, Chang could take a minute or two to move my signed contract to accounting, so my first check could be cut, a two-thousand-dollar payment that had become due upon approval of my outline the previous Friday, to tide me over through the writing of the first draft.

I was told by the operations supervisor that Chang was in Editing Bay Number Four but was not to be disturbed. I thanked her, followed the numbered doors down the hallway, found the right one, and rapped with my knuckles. Inside, I could hear a voice on audio that sounded like Chang's, talking about the importance of research in the documentary process, then a *whir* as the audio was rewound before being played again. I closed my fist and pounded on the door with the meaty part of my hand. This time the audio went silent and Chang pulled open the door.

"Sorry to bother you, Cecile—"

"Didn't you see the note posted on my office door?"

"I'm afraid I need to sign my contract and get a paycheck moving."

"Ask Denise to take care of it."

She started to close the door, which I stopped with the flat of my hand.

"Denise is out sick."

Through the half-open door, I could see an editor working at the knobs and switches of the AVID control panel, making pictures appear, disappear, fade, or dissolve. On one of the two monitor screens, Chang could be seen walking slowly through the crowded research room, dressed in the outfit she'd been wearing the first time we'd met. In the background, as she talked directly to the camera, young men and women worked at their cluttered desks; file cabinets with open drawers were crammed with papers, shelves were filled with videocassettes, and a wall clock indicated the hour of ten-fifteen.

"Your contract is on my desk, Ben. Sign all the copies and leave them on my chair so I don't miss them. I'll take care of it at lunch."

"I appreciate it."

"I should have seen to it sooner. Now, please, I must get back to work. This video is due for presentation on Monday, and we still have my narration to record and lay down before we go to on-line."

Over her shoulder, I watched the editor put his dissolve function to work, blending one cut slowly into the next.

"Maybe I could sit in and observe. Learn some of the tricks."

"I prefer to work without distractions."

The tone of her voice told me the conversation was over.

"Sorry I disturbed you."

She smiled tightly and shut the door in the same manner. I heard a lock being turned inside.

Downstairs, I found my contract on her desk, placed neatly in the upper right-hand corner, anchored by a cigarette packet with the name Capri on the front. I bent over the contract pages, signing where my name was required, and left all three copies on the seat of Chang's chair. I was about to step from her office into an empty hallway, when I changed my mind. I stepped back in, shut and locked the door, placed the contracts on the credenza, and took the chair myself. For the next several minutes, I faced the PC screen, moving through Chang's directories. After failing to find anything interesting, I stepped across to her file cabinets, which looked more promising. I was particularly intrigued by the one marked *Applicants/Resumes.*

I went directly to the files under C; Tommy Callahan's was among those at the front. Inside were three documents: his resume, his application for a job with New Image Productions, and a cover story neatly clipped from *Broadcast Monthly* magazine. It was a profile of Jacob Kosterman, who was identified beneath his smiling cover photo as the president and CEO of the cable Documentary Channel—the same Jacob Kosterman, I presumed, who was also listed in the credits of *On Patrol* as its executive producer. Callahan's resume showed a gap in his employment history of more than a year before he came to New Image looking for work. His last job had been with Jaffe-Edwards Productions on a military history series the company had produced for the Documentary Channel. In the margin were several notes in Chang's distinctive handwriting:

1/23 Callahan interview OK, check J-E Prod.

1/24 Jaffe re: Callahan—blackballed per Kosterman direct order.
1/26 Kosterman details on T.C. firing (off the record)
1/26 Put in Callahan hire ASAP

I scanned the rest of Callahan's work history, which went back twenty-seven years to his first job in television, as an apprentice editor with a local public affairs show in Cincinnati when he was in his mid-twenties. For twelve years from that point forward, his career showed a steady rise, with jobs of increasing responsibility that took him to Chicago, San Francisco, then to L.A., where he hooked up with *On Patrol.* In his resume, he described it as "the first true cinema verité show in the history of network television," and obviously considered it a feather in his cap. After leaving *On Patrol* in its second season, his work record was spotty at best; it appeared that every job he landed was of brief duration, with wider and wider gaps in between. After more than a year without work, his hiring at New Image in late January, along with his subsequent promotion to writer-producer must have seemed like extraordinary luck to him.

I replaced Callahan's resume in his file, removed the *Broadcast Monthly* cover piece on Jacob Kosterman, and photocopied it on the Xerox machine in Denise's office. I replaced the original where it belonged, shut the file drawer, put my signed contracts back on Chang's chair, and went out to find a decent cup of coffee and do some reading.

I took my caffeine at a sidewalk table outside a small joint called Java Time that had somehow survived the Starbucks invasion, and scanned the Kosterman profile, which the editors had rather pompously titled "The Man Who Put Truth Back in Television." The article ran five pages, and was replete with photos of Kosterman aging from a wild-haired sixties radical to a dapper, mustachioed man in his late fifties with a shaved head and a single gold earring in his left ear. It was essentially a puff job, with little in it that was probing or critical, but it told me what I needed to know for the time being: Jacob Kosterman had been a firebrand documentary filmmaker as a young man, with a bachelor's degree in journalism and a master's in film, along with a passion for leftist causes. During the seventies, he had drifted back toward the mainstream, married, and had a growing family to support. A skillful low-budget filmmaker, who knew how to get "maximum bang for the buck," as the article put it, he developed a successful career as a producer of cheap syndicated specials that garnered unusually high ratings. His subject matter tended to be on the sensational side: "Scandals of the Rich and Famous," "Inside the White House Bedrooms," "Mondo Oscar: Behind the Scenes at the Academy Awards." By the early eighties, Kosterman had found his niche in a television world that was rapidly expanding, with new outlets hungry for viewers that lacked the huge budgets of the three major networks. According to *Broadcast Monthly,* that was when Kosterman came up with a surefire concept: Put an athletic cameraman in a police car, have him tape whatever happened on patrol, get the suspects to sign clearances, then edit the raw footage into a fast-paced half hour that captured the action, drama, humor, and pathos in the daily life of the big city cop.

Kosterman called his show *On Patrol,* opened it with a pounding Isaac Hayes R&B score, sold it to the fledgling United Broadcast Network, and struck television gold. The show, more gritty and realistic than any commercial network had ever dared to put on the air, caused an instant sensation. More important, it attracted a loyal audience of male viewers in the fifteen to thirty-five age range that was so coveted by the big national advertisers pushing beer, cars, and razor blades, and became the Sunday night "anchor" program for the fledgling UBN network, second only to *60 Minutes* in the ratings for its time slot. When the show had gone into reruns after its fifth season, as a five-day-a-week syndicated "strip," Kosterman became an instant millionaire, with money flowing in that he literally did not know what to do with. In the meantime, *On Patrol* ignited a wave of so-called "reality" shows that swept the airwaves, as imitators rushed to cash in on the public's appetite for "fact-based" programming.

At that point, when Kosterman could have continued to exploit the reality craze he had helped to spawn, he took a dramatic turn professionally and creatively: He founded the Documentary Channel, a twenty-four-hour cable outlet devoted to nothing but nonfiction films and series. With his vast wealth, abetted by coinvestors, he had returned to his original passion for documentary filmmaking, and was now president and CEO of one of cable television's most successful enterprises. The magazine's editors had pulled one of his quotes and framed it in a box within the article:

> "With *On Patrol*, I brought something fresh to television, giving the audience a dose of truth it couldn't find anywhere else. Now, with the Documentary Channel, I've been able to take that principle of truth in television and build on it, giving viewers the opportunity to see subjects explored in documentary form, where facts are the driving force."
>
> —Jacob Kosterman
> President & CEO of The Documentary Channel

I set the article aside, and stopped to consider what I was doing: sticking my nose where it didn't belong, worrying about matters that had nothing to do with me. Things were going pretty well for me again. I was healthy, living in reasonable comfort, and becoming involved with a remarkable man who seemed at least somewhat interested in me. I had a television show to write, visuals to select, interviews to cull, footage to edit. I was earning a paycheck again, with at least the glimmer of a chance at a new career. I didn't need to alienate Cecile Chang, and certainly not a television big shot like Jacob Kosterman, by asking troubling questions neither of them wanted to hear. What I needed, more than anything, was to work again, and to keep working.

I finished my coffee and walked back to New Image Productions, intending to view my way through more of the videotapes that sat in the three boxes on Peter Graff's office floor—intending to stay focused on the work, and forget the intrigue swirling around the murders of Tommy Callahan and Byron Mittelman. But when I arrived, I found Melissa Zeigler waiting for me in the lobby.

She jumped up from her seat the moment she saw me, her big body jiggling like Jell-O in the same lavender warm-up suit she'd worn the day before. Her dirty blond hair was in even more of a tangle, and she wore no makeup. Her words came in a rush, but halting at the same time, as if the connections between her brain and her mouth were short-circuiting.

"I'm sorry to bother you, Ben. It's just that, I don't know, this whole thing has me—I'm very upset. I don't know what I'm going to do, I just—"

"Take it easy, Melissa."

"I have no right to ask you to help me."

"I don't really know what I can do for you."

She was wringing her hands now, pacing the lobby.

"It's just that, I don't know, you seem the only one who wants to listen. The detective they put on the case, this Sergeant Montego, I don't think he really intends to investigate this at all. I think he's trying to ignore me, hoping I'll just go away."

She whirled on me, her face an anguished mix of grief and fury.

"But I won't go away, Ben! Because what's happening is not fair. It's not fair to me, it's not fair to Byron. Have I shown you a picture of Byron?"

Before I could answer, she rushed back to her chair, where she dug frantically in a large handbag, spilling items onto the floor. Harold, whose spiked hair had gone from lavender to neon green over the weekend, stared at me pleadingly, as if she were my responsibility. She returned with a wallet-size photo of a plump, fortyish man whose unruly dark hair was going thin on top, wearing horn-rimmed glasses with soft, pleasant eyes behind the rims.

"As you can see, he was on the heavy side, like me, though not as big, but that didn't bother him. He saw beyond that, beneath the surface. He said I was beautiful. He saw what was inside, Ben! How many men do you find like that?"

"Too few, I'm sure."

"We were going to be married, have children. I'm thirty-nine. I'll probably never have a child now. Byron's been murdered, and my life's been torn apart, and they aren't doing anything about it! I loved him, Ben! I loved Byron!"

Her voice had risen to a shrill pitch, and Harold suddenly rose behind his crescent-shaped desk. His lisp, always lively, got livelier.

"Thank God, you're back, Mr. Justice! I tried to console this poor woman—I even offered her one of my Valiums. But she only wanted to talk with you."

"Don't worry, Harold. Things are under control."

I convinced Melissa Zeigler to sit, and took a chair beside her. All I could think to do was to make her a promise.

"I'll look into it for you, Melissa. I'll try to light a fire under this Sergeant Montego."

"If you could, it would mean so much."

"I'll see what I can do. On one condition."

"What's that?"

"That you promise to go home and get some rest. Will you do that?"

She nodded, and her shoulders slumped as some of the anger ebbed out of her. After a while, she stood, clutching her purse, and we borrowed pen and paper from Harold to exchange phone numbers. I put an arm around her and steered her toward the door.

"I'll call you as soon as I know anything."

She nodded again, whispered the words *thank you,* and stepped out into the lunchtime heat.

I spent three hours in front of a video screen, writing down time codes and making notes on the last of Tommy Callahan's interviews, while Peter Graff was in and out of the office with seemingly a hundred tasks, patiently answering my questions each time I had one. There were times, when our bodies were particularly close, that I had trouble concentrating on his answers. Finally, he went out for a late lunch, and I started to get some real work done.

The most interesting of Callahan's interviews was with a black guy named Charlie Gitt, who, according to the tape, owned a private sex club in east Hollywood called the Reptile Den, which catered exclusively to men who rode bareback. Gitt was no more or less articulate than any of the others Callahan had interviewed on the issue of bareback sex, which included an impassioned spokesman for an activist group called Sex Panic! that had formed to combat what it called Gay Neoconservatism, lumping anyone into that group who remotely challenged sexual promiscuity as unhealthy.

What made Charlie Gitt so fascinating was his ferocious defense of his right to use his genitals any way he pleased with a consenting adult, condoms and other health measures be damned, and regardless of the HIV status of any of the partners involved. His club had been closed down several times, he said, but he had a smart lawyer who knew the constitutional issues inside and out, and Gitt boasted proudly that he was currently back in business as a private social club, and would continue to operate "until the puritan oppressors shut me down or lynch me." He was a fierce-looking man about my age with a rock-hard gym body, dark, angry eyes, and piercings of various kinds in his nipples, lips, and nose. As an African American gay man, he told the camera, riding bareback was the ultimate expression of racial and sexual freedom, "a testament to the selfhood of a faggot nigger," especially when he was fucking a white man. It was a startling, disturbing piece of footage, and I marked it on my logging sheet for special attention.

As I slipped another tape into the machine, the phone rang. It was Melissa Zeigler, apologizing for her agitated behavior earlier that day and thanking me again for doing whatever I could do to give her some peace of mind. When I hung up, I knew that trying to concentrate on more of the tapes was useless. I left Peter a note suggesting he take the rest of the day off, as I intended to do.

Half an hour later, I was in the lobby of a Century City high-rise that served as the headquarters for Jacob Kosterman Enterprises, Inc. I told the receptionist I was there to see Mr. Kosterman, but had no appointment.

The receptionist was a young black woman with impeccable hair, clothes, teeth, and diction.

"I'm afraid that's impossible then."

"Tell him I'm here to discuss the death of Tommy Callahan. See if that gets his attention."

"Your name, sir?"

"Benjamin Justice."

She made a phone call, spoke softly, nodded, and hung up.

"Please take a seat, Mr. Justice. Someone will be right with you."

For a minute or two, I had the opportunity to sink luxuriously into the lobby's plush furniture, studying the lovely arrangements of fresh cut flowers, and admiring the huge art pieces on the walls, which looked fashionable and fashionably expensive. Without a doubt, in his quest for truth Jacob Kosterman had come a long way from his antiestablishment days in the more idealistic 1960s.

Across the polished terrazzo floor, two men in matching green blazers stepped out of an elevator. One was black, one was white, and both had big chests and shoulders, carried on frames exceeding six feet. They glanced first at me, then at the receptionist, who nodded. Then they were both standing over me. The one who was white, the taller of the two, did the talking.

"Mr. Justice?"

"That's me."

"Stand up, please."

I stood.

"Are you parked in the building?"

I nodded.

"May I please have your parking ticket?"

I found it in a pocket, handed it to him. He handed it to the black man, who handed it to the receptionist, who placed validation stamps on it. Then it was passed back through the same hands, into mine again.

"It was nice of you to visit us, Mr. Justice."

"I guess Mr. Kosterman is having a busy day."

"Mr. Kosterman's days are always busy."

"I'm sure he could find a minute or two for me."

"You should have called first."

"He wouldn't have returned my call."

"Goodbye, Mr. Justice."

"He knows I'm here to talk about Tommy Callahan?"

They did a two-step in their well-shined wingtips and took places on either side of me, close enough that I could see specks of dandruff on the white guy's big shoulders, which were even with my eyes. He lowered his voice, firmly accentuating each syllable.

"Goodbye, Mr. Justice."

I drove home with the top down and Nina Simone crooning "I Got My Man" on the radio, basking in temperatures that hovered near eighty degrees, even this late in the day.

In the trunk of the Mustang was one of the three boxes of videotapes, which I fully intended to finish viewing before the end of the night. My plan was to plop down with my notebook in front of the VCR the moment I got inside the house, push the Callahan and Mittelman murders into a mental compartment far, far away, and catch up on my work.

That was the plan, at least, until I pulled into the driveway and saw Peter Graff in the backyard. He was mowing the lawn, wearing nothing more than a pair of silky running shorts that left only a few square inches of him to the imagination.

He looked up when he heard the car door being shut.

"Ben! I got your note and took your advice. Beautiful day, huh?"

"A feast for the eyes. Need a hand?"

"Sure."

"Let me get out of these clothes."

I disappeared into the house and came back with two cans of cold soda, stripped down to my boxers. Peter had put the lawn mower aside and was raking the cut grass into a pile at the center of the yard. I drank half the contents of one can, put it down, and handed him the other one. He tilted the can and guzzled, and I watched the muscles of his throat work as the soda went down.

"You're sweating, Peter."

I ran my hand up the middle of his chest, through the moist golden hairs, collecting his perspiration on the edge of my finger.

"It's hot."

"Isn't it, though."

His eyes could not have been bluer, clearer, more steady. Our bare chests were nearly touching. The early March breeze swayed the trees, but the heat was unyielding.

"If memory serves, you've never kissed a man, have you?"

He shook his head slowly.

I took his face in my hands and looked into his eyes. We were so close now I could feel his breath on my mouth. Beneath my hands, his closely shaved beard felt like fine sandpaper. I could smell him faintly, along with the fresh cut grass.

"There's nothing to it, really. It's just like kissing a woman."

Thirteen

WEDNESDAY MORNING, I drove downtown to visit Katie Nakamura at the *Sun*, with my head still spinning from the feel of Peter Graff's naked body. I'd explored all of him during the slow, sultry night, the contours and textures, all the secret places. It had lasted like a long, feverish hallucination, full of laughs and kisses, grunts and glorious ejaculations, through the sleepy dawn and into our soapy morning shower. The subject of my visit to the *Sun*, however, brought me quickly back to earth.

Katie and I had planned to meet in the small upstairs cafeteria, over coffee, but we ended up in Harry's office instead, with Templeton present and the door closed.

"What's going on, Harry?"

"Why don't you have a seat? Let Katie tell us about it. She's the one who dug it up."

Katie sat on the edge of her chair with her skirted knees close together, and a file open across her lap. It was hard to believe she had earned her college degree and had a year of police reporting behind her; she still looked young enough to be in high school, writing nice features about spelling bees and cheerleading try-outs.

"I was able to find a copy of the police report from fifteen years ago, Mr. Justice. The one you asked for. I got it through a contact at the Hall of Records. At least I think it's the one you want. The date, location, and description of the incident all match up.''

There were two typed and stapled pages, fairly typical for a standard, uncomplicated police report in the years before the LAPD became fully computerized. She lifted the first page, scanned the second, relaying information as she went.

''The victim was a Chinese-American man, Winston Tsao-Ping. He didn't want to talk to the police or press charges, but the ER doctors at County Hospital insisted on bringing in the cops.''

''Because he was beaten so badly?''

She nodded, and indicated the report.

''There's an inventory of his injuries—a broken nose, broken arm, contusions covering most of his face and much of his body, with some internal bleeding that was considered serious enough to keep him in the hospital for observation.'' She glanced up, wincing apologetically. ''It also says he was kicked repeatedly in the groin area—his testicles were swollen to several times their normal size.''

''Sounds like one of the assailants had a sexual thing going on,'' Templeton said, ''maybe both of them.''

''Not untypical in gay bashings,'' I said, ''where the perps are usually sexually conflicted.''

Nakamura resumed reading.

''The victim was identified as a businessman, age twenty-four, married two years, with a Monterey Park address. He was wearing women's clothes and makeup, along with a wig. One of the nurses called his wife at home. The wife spoke little English, so the victim's mother came on the line—Pearl Tsao-Ping. It says here that she did most of the talking after she arrived at the hospital, doing her best to stay between the investigating officers and her injured son. She insisted he had no idea who his assailants were and did not wish to pursue the matter any further.'' Nakamura glanced up at me. ''That seems odd, doesn't it?''

''Not if the guy was wearing women's clothes and didn't want to make the evening news.''

Harry was watching me with an unlit cigarette dangling from his lips, and a twitch over one eye that I hadn't seen before.

''So why the big interest in this report, Ben? You writing a nostalgia piece about Hollywood cross-dressers in the eighties?''

"Suppose you answer a question first, Harry."

"I'll decide when I hear it."

"Why are we meeting hush-hush like this? With Templeton giving up her precious reporting time to hang on every word. This document search was a simple request, between Katie and me."

"Not anymore, it's not."

Templeton sat forward on her chair.

"Look who signed off on it."

As Nakamura handed it across, Harry filled me in.

"You'll find the name Taylor Fairchild at the bottom of page two."

I took the report from Nakamura, but kept my eyes on Harry.

"The assistant chief?"

"Maybe the next *chief.*"

Templeton corrected him.

"Almost certainly the next chief, Harry."

"Taylor Fairchild must have signed off on hundreds of police reports over the years."

Harry pushed his swivel chair away from his desk and clasped his hands behind his head. The tic over his eye kept on ticking.

"I was on the city desk at the *L.A. Times* fifteen years ago, Ben. You'd just come aboard as a cub reporter, still wet behind the ears. Taylor Fairchild was the newly appointed commander of the Rampart Division when he put his name on this report. I remember, because he was in his early thirties at the time, one of the youngest members of the department ever to make commander. The crime took place in the Hollywood Division—outside Fairchild's jurisdiction. He also had the report stamped Internal and Confidential, which kept it out of circulation."

"Out of the press room."

"Out of general circulation, even within the department."

"You think it smells a little."

"Maybe you know something that suggests it smells a lot."

I glanced around the small office at their three expectant faces. It was Harry's, so gray and drawn, so worn out and sad, that caused me to take the plunge I didn't want to take. It occurred to me that maybe I could feed him a story that would make him feel some hope again, give him a reason to get up in the morning, to think about something besides cutting budgets and pink-slipping reporters. Something to help him get over that damned twitch.

"Here's what I know, Harry, with some speculation thrown in to make sense of it. Fifteen years ago, two cops in an undercover car caught this transvestite in an alley near Hollywood Boulevard. That much I know for sure. Apparently, they started questioning him, maybe harassing him. The guy was a closeted cross-dresser, which back then was a big no-no. He tried to get away, maybe even resisted arrest. The two cops got pissed off, started pushing him around. They got carried away, as cops sometimes do, and basically beat the shit out of the guy. As we all know, that kind of thing gets covered up or goes unreported all the time—especially back then, before the Rodney King incident, when Daryl Gates ruled the roost and had the rubber stamp of the police commission. The problem for the cops was, the beating was captured on videotape."

Harry unclasped his hands and rolled his chair forward, until his paunch was tucked under the edge of his desk.

"I don't remember anything like that. I was on the city desk for Christ sake. That would have been front page. Hell, it would have made the evening news, coast to coast. TV loves nothing better than real violence caught on tape."

"The videotape never saw the light of day, Harry. It was shot by a professional cameraman named Byron Mittelman, who was working for that cop show, *On Patrol.*"

"Doing ride-alongs," Templeton guessed, "taping the action."

"Right. But the tape of the beating incident never got on the air, because *On Patrol* doesn't use footage that casts cops in a bad light. Never has, never will. If they did, no police department in the country would let them ride along with their cameras."

"What's your source for most of this?"

"A very distraught lady named Melissa Zeigler. Byron Mittelman's fiancée."

"You think she's solid? Or maybe hysterical?"

"No reason to disbelieve her at this point that I can see."

Harry's elbows were up on the desk now, and he was leaning forward.

"So what happened to this footage?"

"It got locked away in a vault, with other outtakes. During the show's second season, a videotape editor named Tommy Callahan got fired. Before he left, he stole the tape of the beating, for reasons yet to be determined."

"Callahan's the d.b. they found last week up in Angeles National Forest?"

I nodded.

"Callahan was tortured before he died. About the same time he was getting carved up, Mittelman, the camera guy, took a bullet to the head execution-style."

"Together?"

I shook my head.

"They hadn't been in contact for years. But just before he was killed, possibly as he was about to be abducted, Callahan called Mittelman to warn him that he was in danger, since he was the only witness to the beating fifteen years ago."

"Except for the two cops involved."

"There was a third cop, the one driving the patrol car Mittelman was riding in, who stopped the beating. That's all I know, except that the investigating detective in the Mittelman murder, a Sergeant Montego, LAPD, seems to be keeping a lid on the investigation. Melissa Zeigler tells me he's also handling the Callahan murder, and keeping just as quiet on that one."

"Callahan was a sheriff's find," Templeton said.

"Yes, but he was abducted in Hollywood. My guess is Montego used that as a reason to take the investigation out of the hands of the sheriff's department, which was probably happy to have its homicide caseload lightened, especially one involving a seeming deadbeat like Callahan. Gay, alcoholic, seedy Hollywood motel. On the surface, not a very sexy case."

Nakamura had been quiet for a while. She finally spoke up.

"You did say Sergeant Montego, didn't you?"

"Montego, right."

"Felix Montego?"

"Correct."

"You should look at the names of the investigating officers at the end of the report. Fifteen years ago, a Felix Montego was one of the two patrol officers who went to County Hospital to interview the beating victim."

I turned to the second page and ran my finger down to the last few lines. Above the line where Lieutenant Taylor Fairchild had signed off on the report, the signatures of the two investigating officers appeared. Katie was right: Felix Montego, then an officer rather than a sergeant, had scrawled his name and followed it with the date. But it was the name of the other investigating officer that I found even more intriguing.

Charlie Gitt.

Fourteen

HARRY LEANED on his elbows, his fingers folded neatly together like a well-shuffled deck of cards. I thought I saw a spark in his eyes—a tiny spark, but a hint of fire nonetheless.

"So this Montego was the investigating officer fifteen years ago when this Chinese guy got his nuts crushed? And now he's investigating the murder of the cameraman who caught the incident on videotape, as well as the murder of the editor who later stole the tape? Are we on the same page, Justice?"

"We're on the same page, Harry."

"And Fairchild's name appears at the end of the original police report, fifteen years back, along with Montego's."

"There's another name here, Harry. Charlie Gitt. The other cop who went to the hospital with Montego and took the report."

Templeton joined in.

"That name means something to you, Justice?"

"Gitt runs a gay sex club in east Hollywood. On the rough side, down and dirty. Most sex clubs like this one have been shut down for zoning or health violations, but Gitt's has managed to survive. He claims it's because he's got good lawyers, but maybe it's because he's an ex-cop, although I doubt that gay ex-cops are held in all that high esteem."

"Maybe it's that," Harry said. "Or maybe it's because somebody in the department owes him favors. The question, of course, would be why."

Templeton, scribbling notes, asked me how I knew about Charlie Gitt.

"Tommy Callahan interviewed Gitt before he was killed—for the segment I'm writing now for the PBS series. Gitt's a pretty scary guy."

"Start looking for the original victim," Harry said, "this Winston whatever the hell his name is."

I glanced at the report.

"Tsao-Ping."

"We find him, convince him to talk on the record, we got ourselves one hell of a story." Harry stood. "It might even get the attention of some new investors and save this damn paper from going under."

I rose to my feet, followed by the two women.

"Too late for Katie, unfortunately."

Templeton slipped an arm around Katie, beaming down at her.

"Oh, I think Katie's doing just fine. Didn't you notice her engagement ring, Justice?"

Katie held up her left hand, showing off a small diamond set in gold.

"Congratulations. Who's the lucky guy?"

"My main squeeze from college. He's a reporter with the *Chicago Trib*. We're getting married in June, out here in Little Tokyo. I hope you'll come to the wedding."

"With bells on, Katie." I held up the police report. "Thanks for digging this up. Great job."

Nakamura went out, and I looked questioningly at Templeton.

"Did she say 'main squeeze'?"

"It means significant other, Justice. Lover, soulmate."

"I know what it means, Templeton. I just didn't figure it to come from the lips of Katie Nakamura."

"She grew up in the last three years, Justice, since she started interning here. Came out of her shell."

I smiled sweetly.

"Kind of like you, Alexandra."

She smiled in return, only not as sweetly. We watched Nakamura cross the newsroom to her reporter's pod.

"I envy her," Templeton said. "Starting a new life with some-one she loves at her side."

Harry held out his hankie.

"Thanks, Harry. I think I'm under control now."

"Could we get back to the subject at hand, then? Namely, Taylor Fairchild, who is now on your front burner big time."

She poised her pen over her notebook.

"What else do you remember about him, Harry?"

"Fairchild was smart, ambitious, a climber. Seemed to be gen-erally well liked. Top of his class at the academy back in the seventies. One of the bright young stars rising under Daryl Gates. I do recall that he wasn't a very imposing guy. Not too tall, slightly built, soft-spoken for a cop. More management-oriented than street smart."

"The kind of guy Daryl Gates would have regarded as a sissy," I said, noting the irony. "Now, he's being hailed as the great white hope."

"By whom, pray tell?"

"From what Templeton tells me, by the white rank and file."

"And the invisible white power structure that runs this city," Templeton added. "The men with bottomless pockets, who man-age to keep their names out of the papers while creating vast wealth built on political and financial influence. The bank boys, as I like to call them, who pull the strings from here to the White House and beyond."

"Very erudite, Templeton."

"Thank you, Justice."

Harry wasn't as impressed.

"You have evidence of all this, I guess."

"That's the story no one dares to tell, Harry. Especially a news-paper in need of financial investors and capital loans, which pretty much covers the entire fourth estate."

Harry raised his bushy eyebrows.

"Spare me the conspiracy theories, Templeton, and stick to the facts. Start making some discreet contacts with officers who might have an ax to grind with Fairchild, especially those who've known him since way back when. Chase the facts, see where they lead you."

"Will do, Harry."

Templeton started out. I reached out to stop her.

"And I'm still waiting for the police and autopsy reports on Callahan and Mittelman."

"OK, OK. I'll get on it."

She was on her way out the door.

"Aren't you going to thank me for dumping a hot story in your lap?"

"Not until you tell me what you think of my *GQ* piece."

"Haven't read it yet."

"You're the subject, Justice!"

"What could I possibly learn then that I don't already know?"

"God, sometimes you make me crazy."

"Go!" Harry shouted. "Argue later, on your own time."

She went. Harry's shouting erupted into a coughing spasm. I slapped him on the back until it passed.

"You gotta start taking care of yourself, Harry."

He stuck the unlit cigarette back between his lips.

"I'll think about it while I'm having a smoke."

I walked with him in the direction of the elevators, while he patted his pockets for matches. Roger Lawson strode past us down the intersecting corridor, red-faced, huffing and puffing, his glasses riding on his fat cheeks, half his shirttail flapping. He glanced over, but didn't even have the courtesy to acknowledge Harry.

I punched the elevator's down button.

"I wonder where Lawson's going in such a hurry."

Harry offered a sour smile.

"Probably on his way to stick a knife in somebody's back."

He coughed again, and I suggested he think about getting a checkup. The doors opened and the elevator emptied out. Harry stepped in and pressed the button for the ground floor.

"Stop worrying about me, Ben, and help Templeton put a major scoop on the front page. Before Lawson and the other boys upstairs pull the plug on this sinking old ship."

His smile sagged wearily, like the rest of him, as the doors closed between us.

"Just don't wait too long. The water's already tickling my *huevos.*"

Fifteen

I WANDERED BACK to Harry's office, looked up the number for Melissa Zeigler in my notebook, and called her on Harry's phone. She picked up on the fifth ring, speaking slowly, without energy. She sounded sleepy, maybe even sedated.

I apologized for bothering her at home. She said she didn't mind, that she was hoping to hear from me again before too much time had passed. I asked her when she had last spoken to Sergeant Felix Montego.

"A few days ago. Monday, I think. He gave me the usual runaround."

"I want you to call him back, Melissa. Pressure him to meet with you personally. Set up an appointment at a definite time and place. Tell him you'll be bringing a family friend along."

"Who's the family friend?"

"Me. But you don't need to tell him that."

"What if he puts me off again?"

"Tears usually work, if you're willing to go that far."

"I'll do anything to bring Byron's murderer to justice. I don't even care if it puts me in danger. I really don't have anything to lose at this point."

"I wish you wouldn't talk that way, Melissa."

The other end of the line was silent.

"Melissa?"

"I'm here, Ben."

Zeigler sounded as though she might nod off at any moment.

"Will you call Sergeant Montego?"

"Yes, I'll call him. If you really think it might help."

"Can't hurt to try. We need to pry a few rocks loose. How are you doing, by the way?"

"I've been sleeping a lot. You can probably tell."

"That's better than not sleeping, I guess."

"I've joined a grief support group. I'm attending my first meeting tonight. I'll probably be going back to work next week. I have clients who need me."

"You're not a social worker by accident, Melissa. Maybe you need your clients as much as they need you."

"You're probably right, Ben."

I gave her Harry's number at the *Sun,* should she ever need it, and we said goodbye. My next call was to New York University. After the usual delays and transfers, I was put through to the office of admissions and records. I told the woman at the other end that I was Harry Brofsky, news editor at the *Los Angeles Sun,* attempting to verify some information on an employment application filed by a woman named Cecile Chang. She told me it would take some time. I told her I'd hold.

Then, impulsively, I added a second request.

"We have another application here from one of your former students. Might as well kill two birds with one stone."

"The second name?"

"Oree Joffrien."

I spelled it for her, feeling a little sick about it. There was no reason for me to distrust Oree. Yet it also occurred to me, as I sat drumming my fingers on Harry's desk, how little about him I really knew. Chang was clearly involved in the Callahan matter, if for no other reason than the earring she'd lost in his motel room. She and Oree were tight, which made me want to know more about both of them. Not quite ten minutes later, the administrative assistant came back on the line. She told me that Chang had earned a master's in film in 1988 and Oree Joffrien had been awarded a Ph.D. in anthropological studies a year later. Both had been graduated with honors.

"And before that? Mr. Joffrien's undergraduate study?"

"Let's see. Graduated from high school in Louisiana, accelerated program. Bachelor's in history from Duke University, master's from UC Berkeley in poli sci. Very impressive background, this Mr. Joffrien."

"And Miss Chang? Before she came to NYU?"

Several seconds passed. Then:

"I'm afraid that's marked confidential."

"Is that customary?"

"It's unusual, but not unheard of. It depends on the circumstances."

"And what might those circumstances be?"

"I've really told you all that I can, sir."

"Thanks for your time."

"Not at all."

I rifled the stack of phone books behind Harry's desk until I found one that included the city of Monterey Park, which was situated a few miles east of downtown L.A. Not surprisingly, the heavily Asian-American community had listings for several Tsao-Pings. I didn't find a Winston Tsao-Ping, but I did locate a number for a Pearl Tsao-Ping. The address and phone number matched those on the police report typed up fifteen years earlier, with the exception of the area code, which had changed. I dialed the number.

A soft-spoken older man answered, speaking Chinese. I asked in English to speak with Pearl Tsao-Ping. A moment later, a sharp-voiced woman came on the line.

"Mrs. Tsao-Ping?"

"Yes?"

"I'm an old friend of your son Winston. I haven't seen him in many years and wanted to get back in touch."

"I have no son named Winston."

"But Mrs. Tsao-Ping, the address and phone number I have for you is the same one Winston had fifteen years ago."

"No son named Winston! Only one son, Franklin! Do not bother us again!"

As sharply as she had spoken to me, Pearl Tsao-Ping hung up the phone. By then, Harry was back in his office, with coffee for both of us. The phone rang. He took it, spoke a few words, and handed it to me. It was Melissa Zeigler.

"I reached Sergeant Montego, Ben. He says he can meet with us this afternoon, after lunch."

"Where?"

"Parker Center. I guess that's downtown?"

"Main police headquarters. First and Los Angeles streets. What time?"

"He said two o'clock."

"Care to join me for lunch, Melissa? My friend Harry's paying."

Harry gave me a look over the rim of his Styrofoam cup.

"I have to shower and dress, Ben. I think I'll just meet you there."

"See you at two then."

I borrowed some cash from Harry, cut across the central city in the Mustang to Little Tokyo, and enjoyed a solitary, leisurely lunch at the Mandarin Deli, jotting down names in my notebook and mulling their relationships to one another. At one forty-five, I paid the bill, and walked three blocks to Parker Center by way of Los Angeles Street, stepping over two or three unconscious drunks along the way.

Melissa Zeigler was waiting for me on the walkway in front of the eight-story LAPD building named in honor of William H. Parker, who had served as chief from 1950 to 1965. She was attired in a two-tone dress and low-heeled pumps, and had washed and brushed her hair and touched up her face a little. We showed our identification and signed in at the security desk just inside the front doors, waited while our appointment was confirmed, then stuck blue-and-white visitor passes to our chests that signified the room number of our destination.

Standing in the middle of the busy lobby was a well-built Hispanic detective about my age with a decent haircut and a decent suit. He had a good face, skin the color of light mahogany, and a thick, dark mustache under bright brown eyes.

Those eyes grew keener as we approached. Melissa, who had met Felix Montego briefly once before, handled the introductions.

"Sergeant Montego, this is Mr. Justice, the friend I mentioned."

"Friend, or reporter?"

"You seem to know me, Sergeant."

"Benjamin Justice. With the *L.A. Times* in the eighties. You made quite a splash."

"So nice of you to remember."

He half-smiled.

"Should I repeat my question?"

"Can't a person be both, Sergeant?"

He studied me with his wary, intelligent eyes.

"Let's talk in my office." He started walking. "Coffee?"

"I'm full of green tea, thanks."

Zeigler shook her head.

"Not for me."

He led us into an elevator, then up to the third floor, where we made our way to a large room filled with a dozen rectangular tables in the manner of a library. Heaps of skin magazines were stacked on one of the tables, with photos of naked, hairless children on the covers, smiling coquettishly for the camera. Three cops sat at the same table, eating pizza and taking notes while they watched a videotape of a little girl and a little boy doing things to each other I didn't know about until I was at least fourteen.

"Studying the evidence," Montego said, without a trace of humor. "Justice, you didn't see the pizza."

"Do I make you nervous, Sergeant?"

"All reporters make me nervous. Even the ones who got tarred and feathered and run out of town for screwing with the facts." He glanced over his shoulder at me. "You working again? In journalism, I mean."

"On the fringes, you might say."

"A man's gotta make a living, I guess."

"Do you believe in rehabilitation, Sergeant?"

"For a few. Not for the sick pricks who diddle little kids like the ones we saw back there. For reporters who go astray, maybe. You rehabilitated, Justice?"

"The jury's still out, I guess."

He nodded as if he almost cared, and turned into a small office with a window that offered a view of Chinatown to the north and the green hills of Echo Park, Mount Washington, and Highland Park beyond. Just east of Chinatown I could see the old railyards, a wide, flat dustbin lined with tracks and trains that were doomed by a high-rise development now at the blueprint stage but quietly moving ahead. One day we would turn our heads, then the next day look back, and another piece of the city would have been lost forever to the invisible movers and shakers Templeton liked to call the bank boys.

Montego motioned us to take two chairs facing his desk, while he took the chair behind it. In back of him, on a credenza up against the window, stood a framed family portrait showing five brown-eyed kids, from tiny to teenage, grouped around Montego and a pretty Hispanic woman I took to be his wife. Individual photos of the children in shiny gold frames were grouped around the larger picture like chicks around a mother hen.

Montego leaned back in his chair with his hands folded behind his head, the way Harry was fond of doing when he wanted to rule a meeting like a grand pooh-bah.

"What exactly is it I can do for you, Miss Zeigler?"

"I want to know who killed Byron."

"I understand that. As I've told you, I'm working on it."

She glanced over to me, then back at Montego.

"What have you found out? I mean, about the connection between Byron and Mr. Callahan that I told you about. It's been almost two weeks—"

"It's my top priority, Miss Zeigler. But it takes time."

"You didn't answer her question, Sergeant."

His eyes cut in my direction while the rest of him remained still. They stayed on me a moment, then slid back to toward Zeigler.

"We've confirmed that your fiancé, Mr. Mittelman, worked with Tommy Callahan fifteen years ago, as you suggested. We spoke with the executive producer of the television show, a Mr. Kosterman, who told us he knew nothing about a piece of video-tape being stolen, or anything about a videotaped beating inci-dent that took place fifteen years ago the way you described it."

I sat forward on my chair.

"Did you look for a police report on such an incident?"

"We found no report of a transvestite being beaten by two police officers—not even so much as a complaint. Not on the date or in the location provided by Miss Zeigler."

"What about the report of an incident involving unknown as-sailants, taken by two officers interviewing the victim at County Hospital?"

"That would be a very different situation, wouldn't it? Not the incident Mr. Callahan allegedly described when he called Mr. Mittelman. I should say, 'allegedly' called."

"Back to that videotape, Montego. Did any cassettes turn up among Tommy Callahan's belongings?"

"Nothing like that."

"So it must have been stolen by whoever abducted and murdered him."

"If, in fact, such a videotape ever existed at all."

Melissa Zeigler crossed her big, soft arms over her large breasts, looking both hurt and angry.

"Are you suggesting that Byron made the story up? Or that I made it up? That this phone conversation never took place?"

"This entire scenario about two police officers beating up a cross-dresser fifteen years ago apparently exists only in that conversation, Miss Zeigler."

"And I'm telling you, that conversation took place!"

"But only Mr. Callahan or Mr. Mittelman could attest to that, and, unfortunately, both those gentlemen are deceased."

"There must be records of some kind—"

"We found no phone records of a call being made from Mr. Callahan's motel room to your fiancé, Miss Zeigler. Or from the pay phone at the motel. I'm sorry."

She slumped, hanging her head. Montego's eyes moved my way again, giving away nothing.

"You checked the records for Callahan's cell phone?"

Montego's eyes flickered momentarily. Then, just a tad smugly:

"We didn't find a cell phone among his belongings."

"That doesn't mean he didn't have one. Or that records of his calls don't exist."

"I suppose he might have had one."

"I know for a fact that he did."

"How do you happen to know that, Justice?"

"His employer, Cecile Chang, mentioned it. I checked, and learned that he always carried it with him. That's what you do when you're genuinely interested in getting some answers, Sergeant."

The smugness was gone, replaced by a flash of anger.

"For what it's worth, all the checking into phone records was done before I took over the case."

"Why *did* you take over the case, Sergeant?"

His eyes grew hard, fixed on mine.

"Because I'm a senior investigator in homicide. And because Miss Zeigler suggested that two officers from the LAPD might somehow be involved, stemming from an alleged incident some years ago. We take such allegations very seriously."

"Why would Miss Zeigler make up such a wild story, Sergeant?"

"I'm not suggesting she made anything up."

"Then why would her fiancé tell her such a wild story just before he was murdered?"

"If I had that answer for you, we could probably close these two cases."

"Then you do concede they're connected."

His voice grew sharp.

"I didn't say that."

"I think you did."

"What you think—"

He caught himself, and shut up.

"Perhaps you could show us the police and autopsy reports on the two murders, Sergeant."

"Why would I want to do that?"

"To answer some questions in Miss Zeigler's mind."

"In her mind. Or in yours?"

"Should it matter?"

"That's departmental paperwork."

"They're public records. I'll get copies, with or without your help. What reason would you have for stonewalling, Sergeant?"

His voice was cold.

"I'll see what I can do."

"You might do me one more favor."

"What would that be?"

"Tell me what you know about Charlie Gitt."

Not a muscle moved in Montego's face, not even behind his eyes. But he took a sharp, deep breath, and his nostrils flared.

"What's Charlie Gitt got to do with this?"

"You know him, then."

"I knew him once."

"Fifteen years ago, Sergeant?"

Finally, Montego's eyes moved, sneaking away from mine as he stood. He showed us his back, with his hands in his pockets, jingling change. He appeared to be staring out the window toward Chinatown, although, for all I knew his eyes might have been cast down on the pictures of his family.

When he didn't speak, I did some prompting.

"Fifteen years ago, on the night of April fourteenth, you and Charlie Gitt answered a call at County Hospital and took a police report on the beating of a transvestite in an alley near the Egyptian Theater in Hollywood. Your name is on that report, along with Gitt's. And, of course, the commanding officer who signed off on it, Taylor Fairchild."

Melissa Zeigler's eyes widened as she turned toward me. Montego kept his hands in his pockets as he faced us again. His coloring was no longer so dusky; some of it had drained from his face.

"I was a police reporter once, Sergeant. Commanding officers don't ordinarily sign off on a routine police report. Especially when they're assigned to a different division. As I recall, the exception is when there's some reason to bury a report to keep it out of the wrong hands. My pals at the *Sun* tell me it doesn't happen anymore, at least not that they're aware of. But this was fifteen years ago, before Rodney King, when Daryl Gates was on the throne and things were handled differently."

Montego still wasn't talking. He stared down at me with eyes that suggested all kinds of questions were racing around inside his head.

"For what it's worth, I never knew Gates personally. I never met the man, except for a passing word or salute at a special roll call. A lot of us didn't."

"But you did know Charlie Gitt. Why don't you have a seat, Sergeant, and tell me about him?"

Montego took three strides to a side table, where he unscrewed the cap on a bottle of spring water. He drank some, recapped it, set it down, and returned to his chair. He folded his hands in his lap and took a deep breath before he spoke.

"Whatever I say here is strictly off the record, Justice. Among the three of us."

"Fine."

"Charlie Gitt was a loose cannon in the department. He started off with a lot of promise. College degree, clean-cut, obedient, athletic. Not afraid of anything—the guy had brass balls. Plus, he was black, at a time when we needed more black officers. Rose fast for a young officer, into Metro before he turned thirty.''

"Metro was where the toughest detectives used to go. Stakeouts, violent suspects, that kind of thing.''

"Like I said, Gitt was one tough dude, and he had the physique to back it up. But something happened to him along the way. Citizen complaints, brutality, mistreatment of prisoners, you name it. He became a very twisted guy.'' Montego laughed strangely. "He even scared some of the guys on the force who scared me.''

"I imagine there was a lot of pressure trying to be a polite black cop under Daryl Gates. Smiling and saying yes sir, carrying out orders, while racism was institutionalized all around you.''

Montego looked at me more evenly.

"No comment.''

"Being a closeted gay cop under Gates had to be hell, too. Every day when he came to work, Gitt faced something of a double whammy, didn't he?''

"It seems that you already know quite a lot about him.''

"I know that he runs an underground gay sex club in east Hollywood that seems to have escaped police scrutiny. That kind of makes me curious.''

"He also lives in a house up in the Silver Lake hills designed for S&M orgies, which he apparently hosts on a regular basis. We know about that. But times have changed. It's a private matter.''

"Was the beating of a transvestite fifteen years ago a private matter, Sergeant?''

"The victim wanted to keep it that way. His life could have been ruined by public exposure. At the request of his mother, and out of deference to the victim, we went out of our way to keep the whole thing quiet. That's why Taylor Fairchild put his name on that report—to ensure that a victim's privacy was protected.''

"I don't suppose you know where Winston Tsao-Ping is now?''

"If I did, it wouldn't be my place to tell you, would it?''

"Have you had any contact with him since the night you took the report?''

"Absolutely none.''

Montego looked at his watch, then stood.

"Is there anything else, Miss Zeigler? Mr. Justice?''

"What about Charlie Gitt? Spoken to him lately?"

"He's someone neither I nor the department cares to associate with. That's all I have to say about Charlie Gitt." He turned to Melissa Zeigler, his voice more gentle. "I'm extremely sorry about what happened to your fiancé, Miss Zeigler. If there was anything I could do to change what happened, I would. Please believe that."

"Thank you."

He escorted us down in the elevator, and saw us to the security desk at the front entrance, where we signed out. He stood watching from the middle of the lobby until we were out the door, exactly where he'd been standing watch when we'd arrived.

Sixteen

I PULLED AWAY from the parking lot in Little Tokyo a little after three and several blocks later edged onto the Hollywood Freeway, heading toward the Valley.

There was still time to beat the worst of the afternoon rush, which seemed to be starting earlier and ending later with each passing year. It made me think of that new high-rise complex that would be going up before too long next to Chinatown, filling the railyards with business towers and packing more bodies and automobiles into the central city, while the deep pockets of the developers and their connections got deeper, and life for the rest of us got a little more miserable.

Demographers were projecting that by the year 2025, the current population of California—thirty-two million—would have mushroomed to fifty million, analogous to absorbing the entire population of New York State, with most of the new arrivals crowding into already teeming Southern California. How they were all going to get around remained to be seen, and added an ominous new dimension to the term road rage, which was evident all around me now in the beep of horns, squeal of brakes, and a middle finger extended out the driver's window next to me. At least no one was shooting wildly at a passing car, something that happened often enough in Los Angeles to be on everyone's mind at least some of the time; the driver next to me apparently wasn't among the more cautious, because motorists had been blown away for lesser infractions than flipping someone off. Carjacking was the other local driver's nightmare—if you drove a nice vehicle, you never knew when you might be forced to give it up at gunpoint while stopped for a red light, or even shot to death on a whim after turning over your keys. At least that was one crime I didn't have to worry about, given the condition of the old Mustang.

By four, with a freeway headache setting in, I was back in my office at New Image Productions, closing the door behind me, and giving Peter Graff another lesson in how to kiss a man. He was an apt student, who didn't seem to mind repetition drills. When we finally settled down to work, I asked him if he'd accompanied Tommy Callahan when Callahan taped his interview with Charlie Gitt a few weeks before.

"Sure, that's part of my job. I set up the interview, handled the crew."

"What did you think of Gitt?"

"To be honest, he gave me the creeps."

"How's that?"

"The things he said during the interview, the way he looked at me."

"Hungry, the way I do?"

Peter grinned.

"Sort of, but different. It was this weird, crazy look, like I was something he wanted to control, devour. It kinda spooked me."

"He didn't bother you, though?"

"No, just that look."

"You were OK with the interview?"

"Oh, yeah. Plenty of good sound bites. Why?"

"Just curious, that's all."

We sat down and attended to business, finishing what Peter called a "wish list" of visual material I felt I needed to supplement what Callahan had already pulled together—more footage from the notorious gay sex club scene in New York City, prior to the crackdown by the mayor, along with more sound bites on the pros and cons of unrestricted sexual activity between consenting adults, if we could get them. I also wanted some visual references to similar heterosexual scenes—legalized Nevada brothels, straight porn footage, college spring break orgies, a few *Hustler* and *Penthouse* covers, a headline or two on hetero swinger clubs— to remind viewers that homosexuals weren't the only ones who indulged in multiple partners and multiple orgasms.

The plan was for Peter to submit the list to Cecile Chang for her approval, which would be determined according to the availability and permissions costs of the elements I'd requested, subject to the budget limitations of my show. Meanwhile, I was to begin writing the first draft of my script, which was due in three weeks.

Peter and I worked side by side, bent over his desk. We didn't discuss his sexual initiation of the previous evening, yet every time our bodies touched—a knee, a hand, a shoulder as one of us leaned in—the sexual tension became palpable. We worked through dinner, long after everyone but the security guard had gone, then ordered pizza delivered; we ate behind our locked door, feeding each other the virginal point of each slice, then laughing as we chewed. By midnight, our work was done, our shirts were unbuttoned, and we were on the carpet, kissing and dry-humping with our pants on like two hormonal teenagers postponing the next big step.

At half past midnight, our shirts buttoned and tucked back in, we sauntered out past the security guard, holding our jackets in front of us, hiding our wet spots and trying not to laugh. We kissed again in the parking lot, still tasting of garlic and anchovies, then drove home in our separate cars. As I followed the tiny taillights of Peter's vintage VW bug up through the canyon, I felt as if I were floating in a time warp—a man of forty finally ready to slow down, thrown inexplicably together with a dazzling young colt, into a heady swirl of youth and innocence that was a wondrous blessing and a troubling curse all at once, like the powerful pull of male beauty itself.

The conflicts I was feeling intensified when I arrived back at the house to find the red light on my answering machine blinking in the dark. While I looked out the kitchen window, watching Peter climb the stairs to the apartment, I listened to the deep, warm voice of Oree Joffrien: "Sharing Mose Allison with you the other night was great, and dinner afterward. I haven't eaten Thai in a while, and never with such a personable guy. I need to get out more often, it's been a long time. So please don't misinterpret any reticence on my part as disinterest. Just being cautious, I guess. Did I mention there's a Ruth Brown gig coming up at the Cinegrill? Maybe we can catch it together. I've missed you the last couple days. Call when you get a chance.''

I showered, brushed my teeth, trimmed my beard, then went to bed seeing Peter Graff's body and hearing Oree Joffrien's words in my head. Somewhere in there was the face of Melissa Zeigler, telling me she'd never have a child, now that the love of her life was dead. Peter again, weeping over the loss of his friend Callahan. His girlfriend Cheryl, telling me to take good care of him. Harry, looking like hell. Too much garlic and anchovies too close to bedtime can do that to you, especially when you add a dash of guilt.

I didn't close my eyes until just before dawn. The phone jarred me awake at 10 A.M. sharp. It was Denise, back from the flu. She told me Cecile Chang wished to see me, and asked if I could make it at ten-thirty. I asked for eleven. She said OK.

"I found your wish list on my chair this morning."

"Peter put it there before we left last night."

"You worked late?"

"We left a little after midnight."

"Peter's very conscientious."

"Yes, he is."

Cecile Chang glanced up over the pages of the printout.

"You're getting along well with him then?"

"Quite."

"And what about my friend Oree? No luck there?"

"Are you playing matchmaker, Cecile? Like my friend Alexandra?"

"He's an exceptional person in my view."

"I feel the same way."

"Peter's awfully young."

"Yes, he is."

"But quite extraordinary-looking. Hard to resist, I imagine."

I said nothing. A moment later, she lifted the wish list.

"You kept a copy for yourself?"

I nodded. She slipped it into a file slugged *Bareback Sex/Callahan Segment*. Callahan's name had been crossed out, and mine penciled in above it. She placed the file back into a partitioned file holder on her desk and faced me, folding her delicate hands on top of it and smiling comfortably.

"I took another look at your outline. Along with this list of additional visuals, I believe I have a pretty clear picture of where you're going with your segment. I like it."

"Thank you."

"May I offer some advice?"

"I expect it, Cecile."

"I'd warn against straying too far from the focus of your subject. You seem to want to hammer home the point that we live in a sexually repressive society—that Americans in general are deeply afraid of sex, or at least squeamish about it."

"My grandmother on my father's side was Catholic. She took the view that sex was dirty, and therefore should be saved for marriage. I think a lot of people see it that way, though they might not admit it."

"You're a practicing Catholic?"

"Renegade, gone to hell."

"How long have you been lapsed?"

"I started being a doubter at twelve, when our priest told me he needed to examine my privates to see if I'd been abusing myself."

"How did you respond?"

"I let him. And I liked it. I think he sensed I would. Pedophiles are crafty that way, at least the smart ones."

"You're still angry with him."

"I'm still angry with a lot of people."

"Be careful not to get up on a soapbox."

"I'll die standing on my soapbox, Cecile. They'll have to bury me in it."

Her smile widened.

"According to your outline, you plan to deal with this issue of prurience in the introduction, during the host's stand-up." She tilted her head, like a bird hearing a strange sound. "Did I say prurience? I suppose I meant *prudishness,* didn't I?"

"The two go pretty much hand in hand, don't you think?"

"Develop that thought for me, in the context of your script."

I glanced out the window, across the parking lot, at a rooftop billboard crowded with the images of skinny boys and girls dressed in designer underwear and nothing else. Below it, on the side of the building, was a smaller billboard warning kids about teen pregnancy, with a hot line number. It was no coincidence of the moment—the boulevard, every boulevard in L.A., every boulevard in America, was plastered with similar contradictory messages, most of them used to sell something, to make us want to be someone we weren't, to be envious of someone else's body, or the things they owned. My eyes came back into the room, and settled again on Chang.

"We're a country that constantly thinks about sex, a culture immersed in sexual images, obsessively lascivious. Yet we simultaneously condemn it, pretending that sexuality, especially at its most primal, is something to be ashamed of. We strangle our most basic feelings and impulses in a noose woven from guilt and shame. That's one reason so much sexuality gets expressed in twisted and destructive ways."

"That's how you see bareback sex manifesting itself?"

"In a perfect world, without HIV and AIDS, I'd see bareback sex—any form of sex that doesn't cause injury or death—as a personal choice, even a healthy rebellion against the forces of hypocrisy and repression that try to tell us what to do with our bodies, whom we should love and how. But HIV and AIDS have changed the rules. Those who ride bareback, particularly homosexual men, are acting out their own self-destruction, even the more general destruction of the gay community, no matter how they choose to justify or rationalize their behavior."

"We tread in a sensitive area here, Ben. I don't want to use the Public Broadcasting System to further stigmatize the gay community. Neither as a lesbian, nor as a responsible filmmaker. But I don't want to bow to the PC police, either."

"I'm on the side of personal responsibility, Cecile, not a new repression that shuts down bathhouses and condemns nonmonogamous sexual pleasure. That plays right into the hands of the fundamentalist right and those who embrace conformity to placate their own personal unease with sexuality. But we've also got to take an honest, unsentimental look at what's going on with a number of gay men who seem to be on a suicide mission, willing to take others along for the ride, especially the young. We need to examine the role alcohol and drugs play in that, as well as simple sexual compulsion."

"As they do in the straight world."

"Of course."

"You feel confident you can find that balance, and still maintain your focus?"

"I need to remind viewers at the top of the hour, to *show* them, that in our culture, sexuality scares the hell out of most people, especially if it's outside the narrow boundaries of the so-called norm. That cultural puritanism, coupled with this frightening disease, has resulted in the demonization of gay men, turned them into monsters."

"How would you illustrate that?"

"It's on my wish list—a clip of Jack Nicholson around Oscar time, bragging to the media that he never uses a condom when he screws."

"Yes, I saw that. I'm not sure we can get that clip. How does it underscore your point?"

"Jack Nicholson can brag to the media that he always rides bareback. People laugh—'Oh, that rascal, Jack.' A gay man makes the same comment, the public wants him executed, or at least locked up. Without that clip, or at least a photo of Nicholson, I lose the line, and the thought. Isn't that how it works in TV, Cecile?"

"Unfortunately, without the pictures, it's difficult to tell the story."

"And television is just about all that matters these days, isn't it?" Our eyes met very directly. "It's kind of like that piece of videotape Tommy Callahan stole. If it's never found, never shown to the public, what happened that night fifteen years ago is pretty much a dead issue. So far, I've heard nothing from the police to indicate it's turned up, or even exists."

I noticed the muscles of her graceful neck and jawline tense.

"You've been in touch with the police?"

"Melissa Zeigler and I had a chat with Sergeant Montego."

"And what did you tell him?"

"Mostly, I asked questions. When I brought up the issue of the stolen videotape, he told me Jacob Kosterman denied any knowledge of it. My guess is that whoever did a search and destroy through Callahan's motel room has it in his possession."

She smiled, but the lines below her mouth remained taut.

"Of course, I wouldn't know anything about that."

"Of course."

"Only what I heard from Miss Zeigler the other day when she was here. Frankly, she seemed a bit unhinged. I'm not sure how much faith we can place in her account of things."

"Perhaps you're right, Cecile."

"I'd hate to see you get sidetracked with Miss Zeigler's problems when you have a script to finish. Which brings us back to the point of our meeting." She swiveled in her chair and picked up a three-quarter inch-videocassette from her credenza. "We've finished cutting the fund-raising video, and I wanted to show you the off-line version, to give you a sense of how a video is put together, pictures and words. When it's ready, you can see the on-line edit, with the final technical touches in place."

I settled back into my chair.

"You seem to have lots of time for me today."

"With the piece finished, things have loosened up a bit, thank goodness."

She slipped the cassette into a tape deck at one end of her credenza, next to the framed photograph of Tiger Palumbo, hit the appropriate buttons, and rose to draw the curtains across the window. By the time she was seated again, tugging her skirt down over her knees, the video was beginning. It opened with an establishing shot of the building we were in now, cut to a close-up of the New Image Productions sign and logo, then dissolved to footage of the lobby, where Harold, the receptionist, sat behind his desk trying to look busy. The camera slowly panned the posters and awards decorating the walls, while Chang was heard in voice-over, telling viewers succinctly about the purpose, vision, and accomplishments of her company. She invited viewers to join her on a journey through "a day in the life of a documentary production company," and another dissolve took us to the research department, where Chang was seen walking past her workers, busy at their desks, with the background clock at ten-fifteen. It was the same footage I'd glimpsed Tuesday morning in the editing bay upstairs, before Chang closed the door in my face. She hit the pause button, freezing the video, as the camera captured her in full face.

"Do you think I overdressed for the taping, Ben? I'm always so critical of myself, once I see what the camera saw."

"The suit's tasteful, Cecile, but conservative. The scarf adds a nice touch of color. It looks fine to me."

She glanced at me, then back to the monitor.

"I was thinking more about the jewelry. The jade and gold bracelet and the matching earrings. I hope they're not too much."

I studied the pair of earrings, then Chang herself, who waited for my response with her chin raised.

"You're a lovely woman, Cecile, you certainly don't need any help in that department. But I think the jewelry works fine. Especially the earrings, with your hair pulled back like that."

"Flattery will get you everywhere, Ben—Tiger plies me with it all the time." We both smiled. "Shall I go on?"

"By all means."

She hit the pause button again, and the presentation continued. A number of fades and dissolves took Chang from the research department into the production offices, upstairs into the business and administrative areas, then on a tour of the video library and editing bays, all the while speaking on-camera about the commitment of New Image to quality production and state-of-the-art equipment. There was a cutaway shot from the rooftop of the sun setting over the San Fernando Valley, then an interior of various employees leaving the building, bidding the camera good night. Finally, Chang was seen alone, back in the empty research room, wrapping up the presentation as she faced the camera directly, before the fade to black. Behind her, the hands of the wall clock indicated eight forty-five; someone had left a television set on as well, tuned to an evening segment of the CNN news.

She hit the stop button, rewound the tape to her final moment, and froze on it.

"You're sure the jewelry isn't too much? I may be a lipstick lesbian, but I don't want to come off as too showy."

Again, I studied the two earrings. They were both there, right where they'd been earlier in the day, though something else about the picture wasn't right. Something my untrained eye was missing.

"Honestly, Cecile, you're worrying over nothing. It's fine. All of it."

She smiled modestly, and left the image on the screen.

"You can see, Ben, how much you can say with very few words.

Let the images tell as much of the story as possible. As they say, it's always better to show than to tell."

We were standing, then walking to the door.

"As soon as we finish on-lining tonight, I'll have the editor make a dub. We'll get a copy to you over the weekend so you can see exactly what we accomplish in the on-line process."

"It's already been very instructive, Cecile."

"I'd hoped it would be. Thanks for coming in on such short notice."

I stepped out, and the door was closed behind me. I was nearly to the end of the hall when I heard Denise's voice. I turned to see her closing the gap between us in her wheelchair.

"There was a message for you, Mr. Justice." She handed me a pink slip of paper. "Jacob Kosterman called, from the Documentary Channel. He was hoping you could meet him for lunch, if it's not too inconvenient."

I smiled as I studied the message.

"I think I can find the time for Mr. Kosterman."

Seventeen

J ACOB KOSTERMAN had business in the Valley after lunch, or
so he said, and suggested that we meet at Teru Sushi, a popular
sushi bar where the theatrical preparation of the food was
nearly as good as the menu of raw fish and seaweed-wrapped rice
rolls. The restaurant also happened to be close to New Image
Productions, almost across the street, which suggested that Kosterman was suddenly bending over backward to be accommodat-
ing.

He was sitting at a table in the back when I walked in, pretending to study a menu while I studied a good-looking chef behind
the counter as he carved up fresh *ahi* with flashing knives of
razor-sharp steel. Kosterman stood as I approached, and I was
surprised by how diminutive he was; his cover photo on *Broadcast
Monthly* had caused me to expect a man of considerably more
height and heft.

"Mr. Justice."

He extended a small, well-manicured hand, which I shook.
With a sweep of the same hand, he indicated the other chair.

"Please."

I sat.

"You enjoy sushi?"

"When I'm not paying for it."

He smiled broadly.

"Then enjoy, Mr. Justice. Order whatever you wish."

For all his charm and civility, as well as his surprisingly small stature, he was still an imposing man, with a surplus of what's frequently called charisma, which I've never trusted. His luxuriant gray mustache, shaped and waxed into curling handlebars, gave him a distinguished if slightly comical look, as did the smooth dome of his head. He wore no tie, but his open-collared shirt looked to be cut from good silk, his dark blazer and gray slacks were probably tailor-made and fit his slender frame nicely. His jewelry was all gold: the wedding band, the fine-mesh neck chain, the single stud in his left ear that had replaced the gold ring I'd seen in the *Broadcast Monthly* cover photo.

"Why are we here, Mr. Kosterman?"

"You're not one to waste time, are you?"

"Like you, I'm a busy man, seeking after the truth." I smiled as pleasantly as the situation allowed. "Just not as rich, or as powerful."

"I've worked hard for what I have."

"I'm sure you have. You still haven't told me why we're here."

He looked up as a waiter arrived.

"Why don't we put our order in? Teru Sushi gets awfully busy at lunch, and always on Fridays."

He ordered a mixed platter of sushi and sashimi that included raw mackerel, tuna, and eel, and a small bottle of saki. I asked the waiter to bring me the same, but with hot tea in place of the warm wine.

When he was gone, I tried to kick-start the conversation again.

"I assume you've been in touch with Sergeant Montego, that he's filled you in on the background of the Callahan and Mittelman murders."

"He's spoken to me, of course. As part of his investigation. Terrible, what's happened."

"Has he spoken to you today?"

Kosterman hesitated.

"As a matter of fact, he has."

"So you know what I know, and you've decided maybe you'd better talk to me after all."

"First, Justice, let me apologize for the way you were treated the other afternoon when you dropped by my corporate headquarters. My security people are instructed to screen out anyone who doesn't have an appointment. When you work in the documentary field as I do, you sometimes make an enemy or two along the way. When it comes to security, we prefer the preventive approach."

"You've been producing *On Patrol* for fifteen years. I imagine some of those arrested aren't too happy about having their faces shown on national television."

"They all sign releases giving us their approval. Otherwise, we digitize their faces with a video grid to protect their privacy."

"You could have done that with Winston Tsao-Ping, couldn't you? Masked his face but still used the footage? To protect his privacy. Or maybe what the cops were doing that night wasn't kosher."

The waiter placed a small tray between us. On the tray was a tiny cup without a handle, and a slim pot of saki. When the waiter was gone, Kosterman filled the cup.

"Winston Tsao-Ping?"

"The transvestite who was beaten up fifteen years ago by two members of the LAPD. A beating caught on tape by your cameraman, Byron Mittelman. I'm sure it's come up in your discussions with Sergeant Montego."

Kosterman sipped the cup dry, then held it poised in his slender fingers.

"Ah yes, Mr. Tsao-Ping. I remember the name now."

"That must have been very revealing footage, Mr. Kosterman. Cinema verité at its finest, exposing a social wrong. What every true documentarian must dream of."

"I said I remembered the name of Mr. Tsao-Ping because Sergeant Montego brought it up. I didn't say that any such tape exists, or ever did."

"If we're going to play games, Kosterman, I've got better things to do."

Kosterman filled the cup again, but set it aside.

"You're gay, aren't you, Justice? At least according to what I read in *Gentleman's Quarterly.*"

"It's on the newsstands?"

"Just out. You haven't read it yourself?"

"I'm afraid not. To answer your question, yes, my romantic inclinations tend to be homosexual."

"Then I'll assume you've never been married, with the responsibility of housing, feeding, clothing, caring for, and educating children."

"I've never been blessed with children, no."

"Fifteen years ago, the first year that *On Patrol* went on the air, I had four children. All bright and headed eventually for college. We were living in a comfortable but modest four-bedroom house here in the Valley, and I could barely keep up with the payments. Then, thank God, I got *On Patrol* on the UBN schedule."

"You suddenly saw light at the end of the financial tunnel."

"I had a chance at the American dream, Justice. The American dream of creating an enterprise with my own wits, my own sweat, my own hands, and making a better life for my family. Does that mean anything to a gay man, Mr. Justice?"

"No, all we think about is getting high and trading blow jobs."

He fanned out his small, soft hands.

"Forgive me. My question was unfair and insensitive. I'm just trying to make the point that having those kinds of responsibilities changes one's priorities."

"Which includes burying evidence that two police officers beat the crap out of an innocent man?"

"That's awfully blunt."

"I get irritable when I haven't eaten."

He looked up, smiling as the waiter approached.

"Thankfully, we're about to remedy that."

The waiter slipped in, served our platters, and disappeared as quietly as he'd come. We ate for a minute or two, blending hot green mustard and fresh ginger with our raw fish and rice, before Kosterman spoke again.

"In fact, Justice, Winston Tsao-Ping resisted arrest. He became absolutely hysterical with those two officers. Yes, it was all on the tape. And if you ever quote me to that effect, I'll deny it and call you a damn liar. I don't have to point out that, given your reputation, I already have a considerable edge in the credibility department."

"If he was resisting arrest, and the actions of the two cops were justified, then why not air the tape?"

"The actions of the officers might have been misconstrued. The gay activists would have been up in arms. The department asked us to delete that particular piece of footage from the show, avoid a brouhaha.''

"What was Winston Tsao-Ping being arrested for, Mr. Kosterman?''

He looked at me oddly, and poured himself more saki.

"I'm not sure. It's been such a long time. Loitering, I suppose. Prostitution. I don't really remember.''

"There was never any mention made in any report I could find of criminal activity on Tsao-Ping's part. He was walking alone down an alley wearing women's clothes. For that, he was beaten half to death. And you helped cover it up.''

I added a tiny chunk of the green mustard to a roll of tuna and rice wrapped in seaweed, and popped the whole thing into my mouth, savoring the burst of salt and fire as I chewed. Kosterman stared at his plate a long moment before looking up.

"I'm going to be completely honest with you, Justice.''

"How refreshing.''

He placed his elbows on the table and pressed his hands into a teepee under his chin.

"If I had gone after those two cops with that videotape, turned it over to the district attorney, helped prosecute them, *On Patrol* would have been finished before its first season ended. The access I needed to other police departments would have evaporated, and with it, everything I'd worked for. I'd financed the pilot out of my own pocket, and covered most of the production costs for the first thirteen episodes. What we producers call deficit financing. To lose the show at that point would have ruined me financially.''

"So you ignored the beating incident and kept on shooting.''

"Not with the LAPD. I realized by then that it wasn't a department I wanted to ride along with. Too much of the footage we got was full of racial slurs, sexual harassment of females, antigay behavior, borderline brutality—an attitude of arrogance and machismo that was endemic, fostered from the top down. It made most of what we shot totally unusable, and continuing to shoot with the LAPD would have been cost prohibitive.

"I realized that I had to seek out police departments that were pro-active, and individual officers who treated suspects and the human race in general with respect, or we'd never have enough footage to keep our show on the air. Except for the county, which comes under the sheriff's department, I didn't ride along in Los Angeles again until 1995, after Daryl Gates was out as chief and the atmosphere began to change."

"So you've justified in your own mind what you did with that footage."

"What I did allowed me to continue producing *On Patrol.* The financial windfall from syndicating *On Patrol* financed the Documentary Channel, which broadcasts more fact-based programming than the three major networks combined."

"I've looked at your listings, Kosterman, seen some of the shows. The programming on the Documentary Channel is safe, mainstream, strictly establishment. There's nothing probing or provocative, nothing that remotely reflects the spirit of independence that put you behind a camera to begin with."

"The 1960s are a long way behind us, Justice. One can't hold on to the past. It's unrealistic and unproductive. We were young, idealistic, filled with passion. But just as often, we were naive, misguided, and foolish."

He speared a California roll with his chopsticks, then a slice of fresh ginger and transferred them together into his mouth. I could see several smooth gold fillings lining each side of his jaw.

"Tell me, Kosterman, do the murders of Tommy Callahan and Byron Mittelman even bother you in the slightest?"

His eyes lost their cordial spark, and leveled on me as he chewed.

"I won't dignify that question with a reply."

"I'll try another one then. How well do you know Taylor Fairchild?"

He cleared his throat with more saki before he spoke.

"Our families knew each other when we were growing up. I'm a few years older than Taylor, but we were still fairly close. We were in Scouts together, collected stamps, that kind of thing. Then, in the sixties, our politics and paths diverged. We renewed our friendship during the first year of *On Patrol,* back in the mid-eighties. He's served as our technical advisor for the last few years."

"A minute ago, you were telling me you wanted nothing to do with the LAPD."

"As I said, the department changed."

"Has Taylor Fairchild changed?"

"I'm not sure I understand your question."

"He was one of Gates's fair-haired boys, wasn't he?"

"Whether you choose to believe it or not, Justice, Taylor Fairchild is a fair and decent man, and he'd make a damned good chief. He's had a few problems along the way, had to work through some issues, but that's true of most of us, isn't it?"

"What kind of issues?"

"It's not widely known, because Taylor doesn't like to discuss it, but he lost his father when he was quite young. Fairchild Senior was a captain with the LAPD, on the fast track to the chief's job when he was killed in the line of duty. He had a law degree, was active in civic affairs. There were some who thought he had the stuff to go all the way to the governor's mansion, maybe even to the White House."

"Was his wife, Rose Fairchild, one of them?"

"I'm sure Rose supported him."

"The way she supports Taylor now?"

"Naturally, she wants the best for her son. Wants to see him do well."

"But first he had some issues to work through. I believe that was the way you put it."

"Taylor was twelve when Captain Fairchild was killed, a terrible time for a boy to lose his father. Especially one he worshiped, as Taylor did. He dedicated himself to following in his father's footsteps, being a firm cop like his old man. Maybe he went too far— he went through a period after the academy when he was trying a little too hard to be one of the boys and prove himself as a man. But he got through that, and he's developed into a solid, level-headed leader. He's also a good family man and a sincere Christian. That's the Taylor Fairchild I know."

"Tell me about Tommy Callahan."

"Callahan was a very good videotape editor with a promising future." Kosterman smiled sourly. "Unfortunately, he was also a drunk and a thief."

"When he stole that tape, it must have been very upsetting."

"I certainly wasn't happy about it, but there wasn't much I could do. Callahan had the tape, and he was difficult to find."

"Did you report the tape stolen?"

"No."

"Of course not. But you wanted it back, nonetheless. Especially as *On Patrol* became such a success—the foundation of your entire production empire. If that tape got into the wrong hands, and became a *cause célèbre,* your vaunted reputation as the Man Who Put Truth Back In TV would become something of a joke, wouldn't it?"

He pursed his thin lips dismissively.

"If that's the spin you wish to put on it, Justice."

"You might even have encountered some legal problems for aiding and abetting a criminal cover-up."

"I seriously doubt that."

"When was the last time you heard from Callahan?"

"Fourteen years ago, when I fired him."

"Byron Mittelman?"

"He's worked on various shows of mine through the years. A good camera operator, a nice man. I sent flowers to the service and notes to his family and fiancée."

"Melissa Zeigler believes the two murders are connected, and have something to do with the stolen videotape."

"Yes, that's what Sergeant Montego told me when he first contacted me."

Kosterman poured another saki, drained the cup, and patted his lips with his napkin.

"I understand you're working for Cecile Chang now."

"That couldn't have been in the *GQ* piece, which means you've done some checking up on me."

"It's quite an opportunity, considering what's happened to your career in recent years."

"Yes, it is."

"You might actually climb back to a level of respectability again, Justice, with a little luck along the way. On the other hand, it may be the first and last job you ever have in television. Funny how things often work out that way, isn't it?"

I knew where he was going, felt myself instantly weakening, hated myself for it. I poured and sipped some tea, wishing against my will that it were warm saki instead, with an alcoholic kick to bolster my slipping courage.

"You're probably aware that as president and CEO of a successful cable channel that specializes in documentary programming, I'm in a position to give someone with your background and skills just about all the work you would ever want. Considering the forcefulness of your personality, I have no doubt you're producer material. Who knows? Perhaps you even have the stuff to be an executive producer."

"That's where the money is, from what I hear."

"Quite a lot of it, when a series does well. More, I'm sure, than you've ever dreamed of making, even back in your halcyon days at the *L.A. Times,* when you were on top of the world. From what I understand, even at the top, most newspaper reporters remain stuck hopelessly in the middle class."

"Is that something to be ashamed of, Kosterman?"

"Not at all. But it doesn't buy much sushi, does it?"

"So what is it you're trying to say?"

"Getting a foothold in the TV business is all about contacts and relationships, Justice."

"So I've heard."

"I could do a lot for you." He leaned forward, his eyes as self-assured as they were cool. "I could change your life. Do you realize that?"

I said nothing, just sipped my tea to moisten my drying throat. He sat back, relaxing, his voice and manner becoming almost nonchalant.

"There may even be a place for you in the company itself, near the top. We're growing, expanding internationally as new markets open up around the world. I can always use a man who's decisive, strong-willed, smart."

He pushed his chair back.

"Think about it, Justice. Opportunities like this don't come along too often. For most people, never at all." He glanced at his watch. "You'll have to excuse me. I have an appointment at Universal. Let's be in touch. *Ciao.*"

"Ciao."

The waiter appeared as I was finishing the last piece of sashimi on my plate. He asked me if I cared for anything else.

"Has Mr. Kosterman taken care of the check?"

"Oh yes, sir. It's all on his account."

I smiled, feeling full but not content.

"In that case, I think I'll see the dessert tray."

Eighteen

I WORKED HARD to land this interview, Justice. I want you to
know that."

"You always work hard, Templeton. It goes without saying."

"This time, I had to wheedle and beg. Rose Fairchild hasn't
granted a press chat since her husband was killed back in sixty-
five. And that was a pre-fab statement released through her family
lawyer."

"She's reclusive, then."

"In the extreme."

We were traveling east on the Pasadena Freeway in Templeton's
air-conditioned Infiniti, leaving downtown Los Angeles miles behind. Templeton had reached me at my office when I returned
from my lunch of sushi and coercion with Jacob Kosterman, and
asked me if I wanted to ride along to her interview with the
matriarch of the Fairchild clan. It was not quite 3 P.M., and already the stream of cars on the oldest and narrowest section of
the Southern California freeway system was slowing to a jogger's
pace. Discussing what Templeton and Katie Nakamura had dug
up on the Fairchild family helped pass the time.

"Did Katie fill you in on Captain Fairchild's death?"

"He took a ricochet from a detective's forty-five during a robbery stakeout. Strictly accidental."

"Not the robbery."

"No. They threw the book at the two robbery suspects."

"What was the adjudication?"

"They copped to armed robbery and voluntary manslaughter, got twenty years apiece, and were shipped off to San Quentin. Within a month, one turned up stabbed to death in the shower room. The other was found suffocated in the laundry, with his head shoved into a barrel of powdered detergent."

"At least they died cleanly."

"That's more than can be said about the investigation that followed."

"Smelly?"

"Both killings went unsolved, written off as routine prison violence."

"How convenient."

"Wasn't it?"

"I don't imagine the Fairchilds shed too many tears over what happened up at Quentin."

"Nor the members of the police fraternity who arranged to have those two guys rubbed out."

"Why, Templeton, I do believe you're becoming cynical."

She kept her eyes straight ahead as she drove, but smiled a little.

"Even the press left it alone. This was sixty-five, almost a decade before Watergate. You know how the press handled things like that back then."

"Nothing in the *L.A. Times*?"

"Rose Fairchild came from a prominent family of wealthy landowners. Very cozy with the Chandlers, who owned the *Times*— another prominent family of wealthy landowners, which had also made its fortune in real estate and land development. Not without the taint of scandal and conflict of interest along the way."

"You've been reading your history books, Templeton."

"I try to keep up."

"What about the *Sun*? The *Herald-Examiner*, the *Daily News*? They didn't chase the story?"

"All politically conservative papers, Justice. Very pro-police, cooperative to a fault. Surely you're aware what it was like back then, in the days before Woodward and Bernstein. You've read the history books too."

"Just testing you, Templeton."

"How am I doing?"

"Headed for an accident if you don't watch the road."

She turned her attention back to the traffic and hit her horn as a Porsche cut rudely in front of her.

"So how did you score an interview with the reclusive Rose Fairchild?"

"I reached her through her attorney, convinced her that to draw a more complete portrait of her son as a police chief candidate, I should interview his mother. See where Taylor Fairchild grew up, get a sense of what he was like as a child."

"I guess she took the bait."

"Reluctantly. She kept reminding me that she's an extremely private person. In the end, I guess I wore her down. She conceded that a short interview would be worthwhile if it helped the public get a better picture of her son. She feels he's the top candidate among the bunch, that he'll be good for the city."

"No surprise there."

"She also feels he's destined for even greater things."

"She said that?"

"Oh, yes. She's very much the proud mother, and I played to that. She's giving me one hour, from four to five P.M."

"You're getting trickier and trickier, Templeton."

"I've studied with the master."

We exchanged smiles of mutual appreciation that were greased with bullshit.

"What am I supposed to do while you're chatting up Mrs. Fairchild?"

"I thought you might check out the neighborhood, take some notes. After all, Taylor Fairchild grew up there."

"His mother never moved?"

"Rose Fairchild was born in the house she still lives in seventy years later. It was a wedding gift from her parents, the Maplewoods, who moved to a smaller place nearby. Today, both homes are certified as official historical landmarks, architectural treasures. There's a lot of that out here."

"Old Pasadena money, I think they call it."

"The Maplewood side of the family pretty much defines the term—bottomless wealth, going way back. Along with a tradition of political conservatism, calculated philanthropy, and high social standing. And, of course, lily white, like some of the private golf clubs out this way."

"What else can you tell me about Mrs. Fairchild?"

"There's a file in my handbag, if you want to have a look."

I found it, and started reading. In snippets from books on California history and the social pages of the *Sun* and the *Los Angeles Times,* a profile emerged of Rose Fairchild as a formidable matriarch, in the tradition of another Rose on another coast, with the last name of Kennedy. Photos of Rose Fairchild, most snapped at charity events years ago, showed a slim, graying woman of considerable beauty who appeared patrician but not stiff, with a smile that was wide and warm and a penchant for black gowns and white pearls. When I commented on that, Templeton corrected me.

"Actually, she wears black almost exclusively in the evening, and rarely anything but red during the day. It's rumored that she only wears a piece of clothing once."

"The black widow or the lady in red? Peculiar, either way."

"With her money, Rose Fairchild can afford to be peculiar."

"How wealthy is she?"

"Pretty much off the charts. According to *Forbes,* she's worth so much they can only guess, but it's well into the hundreds of millions. They routinely rank her among the country's fifty richest people, but she manages to keep the exact figure a mystery."

I returned to her file and learned that Rose Fairchild's father was Harrington Cahill Maplewood, son of Taylor Cahill Maplewood, a Union general in the Civil War who had later served in the cabinets of two Presidents. Harrington Maplewood, an engineer, had moved west at the turn of the century and made his own fortune in mining and real estate. He and his wife named their daughter Rose, after Pasadena's Festival of Roses, which had been organized in 1888 with horse carriages festooned with roses, and later became the extravaganza of motor-driven floats known as the Rose Parade. Rose and her husband, Rodney Fairchild, had married in 1951, and named their firstborn Taylor, after his great-grandfather on his mother's side; their second son, Harrington, had died in childbirth, and there had been no other children. Rodney Fairchild, like his younger brother Matthew, had been a lawyer; unlike Matthew, he had considered law enforcement his true calling, and eventually left his legal practice to join the Los Angeles Police Department, against the wishes of his wife and her family. Rose Fairchild continued to oppose his police career until it became clear he was on his way to the high-profile chief's position, which might serve as a springboard for higher public office. When Rodney Fairchild was killed in the line of duty in 1965, she transferred her ambitions for her husband to her twelve-year-old son, Taylor, grooming him to follow, and hopefully surpass, the accomplishments of his father.

It was a lot of family history to digest, and I went over it again, from the top down, before I closed the file.

"Taylor Fairchild may be a cop," I said, "but he was definitely born with a silver spoon up his ass."

Templeton laughed.

"Big bucks and breeding, as Harry likes to say."

"How is Harry, by the way?"

"Not good."

"How bad is not good?"

"Wrung out, losing weight, running a temp."

"Is Roger Lawson still leaning on him, whittling away at his staff?"

"Harry had a major argument with Lawson just after lunch today. Harry called Lawson a bully, told him to get out of his office. Lawson tried to throw his weight around, literally. I think he'd belted down a few scotches with his double burger and fries."

"Lawson's a boozer?"

"Oh, yeah. Gets very boisterous and pushy when he's loaded, especially with females."

"And sixtyish editors on the sickly side, apparently."

"Yeah, he seems to have it in for Harry. He bristles at anybody with an independent streak who speaks his own mind." She glanced over, arching dark brows. "As long as they're smaller than he is, of course."

"If Roger Lawson ever lays a finger on Harry—"

Her eyes went back to the freeway, as she eased the car toward an off-ramp.

"Don't go there, Justice. You promised me those days were behind you."

"Somebody needs to plant his foot on Lawson's fat ass."

"You want to get angry, take a look at the file on Rose

Fairchild's father. He makes the Roger Lawsons of this world look like the petty errand boys they are.''

I found the file in her handbag. There wasn't a lot in it—a few clippings from the *Washington Post,* and one or two from the old investigative magazines *Ramparts* and *Mother Jones*—but there was enough to indicate that Harrington Maplewood deserved to spend eternity in hell. After making tens of millions in California mining and real estate, in his later years he had sat on the boards of several multinational corporations while serving as the conduit between these companies and various dictators in countries where the right to do business was coveted by stockholders for whom being grossly wealthy was not enough. Taylor Fairchild's grandfather had lived into his nineties, and his last accomplishment had been to work behind the scenes as the chief liaison for a number of American corporations with huge investments in Indonesia—corporations that had funneled tens of billions of dollars into the bank accounts of the ruthless dictator Suharto and his family members, while Suharto murdered and imprisoned his political opponents. It was a story I didn't expect to see on the Documentary Channel.

I shut the file and slipped it back into Templeton's handbag. "The man was evil."

"He was a businessman, Justice, without a soul or conscience."

"That's what I said."

We were in Pasadena now, the civic focal point of the San Gabriel Valley, and you could practically smell the old money along the wide, clean, tree-lined residential streets, where the lawns were broad and countless Queen Anne cottages and other historical styles were well preserved. We left the western section of the city, passed through a long, lush parkway, and wound northward into the picturesque green hills of the city's upper Arroyo Seco, one of the richest architectural districts in the country. Dozens of stunning homes dating back to the turn of the century sat proudly atop lush, gently rolling lawns, with Craftsman the dominant style.

Templeton slowed as she stared out, mouth agape.

"I feel like I'm driving through back issues of *Architectural Digest.* "

"I'm trying to picture Taylor Fairchild in these streets forty years ago, playing kickball and riding his bike."

"I've never seen a neighborhood that looked so perfect, so beautiful, yet so unreal. It's hard to imagine anything bad happening up here. I have yet to see a weed or a piece of litter, or hear a discordant voice."

"All the more reason Fairchild must have been shocked by his father's sudden death."

"Good point, Justice."

Down below, the enormous Rose Bowl football stadium came into view, and, in the distance, the less distinguished structures of downtown Pasadena, shrouded in noxious smog. We passed the elegant Gamble House, a two-story Arts and Crafts masterpiece designed meticulously in oak and teak, built in 1908 for the Procter and Gamble family, but now a house museum open to the public. Moments later, Templeton made a turn and drove uphill until she reached the crest, where she cruised slowly past a huge Mission-style mansion so massive and sprawling it might have passed for a great library or church, poised at the top of a sweeping drive. A neatly clipped lawn rolled down to the street in undulating, terraced symmetry, as smoothly as a well-laid carpet.

Templeton noted the street number outside the big gates, drove on for another block, and pulled to the curb.

"That was the Fairchild house, the big one. You should probably get out here." She glanced at her watch. "It's a few minutes before four. I'll meet you back here at five, unless my interview runs over, which doesn't seem likely. Mrs. Fairchild was very specific about the time frame."

Templeton reached into her purse, found a notebook and pen, and held them out to me. I patted my coat pocket.

"Thanks, I carry my own."

I climbed out.

"Wish me luck, Justice."

I gave her a small salute, and she pulled away, making a U-turn to disappear back the way she'd come. When I peered around the corner, she was well down the block, speaking into an intercom positioned to the left of the Fairchild gates. Moments later, the big gates opened, and she drove through, and up.

I surveyed the wide street, then started walking downhill. By the time I reached the Gamble House, I'd spoken with a postal carrier, a painter stenciling street numbers along the curb, and a woman bringing in her mail; none of them had anything to tell me about the Fairchild house or its inhabitants that I didn't already know. I found a tour about to start on the front steps of the Gamble House, and told the official guide I was writing a history of the neighborhood and hoped to find someone who could talk to me about some of the other landmarks in the area. She sent me inside to make inquiries at the front desk, and to look through the historical books on sale. The woman behind the counter heard me out, thought for a moment, then threw her hands up in the air, smiling brightly.

"I know just who you should talk to! Mr. Villereal, our landscape technician."

"He's familiar with the neighborhood?"

"Oh my, yes. His family has taken care of the yards up here for decades. He started as a boy working beside his father, then took over the yards himself as he got older. Eventually, he settled here as our full-time greens man. He's a walking encyclopedia on the botanical history up here."

"I was hoping to ask a few questions about the families as well."

"Dig enough in someone's garden, and you're bound to learn something about the person, don't you think?"

"Wisely put. Where will I find Mr. Villereal?"

"You'll have to look around. He's always about, puttering in the gardens."

Several minutes later, after traversing the southern and eastern boundaries of the magnificent house, and pausing to take in the views of the hills and the valley, I came upon an older man in gray work clothes dumping nitrohumus into a bed of bird-of-paradise plants. His hair and mustache were white, his brown skin burnished deeply and cracked by the sun, his body trim. He moved carefully as he knelt, as if the muscles in his back and shoulders were locked permanently into position.

"Mr. Villereal?"

He looked up without speaking. I complimented him on his well-shaped hedges, and wondered if I might ask a few questions.

He stood slowly, grimacing as he worked out the kinks, and ran his sleeve across his forehead, drawing off the sweat. When he spoke, in perfect English, I heard a Mexican accent that had faded but survived over time, like good adobe.

"What would you like to know, sir?"

I asked him how long he had worked in the upper Arroyo Seco. He guessed fifty years, maybe more.

"Have you ever worked at the Fairchild house? The one around the corner and up the hill?"

He shook his head no.

"Do you know anything about the family?"

He smiled, his teeth bright against his brown skin.

"A little, yes. A very important family up here. Mrs. Fairchild, she's a fine woman."

"You've met her?"

"Oh, yes."

"But you said you never worked for her."

"At Easter, she would have a party for the children. She would wave to us from the balcony. And once, many years ago, we had some personal business between us."

"Do you mind my asking what that was?"

"It was nothing, really. The boy, Taylor, he was riding his bicycle one day. He fell, hit his head on the edge of the street, near where I was trimming the grass. Of course, I hurried to help him. I took my shirt to stop the bleeding and carried him up to the Fairchilds' house. That was how I first met Mrs. Fairchild."

"You carried him in your arms, all the way up that drive?"

He grinned.

"I was younger then. Stronger. *Muy macho.*" I smiled, and he laughed. "They had no gate then, the Fairchilds. I walked right up to the front door and rang the doorbell. The maid answered, of course, and then Mrs. Fairchild came. He was fine, the boy. Scared, a few stitches to the head. But he was all right."

"Mrs. Fairchild must have been very grateful."

"Oh, yes. She was very good to me, to my family."

"She rewarded you in some way?"

He dropped his eyes, and when he brought them up again, they were cloudy with emotion.

"My three children, they all went to college because of Mrs. Fairchild. She pay for everything, the books, the tuition, all of it. A very generous lady, Mrs. Fairchild."

"And the Easter parties you mentioned. Your children were invited?"

"All the children whose parents worked in the neighborhood.

The maids, the gardeners like me, black and Mexican, everyone. Mrs. Fairchild, she would sit up on the verandah enjoying to watch. It was always very nice, hundreds of colored eggs hidden all over, all the children running around with their baskets looking for the eggs, and the chocolate candies wrapped in pretty foil." He smiled, remembering. "You know, up there on the hill, on the rolling lawn. My children very much enjoyed that."

"Mrs. Fairchild wasn't concerned about security? Bringing all those strangers on to her property?"

"There were always policemen there. You know, because of her husband being a police officer. The police, they have always been very good to Mrs. Fairchild."

"Especially after Captain Fairchild was killed, I imagine."

He shrugged, tilted his head, said nothing.

"His death must have been very hard on the boy."

"Oh, yes. It was a very sad time. Very hard on the boy, Taylor."

"The Easter parties ended with Captain Fairchild's death?"

"Oh, no! Mrs. Fairchild, she wanted things to be the same, for the boy. She had one more Easter party for the children, the next year. It was after the other thing happened that the parties were stopped, when Mrs. Fairchild began to keep such a close watch on her son."

"What other thing was that, Mr. Villereal?"

He dropped his eyes again and turned back to his gardening.

"Mr. Villereal?"

"I am not so sure this is something I should speak about."

"Why is that?"

"It is a private thing. A very bad thing, I think. Mrs. Fairchild, she was hurt greatly by it. And, of course, the child."

"If I were to promise to keep it just between us, could you tell me? So I might understand why such a generous woman as Mrs. Fairchild would stop the Easter parties, when all the children had enjoyed them so much."

He dug both hands into the big bag of nitrohumus and transferred a pile of it to the base of a bird-of-paradise.

"Mr. Villereal?"

He glanced up, but only partly, leaving a gap between us. His weather-lined face seemed further creased with pain.

"It was when the boy's uncle did things to the child, and Mrs. Fairchild found out."

"Captain Fairchild's brother, Matthew, the lawyer?"

"Yes, Matthew, I think that was his name."

"Do you know what happened?"

"I only know that in the year following his father's death, the boy was very sad. He seemed to need to be with older boys, and to talk to men his father's age. He would even walk down the street at times and talk to me as I worked in a neighbor's yard. Not about anything, really, just to talk, you know? He seemed lonely, as if he missed his father very much. I would dig in the garden, trim the hedges, and try to be a friend to the boy.

"Then, Mrs. Fairchild, she learned that the boy's uncle had been doing bad things to him, and after that we never saw Taylor again. Mrs. Fairchild kept him inside, or took him to school and picked him up in her big car. He was never out of her sight."

"Do you know how Mrs. Fairchild found out? About the sexual abuse?"

"The boy, Taylor, had a friend, Jacobo. A family friend, an older boy. For some years, I tended his family's yard. Taylor, he told Jacobo what his uncle was doing. This Jacobo, he told his parents. This is how Mrs. Fairchild found out."

"Jacobo. In English, Jacob?"

"Jacob, yes."

"Jacob Kosterman?"

"Kosterman. Yes."

"What happened to the uncle, do you know?"

Mr. Villereal spoke as he bent to the soil, showing me his back.

"That is something of which I know nothing, sir."

"Nothing at all?"

"Please, if you will, I have my work to do."

I thanked him for answering my questions, but he said nothing, just kept his back to me, busy with his plants, until I knew it was time to go.

Templeton was waiting for me at the spot where she'd dropped me off, as I climbed the hill past the Fairchild mansion. I heard the lock on the passenger door electronically unlatch, opened the door, and slid in.

"How did your interview with Mrs. Fairchild go?"

Templeton switched on the ignition and shifted into drive.

"Reasonably well, if I were writing a puff piece. She's very gracious but also keeps a lot to herself. She seemed to know how to give me just enough, while deflecting any questions that started to scratch the surface. I taped our conversation. You're welcome to listen to it at some point, if you'd like."

"I might do that. Was she wearing red?"

"Head to foot."

She turned the wheel and swung away from the curb in a wide arc.

"How about you, Justice? Learn anything interesting?"

"I learned that Rose Fairchild is quite generous to people who do her a good turn. Also, that bad things do happen up here."

"Care to be more specific?"

As Templeton pointed the car downhill, I told her briefly about what Uncle Matthew had done to little Taylor when he was especially vulnerable after his father's death.

"When we get back to the office, I'll ask Katie Nakamura to see what's become of Matthew Fairchild. He might even be worth an interview, if we can arrange it."

We passed the big gates and ascending driveway of the Fairchild place, and could see a gray-haired woman in red sitting behind the rail of a second-story verandah. Rose Fairchild gazed out across the rolling slopes of her rambling property, presiding over her private world, perhaps studying us as we went by.

I wondered if she might also be recalling all those Easter parties of long ago, and hearing the laughter of the children as they scampered up and down the lawns, when her husband was still alive, her son still innocent, her private world still safe and intact.

I wondered about a lot of things in Rose Fairchild's life as we wound our way out of the Arroyo Seco, down into the flats of the city, back to the world of weeds, litter, and discordant voices.

Nineteen

I T WAS ALMOST SIX by the time Templeton and I had covered the ten miles from Pasadena back to downtown Los Angeles, with most of the commuter traffic headed in the other
direction, away from the city. On our way in, we stopped near the
train station for French-dipped sandwiches at Felipe's, where a
cup of coffee was still a dime and the double-dipped pork sandwiches were served with thick slabs of blue cheese that was pun-
gent and sharp. We ate ours with dollops of sweet, crispy coleslaw
on the side, sitting on tall stools at a long table, trying to make
some sense of the Callahan and Mittelman murders, and figure
out just where a few other names figured into the tangle.

Satiated on food, if not conclusions, we crossed the central city
to the warehouse district, and the faded, ornate Romanesque
building that housed the *Sun.* Except for a few sports reporters,
there was almost nobody on the third floor, where editorial was
located. Even Harry had gone home, after leaving a note posted
to his office door: *Getting some shut-eye. Call me at home if there's
another crisis.* It was a desolate setting, all those empty reporter's
pods, some of which might never be filled again. It had my past
and the future of newspapers in general written all over it, and my
lunch with Jacob Kosterman started to grab at me again, as his

tempting talk of power and paychecks danced like sugarplums in my head.

We found Katie Nakamura in the library, bent over a computer, working in Nexus. I put in my request for anything she might pull up on a lawyer named Matthew Fairchild, uncle of Taylor Fairchild and brother-in-law to his mother, Rose. She added it to her list of projects, and went back to work.

After that, I drove home, all the way out Sunset Boulevard to avoid the Friday evening freeway crush, with my lunchtime craving for alcohol coming back a little stronger than I found comfortable. The surface street proved a poor alternative—there were no longer any routes in the city free of gridlock at rush hour—but at least the scenery was more interesting. I passed through neighborhoods that were Latino, gay, Thai, and Pakistani, then lurid with the promise of commercial sex, along the stretch where the Sunset Tiki Motel was situated. Roughly ten miles and one hour after leaving downtown, I was moving slowly along the Sunset Strip, past all the trendy joints that would be filled by midnight with Hollywood's pseudo-hip, while the wannabes lined the sidewalk outside, hoping to be blessed with admittance. There were at least three liquor stores along the Strip with convenient parking that would have made buying a bottle of wine, or something stronger, a two-minute stop on the way to hell. I passed each one with my hands tight on the wheel, my eyes straight ahead.

When I reached the house, I called Oree Joffrien at home, hoping for a dinner companion, or just someone to talk to; he was out, so I left a message. Peter was still at work, so I fed the animals and took Maggie for a walk by myself, greeting neighbors whose identities I knew only by their dogs' names, as most of them knew me. Then, before the loneliness of the empty Friday evening closed in too tightly, and the lingering memory of hot saki began to haunt, I changed into an old pair of sweats and spent fifteen minutes stretching and gutting out my regimen of sit-ups and push-ups, trying to reclaim some diminished muscle mass before it was too late. After that, I took off on a two-mile hike into the hills, all the way to the top where the road ended, punishing myself with a fast pace and not a single break until I reached the summit. A strong March wind was up, blowing the basin clean, and the lights of the city sparkled like a million tiny diamonds. Then I was striding down even faster than I'd climbed, two miles home to a hot shower and a nap, before waking in the disorienting darkness.

I lay for a while naked on the cool sheet, in the small bedroom Maurice and Fred had shared for more than forty years. I felt my body—my chest, arms, belly—and found some firmness coming back, some dormant muscles being revived. Twenty years ago, in my final year as a college wrestler, I'd weighed twenty pounds less at meet time, been twice as strong, immeasurably more quick. I still had dreams in which I was twenty again, in top condition, with a chance to win; sometimes, in my feverish sleep, sweating and turning, I relived certain matches, like old tapes I couldn't shut off. Never the matches I'd won, which had been most of them; only the rare few I'd lost. In the dreams, I'd strain, grope, lunge desperately to make the right moves, undo the outcome. Always, on the brink of possible victory, I'd wake, as I was slowly waking now, realizing I was forty, not twenty; that I would not, could not, change the old scores, could not get back to where I'd once been, could never do things over, differently.

Through an open window, I heard mournful cello music coming from a neighbor's house as he practiced a sonata. I listened awhile, thinking about Oree, how much I wanted to connect with him, if he'd let me, how much I'd like to have him there beside me, if he was willing, as I tried to pull my life together, start over. It had been a long time since I'd admitted my need for another person in my life, a mate, someone strong enough and smart enough to stand up to my bullshit and my fear, to call me on it when necessary. Templeton was getting pretty good at that, and Harry had managed it from the start, but that was different. I needed a man beside me in the total sense; every fiber in me cried out and ached for that. It was something a lot of people wouldn't understand, something many others would condemn, but that didn't change it in the slightest; it never had and never would, and when you reach a certain age you understand that, and stop worrying about the other people, while you still have some time left to make a life for yourself, on your own terms. I hadn't thought about these things for a while; it had taken the emergence of Oree Joffrien into my life to do that. Yet, for all his warmth and wisdom, he seemed disconcertingly distant, always just out of reach. I didn't like to admit it, but I felt more alone now than I had before I'd met him.

The sonata ended, the cello fell silent, and the house grew cold. I got up, put on some decent clothes, and walked down to Tribal Grounds, where a hot mug of coffee in my hands and friendly people around had become a familiar substitute for companionship. I drank my dark roast at a sidewalk table as the men streamed by on their Friday night pilgrimage into Boy's Town, feeling a little older as the night got later and the faces got younger. After that, I sauntered on down the boulevard to the Powder Room in search of Tiger Palumbo.

She was behind the bar, wiping it down while she chatted with a female couple who sat on barstools, holding hands and sharing a pitcher of beer. A few more women were scattered here and there along the bar, while a dozen or so were gathered around the pool table, the players laughing and slapping high fives after sinking difficult shots. A k.d. lang tune played insistently in the background, something about constant craving, but not so loudly that it killed the conversation. As far as I could tell, I was the only man in the place.

Palumbo looked over as I took a stool at the end of the bar near the door. So did the two women she was talking to. She turned back to them, took a minute to finish the conversation, then came in my direction, taking her time while she sized me up. She was shorter than I expected, with wide hips, stubby legs, and an upper body that looked as if it could still throw solid uppercuts if necessary. Her hair was ducktailed, brown with streaks of gray at the sides, her face free of makeup, and her outfit standard issue West Hollywood dyke: Doc Martens, tight blue jeans, a T-shirt with the sleeves rolled up. As she got closer, under the glow of a Bud Light sign behind the bar, I saw that her eyes were green and her brows unplucked. A trace of downy hair was visible on her upper lip and down the sides of her face, like the first signs of a mustache and sideburns on a pubescent boy. As wispy as her facial hair was, my guess was she took some pride in it.

"Can I help ya?"

"Mineral water, if you've got it."

"Got some ID, pal?"

"You're joking, right?"

She stood with her legs slightly spread, her strong-looking hands braced on the bar, and not a trace of humor in her eyes.

"Do I look like I'm joking?"

"I'm not a cop."

She said nothing, just waited. I pulled out my wallet, showed her my driver's license. She barely glanced at it.

"Need to see three pieces of picture ID."

"Nobody carries three pieces of picture ID."

"That's the house policy."

I heard laughter behind me, coming through the door. Two twenty-something men, slim and pretty, and a larger woman in the same age range sauntered past and took stools farther down the bar.

"You going to ask them for three pieces of picture ID?"

"I know them. I don't know you."

"What if I'm a friend of Cecile's? Does that make a difference?"

"If you were a friend of Cecile's, I'd know ya."

"I saw her just this morning. We talked about you as a matter of fact."

"Me? I don't think so."

I leaned toward her, lowered my voice.

"She keeps a framed photograph of you on her credenza, right behind her desk. She mentioned how you like to ply her with flattery when you want to have your way with her."

Even in the muted light, I could see Palumbo blush.

"Go on!"

"I believe you two have a fifth anniversary coming up."

"You do know Cecile!"

"I believe I said that."

"Well, why didn't ya say so sooner?" She shook a playful fist at me. "Damn!"

"Think I could have that mineral water now?"

"Hell, yes. On the house. You sure you don't want somethin' stronger?"

"Not very. That's why I'll have the water."

She grabbed a bottle, unscrewed the cap, wiped the lip with a fresh towel, and set the bottle on the bar, sans napkin.

"Shit, man, you come in here like you're some straight dude wandered into the wrong bar, or out slummin', maybe lookin' for trouble. I was ready to show ya the door."

"I'm surprised there's not a bouncer out front."

"Rhonda don't come on till eight, when we start to get busy. She never woulda let you in—not without the ACLU filin' a lawsuit first."

I laughed.

"I think that's called reverse discrimination."

"I call it protectin' the regular clients from assholes. So just how do you and Cecile come to be pards, anyway?"

"Oree Joffrien introduced us."

"That professor guy, from UCLA."

"That's the one."

She tidied up the bar as she talked.

"They go back a ways, Cecile and Oree."

"Not that far, really. From what Oree tells me, he met Cecile at New York University. You must know friends of Cecile's who go back a lot further. I mean, since she grew up out here and all."

Palumbo shook her head, set out a bowl of popcorn.

"Naw, not really. She was pretty much in the closet till she got to that school in New York. Started makin' friends after that."

"Oree mentioned that you met her on a cruise up in Alaska."

"Yeah, how about that! I got up my nerve one night, asked her to dance. It was cowboy music, you know, line dancin'. She was in heels and I was in saddle boots! Christ, what a pair we was. But once we got to talkin', we just hit it off. Who woulda known?"

"They say opposites attract."

"Well, she got herself one unrepentant butch dyke when she got me, and she ain't never asked me to tone it down yet."

"How's her family accepted you?"

"Cecile's family? Hell, I never met one of 'em. They don't have nothin' to do with her. Never accepted her bein' a lesbian, she told me, not even as feminine as she is."

"That must be painful for her."

"Cecile's fragile-lookin' as a flower, but she's tough inside. Said she got over it a long time ago, that it's just her and me against the world now, which is OK by me. Any of her family come around givin' her problems, they got me to deal with, you know what I mean?"

"I think I do."

"Listen, what's yer name—?"

"Ben. Ben Justice."

"Ben. I gotta get back to the bar, take care of the girls. Includin' those two queens who just come in." She nodded toward the two young men who had just entered, then stuck out her hand. "It's been a pleasure. Any friend of my woman's welcome in the Powder Room. You just tell Rhonda at the door that you and Tiger's pards."

She shook my hand with a grip more powerful than most men's, then returned to business. I emptied half the bottle, left a dollar for a tip, and stepped out into a brisk wind and a night that had grown quickly cold. Only in Boy's Town would you see men in shorts and tank tops in frigid weather, and there were plenty of them now, on their way to and from the gyms or showing it off at Starbucks on the corner while commuters along Santa Monica Boulevard gawked, tittered, or sneaked glances as they passed slowly in the steady traffic. I turned up my collar against the cold and started home.

It wasn't until I was passing the S&M paraphernalia shop the owners called 665—"One Number Short of Hell"—that I sensed someone might be following me. Others were coming and going, but they were moving at different paces; the figure who had caught my attention seemed to be in step with me, while keeping his head down. I confirmed it when I stopped suddenly and looked back, past the white exterior of the Metropolitan Community Church that separated us. I saw a darkish figure in a long heavy coat, the collar turned up around his ears, a skullcap pulled low, his face well obscured as he pretended to study the interior of a massage and tanning salon.

I started back in his direction. He hunched his shoulders and turned his head away from the light. I immediately wheeled and sprinted to the corner, then cut down a side street leading away from the boulevard toward the residential neighborhood to the south. I turned left at the first street I came to, stepped into a dark cluster of arching banana palms, and waited. Not half a minute later, he was turning the same corner. As he passed, I recognized the profile and stepped out to the sidewalk behind him.

"Out cruising, Sergeant?"

Felix Montego stood where he was for a moment, with his back to me. Finally, he wheeled slowly, keeping his mouth shut.

"Really, Sergeant, I'm flattered to be followed by such a handsome man."

"You may think all this is funny, Justice. I can assure you it's not."

"Why don't you fill me in, Montego? Maybe I'll believe you."

"The less you know, the better off you are."

"Why the cloak-and-dagger routine? Shouldn't you be home playing Nintendo with your kids instead of out here playing Keystone Kops?"

He glanced around, then took several steps, closing the gap until there were only inches between us. When he spoke again, his voice was dead serious.

"I'm telling you, Justice, you're poking around where you shouldn't, asking too many troublesome questions."

"Somebody needs to ask them."

"That's my job."

"Then why aren't you doing it, instead of shadowing me like a second-rate private eye?"

"If I told you, you wouldn't believe it."

"Try me."

"Because I don't want to see you get hurt. I don't want to see anyone else get hurt. Not the Zeigler woman, no one."

"How touching, Sergeant, to know how much you care."

"Listen to me, Justice. Please. Butt out of this, let it die."

"You sound like you might have a personal stake in it."

His eyes grew uneasy, the way they had in his office when my comments had cut too close to the bone.

"This thing is far more complicated than you could ever guess. You're dealing with forces much bigger and more powerful than you realize."

"I'm getting aroused, Sergeant."

"This is not a battle you can win, Justice."

"Any other advice? Maybe something a little more concrete? Because the bullshit's starting to run a bit thin."

He looked at the ground, shook his head, muttered something to himself. Then, very directly:

"Just this. Don't even consider looking up Charlie Gitt. I have a feeling he's on your list, but he's one person you definitely don't want to mess with."

"Dangerous, Sergeant?"

"Totally out of control."

"I'll keep that in mind."

His eyes stayed on mine for a moment, and I thought I saw genuine concern in them. Then he stepped around me and back around the corner. I followed more slowly, and when I reached the boulevard, he was nowhere to be seen.

I arrived home to find Peter Graff sitting alone in the swing on the front porch. He'd lit a candle in a hurricane lamp on the rail at the far end and sat in its soft glow, bundled up in a plaid wool jacket with a fleecy collar. He stood up to meet me as I mounted the steps.

"Hi."

"Hi."

"I was waiting for you."

"So I see."

"I was hoping—"

"Hoping what, Peter?"

"You know. That maybe we could spend the night together."

"I'm not sure that's such a great idea."

"Oh."

"Maybe we should think about how involved we both want to get before it goes any further."

"Are you seeing someone else?"

"Not exactly."

"You met somebody?"

"Sort of."

"Maybe I shouldn't be staying in the apartment, then."

"I didn't say that, Peter."

"I'm confused, Ben. Are you seeing someone else or not?"

"It's not that simple."

"I don't expect anything from you, Ben."

"I know that. That's what makes being with you so damned easy." I looked him up and down. "Aside from the other obvious reasons."

He reached for my face, and initiated the kiss. It was his first time doing that with me, with any man, and it was awkward for him. I maneuvered him into the corner by the door, into the deepest shadows and out of the wind, taking over for him, kissing him with real force, pushing past his hesitation. Within moments, I was pressing against him and touching him in such a frenzy I never heard the car door shut on the street, or the footsteps coming up the walk behind me.

It wasn't until I heard Oree's voice that I realized he was there.

"I was in the neighborhood, Ben, and I—"

He didn't see Peter until I took a step back, and Peter emerged, wiping my saliva from his lips. Oree's thin laughter was tinged with irony, maybe some pain.

"Obviously, I came at a bad time. Forgive me."

He turned and started down the walk.

"Oree, wait! I need to talk to you!"

I pursued him to the street, where he turned and put up a hand like a traffic cop.

"No words needed, Ben. It's all right. I understand."

"No, you don't. You don't."

His voice was soft, knowing.

"I think I do."

And, of course, he did.

Then he was in his car, pulling out, speeding away. Gone.

Twenty

I WOKE AT DAWN and drank my coffee on the front porch with the cats nearby, each of us angling for the first of the sun's warmth, while I ran through the events of the previous evening, trying to sort things out. Finally, I decided that if I couldn't get some order into my personal life, I'd at least try to make some headway in the Callahan and Mittelman murder cases. I hadn't forgotten Sergeant Montego's dire warnings to butt out—if anything, they fueled me to push harder, faster.

By 8 A.M. I was on the Hollywood Freeway, cruising toward the San Gabriel Valley, the neon dragons of Chinatown to my left, the downtown skyscrapers to my right. I crossed the Los Angeles River, which had once been lush and green, with Indians camped along its fifty-eight winding miles. Now it was a cement-lined flood channel, as well as a handy canvas for graffiti artists, who used the concrete-covered embankments to spray-paint their messages, and a hangout for skateboarders, who coveted the same steep slopes and were sometimes swept away to shocking deaths when flash floods caught them by surprise. Six miles past the river, across the sleepy barrios of Boyle Heights, I reached Monterey Park.

Variously dubbed "the new Chinatown" and "the Chinese Beverly Hills," the hilly suburb of not quite eight square miles had been reinvented in the 1970s as a haven for immigrants from Hong Kong, Taiwan, and Communist China. So massive was the influx that by the eighties nearly as many businesses were advertised in Chinese as in English, causing a white backlash and failed attempts to mandate English-only sign restrictions. By the nineties, nearly half the city's sixty thousand residents were of Chinese descent, and more than a hundred authentic Chinese restaurants were competing for each other's business. Asian gangsters had moved in to make their shakedowns, and *pai gow* poker became the most popular form of gambling in the city.

At half past eight, most of the business district was still asleep as I passed quietly through. I followed a Thomas Bros. guide that directed me toward the hills rising to the south, separating Monterey Park from the poorer barrios of neighboring East Los Angeles. Most of the street names on the flatter north side were in Spanish, reflecting the city's nineteenth-century land grant beginnings as a Mexican rancho, and later a growing pueblo. Those to the south sounded right out of an Anglo land developer's real estate brochure: Sunny Hill Drive, Cresthaven Way, Glenview Terrace, Rolling Hill Road. Pearl Tsao-Ping, according to my notes, resided on Summit Place, which turned out to be a cozy cul-de-sac tucked into the hillside, with views across the San Gabriel Valley to the snow-capped mountains to the north.

I circled slowly, found the number I was looking for, and parked just outside the mouth of the cul-de-sac, where I could watch the house from a few hundred feet without being observed. It was a compact Tudor-style home of white-painted brick, with an orderly yard of freshly clipped grass ringed by a profusion of blooming flowers in at least a dozen varieties. A brick walkway divided the lawn, leading to a porch on which sat a lounge chair that looked singular and lonely. In the driveway was a truck whose side panels advertised a business—Trade Winds, Fashionable Apparel for the New Century—and listed a toll-free phone number and the addresses of several stores, all of which I wrote down.

At nine o'clock, an hour that seemed reasonably civil, I climbed out of the Mustang, walked to the house, and rang the bell. I could now see a shiny black Mercedes-Benz sedan parked in front of the truck, separated from it by a locked driveway gate. I was about to ring the bell again when the door was opened by a small, wrinkled man of perhaps sixty-five. He had a pleasant, inquisitive face, happy, childlike eyes, and a chin of sparse white whiskers.

"Mr. Tsao-Ping?"

He nodded and bowed slightly.

"I'm looking for your son, Winston."

His smile remained but the happiness went out of it, and out of his narrow eyes as well. He shook his head slowly, almost apologetically, several times.

"Your son Winston no longer lives with you?"

Mr. Tsao-Ping raised his hands like a pair of small, soft wings, and shook his head again, sadly.

"Is Winston still alive?" I recalled how limited his English had been on the phone when I'd called before. I repeated carefully: "Winston—alive?"

Suddenly, the door was pulled wide by a tiny, robust woman with dark, angry eyes, whom I took to be Pearl Tsao-Ping. She appeared to be roughly the same age as her husband, but carried herself with a fury and a force that seemed unimaginable in him. Her face, squashed and buttoned down with a tiny pug nose, was heavily made up under a wig of dark, lacquered hair. Gold jewelry, with stones in several different colors, embellished her wrists, neck, and fingers.

She thrust out a finger with a painted nail long enough to take out my eye, if she were so inclined.

"I tell you not to bother us! I tell you that when you call! Now go away!"

"It's important that I find Winston, Mrs. Tsao-Ping. He may be able to give me some information I need."

"I tell you, I have no son Winston! Only Franklin! Good son! Married boy! No son Winston! Winston dead!"

"I've checked records in the Los Angeles area, Mrs. Tsao-Ping. I found no death certificate for a Winston Tsao-Ping during the past fifteen years."

"Why you want to bother us? Not your business! Go!"

I glanced at the Trade Winds logo on the parked truck.

"Perhaps he works at one of your shops, and I could reach him there."

She glared at me a moment, then disappeared inside. When she came back, it was straight at me, with a broom raised above her head. She brought it down on my back and shoulders—two, three, four times—as I turned and scurried back down the walk. She stood at the edge of the bricks, holding the broom like a bayonet, watching, until I climbed into the Mustang and drove away.

I covered three blocks, using up a minute or two, swung back, parked where I could see the house again, and waited.

Mr. Tsao-Ping came out a few minutes later with a small kneeling stool, which he placed at the edge of a flower bed, and used for support as he pulled weeds. Not quite half an hour had passed when a young Chinese man emerged from a side door. He was on the tall and husky side, but moved with his head slightly bowed, and I guessed he was Franklin Tsao-Ping, which would later prove correct. He climbed into the truck, started the engine, and backed into the street as his father paused in his gardening to wave.

As the truck came in my direction, I rolled up the Mustang's dirty window and slouched low in my seat, out of sight. When it was past, I fired up the engine and gave Franklin a safe lead before I followed. Fifteen minutes later, I was back on the 101 Freeway, heading west across the Los Angeles River, through downtown, into Hollywood. As the freeway veered north, Franklin took the Melrose Avenue exit, continuing west for two miles until he was into the trendiest section of the street, between La Brea and Fairfax avenues. Melrose, as the neighborhood was known locally, was comprised of a dozen blocks of boutiques, cafés, coffeehouses, and record stores that had once catered to an arty, thirty-something crowd but was now a hangout for the funkier teenage grunge set that seemed to have endless money to spend on ridiculously overpriced clothes that were out of style by their second laundering. Most of those clothes were imported, many of them from the sweatshops of Asia—even the grim prisons of Communist China—where workers as young as five or six cut and stitched fifteen hours a day to satisfy the world's voracious appetite for fashion, and to make importers like the Tsao-Ping family rich. The teenage grunge set didn't seem to care much about that. Not many people did, for that matter; they just kept on buying and buying, and looking for another sale.

At a traffic light, the truck's right turn signal began blinking. I surveyed the block ahead, and spotted a store bearing the Trade

Winds logo. The truck turned right, then made a quick left into an alley, and pulled in behind the store. I parked on the street, slipped quarters into the meter, glanced at my watch, saw that it was half past ten, and went looking for coffee and a place to take a leak.

When that was taken care of, I returned to the store. By then, Franklin Tsao-Ping was at the front, unlocking the door. A young woman, also Chinese, was in the window, hanging colorful papier-mâché streamers behind several headless mannequins dressed in outlandish vinyl-covered clothes. A few feet away, a chubby Chinese baby played in a small chair with wheels, pushing it about with his tiny feet and laughing with excitement each time he bumped into a rack of hanging clothes.

I smiled as I entered, said hello, and began browsing.

"If you need any help, just let me know."

Franklin's voice was soft, deferential; unlike many retail sales clerks, he left me to roam on my own while he busied himself behind the cash register. I sauntered down one side of the store, which was filled with garish, retro-seventies nylon shirts that hadn't even looked good on John Travolta when he was svelte. The other side was devoted to women's apparel; I could tell because I saw a few skirts, the kind I thought had disappeared with Twiggy, but which apparently had made a comeback. I checked a price tag on a shirt I wouldn't have been cremated in: ninety-five bucks, plus tax.

I decided it was time to speak with Franklin Tsao-Ping. He had lifted his son from the rolling playchair and was bouncing the giggling baby high above his head on outstretched arms.

"Cute kid."

He lowered the boy and cradled him against his chest.

"This is my son, Dwight—after the great general and president, Eisenhower."

"You look too young to know much about Ike."

"My mother picked the name." He laughed dryly. "She picks all the names in our family."

"What did she call you?"

"Franklin."

"After Roosevelt, no doubt."

"How did you know?"

"A lucky guess."

He glanced toward the shirts.

"Did you find something you like?"

"Not really my style."

"Mine, either, if you want to know the truth."

"Then why do you sell it?"

"Because people buy it. Because my mother owns the store and puts me here."

The young woman stepped down from the window and took the baby from Franklin's arms.

"And this must be your wife."

"Yes. Lu-Ling."

She was a pretty woman, with unusually large, long-lashed eyes set evenly in her pale Chinese face, and a small, heart-shaped mouth. She was dressed conservatively like her husband, her clothes at odds with the styles offered for sale in the store.

She smiled, looking flustered.

"I sorry. I not speaking English very much yet."

"How long have you been in our country?"

She looked at her husband.

"Lu-Ling came over from Taiwan just before the wedding two years ago."

"You met when you were overseas, on a buying trip?"

The dry laugh again.

"My mother chose Lu-Ling for me."

"Ah."

"I met her the day she arrived, three weeks before we were married."

I reached out and touched the baby's tiny nose.

"You have a beautiful son."

"Yes, my mother was very pleased."

There was no laugh this time, and the edge in his voice surprised me. He struck me as a man who had a great deal he wanted to say, but never quite said it.

"Would she have been as pleased if your wife had given birth to a girl?"

"Apparently you know something about the old Chinese attitudes."

"I know that in traditional Chinese families, sons are often fiercely loyal to their parents. Especially to the mother, when the family structure is matriarchal, as it so often is.''

He was looking at me keenly, shrewdly.

''Are you the man who came to our house this morning?''

''You saw me?''

''I was upstairs, but I heard your voice.''

He turned to his wife, speaking Chinese. When she had walked away, out of earshot, he reverted to English, speaking more urgently.

''You know something about my brother, Winston?''

''Not as much as I'd like to.''

''What can you tell me?''

''When did you last hear from him?''

''I was eight when my mother banished Winston from the family. He was twenty-four.''

''Were the two of you close?''

''I worshiped my brother. I miss him more than I can tell you.''

''You said you were eight when your mother disowned him. That would have been fifteen years ago?''

He nodded.

''I never saw him again. He sent me letters, called, until my mother found out and stopped it. In her mind, he's dead; he doesn't exist.''

''He could have found a way to contact you if he wanted to.''

''Something happened. He changed.''

''Changed how?''

''I don't know. The last time I heard from him, when I was ten, he told me I'd never see him again, never hear from him, that it was better that way. He told me he loved me, asked me to always remember him. That was the last time.''

''I understand Winston was married.''

''Yes.''

''Children?''

''His wife got pregnant but miscarried.''

''Boy or girl?''

''Girl.''

''Your mother knew?''

He nodded.

''Natural miscarriage?''

He flushed.

"I was young. I didn't know about those things. I just know she lost the baby."

"What happened to Winston's wife after your mother sent Winston packing?"

"My mother sent her back to Taiwan, paid money to have the marriage annulled." I felt his hand seize my arm. "Tell me what happened, anything you know. Please."

"Fifteen years ago, your brother was beaten up by the police. He was dressed in women's clothes when it happened, something he apparently did fairly often, according to the police report."

Franklin's grip loosened, and he looked away.

"You're sure about that?"

"Yes."

"I didn't know about that."

"Does it make you love him less?"

He faced me quickly.

"No. No, of course not. It's just—I didn't know, that's all."

"Winston told the police who investigated that he was heterosexual, which is quite common among transvestites. That he'd secretly been dressing up this way since high school, that he felt compelled to do it. That he couldn't stop himself."

"My mother found this out?"

I nodded.

"She managed to keep things quiet, cover the whole thing up. Kept it out of the courts, out of the papers."

He crossed his arms and hugged his chest, as if pressing in his emotions.

"I understand now why she always pressured me to marry. Why she started in on me so young."

"You didn't want to marry Lu-Ling?"

"It's not a question of what I wanted. In our family, a son must marry, no matter what his feelings."

"It must be awfully hard on the wives when the love isn't there."

"My mother says there's no such thing as love. That it's a silly notion, foolishness. She says that only three things matter—loyalty to family, making a good business, and eating well."

A car door slammed behind the store. Through the screen of the rear door, I saw the side of a black Mercedes-Benz sedan.

"That's my mother. You'd better go."

"I'll call you here if I need to talk."

"What's your name?"

"Benjamin Justice."

"Why are you involved in this?"

"I'm not exactly sure."

"You knew Winston?"

"No."

"You must have a reason."

"There have been two murders that may be related to the beating incident fifteen years ago. I have friends who'd like to see them solved."

We heard the rear door slam, and I started out. He followed me as far as the front door, grabbing my arm again.

"Do you think Winston is alive? Will I ever see him again?"

"I'm sorry, Franklin. I don't have an answer to that."

He turned back, and I disappeared into the passing crowd. A moment later, as I stood behind the fat trunk of a curbside palm, I heard Pearl Tsao-Ping's shrill voice, screaming in Chinese. I watched her through the window, flailing her hands, castigating Lu-Ling for the work she'd done on the window display, while Franklin took the crying baby from his wife's arms.

Mrs. Tsao-Ping stepped up into the window, tearing down the streamers her daughter-in-law had just hung. She shook them with disgust, then flung them at the young woman, who lowered her head in shame, fighting back her tears.

Twenty-one

I'M OFF the story, Justice."

"What?"

"Roger Lawson told me to back off the Tsao-Ping angle, to cover the police chief story completely straight."

"Meaning what?"

Templeton paced the spacious living room of her Santa Monica condo as a faintly salty breeze wafted in from the big balcony. It was almost noon, and she was still in her bathrobe. I'd never seen Alexandra Templeton in her bathrobe, and certainly not this late on a Saturday morning.

"Lawson ordered me to write a series of evenhanded portraits of all the top candidates. I'm supposed to sum up their backgrounds, with a few quotes from each man about his plans for the department if he's selected. He told me to write each profile the same length to be sure we're not showing any bias toward one candidate over another."

"What about Harry? He's the *Sun*'s news editor. Harry's your boss, not Lawson."

Templeton stopped pacing to face me. There was something missing in her—her usual spirit, her fire. It was gone, extinguished.

"Harry called late last night. A lot has changed since yesterday."

"Like what?"

"Lawson's now the editor in chief."

I'd been sitting on the long white couch. I was suddenly standing.

"Roger Lawson's the editor in chief of the *Sun*? The most gutless guy at the paper?"

"The top man quit, took a payout, got out while he could. Lawson's in charge."

"Jesus fucking Christ."

"Word is, Lawson wants to consolidate his power, look like he's in charge when the paper shuts down. That way he gets to make the farewell speech, make a name for himself before he goes looking for another job."

"What about Harry?"

"Harry has to answer directly to Lawson now, not just on fiscal matters, but editorially. Frankly, when I talked to him again this morning, he sounded ill."

"I'd be sick too if I had to report to a prick like Lawson."

"I'm serious, Justice. I'm worried about him."

Templeton was on the verge of tears. I went to her, slipped an arm around her shoulders.

"So am I." I tried to show her a smile. "At least he's home, getting some rest."

"I hope that's enough, Ben. I've never seen him so stressed out, so down."

"You're not exactly a picture of tranquillity either."

"I couldn't stand it if the *Sun* folded, Ben."

"Better prepare yourself, kid. Happens a lot these days."

She chewed at a nail, her eyes roving the room.

"Or if something happened to Harry."

I had no advice for that one.

"When's your interview with Taylor Fairchild?"

Her eyes came back, and her mind seemed to follow. She separated from me, pulled her robe together, found a photograph of the assistant chief among some papers on the glass-topped coffee table. It was a head shot, a standard handout from the LAPD public affairs office.

"There won't be an interview with Fairchild, or any of the other candidates. Lawson told me to make up a list of questions for his approval. I'm to submit the questions to each candidate, who will then write their own answers, which I'm supposed to insert into the profiles."

"A total puff job, in other words."

"I told Lawson I wouldn't put my name on them."

"Good for you."

"He said I might not have a job that long anyway. He really enjoyed it when he told me that."

"Spineless bastard."

She handed me the photograph of Taylor Fairchild. It showed a lean, sandy-haired man in his late forties whose mild eyes were at odds with his tightly set jaw. He was clean shaven except for a neat mustache; even his sideburns were short, military style.

"I tried to set up an interview with Fairchild anyway, on the Q.T. I got the runaround over at Parker Center. Word got back to Lawson, who warned me to back off. And he told me in no uncertain terms never to approach Rose Fairchild again."

"So they've gotten to Lawson, too."

"Fairchild and the other candidates are all playing in the police-celebrity golf tournament today. Out at Rancho Park. I'd planned to go there, get some color for my series, see how they behaved with a golf club instead of a carefully prepared transcript. So much for that idea."

Templeton sagged wearily into the couch, rifled through the papers.

"I've got the police and autopsy reports you wanted. Katie brought them by this morning. Also, a few clippings on Matthew Fairchild, the brother, which I haven't looked at yet."

She handed over the police and autopsy reports while I sat, and kept talking.

"Callahan suffered pretty badly. Beaten repeatedly about the face and body, broken teeth, broken jaw, fractured right arm. He was also cut up with a razor or a very sharp knife, very methodically."

"Sounds like a thug with a deep sadistic streak."

Templeton pointed to a section of the autopsy report.

"He took a pair of pliers to Callahan's nipples, which were

twisted off. Pliers or a similar tool. Callahan's genitals also got a good going-over. It's all there, if you have the stomach for it.''

Templeton's voice was flat, her litany of torture matter-of-fact.

"You OK, Templeton?"

When she looked at me, it was with the face not of a journalism grad student, eager but wet behind the ears, but of a hardened reporter who had paid her dues on the police beat. In the last three years, without my quite seeing it, Templeton had been developing the tough shell and emotional survival skills needed for the job.

"I'm a news reporter, Justice. Just the facts, ma'am. Isn't that how it's supposed to be?"

"Do you really want to close yourself off behind that kind of armor, Templeton? The way I did when I was starting out."

"Right now, it feels like the only protection I've got."

"You've got me. And Harry." I glanced at the framed photograph of the handsome, middle-aged couple on the mantelpiece. "Your folks."

"But not the *Sun,* Justice. Not the paper anymore. What do we do when the paper's not there?"

"We'll think of something. Don't we always?"

Her smile was small, unsure.

"I guess."

I scanned the police report on Byron Mittelman's death.

"At least Mittelman didn't suffer like Callahan before he died. A single shot behind the ear. Probably never felt a thing. These two murders couldn't have been more different."

Templeton indicated the autopsy reports.

"There is one similarity. On the strange side."

She took the autopsy reports, laid them side by side on the glassed-top coffee table, then put a finger on each one, indicating lines of medical information that said essentially the same thing.

"The rectums of both men showed signs of trauma."

I leaned forward for a closer look.

"They were sodomized?"

"Possibly, if a condom was used. Or else raped with an object, a dildo, something like that."

"No semen?"

She shook her head.

"And no foreign pubic hairs at the site of entry. Mittelman showed the least damage, by the way."

"That doesn't make sense." I thought out loud. "Mittelman was straight. Callahan was queer. If it was forcible rape—"

"The autopsy clearly showed more bruising and tearing on Callahan."

I checked the two reports. Templeton had it right. I sat back on the couch, trying to make some sense of it.

"Presumably, since Callahan was gay, he would've had some practice taking it up the ass. It should have been the other way around—Mittelman would have been the one doing the most resisting."

Templeton offered an explanation, in her chilly reporter's voice.

"Not if he was dead when it happened, Justice."

She handed me several press clippings, paper-clipped together, from the *Sun,* the old *Her-Ex,* and the *L. A. Times.*

"The only thing Katie found on Matthew Fairchild were news reports on his death, and obits. They all give essentially the same facts. He was a moderately successful lawyer, unmarried, who led a quiet life. Kept to himself pretty much, except for his work with the Boy Scouts. He died in a boating accident in sixty-six. About fifteen months after his brother died in that robbery shoot-out."

"And not long after Rose Fairchild learned that Matthew was getting into her son's pants."

I glanced at one of the news clippings, which was boxed as a sidebar:

Attorney Drowns in Boating Mishap off Palos Verdes

REDONDO BEACH—A Pasadena attorney died in a freak boating accident several miles off Palos Verdes yesterday afternoon, despite the efforts of two others aboard to save him, according to Coast Guard officials.

A Coast Guard spokesman reported that at 4:17 p.m. yesterday a Coast Guard helicopter answered a radio call for help and met the 24-foot sailboat as it returned to harbor. The helicopter airlifted the unconscious victim, Matthew Fairchild, 39, to South Bay Hospital, where he was pronounced dead shortly after arrival.

According to the Coast Guard, Fairchild fell overboard during an outing with his sister-in-law, Rose Fairchild, and Larry Bingham, a family friend. Bingham, the skipper of the craft, told authorities that the victim struck his head as he fell when a gust of wind suddenly rocked the boat. Despite wearing a life jacket, and efforts by Bingham and Mrs. Fairchild to rescue him, the victim drowned in the rough seas. Because of the weather, most other boaters had returned to harbor, officials said, and there were no other witnesses to the incident.

Matthew Fairchild was the brother of Mrs. Fairchild's late husband, police captain Rodney Fairchild, who died in 1965 when he was struck accidentally by a bullet fired by a detective during a robbery stakeout in Los Angeles.

I laid the clippings back on the table.

"You're better acquainted with Mrs. Fairchild than I am, Templeton. And appearances can be deceiving. But she doesn't strike me as the type to be out sailing on a small boat in blustery weather. Or any other time, for that matter."

"No, she doesn't."

"And this family friend, Larry Bingham. I wonder what his story is."

"I've already made a few calls this morning, to friendly sources within the LAPD. Larry Bingham was a retired cop."

"You don't say."

"He'd been Rodney Fairchild's partner and best friend before he was killed in that stakeout in sixty-five."

"Maybe we should talk to him."

"Only if you've got long distance to the afterlife, Justice."

"When did he die?"

"He had lung cancer at the time of the boating accident. Knew it was terminal and died within the year."

"Isn't that neat."

"I called the mortuary that handled Bingham's funeral, found an old-timer who'd been around for the services. All he remembers is that Bingham got quite a send-off, a lot of cops showed up for the funeral, and Rose Fairchild paid for everything, sparing no expense."

I smiled, to myself more than anyone else.

"A very generous lady, our Mrs. Fairchild."

Twenty-two

RANCHO PARK GOLF COURSE was part of a spacious municipal park situated south of Twentieth Century Fox Studios along Pico Boulevard, which had once served as the boundary of a Mexican land grant rancho that had been carved up as a subdivision in 1922. By day, the park was a lushly green playground of baseball and soccer fields, basketball courts, slides, and merry-go-rounds, fringed and shaded with more than three dozen varieties of trees. By night, it could be a deadly place, especially if rival gang members happened to show up at the same time, or a drug deal going down in the shadows went down the wrong way.

I'd covered a double murder at the park in the mid-eighties and knew something about the area, including where to find a parking space—even on a balmy Saturday afternoon when a hundred sports and entertainment stars were showing up to play eighteen rounds of golf and hand out free autographs to a couple of thousand fans. The golf course had originally been private, but had gone belly up during World War II; in 1946, it had been purchased by the city of Los Angeles for slightly less than a quarter of a million dollars, which wouldn't buy a house in the surrounding neighborhood today. Hilly and rolling, with very few flat spots, it was famous for its picturesque foliage, small greens, tough approach shots, and a par-four eighteenth hole where the legendary Arnold Palmer had once taken twelve shots before finally getting his ball into the cup. Greens fees were in the bargain range of twenty bucks—cheaper on weekdays, more on weekends—and with four hundred golfers playing through on an average day, Rancho was reportedly the busiest course in the continental United States.

I arrived at half past one, thinking about the questions I might put to Taylor Fairchild if I got the chance. Parents and kids streamed into the park ahead of me, clutching footballs, baseballs, mitts, and autograph books, along with Sharpies for gathering celebrity signatures. I paid my admission, was handed a souvenir book, and stepped through the gates to a placard that announced the Los Angeles Police–Celebrity Golf Tournament, "The Largest Celebrity-Supported Sports Charity Event in the World," in benefit of the Los Angeles Police Memorial Foundation.

Uniformed cops were all about, some with trained police dogs, while clusters of kids petted the pooches. There were also lots of LAPD displays: motorcycles, a black-and-white patrol car, a chopper, a bomb squad robot, special SWAT team equipment, a mobile museum devoted to LAPD history, and several mounted officers, where more kids were gathered, stroking the necks of the big horses. I peeked into the museum, noticed that the Rodney King incident was not among the displays, then cut past the clubhouse and headed for the sloping greens.

What seemed like miles of ropes lined both sides of the eighteen fairways, which were fitted snugly into one hundred thirty-seven acres like long, narrow pieces of a very green crossword puzzle. Hundreds of spectators were gathered behind the ropes; from time to time, a gasp or groan erupted from the gallery, or a smattering of applause. Otherwise the crowd was orderly and respectful. Volunteers scurried about or stood at their appointed positions, recording the length of drives on certain holes and the shots closest to the pin on a chosen par-three hole, or acting as marshals to keep the more exuberant fans from pestering the celebrities or interfering with the play. Some were armed with player rosters, and helped fans locate where a favorite celebrity might be playing, based on his or her starting time, calculated at roughly twenty minutes per hole.

With the assistance of one such volunteer, I found Taylor Fairchild between the third green and the fourth tee. He stood next to his motorized cart, placing a putter into his bag and pulling out a driver, looking every inch the contented weekend golfer. His outfit was comprised of fresh-looking tan chinos and a spotless powder blue polo shirt, with dark glasses and an LAPD cap for sun protection; his white, cleated golf shoes looked freshly cleaned and polished. He was trim as a rail, of average height, slightly bookish-looking, and as neatly clipped and groomed for the golf course as he had been for his official police department photograph.

Judging from his jocular manner, his game was going quite well. Two uniformed officers, both burlier than Fairchild by a good forty pounds, most of it in the chest and arms, stopped to slap him on the back and shake his hand. As I got closer, I heard him being congratulated on his two-under-par score by his partner, a Hercules-style television star whose name escaped me, if I'd ever known it at all. Fairchild seemed to revel in the male camaraderie, almost too eagerly, like a grade school mama's boy who'd finally gotten on a sports team without being picked last.

I called out his name. He bid the two burly cops goodbye, laughing at a joke I couldn't hear, and glanced over.

"Winston Tsao-Ping sends his best wishes, Mr. Fairchild."

"I beg your pardon?"

"Winston Tsao-Ping. I'm sure you'll remember that name, if you think about it."

A trim, attractive woman with silver hair and a volunteer's badge that identified her as Betty Lou Dean held up a Quiet Please sign and put a finger to her lips. Fairchild stood stiffly by his golf cart, staring at me as if I were an apparition. The actor with the Hercules muscles stepped into the tee box and drove his ball, a strong, straight shot that carried nearly two hundred yards down the fairway. The gallery applauded with enthusiasm, but Fairchild hadn't even bothered to watch his partner tee off.

"I believe you're up, Fairchild."

Only then did he come out of his trance and turn away. He

strode to the tee box, placed his tee in the area behind two white markers, set his ball atop the tee, and took his stance.

Instead of swinging the club, he stepped back, pulled out a white handkerchief, and patted his brow, while glancing back in my direction. He tucked the hankie away, resumed his stance, took two practice swings, then made his drive. He struck the ball hard but sliced it badly, sending it off to his right, into the tall trees. The crowd groaned.

Fairchild studied me again as he returned to his cart, his jaw set more tightly now, before he drove away in search of his errant ball. Across the fairway, I watched him select a pitching iron, step in among the trees, and chip the ball toward the fairway, trying to find a clear line through the trunks and branches. His ball dropped feebly in the deep rough, well off the green, and he slammed his club to the ground. Things got worse from there, until he'd expended so many useless shots that he picked up his ball, taking himself out of play until the next tee.

I caught up with him again at the narrow opening in the ropes between the fourth and fifth holes.

"Charlie Gitt also sends his best."

Fairchild whirled, searching the spectators until he found my face.

"Who the hell are you?"

"Someone who wants some answers about the murders of Tommy Callahan and Byron Mittelman."

I could sense the eyes of the closest spectators moving from me to Fairchild, and had no doubt he was just as aware of them. All those eyes, all those ears, along with a couple of dozen media cameras and tape recorders not too far away.

"I'm golfing for charity, sir. You can call me at the office regarding police matters. I'll be happy to speak with you."

"Alex Templeton has tried calling you, Fairchild. You're stonewalling her. And now it's looking like you've got her new boss, Roger Lawson, in your hip pocket."

I heard a few curious murmurs from the spectators around me. A volunteer marshal stepped forward uneasily and asked me to move behind the ropes. I did. Fairchild glared at me, trying to look stalwart, but the look was as shaky as his last chip shot.

He moved to his place on the fifth tee, took a few practice swings trying to get his stroke back, then stepped up to the ball and gave it a whack. This time he pulled it badly to his left, out of bounds and into the crowd, which was too busy ducking and dodging to do much groaning. Fairchild went charging angrily to the vicinity of the renegade ball, removing his dark glasses and scanning the area with quiet fury.

"I think this is what you're looking for, Fairchild."

He looked over to see me standing next to his ball, pointing down at it nestled in deep grass. He pulled himself up and regarded me with small gray eyes as he approached.

"I know who you are, Justice. I didn't recognize you at first behind the beard." His narrow mustache stretched as he smiled. "Unfortunately, it came to me a moment ago just as I was about to tee off."

"It's nice to see you have a sense of humor about the game, Fairchild. Some golfers would have beaten me to death with their nine iron."

"I'm not a violent man."

"You work in a violent profession."

"Violence is a small part of it, to be avoided if at all possible."

"Winston Tsao-Ping might have a different perspective on that."

Fairchild's smile disappeared faster than a bad tan.

"Sergeant Montego has briefed me on your interest in certain matters that were put to rest many years ago."

"Put to rest, or buried alive?"

He had no answer for that, so I tried another question.

"Why did you sign that report fifteen years ago, Fairchild?"

Again, silence.

"If the Tsao-Ping case was put to rest, why were Tommy Callahan and Byron Mittelman murdered fifteen years later?"

"You're referring to something I'm not familiar with."

"As the assistant chief, I believe you have the authority to make special assignments within the department, certainly to influence those kinds of decisions."

"I suppose I do, under certain circumstances."

"If one checked, I have a feeling he'd learn that it was you who had Sergeant Montego assigned to take over the investigation of the Callahan and Mittelman murders."

He cleared his throat, swallowing with some difficulty.

"I might have, for administrative purposes."

"Why, Fairchild? If the two cases are unrelated."

The muscles of his face became taut, and his speech cool and clipped.

"Oh, yes, I remember now. My understanding is that those were both homosexual killings, with some kind of perversion involved. Unconnected to any past cases that we know of, but sensitive enough because of the sexual aspects that I wanted an experienced detective like Sergeant Montego in charge."

"You're going to try to pass those two murders off as sex crimes?"

"Sergeant Montego's heading the investigation. I have nothing to do with it."

"You're a practicing Christian, aren't you, Fairchild?"

"I'm a churchgoing man, yes."

"Devout, from what I've heard."

"I try my best."

"Yet you've just reeled off a string of bald-faced lies. Not very Christian, is it?"

He locked on my eyes, working hard to mask his emotions and hold back what he really wanted to say.

"What will you do with all that blood money your grandfather siphoned off the third world through his corporate connections? Use it to finance your trip to the statehouse, maybe the White House?"

"You're talking nonsense."

"Or maybe you'll serve out your term as chief, retire quietly, and use some of your millions to build a church and buy your way into heaven. Is that how it works, Fairchild? Or is that a decision your mother will make for you? She's the one who pulls the strings in the Fairchild family, isn't she?"

"A wild man." He shook his head, trying to smile. "You're talking like a wild man."

"I'm talking like a reporter asking questions that deserve answers."

"But you're not a reporter, Justice. You're a fraud who got found out years ago and was drummed out of the trade. In your case, all we need do is consider the source."

"You've got me there, Fairchild."

He smiled a little more, and added a slight nod.

"You'll have to excuse me, Justice. I'm holding up play."

He bent to pick up his ball.

"You seem to enjoy the game."

"As a matter of fact, I do."

"Finally feeling like one of the boys, after all these years? After what your uncle did to you when you were a kid, and how troubling that must have been for you."

Fairchild's smile crinkled awkwardly, and his eyes did a nervous dance just before they disappeared behind his dark glasses. He strode briskly back to his cart, climbed in, and made a beeline back to the tee to repeat his drive. I didn't stay around to watch, but another groan from the crowd suggested that he hadn't quite regained his concentration.

I was on my way out of the park when Felix Montego fell into step beside me, talking as we walked.

"I tried to warn you, Justice. You just wouldn't listen, would you?"

"I have a serious hearing problem, especially when I'm getting the runaround."

"You just upped the ante. Way, way up."

"I want a few answers, that's all."

"And I'm asking you one more time—leave it alone."

"Fairchild was scared back there, Montego."

A few seconds passed before he responded; he wasn't looking at me.

"Maybe."

"I think you're scared too."

He stepped around in front of me, planted his feet, and put his left hand firmly on my chest.

"But you're a tough guy, aren't you, Justice? You don't get scared, do you?"

"Maybe I just don't have as much to lose."

"Maybe you don't know it until it happens."

"I think we had this little talk already, Sergeant. The other night, when you followed me around like bad credit."

His voice softened a little, became sly.

"Speaking of financial matters, you aren't exactly living on easy street."

"That's not too hard to figure out."

"I could probably arrange it so you didn't have to be the loser in all this—fix it so you came out of it with something for yourself."

"If I lower my ears, you mean, and slink away with my tail between my legs."

"You could wake up Monday morning, Justice, with a pretty comfortable stake. Instead of wondering how you're going to pay your rent next month."

"Funny, Jacob Kosterman offered me the same kind of deal."

"And what did you tell him?"

"I thought real hard about it, found it more than a little tempting."

"No one could blame you for that."

"Then I got sick to my stomach. Kind of the way I'm feeling now."

"If you keep pushing, you're going to end up feeling a whole lot worse."

"Is that another threat, Sergeant?"

"I'm afraid it's a promise."

A distant roar went up from the gallery inside the park, followed by sustained applause.

"You'd better get back to the course, Montego, to do some backslapping. That could be Fairchild, scoring a hole in one."

He smiled grimly.

"Somehow, I doubt it."

He started to go, but stopped, and looked at me frankly.

"I told you once before that I don't like to see people get hurt. Whether you want to believe it or not, it's the truth." He sounded sincere, almost sad. "But there's not a lot more I can do to help you, if you're bent on putting your ass in the grinder."

"Like I said, Sergeant, I just want a few answers."

He gazed at me a long moment with funereal eyes. Then he turned and ambled away, back toward the polite applause of the crowd.

Out on the street, a long, sleek car passed. It was black and old, in vintage condition, possibly a Bentley. The driver was a clean-cut young man of nondescript Asian features in a chauffeur's cap and coat. In the back seat, an older woman sat peering out the open window from behind dark glasses, her chin held high like royalty. She was wearing an elegant red pantsuit, and was close enough to where I stood that I could see the age lines in her face and neck.

I saw her lips move but heard no words as she spoke in a near whisper to the driver. The window slowly raised, until I was looking at my own reflection in the darkened glass, knowing that Rose Fairchild was on the other side, watching me.

Twenty-three

WHEN I ARRIVED back on Norma Place with a bag of groceries, I found a hand-delivered package from New Image Productions on the porch, leaning against the door. The day's mail had also been delivered, and among the bills was an oversized postcard from Germany, with a note penned by Maurice:

My dearest Benjamin,
    Our journey down the Rhine was absolutely divine. Fred and I sipped soft white wine and munched grapes and the most wonderful little cheeses, and I read from a guidebook about each of the historical castles on the hilltops as we passed, while Fred shot photographs when he wasn't stealing glances at the ruddy-faced German boys. There was a small orchestra playing on board, and when Fred was tipsy enough, I got him to waltz with me, right there in front of everyone—even the blue-haired ladies! (I mean, at our age, who cares what anyone thinks?) Before long, wouldn't you know it, just about everyone on board had gotten up for a dance or two, and it was just like one big, happy family! (One of the blue-haired ladies even asked me to dance, and I can assure you, I showed her a new step or two.) We're off to Paris now, with no set itinerary between here and there except to follow our hearts, and fall in love with each other all over again, the way we first

*did back in the fifties. Please remember to keep the kitty litter clean,
as Fred and Ginger are both quite fastidious in that regard, and
be sure to walk the doggie, whom Fred (my Fred) misses terribly. I
hope you're enjoying the house, and have found someone to warm
the bed with you. See you sometime in the late spring, dear one.
Kisses, kisses, kisses, Maurice.*

I set the mail on the kitchen counter and cleaned the litter box
before I forgot, then opened the package that had been delivered
by messenger. It contained the finished video Cecile Chang had
promised me; I tossed it on the bed in the small bedroom at the
end of the hall, where Maurice and Fred kept their VCR. After
feeding and walking Maggie, I took my notebook and a glass of
cold lemonade out to the quiet of the backyard. At the top of the
stairs, Peter's door was shut, and the curtains were drawn. I
hadn't seen him since last night, when Oree had caught us kissing and driven off in a rush, leaving Peter confused and me
retreating into solitude for a while. At some point, we'd have to
talk it out, but now wasn't the time.

I eased myself into a lawn chair, opened my notebook, and
printed a list of all the players in the Callahan-Mittelman murder
scenario, hoping it might bring some clarity to a blurry picture.

> Cecile Chang
> Tommy Callahan
> Byron Mittelman
> Melissa Zeigler
> Jacob Kosterman
> Winston Tsao-Ping
> Pearl Tsao-Ping
> Franklin (and Lu-Ling) Tsao-Ping
> Charlie Gitt
> Assistant Chief Taylor Fairchild
> Rose Fairchild
> Sergeant Felix Montego

I studied the names awhile, then jotted two more at the bottom: Oree Joffrien and Peter Graff. After each of these, I added a
question mark to indicate how peripheral they seemed, which was
ironic, since they had recently become the two most compelling

men in my life. The difference now was that Peter was still here while Oree was gone, and it seemed probable that I would never see him again.

I was still sitting there, pondering all the names and their connections to each other, when Peter arrived home just before sundown, the tip of his surfboard poking out the passenger window of his old VW bug. He climbed out the driver's side, barefoot and sandy, clad in wet swimming trunks that clung to him like sandwich wrap. Before going upstairs to shower, he stood in the middle of the lawn, revolving slowly, while I washed him off with the garden hose, entranced by the play of cascading water and gentle light on his body, and wanting him more fiercely than ever, even as another part of me resisted him.

Before he mounted the steps, I invited him down to dinner and a viewing of Cecile Chang's video. By the time he was back, showered but still deliciously damp in fresh shorts and sandals but no shirt, I'd fired up the grill on the patio, taken a quick shower myself, and opened up the windows all around the house to let in some air. Peter settled on the bed in the little bedroom, propped up on big pillows, while I slipped the cassette into the machine and hit the play button. I tossed him the remote control, and settled in beside him with one arm slung across his bare shoulders.

The video was essentially the same one that Chang had shown me in her office, but with all the titles and graphics inserted, along with the music, and some audio and visual rough spots smoothed out. By now, I could spot the more rudimentary video effects, such as fades and dissolves, but I asked Peter to point out any he might recognize that wouldn't be familiar to a neophyte like myself. He stopped the tape several times to identify various techniques—crosscutting, flop-over, skip frame, wipe—and I marveled aloud that someone so young could know so much.

"I grew up playing Nintendo and composing on a Mac," he said. "I was creating my own movies on the computer before I was out of high school. Nothing I'd want to show anybody now. But I learned how to manipulate images the way I wanted, which is what video editing is all about."

"Not in the documentary field, though."

"Sure, documentaries too."

"Isn't each shot in a documentary supposed to be the literal truth, exactly as the camera recorded it?"

"Once, maybe. Not anymore."

"Educate me, Peter."

He rewound the tape again.

"Today, you can use pictures to make people think they're seeing something they're not. Woody Allen did it back in 1983 in that movie *Zelig*, where he inserted himself into famous historical scenes. So did the people who made *Forrest Gump*, sticking Tom Hanks into old documentary footage to make it look like he was really there when it was shot. Documentary filmmakers do the same stuff all the time, at least some of them. They just don't want you to know it."

"How?"

"Cheat shots. Like right here."

He stopped the tape, and started it forward again.

"You see how Cecile's standing in the research room at the end of the evening, wrapping up the show? I can tell they created a key effect here."

"A key effect."

"You create key effects with the AVID system in what they call the Media Composer. A key effect separates the foreground from the background, with different effect parameters, depending on whether you create a chroma key, luma key, or matte key."

"You're losing me, Peter."

"It's kind of complicated."

"Start at the beginning. What's a key effect?"

"A special effect that separates the foreground elements in a video clip from the background. That's the basic function."

"Why would you want to do that in a documentary?"

"All kinds of reasons, when you want to integrate two images that in reality are separate. You see it every night on TV, when the weather guy's in front of a weather map. He's not really in front of a weather map, he's in front of a blue screen. By using a chroma key that eliminates the color blue, the video engineer is able to project the weather map on that blue screen, as if it's behind the weather reporter, when it's really not. They can do all kinds of stuff now that's a lot more technically sophisticated than that."

"How do you know Cecile created a key effect here?"

He rewound the tape once more and started replaying it as Chang walked into the research room at the end of the night, to wrap up the shooting.

"Earlier in the show, when she was in the research room—the footage they shot in the morning—there was a natural shadow behind her, created by the camera lights. In this section, which was shot in the same room but at night, when everyone was gone, there's no shadow. That tells me they keyed the image of Cecile against the background."

"They took footage of Cecile's image in the morning, and inserted it digitally against background footage shot at night, when the clock showed the later time, and the evening CNN telecast was on."

"Exactly."

"Interesting."

"Normally, they'd insert the shadow to make it look seamless and natural. They were probably in a hurry, and someone missed it."

"There's even an effect for inserting someone's shadow?"

"Oh, yeah. The technology's amazing now. They can make you believe you're seeing almost anything they want."

The tape faded to black, and Peter hit rewind again. We lay together, listening to the whir of the machine. I stroked his face with the back of my fingers, and let my hand drift to his chest, playing with the silky hairs. He turned his head, and we kissed. A moment later, we were in each other's arms, and my mouth was moving from his lips down to his chest and belly. Then, as quickly as we started, I stopped.

"The coals are probably ready. We should get the dinner going."

He cupped his hand over the bulge in my pants.

"You sure that's what you want to do?"

I laughed.

"No." I kissed him quickly on the lips. "But I think we should."

The big porterhouse, enough for both of us, sizzled as I tossed it on the grill, and Peter placed small rosebud potatoes around it, buttered and wrapped in foil. In the kitchen, we whipped up a salad together, kissing and fondling each other between the romaine and the cabbage, between the broccoli and the bean sprouts, between the tomatoes and the dressing, at which point the notion of undressing strongly insinuated itself into the recipe. Yet each time my hand strayed to the waistband of his shorts, something stopped me from going farther. Then I was outside, turning the charred steak and the potatoes one last time, while Peter brought out the plates and silver.

We ate on the patio with some vintage Sarah Vaughan tunes playing in the background, while feeding scraps to Maggie and the cats. When "Lover Man" ended, along with my old tape, we sat in silence for a while. Finally, I asked Peter if he had something on his mind. He said he thought it was funny that we hadn't talked about what had happened the previous night.

"You like Oree a lot, I can tell." When I said nothing to that, he added, "So why are you with me, if you feel that way about him?"

"That's a complicated question, Peter."

"That's just a way of not answering me, Ben."

I smiled a little. *Well, good for you, Peter.*

"I suppose I'm with you because Oree likes to take his time in matters of love. Which is probably what most smart people do. The way you and Cheryl are doing."

The silence intruded again as he finished the last of his steak. When he spoke again, he was staring off distantly across the yard.

"I called her today," he said softly. "I call her almost every day."

"I know."

His focus pulled back, and he turned it on me.

"How do you know?"

"Because I know you, Peter. And I know how you are with me."

"What do you mean?"

"I'm an adventure for you. A learning experience, a male bonding experiment. But you're not a homosexual man, not at your core."

"Can't a man be more than one thing?"

"Of course. But the fact is, most of the time we're together, with our clothes off, you're as limp as a licorice stick. The only time you get hard is when you close your eyes, when I'm doing what Cheryl does."

"I really like what we do together, Ben. It feels good."

"Of course it does. How can touching the way we do not feel good, unless the mind is set rigidly against it? In truth, though, it takes a woman to turn you on. Am I wrong?"

He grinned and dropped his eyes.

"I guess not."

"Hey." He looked over again. "That's nothing to be ashamed of, having stronger feelings for Cheryl than for me."

"I want to be a whole person, Ben. I want to relate to everyone equally. I don't want to have any barriers holding me back from people."

"You're about the most whole person I ever met in my life, Peter. Stop trying so hard. You're there. You just don't know it."

"So you don't want to sleep with me again?"

"I'll never stop wanting to sleep with you, Peter." I reached across, and our hands joined, fingers entwined. "I'm just not sure it's the right thing for either of us."

I saw his beautiful chest heave as he sighed.

"I do miss Cheryl. Even when I'm with you, sometimes. I admit it, I think about her. Even when you do things to me that, well, that I like, and she doesn't do." He shook his head. "Wow."

"What?"

"Back in Minnesota, I never thought I'd be talking to a guy like this. That I'd be doing the stuff I've been doing."

"Minnesota's got more than its share of queers. You didn't have to come all this way to lie down with a man."

"No, I did. I had to break away first."

"Any regrets?"

A few seconds passed.

"Maybe one."

"What's that?"

"That I never really did everything with you. You know."

"I never fucked you, you mean."

He nodded, almost solemnly, and a moment passed before he spoke again.

"Maybe we could spend just one more night together, Ben."

"Maybe."

"How about tonight?"

"You're sure you want to go all the way, Peter? It's not always a lot of fun the first time out."

"I know you'll treat me OK, that you won't hurt me."

"We'll have to be careful."

"You told me you'd been tested, that you're negative. Same as me. Plus, we can use a condom, right?"

"I insist on it."

"In the documentary you're writing, some of the people we interview say it's wrong to have sex like we're having. You know, what they call promiscuous. Just for pleasure."

"It doesn't feel wrong to me. And it feels like more than just pleasure."

He smiled, just as his eyes met mine.

"Yeah, for me too."

Then he looked away, out to the yard again.

"I read that magazine article about you. The one Alexandra wrote."

"You and a lot of other people."

"I guess it's true, about what happened between you and your old man."

"That I killed him? Yes, it's true."

"I'm sorry about what he did to your little sister. If somebody did that to my little sister, I'd probably do the same."

"Don't be so sure."

"Why do you say that?"

"I enjoyed killing him, Peter. I'd wanted to do it for a long time. Catching him with Elizabeth Jane just gave me an excuse, lit the fuse."

"I'm still sorry. About what happened to your sister and mom and all."

"It was a long time ago."

"Not all of it." He glanced up at the apartment over the garage. "That apartment was the one your lover lived in before he died. Jacques."

"Yes, he lived there, for quite a few years."

"The bed I'm sleeping in now—that was his bed?"

I nodded.

"Maybe that's where you and me could be together tonight. In the bed you used to share with him. If that's OK with you."

"Sure, Peter. That's fine."

He raised my hand to his face, rubbed the back of it against his cheek. Maybe it was because he knew how much I enjoyed the feel of his beard, so blond, so invisible until the sudden roughness of it surprised. Or maybe because he simply liked having my hand there, for unspoken reasons of his own. Either way, it felt just fine.

Twenty-four

AT HALF PAST MIDNIGHT, as Peter slept in the big bed in my apartment, I pulled the sheet up over him, kissed him without waking him, and went quietly down to the house.

I used Maurice's copy of the Gay & Lesbian Community Yellow Pages to look up the phone number of the Reptile Den, and found it under Private Clubs, between Printing and Psychologists. When I called, a man answered on the first ring. I asked for Charlie Gitt.

"I'm afraid Charlie's inaccessible at the moment."

"He's not there?"

"He's always here on Saturdays, after midnight, when the action gets hot. That's why he's not accessible. The bodies are packed pretty tight in here."

"And Charlie could be doing just about anything."

"I have a pretty good idea what Charlie's doing, and he's not the one on the bottom." I heard another line ring. "Why don't I take a message?"

"Why don't I come down and see if I can find him?"

"You a member?"

"Not currently."

The other line rang again; he asked me to hold while he took the call. When he came back on, he told me it would cost me twenty-five bucks to join for six months, and fifteen to get in on Saturday nights after nine o'clock, when the ten-dollar discount rate ended.

"Sounds reasonable."

"Dress code is leather or jeans and T-shirt. No exceptions. Required footwear is boots or athletic shoes. Underwear optional."

"Any other rules?"

"As long as you're reasonably butch, you'll get in. I guess you know this is a private club with a special clientele. You're welcome to bring toys if you want."

"How about condoms?"

"You can bring 'em, but you won't find anybody to use 'em with. You got a name? I'll pass it along to Charlie if I see him."

"Benjamin Justice. The writer who's finishing the documentary Tommy Callahan started, now that Callahan's out of the picture."

"The one on riding bareback?"

"That one, yes."

"You picked the right man when you interviewed Charlie."

"I guess we did."

"Benjamin Justice. I'll tell him."

Half an hour later, I found the Reptile Den on a dark side street lined with cars, which was unusual for that part of town at that time of day. The address was in east Hollywood, just off Santa Monica Boulevard as it angles up toward Sunset, on the edge of Silverlake, what some people call a mixed neighborhood. Warehouses and body shops shared space with gay and Latino bars and low-rent taco stands, along with musty-smelling boutiques that specialized in selling used gowns to budget-conscious Latinas getting ready for their first proms and cross-dressing men trying to look like the Good Witch of the West.

I parked two blocks away, around the corner, and walked back, keeping my eyes open for cruising teenagers looking for a faggot to bash. There was no name on the club, just a stenciled street number on the black warehouse facade and a big Hispanic security guy at the door who nodded but said nothing as I entered. Standing in line ahead of me were three men who looked to be in their thirties, one of whom had a well-starched preppy look and was turned away for improper dress. The man checking ID and taking money stood behind a makeshift window without glass and a counter constructed of cheap plywood painted black like the rest of the place. He was shirtless and skinny, but tight with sinewy muscles; he'd shaved his flat chest and a heavy silver ring hung from each of his well-distended nipples, while his biceps were encircled with barbed wire tattoos like warrior bands. Three more rings, much smaller, decorated the right side of his upper lip, and a pearl-shaped silver stud pierced his tongue near the tip. His goatee was dark and well trimmed, giving him, with his nose ring and buzz cut, a slightly devilish look.

He buzzed the other two men through a locked door one at a time; each time the door was opened, music with an insistent beat throbbed from inside. I stepped up to the counter, the man inside looked me over, then asked for identification and forty dollars. I passed them across and waited for my membership form. By then, several other men were in line behind me, mostly white, ranging in age from late teens to a graying couple, though the older men were exceedingly well muscled and fit. Both were in leather, with matching leather vests and openings in the rear of their shiny pants that showed their hairy butts. Everybody was sizing up everybody else, though some were more discreet than others.

The man behind the counter slid my entry form across, along with a pen. I filled in my name and address, signed and dated it, and passed it back.

"You called earlier, right?"

I nodded.

"Charlie still here?"

"Yeah, he's here." The voice wasn't as friendly now. "I told him you were looking for him, that maybe you'd be in. I got the impression he's been expecting you."

"Is that so."

He ran his hand down over his mouth and chin, smoothing out his goatee.

"He says you've been bothering people with questions, and he figured you'd get around to him sooner or later."

"Maybe he'd like to meet me out here, away from the action. Or in the office, where it's more private."

"He told me to send you on in."

"I guess I go in then."

He raised his devilish eyebrows.

"Have fun."

Between the admissions window and the door was a sign announcing that patrons were in a gay establishment and if they were offended by "consensual social activity between males" they should not proceed further. Another sign warned that drugs and alcohol were prohibited. Nowhere did I see the warnings about HIV transmission or mandates about safe sex, or the big bowls of free condoms and lube tubes that were customarily found in similar establishments.

I pulled open the buzzing door to the pounding music, and stepped inside.

Immediately in front of me was a small, dingy space filled with old couches, where a few men with spacey eyes lounged or dozed, or checked out the fresh meat making its entrance. The light was dim, but even darker beyond, where I could discern the outlines of wall-like partitions painted black, but not much more, except for bodies wandering about zombie-like, in and out of doorways in the partitions. The music continued to reverberate, without variation or letup, and I realized that the same tune had been playing since the first time the door opened a few minutes earlier. It wasn't a song so much as a relentless synthetic rhythm with the same refrain repeated by a tough male voice over and over: *I want to fuck you in the ass.* The last time I'd been in a private club where lonely men went to find companionship and sexual relief with other men of similar desire, it had been a spanking-clean, three-tiered bathhouse replete with steam rooms, Jacuzzis, workout equipment, a snack bar, and fresh towels. Endless disco hits from the seventies and eighties had played on every floor, and in every private room, even in the sparkling, tiled showers. Times, and musical tastes, had obviously changed, at least with a certain crowd. *I Want to Fuck You in the Ass* made *Last Dance* seem almost like church music by comparison.

I stepped farther into the room and waited a minute while my eyes adjusted to the dimness. As they did, I spotted Charlie Gitt. He was standing in a doorway across the room to my left, and looked, from the waist up, exactly as he had in the video interview Tommy Callahan had shot several weeks earlier: muscular, black, abundantly tattooed and pierced, face fraught with anger, maybe violence. He was shirtless, exhibiting a mat of tightly curled chest hair and about as much body fat as a razor blade; from the waist down, he was clad in tight brown leather pants with an opening in the front that exposed his bulbous, uncircumcised cock. As I spotted him, a smile creased his face, showing even white teeth and making him, for a moment, quite handsome. A moment after that, he turned and disappeared.

I went after him, which seemed to be the idea.

As I passed through the doorway, I found myself in an un-lighted room crowded with bodies, most of them moving. The smells of sweat, sex, poppers, and excrement mingled in the hu-mid air, and grunts and cries punctuated the pounding music. Hands found me in the darkness as I passed, touching my chest, arms, butt, crotch, measuring me for muscularity, firmness, hairi-ness, size. I reached out in turn, trying to find a body that felt like it might belong to Charlie Gitt. Gradually, my eyes adjusted, and I could make out shapes and sizes, shades of skin. In a corner, a group was gathered tightly around a muscular black guy who was bent over with his legs spread and his face turned away while a tall, lean blond man screwed him from behind; everyone else touched each other in a frenzy of groping, and a vial of poppers was passed from nose to nose. I pushed my way into the circle of bodies and ran my hand over the black man's chest. No nipple rings, no chest hair. It wasn't Gitt.

I moved on, found an exit, went out of the room into a narrow corridor, past cubicles with locked doors, ignoring anyone who wasn't Gitt's shape and color. Then I saw him ahead of me in the muted light, turning a corner. I moved faster, pushing past saun-tering men, hungry eyes, groping hands. When I got to the cor-ner, Gitt glanced back, then stepped through another doorway.

Through the door was another room. Inside the room was a cage, and inside the cage were several men, taking turns slapping, pinching, and twisting the nipples of their object of desire, a well-built Asian man with a nearly hairless body, on his back in a hammock-like sling with his arms and legs splayed and upraised, his wrists and ankles bound to the straps of the hammock. Some-one waved a vial of poppers under his nose while a beefy Hispanic man with a sizable erection stepped forward to penetrate him. None of them was Charlie Gitt.

I found another doorway, in a far corner beyond the cage, the only one from which Gitt could have escaped. It opened up to a corridor so narrow my shoulders scraped the walls as I moved forward. I squinted in the shadowy light, and as I reached a corner, I saw Gitt again, waiting at yet another corner, grinning. Then he was gone, and I was chasing him, pulled along by the game, driven by the curiosity and fear that were working inside me like a drug. He led me through a maze of claustrophobic corridors, allowing me just a glimpse of him, before disappearing again into a labyrinth that drew me deeper and deeper toward the unknown, toward the dark center of Charlie Gitt's universe, where I wanted to be, if only long enough to better know and understand him, and to challenge his manhood by daring him to tell me the truth about what had happened fifteen years ago.

Finally, with the same tape pounding so loud I could hear nothing else, I found myself going through a narrow doorway into a room that was pitch black.

"Gitt!"

I screamed to be heard above the maddening refrain: *I want to fuck you in the ass. I want to fuck you in the ass. I want to fuck you in the ass. I want to fuck you in the ass* . . .

"Gitt!"

Then, in one well-orchestrated movement, I was seized by several pairs of hands coming from the shadows. I was dragged to the center of the room, forced to my knees, shoved face down on the sticky floor. I felt my pants being ripped open, and began to fight ferociously. The hands on me tightened everywhere.

"No!"

My pants were pulled down around my ankles.

"Gitt! Don't!"

My arms were twisted and stretched perpendicular to my sides, my face flattened to the filthy floor, my legs pried apart.

I felt a body on top of me, a rock-hard body, with two nipple rings digging into my back just below the shoulder blades.

Gitt screamed into my ear.

"Here I am, Justice! Just like you wanted!"

"No!"

I clenched my ass tight, felt his fingers trying to pry me apart, cursed him, then begged him to stop. Then I was pleading with him at least to use a condom, and I heard his laughter cutting through the pulsating noise. Suddenly, the laughter stopped, and I felt a fist, fast and hard to my right kidney; for ten or fifteen seconds my body went slack, as if paralyzed. Within the all-consuming pain caused by the punch was an even more excruciating pain, and I knew Gitt was inside me. By the time my body started to come back to me, it was too late to stop him, too late to bother fighting anymore.

Then he was finished with me and I was alone, while the refrain of the one-line song continued, flailing me with humiliation.

I had no idea what time it was when I staggered from the Reptile Den clutching my jeans to keep them up. I said nothing to the man behind the window, or to the guard outside. There was no point. No point in complaining, or calling anyone, or reporting anything. I had willingly gone to a commercial sex club, purchased a membership, paid my admission. To cry rape now would be a joke.

Besides, I didn't want anyone to know. I felt overwhelmed with fear that I might have been infected with the virus; I shook with the fright of it, was on the verge of throwing up as I reached the Mustang, my stomach was in such turmoil.

More than that, though, I didn't want a single soul to know.

Twenty-five

PETER FOUND ME the next morning, naked on the floor of the shower, where I'd fallen asleep some time around dawn with the hot water streaming down.

He reached in, grabbed my shoulder, shook me awake, then turned off the water, which had long gone cold.

"Ben? Are you all right?"

I nodded without looking at him, and struggled to my feet. He grabbed me under one arm and helped me up, but as soon as I was steady, I pushed him away. He backed off as I stepped out.

"Did you get drunk last night or something?"

"Yeah, drunk on my own bravado."

He handed me a towel, and I buried my face in it, long enough to know that what had happened the night before had not been a bad dream, but still wishing it was. Then I looked at myself in the mirror, mostly into my eyes. The reality sank in more deeply, like a sickening weight settling at the bottom of my gut, anchored by the knowledge of what might be happening inside my body. I felt filthy, diseased, vile, and incredibly frightened all over again. I closed my eyes, trembling.

"What is it, Ben?"

"Fate, Peter. Punishment for a life lived recklessly."

When I opened my eyes, he didn't look any less confused, which was fine. I felt his fingers touching my upper arms softly, like a caress.

"What happened to you?"

He'd found some of the bruises where I'd been grabbed and held down. Ordinarily, the slightest touch from him sent a pleasurable sensation rippling through my body. Now I pulled away, wanting nothing to do with him, least of all his hands on me, or any sign of his sympathy.

I moved past him out of the bathroom, toweling off, feeling icy cold. He followed me into the kitchen, as I wrapped the towel around my waist.

"What's going on? Why won't you look at me, Ben?"

I kept my back to him, filling a teapot with water at the sink.

"Your friend Alexandra's been trying to reach you."

"I'll call her, Peter. Thank you."

"She phoned me upstairs, asked me to come down, see if you were home."

I whirled on him.

"I said I'd call her! OK?"

He blinked sharply in surprise. I put the water on the stove, turned on the gas, wishing he'd go away.

"She sounded pretty upset, that's all."

I dumped a spoonful of dark crystals into a cup, thinking of the old T. S. Eliot line about measuring out your life in coffee spoons, and how much more meaning it had now that instant coffee, neatly and conveniently packaged, had been thrust upon the world. A shiver of dread ran through me like a cold wind through an old, empty house.

I tried to seize on my other life, the one before last night.

"What was she upset about, Peter? Did she say?"

"Your friend Harry."

"What about Harry?"

"She just said you should call her right away, that it was important."

I went to the phone and called her. Templeton got right to the point: Harry was at UCLA Medical Center. He'd suffered a stroke.

Peter stood beside me, listening. When I hung up, he asked what he could do.

"Take Maggie for a walk. Feed the cats. Clean their litter box. And don't ask me any more questions."

I poured boiling water into the cup, stirred it, and carried the cup into the bedroom, where I started pulling on clean clothes. Peter came in, and I caught him staring down at the underwear I'd worn the night before, which was soiled with blood and shit. I kicked it under the bed, and when he reached out again to touch me, I put my hand up to ward him off.

"Please, Peter. Don't."

His voice, like his eyes, were tremulous with hurt, with confusion.

"Don't touch you?"

"Yes, don't touch me."

I finished the coffee staring out the window at the neighbor's fence, while Peter sat watchfully on the small bed. I didn't care now if he was there or not. I grew oblivious to him as I gulped the coffee, oblivious to anything outside myself. I was fixated on the nerve impulses dancing frantically inside my overcharged mind. I suddenly shuddered, close to tears.

I went into the bathroom, sat down on the toilet, and endured a minute of tearing pain as I shit blood and semen into the bowl. Then I cleaned up again, hurried from the house, and drove the twelve minutes to the hospital trying to pay attention to the traffic signals along Santa Monica and Wilshire boulevards. The medical center sat along the southern boundary of the UCLA campus, a massive complex of buildings that were enveloped in the quiet of the Sunday morning. Harry was in the neurology ward, on an upper floor. Templeton was waiting for me near the nurse's station when I stepped from the elevator. She was dressed in a classy beige pantsuit with big dangly earrings and open-toed pumps, as if she were on her way to a Beverly Hills brunch. I hugged her perfunctorily, feeling robotic.

We began walking down a corridor. I had no idea where we were going, I was just following. I saw Oree Joffrien ahead, standing at the entrance to a visitor's hospitality room. He was wearing stonewashed jeans and loafers without socks, a pin-striped cotton shirt, blue on white, and a darker blue striped tie knotted loosely at his open collar, a splendid specimen of a man. It occurred to me that he and Templeton were going to brunch together, perhaps after they visited Harry, and the possibility of that angered me, although I wasn't sure why. They had a right to look handsome, a right to eat. All the nice white people could stare at them and think what a lovely black couple they were, what a credit to their race, what beautiful babies they would make together. The nice white people could lower their voices and talk about how encouraging it was to see a black couple paying with cash and not food stamps before going back to their sanitized lives feeling proud about how tolerant and progressive they were.

Templeton was talking.

"Harry's in ICU. He suffered a blood clot in his brain, something about the carotid artery, I didn't get all of it when I spoke with the doctor."

"Can he talk?"

She pressed her lips together, and shook her head.

"What else?"

"He's paralyzed, Ben. On his right side. His arm and leg, most of his face."

I didn't say anything, so she kept talking.

"The doctor said the stroke hit the motor fibers to his right arm and leg, but it also hit his speech center, which is on the left side in right-handed people. Harry's right-handed. I'm not sure why it affects the right side when it hits the left side, but that's what the doctor said. Unless I'm getting it all wrong."

She started to cry, and I put my arm reflexively around her. We stopped when we reached Oree, and he put out his hand, which I shook.

"Sorry to be meeting again under such circumstances, Ben."

"Sorrier than the last time?"

My tone was flip, and I instantly regretted it. He said nothing, just blessed me with his calm gaze, which infuriated me, even though he was the one with every right to be angry.

Templeton dabbed at her eyes with a tissue, then offered more details.

"They said that in a case like this the prognosis is totally open. They have no idea what to expect. With therapy, he could regain all of his mental and physical capabilities. Or he could just stay the way he is—even get worse, completely comatose."

"What do you mean, the way he is?"

"He's not responding, Ben."

"Not responding to what?"

"He can't communicate."

"At all?"

She shook her head.

"He can't write notes with his left hand?"

"They tried that. All they got was some gibberish. They said his hand may not be doing what his brain tells it to, if the brain is putting out any kind of signal at all."

My voice rose.

"He can't even blink for a yes or a no?"

Templeton clouded up again, and looked away. Oree took my arm and led me several steps down the hall, lowering his voice.

"He's pretty much out of it, Ben. What the doctor called a semivegetative state. They think he can hear what's being said to him. They aren't sure how much, if anything, he understands."

"Semivegetative."

"Not a very pretty term. But honest, I guess."

I attempted a smile.

"Three cheers for honesty."

"How are you holding up? You seem a bit remote."

"I'm fine, thanks."

"You don't sound fine."

His brown eyes were keen with concern, trying to bridge the gap. I'd wanted that so much such a short time ago, which now seemed like a lifetime away.

"I'd like to see Harry."

"They're not allowing visitors yet, Ben."

"Just to look in."

He gave me a room number and pointed down the hall. From the doorway, I saw Harry in a room by himself, stuck full of needles and tubes, surrounded by monitors and gauges, and a nurse, who was adjusting his IV drip. He was covered up to his neck with a sheet, and his eyes were open but expressionless. The color was gone from his face, and the right side of his mouth was pulled down, as if invisible fingers were tugging at it. A male nurse with a setup for a catheter entered past me, went to Harry's side, and pulled up the sheet. I turned away, unable to watch, sickened by the whole thing.

That's when I saw Roger Lawson stepping from the elevator far down the hall and lumbering in Templeton's direction. He was moving at his usual agitated clip, as if something were chasing him, tucking his flapping shirttail into the big waistband of his ill-fitting slacks, red-faced, glasses riding on his big apple cheeks, trademark ponytail bouncing behind him.

Before he reached Templeton, I was there to meet him.

"Why the hell are you here?"

"To see Harry Brofsky, of course." Lawson pushed past me, toward Templeton. "How is he?"

"He's in ICU, Roger. Not doing well."

"How soon can he have visitors?"

"They aren't sure."

"I just need a moment with him. I only have a question or two."

"He can't talk, Roger."

"Oh." Lawson shoved his hands into his pockets and paced in front of us, chewing the inside of his jowly cheeks. "We could give him a notepad, have him write down the answer I need."

I put myself in front of him again.

"What exactly is it you need, Lawson?"

"Some information of importance to the paper. Nothing that concerns you, Justice."

"Anything you say to Harry from now on concerns me."

"Oh, really? And why is that?"

"Because you helped put him here, more than anyone else."

"Don't be ridiculous."

"The pressure you've been putting on him—"

"We've all been under pressure."

"The jobs you've made him cut."

"We're trying to save a newspaper, Justice, not destroy one, which is more up your alley."

"Trying to save the paper, Lawson? Is that why you put the kibosh on the Fairchild investigation? One of the big boys downtown get to you? Tell you to back off, that Taylor Fairchild is off limits? Or maybe Rose Fairchild wrote you a nice check."

We were nose to nose. He sucked in his big gut and puffed up his chest, but he still looked to me like the nervous, flabby guy in high school who always rode the bench, always had the cleanest uniform. I smelled liquor on his breath, despite the early hour, which helped explain the profusion of broken capillaries across his crimson cheeks and nose.

"If anybody's responsible for putting Harry Brofsky where he is, that would be you, Justice. His slide didn't start at the *Sun*. It started eight years ago at the *Times,* when you copped a Pulitzer you had to give back, and took Brofsky down with you."

I grabbed Lawson by his shirtfront, propelled him backward, and slammed him against the wall, hard enough to dislodge a hospital commemorative plaque that clattered to the floor.

"You want to hear my definition of a bully, Lawson?"

He was breathing hard, and his soft chest had dropped back into place, nearer his waistline. Rivulets of sweat appeared on his broad forehead.

"Not particularly."

"A guy who enjoys abusing people, but who never challenges anyone his own size." I tightened my grip on his shirt, and pulled it up under his chin. "Tell me, Lawson, when was the last time you picked on somebody your own size?"

He snorted derisively, but had no words to go with it.

"Ben, let him go."

Templeton wedged herself between us, prying me off. When I wouldn't let go, she leveled her eyes at me.

"Ben, this is neither the time nor the place."

"He helped kill Harry."

"Harry isn't dead, Ben."

"He helped kill his spirit."

"Roger is working to keep the paper solvent, Ben. In his own way."

"This prick doesn't have the heart and soul of a newspaperman."

"Ben, please—"

"He's a cowardly, career-climbing autocrat who spends his life kissing management's ass and doing its dirty work while he keeps one eye on the next open rung."

"Goddammit, Ben!"

I heard her pleading for her job as much as anything else, and it got to me a little, even if I didn't respect it much. I let go of Lawson, backed off a few steps. He glared at me while he put some order to his necktie.

Templeton asked him what it was he needed from Harry.

"His password."

"To his computer?"

"I need to get into his system, move some stories he's been working on."

"I know his password. He gave it to me when he was out last year with the flu, when I needed to retrieve a story for updates."

Lawson suddenly looked very pleased.

"I can get it from you then."

"Like hell. That's Harry's password, nobody else's."

Lawson curled his mouth like a tough guy, but kept his distance.

"Nobody's talking to you, Justice."

"He's right, though, Roger. Our passwords are confidential."

When Lawson spoke again, he sounded genuinely flustered.

"Alexandra, try to see this from my side. I have to shoulder Harry's responsibilities now. He's got several hundred inches of copy in his system that are already edited and fact-checked, ready to be moved. We need that copy ASAP. Honest to God, I wouldn't be here bothering him otherwise. Not at a time like this."

Templeton glanced at me.

"It makes sense, Ben."

It troubled me that she was even talking to Lawson in a civil tone.

"It's your call, Templeton."

"I think Harry would want those pieces published, Ben. If nothing else, to help get the paper out. That's what always mattered most to Harry."

My gaze became as chilly and disgusted as my voice.

"Like I said, Templeton, your call."

She found a notebook and pen in her big purse, wrote down Harry's password, ripped off the page, and handed it to Lawson.

"Anything else, Roger?"

Lawson turned his eyes on me.

"I'd suggest you be more selective about your friends."

He hitched up his sagging pants and swaggered off, a big man who had spent a lifetime trying but failing to live up to his size, and taking out his frustration on anyone he could. We watched him stop at the elevator and impatiently punch the button.

"Congratulations, Justice. You certainly handled that in a mature manner."

"I got rid of him, didn't I? The last person I want Harry to see when he's allowed visitors is Roger Lawson."

The elevator doors opened, and Lawson stepped between them. They closed, and he was gone from our lives, at least for the moment.

I loathed Roger Lawson, or at least I loathed people like him. But I couldn't deny the truth of what he'd said: I, more than Lawson or anyone else, was responsible for putting Harry where he was—at the lowly *Sun,* which was killing him.

I had to live with that, the way I had to live with a lot of things.

Twenty-six

I SPENT MOST of Sunday afternoon at the house, leaving messages for Sergeant Montego at Parker Center and Cecile Chang at home and at her office, trying to work on my television script while I waited for them to get back to me. That wasn't too productive, so I pulled out the list of names I'd jotted down the previous afternoon, and went over it, again and again and again. When that failed to render much that I hadn't already figured out, I added the name of Roger Lawson, just for spite.

Shadows were deepening inside the house, and with them an unsettled mood that comes with the approach of nightfall when there's something going on in your life that feels dangerous and out of control, that you don't want to think about but can't get out of your head. The thing that most troubled me at the moment was the last thing I could escape, which was my own body and what might be happening to it. As I sat in a corner of the darkening living room, on the floor where I couldn't be seen through the windows, I had the irrational notion that I could sense the virus working inside me, riding my bloodstream to every part of my body, attacking tissue, attaching to the T_4 cells that served as the building blocks of my immune system, moving voraciously, staking its claim on me.

When the phone finally rang, it made me jump. I got up and took the call in the kitchen. It was Montego.

"Sorry I didn't call earlier, Justice. My family and I went to church, then out to the Santa Monica Pier so the kids could go on the rides. We like to do that on Sundays when the weather's nice."

"Spare me your sweet family portraits, Montego."

"You don't sound too happy."

"I met Charlie Gitt. It didn't go well."

"I warned you to stay away from him."

"Somebody's been talking to him, getting him riled up about me. I'd like to know who it is."

"Sorry, I can't help you there."

"Because you don't know, or because you don't want to tell me more than I already know?"

"You OK, Justice? You sound seriously on edge."

"Tell me more about Gitt—like how he came to be the way he is."

"I don't usually do psychological profiles on ex-cops."

"Take a stab at it."

"Why, Justice?"

"Because I asked."

"I don't know that much about his childhood, if that's what you're after."

"Start twenty years ago, then, when he was a young cop."

"You taping this?"

"No."

"If you are, I disallow myself to be taped, which makes anything I say illegally obtained and unquotable."

"Fine. Just talk."

I heard a child's insistent voice in the background, then a woman saying, "Shhhh—Daddy's on the phone, sweetie." Montego told me he was going to switch to a phone in another room. A half minute later, he picked up, and hollered to his wife that she could hang up the other line. I heard a door being shut, a click on the line, and then Montego's voice again.

"Gitt was recruited during a period when the department was under pressure to add more minority officers. It wasn't any secret that the LAPD was heavily white, and that Gates wasn't in a big hurry to dramatically change that. I joined around the same time, when they needed more Hispanic faces."

"When did you meet Gitt?"

"At the Academy. He signed up right out of college, where he'd played football. I was already married, had my degree, was thinking about going to law school. Then my first child arrived and being a lawyer was just another dream. I applied with the department, passed the tests, and started training at the Academy, along with Gitt and a few other minority guys."

"How did Gitt get past the psychological evaluation?"

"He was a straight arrow back then, like I told you before. Clean-cut, intelligent, polite, took orders and kept his mouth shut. The way you had to be if you were black and wanted to be in the department in those days. There were two standards, one for white officers, another for black and Latino officers. If you were white and had a mouth, you were considered outspoken, maybe even brash. If you were a minority, especially black, you were considered arrogant, a troublemaker. Charlie was polite to a fault in the beginning, all smiles and yes sir and no sir. He wanted very badly to be a cop."

"But something happened."

"Being a black cop under Daryl Gates took its toll on a lot of officers. You could see what was going on, the way blacks were treated on the street and in jail. You could feel it in the station house, the locker room, everywhere. Some of it was subtle, but a lot of it was overt. You heard the word nigger almost as often as you heard the word black. It wasn't much different for those of us who were Hispanic. You had to learn to keep a lot inside if you wanted to keep your job, have a decent future in the department. It could eat at you if you let it."

"Apparently, it bothered Gitt more than it did you."

"I had a growing family. My priorities were different. The job meant something else to me—a living, college for my kids someday. For Gitt, I think it was all he had."

"When did he start to change?"

"In the early eighties, a few years out of the Academy. I could see it, the tension building in him. Sometimes I felt like the guy was boiling with rage, a real time bomb. Some of the black cops coped better than others. Some of them seemed to be able to ignore what was going on. Charlie was like that in the beginning, but then he changed."

"Plus, he was gay, in the closet."

"That had to be making the guy crazy. In those days, Gates said publicly he wouldn't tolerate any gays or lesbians on the force. Charlie was leading a double life two times over. I think it twisted him all up inside."

"He kept it hidden?"

"Not really. He developed a reputation for being too aggressive, taking it out on prisoners, suspects. The brutality complaints started mounting. After the Rodney King incident, he was put on the list of forty-four, which ended his work in the field."

"The list of forty-four?"

"Where have you been the last few years, Justice?"

"Not working as a reporter, that's for sure."

"I guess not."

"So explain."

"After the King incident, the Christopher Commission ordered an investigation into citizen complaints against the department, going back quite a few years. Forty-four officers were found to be too violent to be trusted in the field. They were given the chance to take administrative or instructor assignments, or to resign. Gitt lived to be where the action was, out on the street. So he quit."

"In case you hadn't noticed, he's gotten worse."

"He's trouble, yeah. I guess you found that out."

"What do you know about Roger Lawson?"

"Don't know the man."

"But you know who he is."

"The big blowhard at the *Sun?*"

"That one, yeah."

"I know who he is, sure."

"What's his connection to Fairchild?"

"My wife's got dinner ready, Justice. Kids are waiting."

"The conversation's suddenly over?"

"I didn't have to talk to you at all."

"Why did you?"

"I told you before, I don't like to see people get hurt. I hope that whatever went down between you and Gitt convinces you to keep your nose where it belongs from now on."

"I don't think it's going to work that way."

"I'm sorry to hear that, Justice. I really am."

"*Adios,* Sergeant. Enjoy your dinner."

I hung up, feeling so anxious, so restless, I thought I might crawl right out of my skin. Beneath the restlessness was an anger I hadn't felt before, growing inside me the way it must have grown in Charlie Gitt when he didn't know what to do with it, and it helped make a monster of him. I intended to do something with mine, which included getting some information that was long overdue. If that meant losing my TV gig, my big chance, fuck it. I had more important matters to think about now.

I picked up the phone and called Cecile Chang again. When I got her answering machine, I slammed down the phone and stalked out of the house, heading in the direction of the Powder Room.

Tiger Palumbo was bent over the pool table when I entered the bar, sending a solid into a side pocket with a sharp, clean stroke.

"I need to talk to you, Tiger."

She glanced at me as she moved around the table, chalking the tip of her stick.

"More to the point, I need to talk to Cecile."

"I'm busy at the moment."

"You remember me, from the other day?"

She bent over the table again, lining up another shot from the far end.

"I remember. I mentioned to Cecile that you'd been in here asking questions. That didn't make her very happy."

"I've been trying to reach her. She seems to be avoiding me."

"That's her business."

She sent the ball rocketing toward the corner closest to me. As the ball reached the lip of the pocket, I grabbed it. I finally had Palumbo's complete attention.

"I've gotten into some deep shit, Tiger. Very deep shit. I need to talk with Cecile, and I'm running out of patience."

"Put the ball back on the table, mister. Then turn around and haul your ass outta here."

"Not until you help me find the little woman."

Tiger turned and handed her cue stick to a tall, long-haired woman dressed incongruously in an evening dress and high heels, then came around the table in my direction, rolling up the sleeves of her denim shirt.

There were perhaps a dozen other women in the bar, and all eyes were on Palumbo, including mine. When she was in front of me, she shoved me in the chest with both hands, hard enough to back me up a step or two. By the time she did it again, then again, I was standing in the middle of the dance floor, with a pretty good idea why.

"I'm givin' you one more chance to catch the bus, mister, and then I'm gonna put you on it myself."

"I don't want trouble, Tiger. I'm in enough trouble already. But I do need some answers, and I have a funny feeling Cecile's the only one who can give them to me."

"Two seconds from now you're not gonna be feelin' so funny."

She counted to two, then whirled with a roundhouse kick, which had been her specialty during her ring days, when she'd been considerably quicker. I caught her boot at the ankle with my left hand as it came around and coldcocked her with a straight right to the chin, the cue ball still curled inside my fist. She went down like a sack of potatoes, and stayed there.

Every woman in the bar was on me in a heartbeat, punching, kicking, clawing at me as I tried to get to the door. The one with the cue stick did the most damage, bringing it down across my back and shoulders half a dozen times or more, even getting in a lick or two across my chops when the crowd turned me around to take target practice on my face. When the woman with the cue stick was right on top of me, I saw an Adam's apple and suddenly realized that she was a *he,* probably a pre-op on the hormone regimen, since the facial hair was minimal and the breasts looked real enough.

Then I was out on the sidewalk, sprinting down Santa Monica Boulevard, thankful the guy with the cue stick was wearing high heels instead of Nikes.

Twenty-seven

MR. JUSTICE! What happened to your poor face!"
"A pool shark in high heels tried to redecorate it with his cue stick."

Harold rose behind his receptionist's desk and came around to meet me, looking genuinely alarmed. His hair was two-tone this morning, shocking yellow on one side, bright chartreuse on the other, with the gelled points shooting in every imaginable direction like the spikes on a psychedelic blowfish. He'd pierced his lip over the weekend with a tiny gold ring, and may have added to the rings in his ears, though I couldn't be sure. During the short time I'd known him, I'd lost count.

"You need to do something about your face, Mr. Justice."

"Yeah, like trade it in for a new one."

"Seriously."

As I came across the lobby, he reached up to touch the souvenirs I carried from my visit to the Powder Room the night before. I raised a hand to keep him at bay.

"I'm fine, Harold. Nothing that hasn't happened before. Cecile in?"

"Down in the conference room, getting ready for the big lunch meeting. You know, the fund-raiser with the rich liberals who like to give away a little tax-deductible money every now and then to a worthy cause—so they can pretend they're different from Republicans. Then, afterward, they can drive away in their nice cars and go shopping on Rodeo Drive without so much guilt.''

"If I didn't know better, Harold, I'd say you were turning into a political animal.''

I started toward the stairs. Behind me, his voice became snippy, maybe a little hurt.

"Just because I like to change my look and express myself with unconventional jewelry doesn't mean I'm a total airhead, Mr. Justice. Appearances can be deceiving.''

"I'm sorry, Harold. I didn't mean to imply that.''

The sharpness went out of his voice as I continued up the stairs.

"If you'd like, you can call me Harriet.''

I stopped in my tracks.

"What did you say?''

I turned; he stood at the foot of the stairs, looking up.

"When you first came to work here, Mr. Justice, I told you I had a special nickname. That I'd share it with you if we became friends.'' He threw up his flighty hands. "Well, that's my secret name—Harriet!''

I came back down the steps slowly, my mind racing.

"And before that—what was it you said?''

"Mr. Justice, you're looking at me like you've seen a ghost.''

"Before that, Harold.''

"Appearances can be deceiving.'' He giggled self-consciously, and threw a wave at me from the end of his loose wrist. "It's just a joke, silly. I haven't had surgery, or anything like that—I can't stand the thought! I don't even like to *shave* down there!''

He glanced at me sideways, batting his lashes.

"Trust me, Mr. Justice—under all this glitter, I'm every inch a man.''

I was smiling, but my mind was a million miles away, rocketing to another galaxy.

"I have no doubt that you are, Harold. I mean, Harriet.''

"We're friends, then?''

"Bosom buddies, so to speak.''

I took his face between my hands and planted a grateful kiss on his forehead, which left his mouth agape. Then I turned back up the stairs, reminded once again that things are rarely what they seem at first glance. A minute later, I was entering the office of the operations supervisor, which was positioned between the videotape library and the editing bays, so she could track the tapes as they were checked in and out. I told her I needed to see the time codes and tape numbers used in putting Cecile Chang's fund-raising video together. She suggested we check the editor's digitized log, which listed every cut in the videotape and the original source tape from which it came.

She crossed the room, to a bank of file cabinets.

"This is OK with Cecile?"

"She personally gave me a tape of the show to study, to learn how it was put together."

"You're certainly being thorough, going back all the way to the source tapes."

"You can learn a lot seeing how something's built from scratch." I smiled mildly. "Kind of like writing articles."

"That's right, you worked in journalism before coming to us, didn't you?"

"You probably saw the *GQ* piece."

"It's been passed around. You have a fascinating background."

"Fascinating hardly covers it."

"You were fortunate to meet Cecile, Mr. Justice. She's very good about giving people second chances."

"Like she did Tommy Callahan."

"Exactly." She shook her head as she rifled through the file drawer. "A shame what happened to Tommy."

She found the file she was looking for, opened it, and pulled out some stapled sheets printed with columns and grids that were filled with brief shot descriptions, followed by tape source numbers, and time codes down to the split second.

"This is a digital printout of the editor's log, in the order the show was cut, shot by shot. I'm not sure what you'll learn from it, but you're welcome to make a copy."

I ran my finger to the last shot on the final page, before the fade-out.

"If I could, I'd like to look at the original tape used for this particular shot."

She glanced over my shoulder at the column.

"That appears to be a fairly complicated edit. It looks like they did some kind of image nesting, or maybe a matte shot. Chroma key possibly. Those tapes would be in the library."

I followed her down the hallway to the videotape library, which she unlocked with a set of keys that jangled on a big ring. Inside were rows of tall shelves filled with videotape cassettes organized by code letters and numbers for easy reference. The room had a section for tapes in the beta format on the right, and three-quarter-inch VHS tapes on the left. She found the ones I needed, locked up, and we returned to her office, where I signed for them.

"Those are masters, Mr. Justice. They aren't to leave your sight. I'd prefer it if you viewed them up here, where I can keep an eye on them."

"No problem."

An hour later, after I had confirmed what Peter Graff had already suggested, and with the lunch hour already under way, I signed the tapes back in.

"So what did you learn, Mr. Justice?"

"What amazing things can be done with the AVID."

"Remarkable, isn't it, how creative an editor can be?"

"Or the producer who's calling the shots."

I thanked her for her help and took the stairs down to the first floor. A corridor led me to the conference room on the north side of the building. The hallway ended in a small lobby where a buffet lunch had been set up, with two servers standing behind the food trays and plates. Across the small lobby space was the meeting room I was looking for. As conference rooms go, it was modest in size and appearance: a practical, undecorated room with a glass wall that revealed a long oval table surrounded by fifteen chairs, a podium, and a large video monitor at one end. Heavy curtains were drawn across the windows on the far side, shutting out the sunlight, and the overhead lights had been dimmed.

Chang stood at the podium while her fund-raising pitch played on the high-definition screen, accompanied by her recorded narration. She wore high heels and a flowing dress of apricot chiffon that was bare at the shoulders and belted snugly at her slim waist, an outfit that accentuated her femininity and grace yet wasn't so frivolous that her business acumen and leadership skills were forgotten. Seated in the fifteen chairs were her prospective grant donors, an assortment of women and men of varied ages and attire, who nibbled at their food as they followed the story unfolding on the screen. I stood at the glass wall, looking in, until Chang noticed me and reacted. She didn't look pleased to see me.

I stepped to the open door, where I waited until the twenty-minute presentation came to an end. The group put down its forks and applauded.

Chang's eyes left me with some reluctance and returned to the room.

"That's the story of New Image Productions, what we do, and how we do it. While we're a nonprofit company dedicated to examining controversial issues and alternative viewpoints, we hold ourselves to the highest technical standard. The new technology, from digital cameras to digitized editing, allows us to do things we never could have done a few years ago, at a fraction of the time and cost. Still, the kind of equipment needed to maintain those standards comes at quite a price, which is why your financial support is so important to us."

I stepped into the room.

"I believe that's my cue."

Sixteen heads, including Chang's, turned in my direction.

"Ben, we're in a private meeting."

I crossed to the VCR, pushed the rewind button.

"Ladies and gentlemen, there's a rule in documentary film-making—show, don't tell. It's an adage that holds true for all writing, all storytelling, but it's especially vital in film and video, where pictures are so important. Cecile herself taught me this valuable lesson—whenever possible, show by concrete example. So let's illustrate just what she means when she refers to the wizardry that can now be performed in the new digital age."

"Ben, please—"

"Notice toward the end of the presentation when Cecile is in the research room at the end of the night, closing the show. It's late, eight forty-five according to the clock in the background, as well as the CNN program seen on the TV set. The footage was shot on a Monday, two weeks ago, when most of the staff had gone home for the night and the camera crew was in its last hour of a twelve-hour day. But that's not really Cecile you see in the shot."

I hit the pause button, freezing the image.

"Let me correct myself. It is Cecile, but the Cecile you see was videotaped that *morning*, before she lost one of her lovely jade earrings prior to the evening's taping. To avoid a continuity problem with her physical appearance, she simply ordered her camera crew to tape the research room without her in the picture. Then, during the editing phase, she ordered a special effect that allowed her morning image to be keyed in against the background shot at night, covering up the little problem of the missing earring. Any references to the late hour were covered in voice-over. Isn't that clever?''

There were impressed murmurs around the table. A well-dressed, matronly woman raised her hand.

"You mean you can actually take different pieces of footage, shot in different times and places, and mix and match to make it appear it's all one shot?''

"Exactly. The only problem in this case is that the editor neglected to put in a shadow behind Cecile in the evening shot, a minor oversight that could be corrected with another special effect. Otherwise, the morning and evening shots would have been a perfect match, and no one would ever have known the difference. In the unreal world of video, Cecile never would have misplaced that earring at all.''

I turned to Chang, who had a death grip on the podium.

"Isn't that true, Cecile?''

"An excellent catch, Ben. And very nice of you to share it with us.'' She turned to the room again. "Enjoy the rest of your lunch. I'll take your questions over dessert and coffee, in just a few minutes.''

Chang took my elbow and turned me out of the room. She led me down the hall, found an empty office, maneuvered me inside, and closed the door.

"You're completely out of bounds.''

"I've been trying to reach you, Cecile.''

"Yes, Tiger told me. She also told me you went to the Powder Room and physically assaulted her.''

"It was self-defense, but I'm still not proud of it.''

"You had no right—''

"I've left you a half-dozen phone messages in the past twenty-four hours.''

"I'm a busy woman. I don't have any obligation to—''

"Cut the crap, Cecile."

She paced in her tall heels, rubbing her hands together.

"I don't know what you want from me."

"How about the truth, for starters?"

She kept pacing, rubbing, but said nothing.

"Let's go back to the day I first met you, Cecile. The day when Peter Graff mentioned that he hadn't heard from Tommy Callahan for several days. The minute you heard that, you shot out of here like a bat out of hell. I saw you drive away burning rubber. An hour later, Peter and I ran into you as you hurried back into the building, lying about where you'd been. I didn't notice at the time that you were missing one of your jade earrings, but you did. Not half an hour later, I saw that earring on the floor of Callahan's motel room. You went to extreme lengths to show me your fund-raising video, to point out your jewelry, hoping I'd be convinced you still had both earrings when you'd taped that evening, should the subject ever come up with the cops. Unfortunately, the truth is in the missing shadow, isn't it?"

"And what truth would that be, Ben?"

"You were in that motel room that afternoon, Cecile. What I want to know is why, and what you did there."

"If you think that's so, why didn't you tell the police?"

"Because I didn't want to get involved. Because my life's a mess, and I'm trying to straighten it out, and I needed this job in the worst way. The last thing I needed was to get drawn into another nasty murder investigation. It's a bad habit of mine I'm trying to kick. But I did get involved, little by little, and now I'm in it up to my balls and then some, in worse ways than you can imagine."

"I wish I could help you, Ben—"

"You can. By telling me what the hell is going on, fitting the pieces together for me. All of them, starting fifteen years ago."

She shook her head resolutely, but her eyes were frightened.

"No, I can't. I can't."

"You'd better rethink that one, Cecile."

"Please leave. Now."

"I'm not going away, no matter how much that inconveniences you, or the cozy life you've created for yourself with Tiger Palumbo."

Her eyes flashed with a deeper, more dangerous fear.

"Why can't you just leave us alone? We love each other, we have something good together. Do you have to destroy that?"

"I have to know the truth. All of it."

"Why?"

"What an odd question to come from someone in your line of work."

"It's sad what happened to Tommy Callahan. I mean that sincerely. But he didn't mean anything to you, Mr. Justice. You'd never even met the man. Can't you just leave it alone?"

"And Byron Mittelman? He doesn't matter, either, Cecile? Shall I tell Melissa Zeigler to forget about the murder of her fiancé so you and Winston Tsao-Ping can continue to play out your masquerade?"

"You know the truth about my past then—about both of us?"

"Yes, I've figured that much out."

Her eyes filled with conflict for a moment. Then she pulled herself up tall, raised her chin defiantly, and squared herself to face me.

"You're terminated, Ben. You'll be paid the second installment on your contract, and that ends your involvement with us. I'm sorry it didn't work out."

I grabbed her roughly by the upper arms, which were slim and soft, and looked into her troubled eyes.

"You're in this awfully deep, Cecile. Both you and Winston Tsao-Ping. I'm running out of patience. I don't care which one, but one of you had better start talking to me."

Twenty-eight

I DROVE AWAY from my encounter with Cecile Chang wound tighter than the copper coiling on an armature, charged with energy that had nowhere to go. When I came down out of bucolic Laurel Canyon into busy West Hollywood, I felt darker currents surge through me as I spotted a billboard warning of HIV transmission and urging early testing and treatment.

More references to the virus caught my attention as I made my way along Sunset Boulevard to Norma Place: advertisements on bus stop benches, placards in store windows, leaflets tacked to telephone poles, even an outlandish, comic-style condom reminder rising on a tall wall above Tower Records: *No Glove, No Love!*

I felt that every message was directed at me personally, yet the last thing on earth I wanted to face was the possibility that I might be infected. How ridiculous, how utterly senseless, to become infected now, this late in the game. HIV and AIDS had been the one thing I felt I'd left behind, along with countless others in my community who had somehow survived. After living nearly two decades in crisis mode, with a crisis mentality—and all the emotional havoc that implied—the crisis was supposed to be behind us. It was supposed to be a time of celebration, of living again, as the old century wound down and a new one beckoned, bright with promise. It seemed so unreasonable to be facing the plague again now, so improbable and unfair. If I was infected, how would I explain it to anyone? How could I justify it? Live with it?

I felt some relief as I turned off Sunset and dropped into the pleasant neighborhood of the Norma Triangle, where the quaint little houses and well-tended yards offered a sense of order and safety, none more so than the fifty-year-old Craftsman on loan to me by Maurice and Fred while they idled away in Europe. That feeling of security was quickly shattered, however, when I realized that during my brief absence that morning, someone had broken into the house.

It was a neat, professional job, a quick, clean in-and-out. The intruder had broken in through the back door, past a dozing, half-deaf Maggie, who slept these days as if she were in a coma. Nothing in the house was messed up and not much had been taken—just my copy of the fifteen-year-old police report on the beating of Winston Tsao-Ping and the notes I'd been making, trying to connect that incident to the murders of Tommy Callahan and Byron Mittelman.

I immediately called Templeton at the *Sun,* ignoring the telephone messages collected on my machine.

When she picked up, her voice was as edgy as chewed nails.

"I've been leaving messages for you, Ben. Things have gotten really weird down here."

"What's going on?"

"I got laid off, for one thing. Which isn't all that surprising, I guess. The strange part is that my computer files have been virtually erased, or else transferred elsewhere. When I went to retrieve some files, I discovered someone had been in my system, plundering as they pleased."

"Roger Lawson."

"I can't imagine who else. Harry kept a number of reporters' passwords in one of his files, in case of emergency. I had no problem with that, just as he had no problem with me knowing his."

"I warned you not to give Harry's password to Lawson."

"I don't need a lecture right now, Justice."

"So Lawson got into Harry's system, found your password, and decided to clean out your files, as long as he was giving you the pink slip. Maybe take a look through them to see if there's anything he doesn't want anyone else to see.''

"My computer files aren't the only thing missing."

I took a guess.

"Somebody snatched your copy of the police report on the Tsao-Ping beating, the one with Fairchild's signature."

"How did you know?"

"Someone broke into the house this morning and got mine."

"We should have made extra copies."

"It's a little late for that."

"I'd tucked mine away in a special file I'd deliberately mislabeled, thinking it would be safe. They got it anyway. Someone had to want it very badly."

"We need to talk to Katie, have her contact her source at the Hall of Records and get another copy."

"I already did, Justice. It was the first thing I thought of."

"I hope you're not going to tell me what I think you're going to tell me."

"When her friend went to check, the original report was gone. Someone had removed it."

"So, for all intents and purposes that report doesn't exist anymore, and never did."

"They're covering their tracks fast, Justice. Whoever *they* are."

"Have you tried to confront Lawson about any of this?"

"He's incommunicado on one of the upper floors. They've brought in special security to keep people out, claiming that with all the layoffs they have to be extra careful. I can't get near the sonofabitch. Which might be good, considering how I'm feeling. I've never scratched a man's eyes out, but there's a first time for everything."

"If you claim he stole your copy of the report, or had someone do it, he'll just deny it, say that you're a disgruntled ex-employee making crazy charges."

"No doubt."

"I'd like to know why he's stooping to this kind of nonsense. He's taking some risks himself, treating a reporter like that."

"I did some checking along those lines, too. I have a source over at Parker Center, fairly high up, who's been in the department twenty-three years. He tells me that back in the late seventies, when Lawson was a police reporter with the Southland News

Service, he regularly got pulled over for driving while intoxicated. Back in those days, the press and the police were a lot cozier, especially the reporters who worked the cop shop. It was routine for reporters to have their parking and traffic citations taken care of by a contact person within the LAPD."

"I've heard that from Harry, when he was talking about the old days."

"So guess who took care of Lawson's tickets."

"Felix Montego?"

"Higher up."

"Taylor Fairchild himself."

"That's what my source says. Fairchild even got Lawson out of the drunk tank one night, without charges being brought, after Lawson had been involved in a minor hit-and-run."

"So Lawson owed Fairchild."

"Big time, considering Lawson's ambitions in journalism and how the attitude toward drunk driving has changed in recent years. It would be a black mark that certainly wouldn't help his career."

"It looks like Fairchild decided to call in his debt, use Lawson to tidy up the mess where he could. I think that's what they call the old boys' club in action. Kind of inspires you to search out a manual on how to make bombs."

"Speaking of explosives, I found something interesting in the public documents filed by the Documentary Channel. Jacob Kosterman may have used some of his own money from *On Patrol* as seed money to build his corporation, but he's got a major silent partner."

She gave me the name of the shareholding company and I wrote it down.

"This is a communications company? I've never heard of it."

"You're not supposed to. It's one of the numerous companies set up by the late Harrington Cahill Maplewood."

"Rose Fairchild's father—the one who liked doing business with dictators."

"The very same. Of course, the company's now in her hands, a small piece of the Fairchild empire."

"Which makes her Jacob Kosterman's partner in the cable venture."

"His primary financial backer."

"Maybe I'll have another talk with Kosterman."

Templeton's voice softened.

"Maybe you should pull back for a while instead."

"Now? After what they're doing to us?"

"I don't like that craziness I hear in your voice, Ben. And you seemed a little shaky at the hospital yesterday."

"Is that you talking, or Oree?"

"He mentioned it. He's concerned. But I could see it too. What's going on?"

I had to tell her something, so I thought fast.

"I'm also out of work, as of today."

"What happened?"

"I pressed too hard, and Cecile Chang cut me loose."

"You think Chang's involved in all this?"

I told Templeton about the jade earring I'd discovered in Tommy Callahan's motel room, and the elaborate steps Chang had taken to cover up its disappearance. I also told her that Oree Joffrien hadn't been straight with me about his old friend from NYU, that there was a lot more to her than met the eye. I didn't get more specific than that.

"You sound angry, Justice. No, that's not it. Bitter, you sound really bitter."

"Bitter doesn't even begin to describe what I'm feeling."

"Something's happened that you're not telling me about."

"How's Harry?"

"You're throwing up that old wall, Justice. The one you were warning me about just a couple of days ago."

"The subject's Harry."

"He's pretty much the same. Still unresponsive."

"I'll go see him."

"He probably won't know you're there."

"I'll go anyway."

"Maybe I'll run into you. We'll get some coffee or something."

"Sure, we could do that."

"This whole thing really troubles me, Benjamin."

"Be careful from now on, Templeton."

"Careful how?"

"Who you talk to and what about. We probably shouldn't even be talking on the phone like this, given the LAPD's wiretap capabilities."

"There's not much more I can do with it now, anyway. Without that police report, without a job. Maybe you should lie low for a while too, Ben. Until things quiet down."

"It's a little late for that now."

"What do you mean by that? Damnit, Justice, talk to me!"

When I didn't reply, she repeated my last name again, more insistently, but by then I was hanging up the phone.

Twenty-nine

WITH SOME DAYLIGHT left, I called Jacob Kosterman to tell him I'd thought about his offer and wanted to see him again. I didn't know exactly why I wanted to see him face to face, other than a vague feeling of anger that was growing combustible and a restlessness that had me crawling the walls. Also, answers; I wanted answers.

Kosterman's office told me he was out, but relayed my message to him at the Getty Center, the massive museum complex that sat on a Brentwood hilltop overlooking the city, where Kosterman was in a business meeting. The center, built for a billion dollars, served as the new home of the J. Paul Getty Trust, which was endowed with more than four billion dollars from the Getty oil fortune, making it the world's richest private art institution, with roughly three billion left over for the oil magnate's heirs. Kosterman called me back personally and suggested we meet there at 6 P.M., in the Central Garden.

I pointed the Mustang west along Sunset Boulevard, past Bel-Air Estates and UCLA, then turned north on Sepulveda Boulevard until I reached Getty Center Drive a half mile farther on. I swung left and crossed under the freeway, then climbed the road-way that had been carved up the side of the mountain, as the center's beige-colored buildings loomed larger above me. Because of the museum's popularity, parking reservations were recommended, but Kosterman had left a special pass in my name at the main gate, which got me into the parking garage. Minutes later, I was riding a slow, winding tram the rest of the way up the mountain. At the top, I stepped out into an expansive plaza paved with stone.

The Getty Center was truly Olympian, a villa-like complex built from massive travertine blocks and curving aluminum panels that sprawled across more than a hundred lushly landscaped acres. The buildings were Modernist in design and somewhat austere— neutral in color and geometrically precise—but nonetheless breathtaking in their scope and imaginative use of space and light. They included a monumental museum comprised of five pavilions, a research institute that housed nearly a million books, restaurants with sweeping views, a lecture and performance hall, and two enormous buildings to the north and east that were closed to the public and housed the offices of the Getty Trust, which was required by law to spend roughly four percent of its wealth each year to acquire, preserve, and support international art and culture.

I'd been here once before, with Templeton, and pretty much knew my way around. It was a quarter to six by my watch, so I walked to the Central Garden, which was situated in a canyon between the angular Getty Museum and the drum-shaped Research Institute. The garden, which provided expansive city and ocean views at the top, was in the general shape of a terraced amphitheater, but unlike any other horticultural creation I'd seen, as imaginative and fantastic in design as the dramatic structures above it were institutional and aloof. Hundreds of plant species were visible along the terraced slopes, but the most vibrant colors were provided by bougainvillea, iceberg roses, and azaleas, hardy, long-blooming plants that were tended five days a week by several gardeners, yet seemed to grow in wild profusion. The bowl-shaped garden was anchored at the bottom by an intricate maze of flowering azaleas that appeared to float on a pond fed by a waterfall, and drew both the eye and the mind deeper and deeper, away from the fortress-like buildings and awesome vistas above, toward something more personal and serene.

I recognized Jacob Kosterman's bald dome as he stood gazing

down at the waterfall, and started toward him, descending along a gently sloping path. It zigzagged across a meandering stream and clusters of large, natural stones placed artfully in the hilly terrain. When I was standing beside Kosterman, I noticed that his pierced ear displayed neither the ring nor the stud I had seen on him previously, and he was wearing a conservative tie with his well-cut business suit. The effect was to age him several years and blunt his distinctive look, no doubt for the sake of doing business with an organization as formidable as the Getty Trust.

When I was standing beside him, he looked over at me, then back to the floating azalea maze below.

"It's nice to see you again, Justice. Have you been here before?"

"Once."

"It's a remarkable achievement, isn't it?"

"The garden, or all of it?"

He looked up, swept his hand.

"Everything. A fantastic legacy, a priceless gift to mankind." Then he was looking at me again. "Something only great wealth could achieve."

"Wealth at what cost, and to whom?"

His eyes stayed on me a moment, before they turned back to the floating flowers.

"I suggested we meet in the garden, Justice, because I felt it would appeal to the more—how shall I put it—the more free-spirited side of your nature."

I glanced around at the lush flora, listened to the falling water.

"I find it makes me contemplative."

"Perhaps you contemplate too much. There are times when one must accept reality as it is." He smiled. "Go with the flow, as we used to say."

I said nothing, and he posed the question I'd expected.

"Have you thought about what we discussed the other day at lunch? Your future in the telecommunications business."

"About that lunch, Kosterman."

"Yes?"

"The sushi was excellent, but there was a little too much obfuscation in the conversation for my taste."

"I thought I answered your questions rather clearly, once we had an understanding."

"You told me Taylor Fairchild had a rough time of it when his father was killed in the line of duty."

"He did."

"You implied that was the reason he might later have gotten off the straight and narrow, trying too hard to be one of the boys."

"Yes, that's what I said."

"You failed to mention that he'd been sexually molested by his uncle in the year following his father's death."

There was a pause, filled by the babbling of the artificial brook behind us and the splash of water below.

"I don't see that that's any of your business, Justice. Or mine."

"It was enough of your business for you to tell your parents about it, and enough of their business to report it to Rose Fairchild."

"I thought someone should know."

"Which is to your credit. Too often, that kind of abuse gets ignored."

"Thank you."

"Did you also think someone should know when the uncle died under mysterious circumstances in a boating accident a few months later? Not unlike the two robbery suspects had died in prison, the two men involved in Captain Fairchild's death."

"You're treading in deep water, Justice."

"You didn't answer my question, Kosterman."

"It never occurred to me to wonder about the uncle's death. I was very young at the time, still in my teens."

"It hasn't occurred to you since?"

"Not in the slightest."

"You don't find the convenient deaths of the three men a rather strange coincidence?"

"I'd hoped this meeting might be more productive, at least from my standpoint." He raised the sleeve of his jacket, glanced at his gold Rolex. "It's getting late. I'm meeting my wife for dinner. I'm afraid you'll have to excuse me."

"That's a fine timepiece you're wearing, Kosterman."

"Yes, it is. A gift from my wife, if it matters."

"What does a watch like that set you back? Ten grand? Twenty?"

"In that range, I suppose."

"You probably don't have to be concerned with price tags anymore, do you, Kosterman? You can pretty much have what you want."

"Fortunately, I've done well."

He turned to go.

"Having Rose Fairchild pour some of her millions into the Documentary Channel must have eased your burden."

He stopped in his tracks, regarding me coolly. I mentioned the name of the company Templeton had found in Kosterman's corporate reports.

"When we had lunch, you neglected to mention that Rose Fairchild is your business partner."

"She's an investor, yes."

"The primary stockholder."

"As I said before, she's an old family friend. I gave her the opportunity to become involved. Just as she invited me to do some documentary work for the Getty. Which is why I'm here today."

"Rose Fairchild set up your meeting?"

"Rose Fairchild was *at* the meeting, Justice. Her friendship with certain families connected to the Getty Trust goes back many, many years."

"I should have guessed that."

"In a way, she's with us at this moment, sharing the experience of the Central Garden."

He glanced up the sloping hillside to a stone bench where Rose Fairchild sat, resplendent in a dark red business suit. Next to her was a man who looked familiar, but whose face I couldn't place. Kosterman filled in the blank.

"That's the mayor beside her, in case you're wondering."

"She gets around, doesn't she?"

"She's quite a remarkable woman, Justice. In a position to accomplish a great many things."

"Like helping you put the truth back in television?"

He smiled.

"Her investment in my cable venture was fortuitous. I won't deny that."

"You have no problem taking blood money, Kosterman? No problem getting fat off the backs of the third world?"

"Don't be ridiculous. I have no connection to any of that."

"It's all connected, Kosterman, and you know it. Every bit of it, right down to that fancy gold watch you're wearing."

His smile was smug now.

"Does this mean you won't be coming to work for me?"

"It's even connected to the beating of Winston Tsao-Ping, and the murders of Tommy Callahan and Byron Mittelman. All of it's connected, all of it neatly covered up. And you played your part, Kosterman. You're still playing it."

His smile froze, but the smugness was gone, replaced by contempt that looked like it might be dangerous.

"You're trying to take on something that's much bigger and more powerful than you or I will ever be, Justice. You're a fool to think you can win, or that you can even alter it a whit."

"You and Felix Montego seem to be working from the same script."

"Maybe you should start paying more attention to the words."

"Maybe I have, and that's the problem."

He turned and started up the pathway. I lost sight of him as he crossed the stream and rounded a green hillock where a bower of bougainvillea exploded with color. I raised my eyes, searching for Rose Fairchild. The bench where she'd been sitting was empty.

I listened to the falling water for a while, then climbed back up and took her place on the bench, gazing out across the megalopolis at a burnt orange sun setting on an azure sea, feeling moved by the beauty around me, but crushed by the hidden power.

Thirty

I SPENT the next few days locked up in the house finishing the first draft of my script, and using it as an excuse to keep my distance from Peter. It seemed the right thing to do, completing the script, given how much I'd already put into it, and I felt obligated, since Cecile Chang had promised to pay me for my work. Besides, I'd never liked leaving a piece of writing unfinished; the rare times I did that, it nagged at me like an unfinished thought or an unexpressed emotion. So, day after day, I wrote.

Nights, I visited Harry. His condition gradually worsened, which included a second stroke that left him with nearly as little movement on his left side as he had on his right. He could neither speak nor make signals of any kind, although his eyes moved. Just his eyes, shifting right and left, making us guess what they were trying to say. Just his eyes, that was all that was left of Harry.

On Friday afternoon, I put a hard copy of the finished script in the mail to Chang, along with a version on diskette, an invoice for payment, and a note telling her she could use the script or not, as she pleased. There was still something about it that was not right, not complete; I'd never quite nailed down my theme, found the underlying meaning of what I was trying to say on the troubling issue of bareback sex. That's what rewrites are for, and rewriting was no longer an option for me. So I sent my first draft off, finished yet frustratingly unfinal, and faced being unemployed and without job prospects once again.

That night, six days after Charlie Gitt had raped me on the grubby floor of the Reptile Den, I came down with what felt like influenza.

The symptoms, which typically signaled a recent exposure to the HIV virus, were also typically flu-like: headache, congestion, low-grade fever, aching, fatigue. But there was something else—a telltale rash, pinkish spots that spread over my upper body like freckles, heaviest on my chest and neck. When I first saw them in the mirror as I stepped from the shower, I felt as if everything were speeding out of control and coming to a standstill at the same time, as if I were on a wild roller coaster ride in pitch-dark space. I'd been infected with HIV, I was certain of it. Reality slammed into dread like two dark comets on an inevitable collision course, and my body, my being, was the universe that absorbed the explosion, and the billowing toxic cloud it produced.

Then I stopped myself: *Or was I infected?* The flu was going around, lots of people had it, and I might be one of them. As for the rash, I'd been popping much more ibuprofen than I should have for the pain I'd been suffering from my run-in at the Powder Room, and for the headaches I experienced every time I came away from another depressing visit with Harry. When I checked the warning label, I found that a light rash was among the possible symptoms of ibuprofen overdosing. So I wasn't infected with the virus after all; I was simply worrying too much, obsessing on the negative.

That was how it went: One moment, I was certain I was HIV-positive; the next, I was trying to convince myself it couldn't be happening, not now, not after so many years of dodging the virus. The rash and other symptoms were simply a passing flu; I'd be fine. The virus was spreading like wildfire in my body; I'd be dead in a few years, regardless of the new treatments that were saving so many. I'd be one of those who couldn't tolerate the drugs or their myriad side effects, who couldn't afford them, couldn't find the exact combination I needed. I was being silly, letting my imagination get the best of me. I was OK. Everything would be OK. I was sick, headed toward a hideous death. Every reasonable mode of suicide passed through my fevered imagination, at the oddest moments, unannounced and without reason, night and day, endlessly.

My mind played Ping-Pong with the options until I was sleepless, exhausted, feeling on the brink of going mad. The rash and flu-like symptoms passed, which was typical of both the flu and the onset of HIV. I stayed in the house with the shades drawn, letting the answering machine take calls, avoiding everyone, even mute, motionless Harry; I could no longer stand to go into the hospital, because of what it represented now; when I thought about returning there, I saw myself in Harry's bed, helpless, dying. I'd been thrust back into crisis mode, crisis thinking, and I couldn't escape it, no matter how hard I tried.

Peter took care of the animals, coming in through the broken back door, which I hadn't fixed since the burglary. I could see him from where I hid in the shadows of the house, knowing he couldn't see me. He'd glance around when he came in to open the cats' food and put it in their dishes, or to clean their litter box, or to get Maggie's leash and a plastic poop bag to walk her; I'd see him looking around for me, and I'd draw back, deeper into the shadows, until he was gone.

It went on like that, day after day. I knew there was no point in being tested this soon; the incubation period for HIV was several weeks to several months from the date of infection; then the body began producing antibodies to the virus and it became detectable in the blood. That seemed an eternity to wait, an intolerable chasm of time. It seemed a blessing, a wondrous, welcome reprieve. I was a man ripped down the middle, with each side flailing away at the other. I grew very, very tired.

Most of the phone messages that piled up were from Templeton, and through the days I could sense her own comets colliding:

Justice, I haven't seen you at the hospital. Have we been missing each other? Call me at home, OK?

Justice, where are you? Harry's condition hasn't changed, and it gets harder and harder to see him like that. I could really use a friend right now, Benjamin. Please call.

I haven't heard from you. Did you go out of town, take a fling with your TV money? It's weird not having a job. I went down to apply for unemployment today, but I couldn't do it. Listen, I hate talking to a machine like this. Call me when you get back, will you?

Justice, it's been a week since I've heard from you. I came by the house but it was all closed up and no one answered the bell. Are you all right? I'm getting worried. Please, please call me.

The Sun *folded today. They couldn't find any investors to save it. Roger Lawson released a prepared statement calling it a sad day for Los Angeles journalism, or some crap like that. This is all FYI, should you care.*

Justice, if you get this message, or bother to listen to it, I'm at my wit's end. I'm going home for a while to spend some time with my parents. We have to do something with Harry, Justice. He can't stay in the hospital much longer, and I'm afraid they'll stick him in a warehouse somewhere if we don't do something first. I've never had to deal with anything like this, Ben. I could really use a friend now, you know? Oh, Christ, I'm starting to cry. Damnit, I hate this. Where the hell are you?

Mixed among Templeton's messages were one or two from Oree Joffrien and several from reporters across the country who had read the *GQ* article and wanted to grill me about the Pulitzer scandal of eight years ago, now that I'd finally been dragged by Templeton out of the woodwork. I ignored them, along with all the others. There were no calls from Cecile Chang, Sergeant Montego, or Melissa Zeigler; it was as if they had all receded into the past, into another time that had nothing to do with now.

Once or twice, I found myself at the kitchen window, watching Peter mowing the lawn, or watering in the early evening, usually in his swimming trunks or running shorts, without a top. Physically, he hadn't changed; he was as lean and golden and flawless as ever. Yet I didn't feel a thing for him physically now; my eyes roved his body, his face, every inch and contour of him, looking for something that might ignite a spark of desire. Once, he turned with the hose and saw me at the window, looking out. This time, he didn't bother to call my name, to pry at me for answers or explanations. He allowed me to see the pain in his eyes for a moment, and then he turned away to continue his watering. In that moment, when I saw his eyes, he seemed years older, seasoned by the life experience he had come to L.A. seeking with such earnest resolve.

Sometime toward the middle of the next week, there was a knock on the front door. After that, the doorbell rang. Then I heard footsteps leave the porch and move around the side of the house, to the back. I wasn't sure of the time; the shades were down, but sun glinted in at the edges of the windows, so I knew it was still daylight, but that was all. There was a clock ticking somewhere in the house. I had grown frightened by clocks, by the ticking away of time, and didn't look.

The back door opened. A tall, broad-shouldered figure filled the doorway, silhouetted against the light.

"Ben? Ben, it's Oree."

He stepped in, calling my name, checking about the house, until he found me huddled on the floor in a far corner of the living room. I hadn't bathed or trimmed my beard or changed my clothes in days, nor eaten much, for that matter; I could only imagine what I might look and smell like. I didn't really care at any rate.

"Ben, what's going on?"

He pulled up a chair facing me and folded his lanky frame easily into it, as calm and centered as the night I'd first met him over dinner at the Addis Ababa.

"Ben, talk to me."

"Why?"

"I'm concerned about you. We all are."

"If you're so concerned, why did you send me to Cecile Chang? Where was your concern then?"

"What's Cecile done that's so terrible?"

"Where do I start?"

"Start wherever you need to, Ben."

"Why didn't you tell me the whole truth about her, before I got myself into this mess?"

"I'm not following you, Ben."

"If I'd known sooner who she was, I wouldn't have gotten myself in so deeply. I would have had all the answers I needed right there, with her. I never would have needed to talk to Charlie Gitt, to go anywhere near him."

"You're losing me again, Ben. Who's Charlie Gitt?"

I sprang like a cornered animal, straight at him. The chair went over backward and I was on top of him, my hands on his throat.

"Stop lying to me, you sonofabitch!"

He was a big man, probably as strong as me, possibly in better shape. Yet he didn't try to move, just fixed me with his calm dark eyes.

"Take it easy, Ben."

I was crying angry tears now, and spitting my words through clenched teeth.

"When you sent me to Cecile Chang, you sent me straight to the devil, straight into hell!"

"Calm down. Tell me what's happened."

"You knew that Templeton and I were trying to find Winston Tsao-Ping. I remember talking to you about it that night we had dinner at Chan Dara."

"Yes, that's true."

"You knew that Winston Tsao-Ping, better than anyone, could tell us what happened that night fifteen years ago. That he's the only one left alive who can do that."

"I understand, yes. But how does this involve me? Or Cecile?"

I tightened my hands on his throat.

"Stop lying to me!"

He gripped my wrists with his big hands, kept me from killing him.

"I swear to you, Ben, I'm completely in the dark."

"You're saying you didn't know that Cecile Chang and Winston Tsao-Ping are the same person? You're saying you didn't know she's not a lesbian, not the woman she pretends to be?"

A stunned expression crossed his face, and his eyes showed shock. When he spoke, it was almost a whisper:

"What are you talking about?"

"You're telling me you didn't know that Cecile's a transsexual?"

"What?"

"That she's probably had the full surgery?"

"My God." He turned his head, his eyes searching the air for answers, or maybe questions. Then he looked at me again. "Ben, I swear, I didn't know. Are you sure?"

"It took a chance comment by a funny kid named Harold to open my eyes. To see what I should have seen a long time ago. Yes, I'm sure. She's fooled a lot of people—apparently, even Tiger Palumbo."

"My God. Cecile. All these years."

He let go of my wrists, and my hands fell away from his throat.

"You never knew?"

"When I met Cecile, she was a woman."

"A woman without a past."

"Without a past, yes."

I sagged, feeling close to collapse, and braced myself with my hands on his chest. Then I rolled off him, onto my back on the hardwood floor.

"I'm sorry, Oree."

I stared at the ceiling, listened to the ticking clock.

"I've been going through a bad time."

"I can see that."

"Not dealing with things very well."

He reached out to touch me, the way Peter had tried to do. Once again, I put up my hand.

"Please, don't."

"What can I do, Ben? Tell me how I can help."

"I just need one thing from you, Oree."

"If I can do it, I will."

"Talk to Cecile. Convince her to see me again, to tell me the whole truth. To tell me exactly what happened that night fifteen years ago."

Thirty-one

"MELISSA ZEIGLER?"

"Yes, this is Melissa."

"Benjamin Justice."

"Ben. How are you?"

"Getting by, thanks. You?"

"Back to work, staying busy."

"I'm sorry I haven't been able to help you more. I was hoping I'd have some answers for you by now. About Byron's death, I mean."

"You tried. I appreciate it."

"You've put it behind you, then?"

"Not really, not with all the questions that were left unresolved."

"I hope you're not alone with this."

"I'm in a grief support group now. I have some wonderful friends and a very supportive family. My synagogue's been important during the worst of it. Byron's family, too. We're very close."

"You're lucky in that sense."

"Yes, I know that. Very lucky."

"I have a favor to ask, Melissa. If it's not too much."

"Certainly, Ben, if I can."

"A friend of mine, Harry Brofsky, had a stroke. He's lost his speech function, isn't communicating much. Not at all really."

"I'm sorry."

"He just lies in his hospital bed, paralyzed, not responding. The thing is, he has to be moved. Isn't that a horrible word, moved?"

"Yes, it is."

"Anyway, for personal reasons I won't go into, I haven't been going in to see him. Right now, hospitals are, let's just say, out of bounds for me."

"That's common for many people, for all kinds of reasons."

"You're the only social worker I know. I was wondering if you might be able to help find a place for Harry. Someplace that's—"

"Comfortable, with good care?"

"Yes."

"I've done a good deal of work involving nursing home placement. I'll be happy to help out."

"I don't know how we're going to pay for it. We're not sure what his insurance situation is. My friend Alexandra has some money. She said she'd be willing to help with the bills as long as she's able."

"I'm sure we'll be able to work something out."

"I'd go to visit Harry, but I just can't bear to see him like that. And the hospital, so many sick people, I—"

"I understand, Ben. Just give me the details I need, and I'll see that Mr. Brofsky is placed in a setting where he's well cared for."

"A setting. That's another one of those words, isn't it?"

"I'll take care of everything. We'll find a good place for your friend."

Thirty-two

FOR SEVERAL WEEKS, I waited.

Waited for word from Cecile Chang and the information only she could give me. Waited for a change of heart and some help from Sergeant Felix Montego. Waited for enough time to pass so that I could take the blood test that might tell me something about my future, one way or the other.

Now that I was desperate for conclusions, desperate for time to speed up, it slowed to a maddening crawl.

A French notecard arrived from Maurice:

My dearest Benjamin,

As you can see, Fred and I have finally completed our journey to the heavenly City of Lights and the wonderfully kitschy Eiffel Tower. We climbed all the way to the top for the view, where we shared a long, smoldering kiss, just like Doris Day and Ray Bolger in April in Paris *(or am I thinking of Audrey Hepburn and William Holden in* Paris When It Sizzles*?). Anyway, a nice lesbian couple from Sweden was kind enough to take the photograph I've waited so long for, and we obliged by snapping one of them. We're having the time of our lives, taking long walks through the Louvre and along the Seine, with everything abloom, including our undying devotion to each other, which means more*

*now than ever, with so much of our lives behind us rather than
ahead. Fred has never been more romantic—well, at least not for a
decade or two—and I'm rewarding him each morning with a
pastry that's definitely not on his diet, which we cut in half and
share at a sidewalk table with our coffee, watching Paris come to
life. Look for us to be home sometime in May, back to our little
nest on Norma Place, where I trust you're enjoying your own sweet
spring, my dear one!*

As ever, your ardent admirer, Maurice

I spent my days reading, working my way through the books
Jacques had left me before he'd died, and my nights parked
outside the Reptile Den, contemplating murder.

Each evening, I arrived about ten and parked half a block away,
hunched down in the shadows, armed with one of Fred's big
fishing knives, the kind with the wide blade and serrated edge for
serious slashing. I'd sit in the dark, listening to the frenzied synco-
pations of Thelonius Monk and Ornette Coleman on my tape
deck, watching for Charlie Gitt to arrive, and when he did, wondering if it would be worth it to kill him—if it would feel as good
as it did each night when I closed my eyes, going through the
motions in my head, trying to find some sense of resolution, no
matter how fanciful, so that I might steal a few hours' sleep before
the next light. I saw Gitt a number of times, late at night, arriving
at the club in his black Jeep Cherokee. He was always alone,
sometimes in tough guy leather garb, sometimes dressed like a
construction worker, always with enough of his hard body showing to warn you who was boss. At some point, he had to be shown
otherwise. I'd decided that much; I just hadn't decided when or
how.

Six weeks from the day he raped me, I drove to the Jeffrey
Goodman Clinic at the Los Angeles Gay and Lesbian Community
Services Center. The building was located in a low-rent neighborhood just south of Hollywood Boulevard, on Rand Schrader Boulevard, a street named in honor of the first openly gay appointed
judge, an old friend who had died from AIDS complications fairly
early in the epidemic. I took the elevator to the second floor,
filled out forms with code numbers that guaranteed anonymity,
as I'd done half a dozen times before over the years. I sat through
an AIDS and HIV information film I'd seen previously and talked

once again to a counselor; when he asked me, among his many required questions, if I'd recently engaged in unprotected anal sex, I simply answered yes. My blood was drawn, and I was told to come back in one week for the results, although I was warned that it could be several more months before my body began to develop antibodies to the virus, which the test was designed to detect.

When I arrived back on Norma Place, I found Templeton's Infiniti parked at the curb in front of the house, under the star-shaped leaves of a California sycamore. I pulled into the drive, listening to the gravel crunch as I slowly braked, realizing what a quiet afternoon it was. I sat for a while, not sure I wanted to see Templeton, not sure I wanted to face her insistent questions. Finally, I got out and went into the house. When I didn't find her there, I poked my head out the back door and looked around the yard. At the end of the drive, to the right of the double garage doors, her big handbag hung by its strap over the post at the bottom of the stairs. At the top, the door to the apartment was open behind a closed screen.

I mounted the stairs quietly and looked in.

Templeton was on the big bed, naked. Peter Graff, also naked, was on top of her. Her long brown legs were wrapped around his waist, and her fingers were thrust into the mass of golden curls at his neck. Each time he thrust his hips, his butt tightened, creating twin dimples in the smooth cheeks, but his stroke was as gentle, as considerate of her as it was strong. Their beauty, dark and light, supple and powerful, the wild freedom yet perfect cadence of their movements, the way they fit together so snugly, all of it was simply dazzling. My head grew light as I stood spying on them, listening to their cries and murmurs. Their sounds joined and rose like a lifting chorus, a lovely keening fused by the sensation they shared, and the muscles of Peter's legs and butt became corded and pronounced as he thrust into her more quickly, while Templeton cried out for more, her hands on his buttocks now as she arched upward and pulled him more deeply into her. I turned away and went back down.

I was sitting on the front porch, scratching Maggie's head, when I heard the screen door open, and turned to see them coming out of the house. They had both showered, and their hair was damp; Templeton had slipped into a fresh sweat suit of Peter's, and looked lost and adorable in it. He sat on the railing at a distance, in gym shorts and a T-shirt, while Templeton slid in beside me on the hanging swing.

"I've missed you, Benjamin."

"I went AWOL for a while."

"Peter's missed you too."

"How's Harry?"

"He's been moved to a convalescent home in the Fairfax district. Melissa Zeigler took care of it. Thanks for calling her. She's been a godsend."

"I haven't been too reliable, I'm afraid."

On the floorboards of the old porch, Maggie shifted in her sleep and treaded air with her paws, as if chasing cats in her dreams. Templeton took my hand.

"Peter and I slept together this afternoon."

"I know."

She smiled, sweetly and sadly at the same time.

"You always know so much, don't you?"

"Never as much as I'd like."

"Are you angry with us—with me?"

I shook my head.

"I came by looking for you, Ben. You weren't here. Peter was."

"Serendipity, I think they call it."

"I needed someone, Ben. Someone to hold me. Someone who wouldn't shut me out."

"You don't have to apologize, Alexandra."

"I'm not apologizing. I'm explaining."

A hummingbird buzzed under the porch, suspended itself in space for a few seconds, then zipped away. Templeton watched it go, then turned back to me.

"Are you going to visit Harry?"

"No. Not now, anyway. Not for a while."

"Are you going to tell me why?"

"I have some things to sort out first. Private stuff."

"That's it?"

"I'd like to leave it at that, if it's all the same."

I motioned Peter to join us on the swing. Templeton made room between us, and when Peter sat, we slipped our arms around him, and then we laughed all at once, as if on cue. He kissed me on the cheek, and Templeton the same way. Then he sat back, pushing the swing with his bare feet, rocking the three of us gently.

A breeze whispered across the porch, and through the leaves that draped the house. Templeton lifted her nose to the air, and the sweet scent of a blooming jasmine vine that Maurice had planted long before she was born.

"I love spring," she said, "more than any other time."

Out on the street, a black Jeep Cherokee drove toward the house. The driver slowed almost to a stop as he passed, staring hard in our direction. I recognized him instantly, even behind his angular dark glasses, and it was obvious to me that he wanted me to see him. I might have been wrong, but I felt certain his eyes were fixed more on Peter than on me. Peter recognized him too.

"Isn't that Charlie Gitt?"

Gitt hit the gas pedal and sped away while I kept silent, lulled by the rhythm of the swing, unwilling to disturb the quiet, the blessed peace.

Thirty-three

L ATE THAT EVENING, after I'd grabbed some dinner with
Templeton and Graff at Boy Meets Grill, I went for a long
hike in the hills. It had been a few weeks, and it felt good to test
my muscles again, to feel my body carrying its weight, as I sought
to reassure myself that the organism was intact, alive, functioning
properly.

By the time I came back down, a wind had kicked up, chilling
the moonless night, shivering the trees. The neighborhood was
characteristically quiet, and as I approached the house, I heard
little more than the leaves rustling and my own footsteps striking
their persistent pattern along the sidewalk. Then, just as I turned
up the front walk, something inside the dark house caught my
attention.

A curtain moved at the edge of the front window, as if someone
had been waiting. I kept my eyes on the window, saw no more
movement, nothing to suggest I was being watched. It might have
been a dervish of air slipping through the drafty old house, a
mischievous breeze touching the edge of the curtain like a human hand, before letting go and moving on. But caution seemed
a wise course.

I altered my path, cutting across the small yard to the gravel
drive, where I made some quick observations. Templeton's Infin-

iti was gone. Peter's VW bug was parked at the curb. I saw no other cars that I recognized, except my own in the driveway. Above the garage in back, the lights in the apartment were out. Other than a front porch light, and another light fixed high over the driveway, the house was pitched in darkness.

Under the front seat of the Mustang, I found the big fishing knife with the jagged edge where I'd kept it handy on my nightly vigils outside the Reptile Den. Maggie was asleep on the patio and never stirred as I passed. I opened the broken back door soundlessly and stepped inside.

From the kitchen, across the living room, I could see the curtains where I had noticed movement, covering the front windows. I moved silently through the kitchen and into the living room before I stopped. To the right, across the room, the curtains of a smaller window, one that looked out on the drive, were drawn open. In the faint light, a figure stood in silhouette, as slender as a surgeon's scalpel.

"You should fix that back door, Ben."

"I've been meaning to."

Cecile Chang stepped away from the window, to the center of the room. She glanced at the big knife as I laid it on an end table, just visible at the outer reaches of the remote light.

"You were expecting someone else?"

"You never know."

"Or perhaps you're tempted to use the knife on me."

I wasn't in the mood for jokes, if that was what it was, so I said nothing.

"Oree came to see me. About the secret I've been keeping."

"Only one, Cecile?"

"Plural, then. Secrets. Is that better?"

"More accurate at least."

"Oree seems to feel that my deception has caused you to get into some kind of trouble."

"Some kind of trouble, yes."

"Deep trouble was actually the way he expressed it."

"Closer to the truth."

"If not very specific."

"Did you come to play word games, Cecile? If so, you can use the front door on your way out."

"You're not happy with me, I know that."

"I'm tired of your games, Cecile. All of them."

"Oree was quite upset with me as well. With the pretense I've kept up all these years. He was quite hurt by that."

"I can imagine."

"He urged me to come see you, Ben. To talk more openly. Oree's a very good person. He likes you quite a lot, you know."

"That could change, when he gets to know me better."

"Do you mind if I smoke?"

"No."

A match flared, briefly illuminating the delicate features of her face. Then the shadows consumed her again.

"It's not easy, Ben. The transgender life."

"I imagine not."

"I'm sure you've heard the clichés, the generalizations—that transsexuals are men or women who feel trapped in the wrong body. That transgender men feel like women inside, that we identify with women emotionally, and need a woman's body to feel complete."

"Yes, I've heard all that."

"It only scratches the surface of who we are, and what we feel. It's impossible to explain it to someone who's never felt the same, never shared the experience. Impossible to make rational the notion that you want to completely alter your body, change your sex, through surgery and chemicals."

"I do have some problems with it, though I don't claim to understand everything."

"You can imagine, then, how difficult it is for the straight world to accept what we feel compelled to do. To accept us as we need to be."

"Is that what you want, Cecile? Acceptance from the straight world? Assimilation into mainstream life? If so, you seem to have done rather well for yourself."

Her long, slim cigarette glowed as she drew on the burning tobacco.

"Is that meant as an insult?"

"I'm not sure."

"I've done my best to build a life for myself the only way I knew how."

"You've lied to a lot of people, Cecile. You've hurt a lot of people. Your brother, Franklin, for one, who's desperate to know

what's become of you. Oree, for another, who gave you his friendship. Certainly Tiger Palumbo, when she finds out."

The cigarette glowed again, and Chang began to pace the
room.

"Are you going to be the messenger of bad tidings, Ben?"

"I hadn't planned on it."

"You feel I should be the one."

"That's your business. Deception inevitably causes pain, to everyone involved. The longer it goes on, the more damage it
does."

"You think I've used Tiger, don't you? Used her to put in place
the last missing piece of my rearranged life."

"That sounds more like a confession than a question."

"Let me correct a misconception that you might have, Ben,
you and countless others. Many people assume that with the right
surgery and a good support group, a transsexual's life changes
for the better. All those well-meaning but simplistic talk shows
parading their supposedly happy transgender role models—they
offer a terrible distortion of the truth. Nine out of ten people
who undergo gender reassignment are miserable for all kinds of
reasons, and many never get better. They bring with them enormous emotional baggage to begin with, frequently terrible childhood abuse, obviously deep sexual identity conflicts. Many
fantasize that having their male organs refigured to female and
growing a pair of breasts is going to give them instant self-esteem
and inner peace, to make them suddenly whole."

Her back was to me, but she kept talking.

"But it doesn't work that way, not for most. And it's never easy,
not for a single one of us. The emotional pain, the social rejec-
tion, are immeasurable."

"Then why do it?"

She whirled on me.

"Because we have to! Because this is what we are!"

"And how have you managed to adjust so well, Cecile, when so
many others have such a hard time of it? Besides passing yourself
off as a lesbian, I mean."

She glanced at a rattan chair.

"May I sit?"

"Of course."

She seated herself in the soft cushions, crossing one leg over the other, dangling a high heel, smoothing down her tight skirt. I sat at the end of the couch nearest her, facing her across the coffee table.

"Whatever lies I've told, whatever truth I've left unspoken, it was to survive."

"When exactly did the lies start?"

"The first lie a transgender person understands is that we are not what we appear to be on the outside, to others. The flip side of that is the truth we know about ourselves, or at least sense, on the inside. But in this world, where gender roles are so rigidly defined and enforced, with so little room for humanity and diversity, our inner truth is at constant war with the lie outside. It causes transgender children untold confusion and grief. Our sense of reality, of self, becomes terribly fractured."

"How did you survive, Cecile? As a child, I mean."

"The first relief we have, at least in my case, is to experiment secretly with our mother's clothes. Then with the makeup, and the hair. I first tried it as a young teenager. I can tell you, the freedom I felt was exhilarating beyond anything I'd expected. I was a completely different person in women's clothes; my personality and character, the way I spoke and carried myself, changed completely. I was myself, at last. As I got older, I became only more certain of that."

"Yet you continued to live a heterosexual life."

"I loved women, Ben. I was sexually attracted to them. Never men. I realize that makes me an anomaly, but that's how it is."

"So marrying was not such a problem."

"I was the first son in a traditional Chinese family. It was expected of me. Anything else was unthinkable."

"You and your wife had normal sexual relations?"

"Under the circumstances. It was a marriage arranged by our parents, between the families. There was affection but no passion, no 'heat,' as they like to say. I cared for my wife, but there was always a distance, an artificiality born of so much pretense."

"You were never able to share your secret with her, then."

"Not with anyone. I could never be myself, except with strangers who were like me."

"And with the mirror."

"The mirror can be as cold as it is clear. A lonely place in which to dwell."

"So you lived a double life, playing the dutiful husband and son on the one hand, and the adventurous cross-dresser on the other."

"I never went out in women's clothes looking for men. I only went out to be seen in natural dress and makeup, like other women. To be myself for a few precious hours. Is that so much to ask?"

She took a long drag on the cigarette, then looked around for an ashtray that wasn't there.

"You'll have to use the sink. In the kitchen. I can turn on a light if you'd like."

"I'd rather you didn't."

"You prefer the shadows?"

"They can be comforting at times."

She got up and crossed the room, her heels tapping neatly across the hardwood floor. I heard the faucet being turned on, and the sizzle as she doused her cigarette. When she returned, she had a saucer with her, which she placed on the coffee table. She sat opposite me at the other end of the sofa, draping a slim arm and set of bracelets along the back.

"It's much easier talking to you than I expected, Ben. You're leading me along quite skillfully."

"It's my background, I suppose. My training."

"Yes, of course."

"As long as we're moving forward so smoothly, why don't you tell me about the night of April fourteenth, in Hollywood, fifteen years ago."

She crooked her elbows, and joined her hands, weaving her fingers together, the long painted nails blood red against her alabaster skin.

"It really all comes back to that night, doesn't it? All that's happened."

"Just about."

"The weather was pleasant that evening, warm but with a nice breeze, and almost a full moon. My wife had planned a visit with her sister for a few days. I was to have the apartment all to myself. We had separate closets, in different rooms. Inside my closet, I'd constructed a secret compartment where I kept my female things. My wife was away rarely, but I waited for those times the way one anticipates a holiday or vacation. In my mind, I lived for those opportunities to dress up and go out. That night, after she'd gone, I took a great deal of time with my makeup and hair, two hours or more, until I looked, well, acceptable.''

"You've been blessed with good features.''

"I was slim, as I am now, and had almost no beard, even back then, long before I began taking estrogen. It was much easier for me to pass than many cross-dressing men.''

"So you went out, to Hollywood.''

"I wanted to be where there were lots of people. Also, where I knew I'd see other men like me, wearing women's attire. I wanted to compare myself to them, to affirm my own attractiveness, my ability to pass. I had coffee, then went window-shopping along the boulevard and looked at the famous names in the stars along the sidewalk. I stayed in the busiest section, where it was well lighted and I felt safe.''

She paused to take a deep breath and steady herself.

"Then I noticed a car passing slowly, with two men inside, staring at me. They were in regular clothes, but it appeared to be an undercover car. I suspected they were policemen, they just had that look about them. I became quite rattled and kept walking, keeping my eyes straight ahead.''

"This was in the area near the Egyptian Theater?''

"Yes, across the street. I remember it quite well, because the theater was in a deteriorated state at that time. It might even have been boarded up, I'm not sure. When the same car came by again, a minute or two later, I became frightened. When it had gone by, I quickly crossed the boulevard and hurried down a side street. It was foolish to act that way, but I was desperately afraid of being exposed. You can't even imagine the terror of that, particularly back in those days.''

"You turned into an alley?''

She nodded.

"If it hadn't been for my heels, I would have taken off at a run.''

"The car caught up with you?''

"In less than a minute. The beams of the headlights flooded my back and the pavement in front of me, and I became paralyzed with fright. I looked back and saw the car, and the two men inside. They drove slowly past and stopped at an angle in front of me, and both got out. I remember clutching my purse and blurting out, 'What do you want? I haven't done anything!' It was all I could think of to say. My voice was deep then, it gave me away instantly. I was trembling, shaking all over.

"The first officer, the one who was driving, came over and asked to see some identification. Again, I asked why, what had I done wrong? He stroked my face with the back of his hand, my cheek, then my chin. I'd shaved, of course, and my face was quite smooth. I thought perhaps I wouldn't be discovered, I prayed for that. Then he reached down and lifted my dress, and grabbed my crotch. When he felt what was down there, a grin spread across his face. It was the most hateful grin I'd ever seen. I still can't get it out of mind."

"Where was the second cop?"

"He stayed a few feet back, as if he weren't quite sure what to do."

"As if he was following the other's lead?"

"Yes, exactly. He even seemed a little unnerved himself by what was happening, like he was uncomfortable being there."

"At what point did they start beating you?"

"Right away. The first officer, the muscular one, hit me in the stomach. It took the wind out of me, I was gasping just to get a breath. Then he ripped my wig off and began slapping me around. At some point, he closed his fist and began striking me hard in the face and the stomach, and then he was urging the other officer to join in."

"Did he?"

"Yes, though reluctantly. When I was on the ground, he backed off, didn't want to do anything more to me. I remember the first officer taunting him, calling him a 'pussy,' and grabbing him by the arm. He shoved him forward, calling him more names like that, until the other officer kicked me a few times. They were both kicking me when a patrol car pulled up and a third officer jumped out. I was already bleeding heavily, in a great deal of pain, and I thought this third officer had come to join in the fun. I thought that was the end, that I was going to die right there."

"Instead, he put a stop to it."

She nodded again.

"He didn't hesitate for a moment. He was loud, very forceful. He pulled both officers off me and pushed them away. He told them to get back in their car and leave, assured them he would 'take care of things.' Those were the words he used. Take care of things. Which is exactly what he did.''

''You haven't mentioned the man with the camera—Byron Mittelman.''

She looked at me for a moment, then away. She drew another cigarette from her pack of Capris, struck another match, inhaled.

''Yes, Byron Mittelman was there. Though, of course, at the time, I didn't know his name. I wouldn't learn his name until a few weeks ago, when Melissa Zeigler came to my office for the first time.''

''But you knew back then that he was a cameraman for *On Patrol,* riding along with the LAPD.''

She smiled ruefully.

''I certainly learned it soon enough, as if I didn't have enough problems already.''

''What happened next?''

''The other car sped away, and the third officer, the one who saved me, told Mr. Mittelman to stop taping with his camera. Then he tried to make me comfortable and called for an ambulance. While we waited, he suggested that it might be in my best interest to create a cover story, to keep the incident as quiet as possible. He pointed out that if I pressed charges against the two officers who beat me, it would become a matter of public record, open to the press, and that all the facts would have to come out.''

''Including the fact that you were dressed as a woman that night.''

''Of course, which I wanted to avoid at all costs.''

''So you helped him create a false police report blaming an unidentified assailant for the assault.''

''My mother handled that, actually.''

''Pearl Tsao-Ping.''

Chang drew in more smoke as she nodded.

''At the hospital, they told me I was seriously injured, that I'd need to call someone. Finally, under great pressure, I gave them my wife's name and number. It was my mother who took the call. When she arrived and learned the details, she took over without even talking to me. She's a very formidable woman, my mother. She managed to tidy everything up quite nicely.''

''Including banishing you from the family.''

''She agreed to pay for the sexual surgery I wanted if I agreed to go away and never have contact with anyone in the family again. I would have to change my name and start life over as a different person."

"And your wife?"

"My mother took her back to Taiwan, had the marriage annulled, and paid her family to keep quiet. I'm not even sure my wife ever learned the whole truth."

"And after the surgery, and enrolling at New York University, you decided that passing yourself off as a lesbian was easier than trying to make it as a transsexual."

"I was romantically attracted to women; that didn't change with the loss of my male organs, or the estrogen treatments. So it seemed like a logical approach. I was immediately accepted by the lesbian community. I found wonderful support there that I never would have experienced as a transsexual trying to live in straight society."

"You must have been concerned about the footage Byron Mittelman shot the night you were beaten."

"Jacob Kosterman, the executive producer, assured my mother the taping would never be aired, that it would be locked away and never seen by anyone. That it would never be a problem."

"Kosterman was involved in the cover-up from the beginning?"

"Oh, yes."

"Why didn't he just destroy the videotape?"

"I'm not sure. He may have seen some future value in it—the financial leverage it gave him with Rose Fairchild."

"It might never have been a problem if Tommy Callahan hadn't stolen it the next season, then tried to cash in on it all these years later."

"Yes, Tommy spoiled the plan, I'm afraid."

"Let me see if I've got things in order, Cecile. A few months ago, after he'd exhausted all his opportunities in commercial television, Callahan came to New Image Productions, desperate for a job. You saw on his resume that he'd once been a videotape editor for *On Patrol,* but you had no idea of his connection to that missing piece of videotape, or even that it was missing at all. Not then."

"I'd pretty much forgotten about it, put it out of my mind. I had a new name, a new identity, a new life. It no longer seemed like a threat to me.''

"Callahan didn't recognize you?''

"Fifteen years and expert surgery, above the waist as well as below, can do a lot to alter a person's looks.'' Again, the thin smile. "Also, I have better taste in clothes these days.''

"When you checked Callahan's references, you learned that he'd been fired from his last job with Jaffe-Edwards Productions. You checked with Jaffe-Edwards and found out that Jacob Kosterman had ordered him fired, probably after Kosterman had seen his name in the credits on one of the shows Jaffe-Edwards produced for the Documentary Channel.''

"That's very close to how it happened, yes.''

"You talked with someone you knew at Jaffe-Edwards and discovered that Kosterman had blacklisted Callahan because he'd stolen a piece of videotape fourteen years before—videotape of two LAPD cops beating up a transvestite. It wasn't too difficult to put two and two together, and realize it was the same video Byron Mittelman had shot during his ride-along, with you as the featured victim.''

A reluctant smile formed on her pretty lips.

"I'm impressed, Ben. I really am.''

"Suddenly, that nasty piece of videotape reared its ugly head.''

"Not really. As I said, I'd started a new life as a different person.''

"But if the media got hold of it, a lot of very nosy reporters might start doing some digging, and do their best to find out what had happened to the victim, Winston Tsao-Ping.''

"I'm not so sure. It was an old incident. Police brutality in those days was commonplace, at least within the LAPD. Anyone with any awareness of what's going on knows that by now. After the video of the Rodney King beating, half a minute of a transvestite getting kicked would hardly be considered newsworthy.''

"Unless the officers involved were still on the force, maybe even prominently.''

Chang shifted uneasily, and kept silent.

"Why not name the officers, Cecile? Why not tell the story, expose the bad guys? Isn't that what a documentarian should do?''

"Without that videotape, there is no story. It's just the word of a troubled transsexual making wild claims fifteen years after the fact. Think about it. If that man who captured the Rodney King beating on his new camcorder hadn't stepped out on his balcony that night, the public never would have known about the beating at all. King would have been jailed for resisting arrest, his word against the officers', and that would have been the end of it. Just like hundreds of other incidents of brutality the police have gotten away with in this city over the years. Without pictures, you've got nothing."

"I imagine a tape like that could be worth a lot of money to the right person."

"Possibly."

"You must have wanted it awfully badly yourself."

Chang studied me closely, keeping quiet.

"When you hired Callahan, you hoped to get your hands on that missing videotape, didn't you, Cecile? Maybe offer him a trade, give him another shot at a career in exchange for the master tape, or just write him a fat check."

"I don't have that kind of money."

"Money can always be diverted in a nonprofit organization when the donations roll in, if the head honcho is clever enough. And you're a very clever person, Cecile."

"When Oree asked me to come see you, to talk to you like this, he said you needed to know the truth. But the truth is, I didn't know exactly why I wanted that videotape or what I was going to do with it. My mind was in a state of confusion and despair, something I thought I'd left behind all those years ago. There were moments when I thought I would destroy the tape if I could get hold of it, so that Tiger could never find out about my real identity. There were other times when I burned with desire to use the tape in a documentary on police brutality, even if I got hurt in the process.

"At the same time, I didn't want to harm the career of the third officer, the one who saved my life, which would surely happen if the complete facts ever came out. He did, after all, participate in a cover-up, to protect not just me but his own. My head spun with the possibilities, the ramifications. All I knew for sure was that I wanted to get control of that tape, before someone else did."

"Which is why you raced out of the office that day when Peter Graff told you Callahan was missing in action. To confront Callahan about the tape, which you wished you'd done before. To get it from him if you could."

"When I got to the motel, he was gone. Someone had ransacked the room before I arrived, turned everything upside down. I searched through his belongings myself, just to be sure the tape wasn't there. That must have been when I lost my earring. Then I saw the blood on the mattress and fled. I had nothing to do with Tommy Callahan's disappearance or death, Ben. I swear to you, that's the truth."

"I suspect you have a pretty good idea who did, though."

"It's better not to speculate. Worse, to know. It's dangerous, especially for me, if they ever link me to Winston Tsao-Ping. Look what happened to Callahan and Mittelman. Do you want the same thing to happen to you?"

"It very nearly has, Cecile."

"Then why persist?"

"Because Charlie Gitt's an animal who hurts people, and I don't like that."

At the sound of Gitt's name, her head jerked like a finger snap.

"He was one of the two cops who kicked the hell out of you that night, wasn't he, Cecile? The leader, the brutal one."

She shivered, crossed her arms, rubbed them as if a sudden chill had filled the room.

"I'm not going to answer any more of your questions. I'm not going to tell you any more. It's safer the less you know."

"Where's the courage and conviction you're known for, Cecile? Or was that just another part of the masquerade?"

Her eyes were on me, searching for sympathy.

"He'd kill me if he knew I was once Winston Tsao-Ping, and that I'd been talking to you like this."

"Maybe."

"I've never been so frightened of a man. I still see his face in my nightmares, that horrible grin, the way it widened each time he drew back his foot and kicked me again. For fifteen years I've seen it every time I close my eyes."

She shivered again, and clutched herself tightly.

"He scares me so much that when I saw him here two hours

ago, I drove on as fast as I could. I didn't come back until I knew for certain he was gone. Even then, I parked my car two blocks away, where he wouldn't see it.''

I reached out and grabbed her wrist.

''Charlie Gitt was here? Tonight?''

''When you were out. As I drove up, I saw his Jeep in the drive. Then I saw him out toward the back, climbing the stairs.''

''Jesus Christ.''

I leaped over the back of the sofa and was out the kitchen door, across the patio, and up the stairs in a matter of seconds. The screen to the apartment was unlatched, and the door wide open. I reached in and switched on the light.

Peter was gone. There had been a struggle.

Thirty-four

W HEN I ARRIVED at the Reptile Den, only two or three cars were parked on the street out front, and the black Jeep Cherokee wasn't one of them.

It was a weeknight, relatively early, and the big Hispanic guard hadn't yet taken his post at the front steps. That left the wiry white guy with the warrior tattoos and the nose ring to deal with. He was inside the office booth, behind the counter, organizing porn tapes while he absentmindedly stroked his shaved chest and belly. I approached with a pliant smile and the big knife hidden at my side, and asked if Charlie Gitt had come in.

Nose Ring must have recognized me as he glanced up, because he looked perplexed.

"No. Not yet."

"You seem surprised to see me."

"We didn't figure you to make an encore."

"Maybe I liked Charlie's action."

He laughed a little, but warily.

"A lot of guys do."

"So where is Charlie anyway?"

"Weekdays, he usually does his own thing. You know, a private party up at his place, if he's in the mood. We don't see him much except on weekends."

"I imagine you've been up to his place yourself."

"Once or twice, sure."

"I really need to see him again." I winked. "In the worst way, if you know what I mean."

He set the tapes aside and leaned forward on the counter, getting friendlier.

"So you really liked your first visit with us?"

"Oh, baby, did I ever."

"From what I hear, Charlie didn't exactly go easy on you."

"That's why I came back—for more." I looked him up and down. "That is, if I can find a guy who's man enough to give it to me."

He studied me closely, first my hairy face, then my thick chest and shoulders. His eyes started to sparkle, like a drug had just hit him.

"We're not too busy at the moment. I wouldn't mind spending a few minutes with you, if you could dig that."

"You wouldn't have a pair of cuffs, would you? Cuffs really get me off."

He grinned, reached behind him into a drawer, and brought out a pair of gleaming steel handcuffs. His mouth seemed to be getting dry; when he swallowed, he had to work at it, and his tongue stayed busy keeping his lips moist.

He tossed the cuffs onto the counter with a clatter.

"Will these do the job?"

"I'm getting hard already."

I glanced around, then leaned in, whispering conspiratorially.

"You know what I really want, hot man?"

His Adam's apple bobbed as he forced saliva down his parched throat.

"Name it, buddy."

With my left hand, I grabbed his nose ring, which pierced the cartilage between his nostrils and was just large enough to accommodate my finger. With my right hand, I showed him the lethal-looking knife.

"I want you to climb into those handcuffs, PDQ."

He grinned, like it was a joke.

"That wasn't what I had in mind. I'm strictly a top, the guy in charge."

I dragged him by his nose ring halfway over the counter, while he hollered and moaned. When our eyes were an inch apart, I placed the serrated blade between them so he could focus on the peaks and valleys of the cold steel.

"I'm giving the orders now, Topper. If you want to remain in one piece, you'll do exactly as I say. I don't have a lot of time."

"What are you, some kind of freak?"

"Keep talking, and I start cutting."

"You're making a big mistake. When Charlie finds out about this—"

"Charlie's going to find out real soon, because you're taking me to him."

"No way, man."

I inserted the tip of the blade into his left nostril and sliced it open, just the way Roman Polanski did to Jack Nicholson in *Chinatown*, only this time, the pain and the blood were real. Nose Ring started trembling, and doing a better job of listening.

"Put on the cuffs, pronto."

He slipped a wrist into one of the rings, and I helped him into the other one before clamping the bracelets shut. Then I dragged him the rest of the way over the counter and down to the floor. I pressed the prickly blade against the big, pumping vein in his neck.

"I've killed before. You didn't know that, did you?"

His voice was tiny, faint.

"No."

"It was a long time ago. I was very angry. I'm very angry now."

"Look, I just work here, that's all."

"You didn't know what Charlie had planned for me that night. That I was going to get ambushed by some muscle boys and have my ass reamed bareback style by the big man himself."

"No, I swear. I never knew."

"It wasn't a question, asshole."

"OK, maybe I knew. But, but, Jesus, please don't cut me up."

"You really want to stay in one piece?"

He nodded furiously.

"Then take me to Charlie Gitt. Now."

I led him by his nose ring across the street, strapped him into the Mustang with a seat belt so he couldn't jump out, and handed him a rag to hold to his face and stop the bleeding. I also told him that if he didn't get me to Gitt's place in ten minutes, I'd cut off each of his appendages, starting with the one between his legs. His directions after that were very precise.

We raced up to Sunset Boulevard, headed east for a few blocks, then cut over to Griffith Park Boulevard, which we followed north until Nose Ring pointed me onto a winding side road that took us into the hills. Five minutes later we were at the crest, looking down on the tree-ringed Silver Lake Reservoir with the hot lights of Dodger Stadium two or three miles to the south and the downtown skyscrapers a mile beyond that, rectangular columns of light twinkling against the black sky.

We didn't pause long to enjoy the view. Nose Ring kept giving directions, and I kept driving, until we were winding up a narrow street without curbs or lights, where the trees were tall and thick, deepening the shadows already dense in the moonless night. There seemed to be no houses here, only steep slopes and heavy foliage on either side of the road, until it ended abruptly at a cast-iron gate erected between two concrete pillars. Beyond the gate, a driveway of crooked, cracked bricks ascended for about a hundred feet, leveling out as it reached a house that was little more than a ghostly outline through the darkness and the untended growth. Parked at the top of the drive was a black Jeep Cherokee.

Nose Ring was staring at the knife in my hand.

"This is where Charlie lives. Those are his wheels."

I reached across, unstrapped him, pushed open the door.

"Get out."

He swung his booted feet to the ground, and stood staring at me, his wrists cuffed in front of him. I climbed out, came around to where he stood, and placed the tip of the blade against his flat belly, pressing the taut skin, pricking the hard layer of muscle beneath. He winced, and started trembling again.

"I did what you asked. I showed you where Charlie lives."

"What do I need to know about the house?"

"There's a dog. Big and mean, trained to kill."

"Alarm system?"

"Not that I know of."

"What else?"

"Charlie has a dungeon. Fully equipped. You know, for orgies and stuff. In the basement."

"How do I find it?"

"There's a door under the stairs, if you go through the house.

Or you can use the steps from the outside, around to the right.
You won't tell him I brought you here, will you? God, if he ever
found out—''

I pushed the tip of the knife deeper, just enough to tap blood.

"If I ever see you again, I'll gut you like a fish. Got it?''

He nodded, short little jerks of his head, like the affirmation of
a terrified child. The same way I'd tried to appease my father
when I was a little kid and he was drunk and stood over me with a
doubled-up belt in his hand, slapping it across his big palm.

"Start running, and don't stop until you're in Orange
County."

I took the pressure off his belly and he ran, galloping down the
hill. I watched as the shadows swallowed him up, and listened to
his boots thudding on the asphalt until they faded away, and I
knew I was alone.

I turned back toward the big gate. It was in the range of seven
feet, and spiked on top like the matching wrought iron fence that
extended to the right and left. On one of the pillars was a street
number, on the other a posted warning:

Private Property
No Trespassing
Beware of Dog

I found a section of the fence where a knee-high boulder provided a boost, and I was over the spikes a minute later, winded but
unscratched. As I hit the ground, I heard the dog, great angry
barks cracking the darkness up around the house and coming fast
in my direction. I stripped off my sweatshirt, wrapped it around
my left hand and arm, planted my feet, and waited.

The dog came tearing down an overgrown path to my right. It
was a Rottweiler, dark in color, massive in the chest, with heavy
jowls already drooling thick strings of mucus as it bared its teeth.
The dog never slowed, just came straight at me, snarling as it
sprang. I raised my wrapped arm, feeding it into the huge jaws.
When the animal's teeth were set, I brought the knife up with one
sharp, clean stroke, under the dog's chin, across the meatiest part
of its throat. It went down quickly, got up, wobbled for a moment,
then collapsed. It thrashed for half a minute, then lay still, while
its blood seeped into the loamy earth.

I used my sweatshirt to clean the blood off the knife, discarded the sweatshirt, and followed the same path the Rottweiler had used coming down. As I climbed, more of the house came into view. It was constructed of square-cut stones and consumed by wisteria that masked most of the facade, which rose to a sharply peaked roof. Two dark windows stared down from either side of the heavy wooden front door. The path flattened out, and I found myself in an area that had apparently once been a garden, with a stone bench and a birdbath at the center that were now lost in the wild foliage. Past the house and through the trees, I could see other houses on the hills across the canyon, which told me the man-made lake I'd seen earlier was just below, down by the main road. The wind had died, no longer molesting the leaves, and the world around me had grown deathly still.

I made my way past the garden, halfway to the house, and stopped again. Ahead of me, I saw a light, indistinct through a low, narrow doorway at the bottom of a flight of cellar steps. I moved toward the muted light, quietly. As I reached the steps, I heard what sounded like moaning. A human voice, male, someone in pain.

I was about to step down, to follow the voice, when I was seized from behind. A hand as powerful as any I had ever encountered gripped my right wrist, immobilizing the knife. In the same instant, my neck was secured in the crook of an arm, and a huge bicep expanded against the main artery, pressing down to stop the flow of blood to my brain. I clawed at the arm, tried to kick the legs behind me, felt my head grow light, my reactions slow and unconnected to the orders I was trying to send to my body.

Facts flashed in my shocked brain, a reporter's fractured memories: I was being subdued with the police choke hold that had been outlawed by the Los Angeles Police Commission back in the 1980s. Daryl Gates had fought to keep the lethal hold in use while he was chief. Charlie Gitt was surely one of those cops who had cursed the commission for taking away one of his most effective combat tools. But there was no police commission here to censure or reprimand him. I was in Charlie Gitt's world now.

Charlie Gitt's world.

That was my last thought as my vision became a blur of bright stars and a feeling of weightlessness swept over me, just before everything went black.

Thirty-five

T HE FIRST PINPRICK of consciousness I felt was the sensation of pain in my arms and shoulders.

Even before I opened my eyes, the pain had spread like a slowly moving fire down and across the knotted muscles of my back. I became aware that I was suspended, hanging by my bound wrists in a cold place that smelled dank.

I opened my eyes, and saw Peter.

There was a steady ripple of movement in his chest and belly, so I knew he was at least alive, and breathing. He wasn't far away—six or eight feet, perhaps, across the rough cobbled stones of Charlie Gitt's cellar floor—but there was nothing I could do for him. I was strung from an overhead beam like a butcher's side of beef; my ankles were also tightly bound, with the same kind of nylon rope that secured my wrists, all of it wrapped and knotted in neat double strands that allowed sufficient circulation, but no movement. Clearly, I had been bound and strung up by an expert.

Peter's constraints were more elaborate: He hung facing me from a steel bar that was secured to a wooden beam by a chain link and wire pulley system, which presumably allowed the bar to be lowered or rotated. His upper body was stretched out crucifixion style, his wrists locked into leather cuffs attached to the ends of the steel bar, while his ankles were lashed together by the same type of rope that bound my own. A black spandex hood with a single opening for the mouth and nose covered his head so snugly it accentuated the sharp contours of his forehead and chin. Around his neck was a leather collar with a brass ring in the front, for leashing. Steel spring clamps pinched his nipples. Otherwise, like me, he was naked.

"Peter? Peter, can you hear me?"

I was whispering for no good reason, so I raised my voice.

"Peter! Can you talk?"

His hooded head hung to one side, unmoving. I knew it was Peter because I recognized his unclothed body, although Gitt had performed some cosmetic alteration in the manner of knife or razor cuts. There were forty or fifty, concentrated on the torso; each slice in Peter's flesh was straight and precise, roughly two inches in length and drawn at the same downward angle, right to left, which meant the incisions must have been made slowly. The cuts had recently been washed clean, but had started to bleed again, and the blond hairs of Peter's chest, crotch, and legs were matted with his sticky blood. I dreaded what his face might look like beneath the hood.

I did this to you, Peter. It was the first thought that came to me as I saw him strung up and bleeding like a modern Christ in the dark heart of medieval Los Angeles, where he had come to explore everything life had to offer, and had chosen me as his guide. *My recklessness did this to you. I couldn't leave you alone, when I knew I should. I had to have you, so I did. I all but led you to this place.*

"Peter?"

Flaming torches on the stone walls cast their flickering light across Gitt's private dungeon, revealing how dedicated he was to the religion of pain and pleasure. Arches had been constructed throughout, opening to dark passages and alcoves barely visible at the edges of the jumpy light. Each alcove was furnished with sadomasochism in mind: a cage, a pillory, a bondage chair, a horizontal rack, an arched wooden block with leather restraints for spanking, a sling equipped with wrist and ankle cuffs like the one I'd seen at the Reptile Den. Here and there, stone gargoyles looked down from the walls between collections of leashes, whips, and flogging canes, and a shelf lined with collars, cuffs, nipple clamps, and cock rings.

"Peter, please talk to me."

I heard footsteps, and turned my head to see Charlie Gitt descending his cellar steps.

"I'll bring him around for you, Justice, if you'd like. He's been asking for you, as a matter of fact."

"You're in danger of giving S&M a bad name, Charlie. The leather community won't be pleased."

Gitt smiled briefly as he crossed through the shadows and into the dancing light. He was dressed in black leather this time, rather than brown, but otherwise the outfit was much like the one he'd worn the night we'd last met: vest unfastened to show off his furry, muscled torso, pants open at the crotch to display his impressive cock and balls, boots heavy enough to crush a head against the cold stone floor, if he so desired. In one hand, he carried a latched metal box about the size of a child's lunchbox; in the other, a small glass vial. He placed the box on a rough-hewn wooden table next to Peter, then unscrewed the cap on the vial and inhaled from it. Within seconds, the smell of amyl nitrate permeated the air. He inhaled the poppers again, more deeply, then caressed Peter's genitals gently, with admiration, as if he'd forgotten I was there.

"Has he seen you, Gitt? Or did you manage to take him from behind, the way you did me?"

When Gitt turned, his pendulous penis had started to rise, the purple head peeking out of the foreskin like the head of a snake looking for prey.

"Has he seen your face, Gitt? Does he know it's you?"

Slowly, he began to smile. He hadn't shaved in a day or two, and his heavy beard cast the square lower portions of his face in black.

"I'm afraid he has, Justice."

Inside, it felt as if everything had suddenly gone dead. Still, foolishly, I hoped.

"You could still let him go. I'll convince him not to talk. Both of us, we'll keep quiet."

Gitt looked hard at me, and the smile disappeared. He stepped to the wall where he kept his collections of whips, and looked them over. He quickly passed by those that were braided and multithonged, stopped to consider a fearsome-looking bullwhip, then selected a signal whip, the kind with a single lash used for training dogs.

He took a position several feet in front of me and slightly at an angle, with his legs spread. He drew his arm back and cracked the four-foot whip. I turned my head and felt the tip of the leather cut my chest. Four more lashes followed, each taking a tiny bite and drawing blood. When Gitt was finished, he coiled the whip and replaced it on the wall, the way a doctor or dentist might replace an instrument in its proper place.

"Don't talk to me like I'm stupid, Justice." The grin came back, more twisted this time, more malevolent. "I'm crazy, maybe. A crazy motherfucker on the fast road to hell. But I can tell you, it's a fantastic ride, a roller coaster flameout, and I'm the holy devil in the front car."

"Which is a fancy way of saying you know exactly what you're doing."

He grabbed my mouth in one of his big hands, squeezing it like a soft peach.

"That's right, motherfucker. None of this is happening by chance, or on a whim. So don't treat me like I'm a stupid nigger, because this is one nigger who is definitely not Stepin Fetchit. Maybe once, when Gates was the boss man, but never again. Capice?"

He took his hand away, but his eyes stayed on me, burning like a dark fire.

"Capice?"

"Capice."

He turned away, went to the table, opened the metal box. He found another vial, unscrewed it, and tapped what appeared to be crystal meth into a tiny spoon, though it might have been cocaine. With a wet finger, he dipped into the white powder, then rubbed it over his gums, before snorting the rest. He tilted his head back and closed his eyes, savoring the rush. Then he stood in front of Peter, looking him up and down, running his hands over Peter's body, smearing the blood, licking it from his fingers.

He removed the clamps from Peter's chest, one at a time, inspecting the swollen nipples.

"I think your friend's ready for piercing. What do you think, Justice?"

"Why don't you forget about Peter for a minute, Charlie? Tell me about what happened to Winston Tsao-Ping. Fifteen years ago, over in Hollywood. That must have been a memorable night for you, beating him half to death with Taylor Fairchild. Why don't you tell me all about it?"

He removed a needle from the box, then two gold nipple rings.

"You seem to know plenty already, Justice. So why don't you tell me?"

He pinched Peter's left nipple, rolling it in his fingers, making it more pliable. Peter's head still rested to the side, on his shoulder; he hadn't yet made a sound.

"Please don't hurt him, Gitt. Hurt me, if you have to. Do anything you want to me. Just leave him alone, please."

He drove the needle in, yanking Peter back to consciousness, causing him to raise his hooded head and cry out.

"I'm waiting, Justice. Tell me your story."

"Benjamin? Are you there?"

"I'm here, Peter."

"What's happening? Why is he doing this?"

"Because he's a pathetic, self-loathing sonofabitch. Because he's so cold inside, so full of self-hatred, that inflicting pain is the only thing he knows how to do. Because he's a coward who can't face anyone who isn't submissive, under his control."

"I warned you not to insult my intelligence, Justice." Gitt's voice was calm as he glanced at me over his shoulder. "Tell me your story. Show me how smart you are. Or I won't be so gentle with your pretty blond friend."

He pinched Peter's other nipple to make it protrude, and drove the needle through. Peter's cry cracked against the close walls, and then again as Gitt pulled the needle out. Peter's head sagged forward onto his chest, his quickening breaths escaping through the hole at his nose and mouth. Gitt inserted the first ring, working it through the bloody nipple, while Peter hung motionless, accepting it.

"Entertain me, Justice, while I do my work."

"I think Taylor Fairchild started hanging out with you because he admired you. You were tough, physically strong, athletic, for all appearances a man's man. Everything Fairchild wasn't but longed to be. You got off on a meek and mild-mannered white guy higher in rank wishing he could be more like you, wanting to be your buddy. At the same time, you were a man in secret torment, a gay closet case, having to hide your sexuality in a department whose chief publicly ridiculed homosexuals. Your sense of personal power and self-esteem was further eroded by having to do the Uncle Tom routine in a department that was notoriously white and racist, from the top down. It twisted you all up inside, filled you with a slow-boiling rage."

Gitt worked the second ring through Peter's other nipple. I heard Peter draw in a sharp breath, but that was all.

"Keep going, Justice. I'll tell you when to stop."

"I don't know exactly how you and Fairchild happened to be in your undercover car that night. Maybe the two of you got together for drinks after work, had more than you could handle, then decided to go cruising for a faggot or cross-dresser to kick around. My guess is you talked Fairchild into it, to prove to him, maybe to yourself, that you couldn't possibly be queer. You wanted to forget who you really were for a while, take out your self-hatred on the most vulnerable person you could find, one who mirrored what you were, what you hated so badly."

"Not too original, Justice."

"But true nonetheless. Right, Gitt?"

He said nothing, so I went on.

"Fairchild went along reluctantly, not wanting to look weak. I don't know, maybe he was secretly queer himself. Maybe he was sucking your dick in the back of your unmarked car. Or maybe you were sucking his, hoping he'd help you win a promotion."

Gitt turned on me, tightening his right fist into a ball, drawing it back. Before he whacked me, though, he stopped himself, and smiled. I saw his fist relax.

"Clever, Justice. Trying to rile me up like that, get me to lose my cool. Draw my attention away from your beautiful boyfriend for a while."

"That's what happened that night, isn't it, Gitt? Things got out of hand. You got a taste of Winston Tsao-Ping's blood, and you went crazy. You might have killed him, except that Felix Montego showed up in his patrol unit and pulled you off."

Gitt licked his finger and drew an invisible stroke in the air.

"Very good, Justice. You get a gold star for deduction."

"Montego orchestrated the cover-up, saved Fairchild's ass and

yours. He even made sure Jacob Kosterman pulled the videotape
Byron Mittelman had shot and stashed it away where it would
never be seen. Since Montego worked in the Hollywood division,
like you, the two of you conveniently became the investigating
officers. Fairchild added his name and rank to the report, and
saw that it was buried. Winston Tsao-Ping gratefully disappeared,
and Fairchild continued his stellar career. Meanwhile, you just
got meaner, beating up suspects, piling up citizen's complaints
until the department had to get rid of you."

"Two gold stars, Justice."

He stepped back to Peter, and turned the steel bar a hundred
and eighty degrees.

"Finish your story, Justice. You're almost there."

"What's the point, Gitt? We're not getting out of here alive, are
we?"

"The point is, I want to hear the end of the motherfucking
story. That's what you writers are supposed to do, isn't it? Put all
the facts in nice, neat order so you feel better about things when
you're done."

"Let him go, Gitt. Do that for me and I'll tell you everything I
know, everything I've figured out. You've done enough to him
already."

"I'm in charge now, Justice. I decide what's enough."

"That's not the way S&M is supposed to work, Gitt. The way I
understand it, the slave has a right to state his limits. He has to
trust the master to respect those limits, to respect him as a person, to see him as something more than just an object of sexual
gratification. That's the basic tenet in your world, isn't it?"

"When I left the LAPD ten years ago, I left behind a world
where there was no respect for me. Not as a black man, not as a
queer. Every day when I went to work, in the locker room, behind
my back, somewhere, I heard the word nigger, or the word faggot. Even in front of me, I heard the word nigger, like I didn't
matter, or my skin was white, or I was invisible. So I created my
own world here, where I make the rules. Where I hand out the
humiliation, the pain. You understand now, Justice? You get how
it works?"

Gitt ran his hand over Peter's unmarked shoulders, down his
back, over his ass.

"So clean and pure, such a perfect canvas. The first time I saw this kid, when that Callahan guy interviewed me, my jaw just about dropped. Then, when I saw him at your place that day I drove by, and I knew where to find him, oh my, I just knew I had to have him, all for myself."

"Please, Gitt."

He sauntered to the wall, reached up without hesitating, and brought down a rattan cane. It was in the range of two to three feet, not quite a half inch in width, showing some flexibility as Gitt came back, slapping it against his hand.

"They call this one White Lightning. Imported from Singapore. Now there's a country that knows how to dish out punishment, how to keep the people in line."

He caressed Peter's buttocks.

"Take a good look, Justice. These'll never be the same again."

"Gitt, I'm begging you—"

"Cane strokes have to be done properly. It's an art form, really, an elegant craft. The strokes have to be delivered at well-chosen intervals, with real passion. All those sexually repressed English schoolmasters understood that. Interesting, isn't it, how the most civilized countries are so in love with simple instruments of torture, not to mention the bare male butt."

"Gitt, please don't."

He stepped back, took two quick steps forward, and lashed Peter across the ass. Peter clenched his fists, the muscles in his shoulders knotted, and from under the mask a slow, guttural groan rose from his throat.

Gitt waited half a minute, then delivered another blow, slicing open the skin. I heard Peter whimper, saw his muscles tighten as he braced for the next flash of pain. Half a minute later, he screamed as Gitt flailed him again, peeling back more flesh.

"No more, Gitt. For God's sake."

"The sooner you finish your story, Justice, the sooner I stop using my toys."

"Do I have your word on that?"

He swung his arm again, sending the cane whistling through the air, leaving a rising welt across Peter's thighs and another cry dying on the air.

"You got my word, motherfucker. Now talk."

He spun, and sliced Peter once more across the buttocks with tremendous force, much harder than before. Peter's head fell to the side and stayed there. I started talking.

"I'm guessing that Tommy Callahan recognized you as one of the cops on the videotape when he came to interview you about your views on bareback sex. Or maybe he knew about you already, because of his fetish for leather and bondage."

Gitt delivered another sharp blow across Peter's backside. Peter remained unconscious, and Gitt seemed to lose interest. He laid the cane on the table, tapped more of the crystalline powder into the spoon, and snorted. Then he reached up and pulled the mask off Peter's head. He grabbed a fistful of hair, and pulled Peter's head back.

"They don't come any finer than this, do they?"

Gitt's eyes had glazed over, and his speech was thick and slow. He twisted Peter's head and kissed him on the mouth. What I could see of Peter's face was intact, unmarked. When Gitt glanced in my direction, his own face was flushed with lust.

"You understand what I'm talking about, Justice. I made him tell me if he'd been fucked or not. So I know you had him."

"I didn't hurt him, Gitt."

"You used him for pleasure, though."

"Maybe. But I didn't hurt him. There's a difference."

"Now it's my turn to use him, for my kind of pleasure."

Gitt was stroking himself, getting hard. With his free hand, he held the vial of amyl under his nose, inhaling the vapors, groaning as his blood began to rush.

I spoke quickly.

"After Callahan recognized you, he made some kind of overture in private, letting you know he had the tape. By then, Fairchild was a front-runner for the chief's job. It was obvious he had powerful backers; a lot was on the line. If that tape was ever made public, broadcast on television, it would have ruined him. Callahan suggested that you act as the messenger, let Fairchild know the tape was for sale. Maybe he offered to cut you in on the deal. Listen to me, Gitt!"

Gitt looked over, halfway out of this world and into another, traveling on the crystal and the amyl.

"You double-crossed Callahan and cut a deal with Fairchild. He paid you to get the tapes from Callahan. That's why the autopsy reports on Callahan showed that he was tortured before he died.

He had to be persuaded to give them up, didn't he? Byron Mittelman, on the other hand, merely had to be eliminated, so he was taken care of with a single bullet to the head. Is that how it went down, Gitt?"

Gitt spit into his hand, lathered himself, and positioned himself behind Peter.

"You gave me your word, Gitt! I told you all of it, everything I know! You promised to stop, to leave him alone."

I saw a different smile this time, the hideous grin Cecile Chang had described to me, the one she still saw in her nightmares.

"I told you I'd stop using my toys, Justice." Gitt turned to show me his erect penis. "This is no toy."

"He's never done anything to you, Gitt. Why do you have to hurt him?"

"With pain comes pleasure. He'll learn that soon enough. Don't pretend you don't understand." He crossed to where I hung, and I felt his fingers close around me where I was stiff. "We're not so very different, you and I. Now are we, Justice?"

I spit into his face, hoping he'd turn his rage on me. Instead, he grabbed my head and kissed me hard, his rough beard scratching my mouth. Then he sauntered back to Peter and stood inhaling the poppers until he swayed unsteadily and had to put a hand on Peter's shoulder to steady himself. When he'd gotten his balance, he spit into his hand and lubricated himself again.

"Not bareback, Gitt. He's just a kid, a naive kid who wanted to get a taste of life, see what was out there in the world. He doesn't deserve this."

"It feels so fucking good without a condom."

His voice sounded small, distant, as if he were receding from me.

"I never hurt him, Gitt. That's the difference between you and me. I never exposed him to the virus, never raped him. I treated him like a human being. Like he was worth something."

Gitt wasn't listening. It was as if I wasn't there, as if nothing mattered to Gitt any longer except Peter, and Peter's rectum.

"Not bareback, Gitt! He's worth something. *You're* worth something!"

But Gitt was gone, reduced to nothing but sexual desire, with nothing beyond it that was human. Not intelligence. Not responsibility. Not empathy. Not a single feeling beyond the sensation in his body, in his cock and balls, beyond his narcissistic need. He was a man who felt no worth, so he was unable to see any worth in Peter. A man who had reduced himself to the piece of meat between his legs and felt compelled to reduce Peter similarly, to justify the coldness in his soul, the emptiness. It was all so clear to me now, what I had wanted to say in my script for Cecile Chang: Unless and until we could value ourselves in our entirety, we could never value others. It was an age-old problem, between men and women, parents and children, bosses and workers, rich and poor, whites and nonwhites. But among homosexual men, with AIDS in the equation, it was not just a matter of respect versus degradation, but of life and death. It was all so clear to me now, and all too late.

Gitt wrapped his right arm around Peter's waist, and began guiding his cock where he wanted it to go, until it began to pry apart Peter's bleeding cheeks.

Then a gunshot exploded, and I ducked as bullet fragments ricocheted off the floor and walls. Gitt went down, clutching his right leg, writhing, wailing through clenched teeth.

Sergeant Montego moved quickly across the cobbled stones, his revolver aimed at Gitt's head. It was an old-fashioned thirty-eight Detective's Special, the kind my father had carried twenty-three years ago before I'd used it to end his life. In his other hand, Montego clutched two videocassettes, which he placed on the table next to Gitt's pharmaceutical supply. He ordered Gitt to lie face down, and when Gitt failed to comply immediately, Montego kicked him viciously in his wounded knee, which got him moving. Seconds later, Gitt was sitting up against a pillar, his hands cuffed behind him, his eyes clamped shut, his face twisted with pain. I could see the full damage now: The bullet had made a small entry wound at the back, in the fleshy joint of Gitt's leg, but had exploded out the front, leaving an ugly, gaping hole, a mess of shredded tissue and splintered bone where Gitt's knee-cap had been.

Montego shouldered his gun, found a pocketknife, began cutting my ankles free.

"Winston Tsao-Ping called downtown, told them they had to get a message to me ASAP."

"Tsao-Ping called you?"

"That's how the caller identified himself."

"A voice from the past. He has good timing."

Montego nodded as he cut.

"The message was short and simple: 'Benjamin Justice has gone after Charlie Gitt. You'd better hurry.' I was at home when communications reached me."

"I hope they didn't interrupt anything important."

"My kids' homework. They didn't mind." Montego freed my feet and stretched up to cut the rope binding my wrists. "I don't know how you found Winston Tsao-Ping after all these years, or where he was calling from, but he saved your ass."

"So did you, Sergeant. Have I thanked you yet?"

"You can thank me by getting out of here and forgetting you ever met me."

"What about the videotapes?"

He grabbed me around the waist and eased me down. My pants and shoes were in a pile nearby, and I started pulling them on. Montego picked the tapes up from the table.

"These? *Pocahontas* and *The Lion King*. For my kids."

"That's not what the labels say, Montego. I see the words *On Patrol* and *transvestite beating*. That would be the master, I imagine. The other one's a copy."

"Let's ask Mr. Gitt. I've been meaning to, anyway." Montego turned and looked down at Gitt, whose face was sullen, contemptuous. "Charlie?"

"Fuck you, Montego."

"I came across these when I was searching for you and Justice upstairs. Are these the only copies?"

When Gitt said nothing, Montego drew his revolver, kneeled down, and pointed the muzzle directly at Gitt's genitalia.

"I could really mess you up, Charlie."

"You're going to kill me, anyway."

"Yes. But it can be easy or it can be very unpleasant."

Gitt looked away, swallowing hard. Several seconds passed that must have been very difficult for him. Then, in a subdued voice:

"Yeah, they're the only copies. Just the two."

Montego rose and handed me his pocketknife.

"Take care of your friend there."

I bent to cut the rope around Peter's ankles.

"You're working for Taylor Fairchild, then."

"Don't assume you know everything, Justice."

"Someone sent Gitt to take care of Callahan and Mittelman. If not Fairchild, who?"

"Gitt was supposed to pay for the tapes, that was it. He got the tapes, all right. But after he overheard Callahan on the phone, warning Mittelman, he decided to take out Mittelman as well, all on his own. Then, with things really messy and the stakes higher than ever, he decided to pull yet another double cross, sell the tapes to the highest bidder. He's been negotiating, right up until today."

When the ropes were off Peter's ankles, I rose and turned the bar so he was facing me. His head was to the side, still without movement. I reached up to work at the leather wrist cuffs, and Montego kept talking.

"When we got into business with Gitt, we didn't realize how far off the deep end he'd gone. No one was ever supposed to get hurt. You can believe that or not, Justice, but that's how it is."

"Fairchild's the one who benefits from all this."

"Taylor Fairchild is a decent man. He's going to make a fine chief. He'll be good for the city."

"A good cop who helped beat Winston Tsao-Ping half to death, then participated in a cover-up so he could get on with his career."

"He made a mistake, a long time ago."

"I imagine your career rises with Fairchild's, doesn't it?"

Montego didn't reply to that. Peter's hand and arm fell limply, and Montego held him up while I worked on the other wrist.

"Somebody has to be calling the shots in all this, Montego."

"That goes without saying."

"But you're not going to give me a name."

"The name doesn't really matter, Justice. We're all just pawns in a bigger game. The people who run the show, they don't have a name, not even a face. I get cryptic messages, phone calls from strangers in the night, attorneys maybe. I don't know who they are or who they work for. I don't want to know."

"So you become a part of the big lie."

"We're all part of it, Justice. They own us, the faceless, nameless people. Half the world's wealth controlled by one percent. That's how it's set up, how it works."

"And Taylor Fairchild's just another pawn?"

"Just another pawn."

"Pawn to queen, perhaps?"

"Why do you have to push it so far, Justice?"

"Fifteen years ago, when Winston Tsao-Ping was calling his mother from the hospital, you were calling Taylor Fairchild's mother, weren't you? Rose Fairchild knew how to take care of things, especially when it came to protecting her own. You called her again a few weeks ago, when you learned that Callahan had the videotape."

Montego's eyes were steady, untroubled.

"Your friend needs your help, Justice."

Peter came down, motionless but breathing steadily, and I caught him in my arms. Montego removed his jacket, emptied the pockets, and used it to cover Peter.

"How do you get through the day, Montego? As a cop, I mean? Knowing what you know?"

His eyes never wavered.

"By going home every night and kissing my wife, and playing with my kids, and tucking them safely into bed. By taking them to church on Sunday, and kneeling down, giving thanks and praying to God to protect them. That's what's real to me, Justice. The rest is just a big game, smoke and mirrors, completely beyond my control. Or yours."

I nodded at the cassettes.

"What happens to them?"

"These tapes don't exist. They never did."

"And Gitt?"

"Don't worry about Gitt. I'll take care of Gitt."

I glanced around, at the blood, the sex toys, the drugs.

"Could be messy."

"Callahan and Mittelman died at the hands of a sex deviate. The autopsy reports showed both men were sodomized. The evidence pointed overwhelmingly to Charlie Gitt. When I came here to question him, he tried to kill me. I defended myself."

"You're committing murder, Montego."

"I'm saving your life, and your friend's. I'm providing Melissa Zeigler with some closure. End of story."

I carried Peter up the cellar steps, out to the yard, and down the viny pathway past the dead dog. Peter started to come around and mumbled my name. I told him he was going to be all right, that we were going home.

Montego had sprung the big gate and left it open. As I passed through, I heard a single gunshot, and knew that Charlie Gitt was dead. My only regret was that I hadn't been there to watch him die.

Epilogue

AYLOR FAIRCHILD was sworn in as the new chief of police on the same day I was scheduled to receive the results of my HIV blood test.

By then, several other events had taken place. Peter's girlfriend, Cheryl, flew out from Minnesota, and took him home. With the *Los Angeles Sun* shut down, Roger Lawson accepted a position as the mayor's top public relations officer, and moved into a bigger office and better-paying position at City Hall. Katie Nakamura and her fiancé left for Portland to start a new magazine on the Internet. Alexandra Templeton went home to be with her parents and think about her future.

To my surprise, Cecile Chang called, offering me the opportunity to complete the revisions on my script and see it through production. I gratefully accepted although, in the end, PBS would consider my segment too controversial for broadcast, especially with my tarnished name attached, and would eliminate it from the series. Reporters continued to try to reach me with questions related to Templeton's *GQ* piece, and a producer or two even hinted at possible film projects, but I didn't return any of their calls. As for the article itself, I never did get around to reading it, and Templeton never brought it up again, although I did finally break down and tell her what had happened to me at the Reptile Den.

My appointment at the Jeffrey Goodman Clinic was on a Thursday at 4 P.M. I talked long distance with Templeton about it, then drove to the clinic alone, telling myself I was prepared for the worst but not really believing it. I took the elevator to the second floor, as before, and signed in, again using my numbered code for anonymity. A few minutes later, a young Filipino man with a round face and a wispy mustache stepped from an office and called out my code numbers in a neutral voice that troubled me.

I sat in a chair next to his desk. The office was so small, our knees nearly touched. He looked through the form I had filled out previously, and noted that my last test had been negative. He explained that my blood had been sent through two separate testing procedures—the ELIZA and the Western Blot—to rule out the chance of false negatives and false positives. The short time he took to explain these things, no more than a minute or two, seemed interminable. Worse, with all my previous tests, when the results had come back negative, the explanation leading up to the test results had not been so lengthy and elaborate.

Finally, he got to the point.

"I'm afraid the results of your tests are inconclusive."

"Inconclusive."

"One of the tests was negative, the other came back inconclusive. So we're unable to verify for certain whether your blood is clearly with or without antibodies at this point."

"What does that mean, exactly?"

"It could mean a number of things."

"Could it mean that I'm sero-converting?"

He hesitated, for half a second.

"It's a possibility."

"How much of a possibility?"

"I can't really put a statistical figure on it."

His eyes shifted uneasily. I didn't need a figure. I suddenly felt as if I were suffocating in the tiny office. I stood, and he stood with me.

"We'll need to take another blood sample, run the tests again."

"I think I'll wait a few months, if it's all the same. Enough time so the results are conclusive, one way or the other. I don't like jumping through these emotional hoops.''

"I understand.''

"Thanks for your time.''

"Just don't wait too long. With early treatment—''

"Thanks, I know the speech.''

I pulled open the door and went out, past men and women sitting on benches who all looked up, all studied me, to see if they could tell. There was fear in some of the eyes, stark fear, which I'm sure they saw in mine.

I walked briskly down the hallway, not looking anyone in the eye, and through a rest room door. I went straight into the stall, locked the door behind me, dropped my pants, and just made it onto the toilet seat as my intestines emptied themselves clean. It was a large stall, designed for wheelchair use, with sanitized white tiles on the floor and a screened window open on the far side for fresh air. Through the window, I could hear the sounds of the city. The rumble of car engines, a horn.

I'd never felt more alone, more afraid.

When I felt the walls closing in, and a strange voice speaking inside my head so fast I couldn't understand the words, I cleaned up and went out. I rode down in the elevator, avoiding more eyes. When the doors opened, I saw Oree Joffrien across the lobby, waiting for me.

I wanted to walk past him, to get some air, but he moved at an angle toward the door and blocked my path.

"Alexandra called. She thought someone should be here for you, just in case.''

"That was thoughtful of her.''

"It didn't go well, did it?''

"Is it so obvious?''

He nodded, and smiled sympathetically. I told him the exact results, that nothing was settled yet, that there was a small chance I wasn't sero-converting and the next tests might come back completely negative. He didn't say anything to that.

I took a deep breath, let it out slowly. Trying to pull myself together, trying to stop the speedy voices bouncing around inside my skull.

"It was nice of you to come, Oree.''

"I've been through this myself. I know how it feels.''

"Was someone waiting in the lobby for you?"

"Cecile."

We started walking, through the double glass doors, out to the sunny street. Oree put a hand on my shoulder.

"I think this is the point when you're supposed to ask me if my results were negative or positive."

"That's your business, Oree, not mine."

"Not if we're serious about seeing each other."

"Are we serious? Both of us?"

We were on the sidewalk, next to the Mustang. He stopped and faced me.

"I tested positive, Benjamin. Not quite four years ago."

I swallowed a lump in my throat, confused by my feelings, not sure if I was relieved or saddened by what he was telling me.

"Is that the secret you were holding back? The fact that you're infected?"

He nodded.

"That's why you didn't want to get involved too quickly?"

"I wanted to become friends first, Ben. Before sharing my secrets. Before becoming romantically involved. That's the way I've always been, even before I sero-converted."

"It was a lover who infected you then? Someone you were serious with?"

"We were a couple. We'd both tested negative. By chance, he was one of those rare people with advanced AIDS but no symptoms, who tested falsely negative because his system was no longer producing antibodies to the virus. It happens from time to time. Unfortunately, I got caught in one of those times."

"Tough break. I'm sorry."

"We thought we were safe as a couple. We got careless, foolish, assumed too much. I became infected, not long before he came down with pneumocystis."

"I take it he's gone."

He nodded. A truck rumbled by on the street and backfired, making me jump.

"I don't know what to say, Oree. Right now, things are—I don't know—up in the air."

"Worse than that, I imagine."

I tried to smile.

"Worse, yes."

"Could you use another friend, Benjamin?"

He held open his arms, and took me to him. His arms, his chest, everything about him, were strong. Yet he was unabashedly gentle, at ease with his humanity, his feelings. A man, in the true and complete sense.

"I don't know what's going to happen, Oree."

"None of us does, Ben. None of us does."

"I need some time."

"You're finally learning patience, then."

He was smiling as he said it, and the warmth of his smile washed over me, helping me to forget some of the coldness I was feeling. We stood holding one another for what seemed like a long time, until some of the turmoil inside me began to dissipate, and I felt my equilibrium coming back.

Oree asked me if I wanted to get an early dinner, maybe down in Little Ethiopia where we'd first met.

"Tomorrow, maybe. Right now, I have an errand to run."

"Tomorrow, then, if you still feel like it."

I climbed into the Mustang and pulled away, watching him wave in my rearview mirror until he was a speck in the distance. Fifteen minutes later, I was on Fairfax Avenue, driving south past the kosher bakeries and delicatessens, following Templeton's directions. When I saw the street sign I was looking for, I made my turn, and found the Golden Harmony Convalescent Home midway down a block lined with oaks and maples, and frail older couples shuffling along the sidewalks with small dogs.

The lobby felt cool and crisp as I entered, and smelled clean without seeming disinfected. I spoke to a woman behind a counter, who directed me to an inner office. There, another woman greeted me pleasantly and answered my questions politely. I was concerned about Harry's insurance limitations, about how we were going to pay for his long-term care, if it came to that. The woman called up Harry's file on her computer, then told me there was nothing to worry about, everything was taken care of.

"I don't understand."

"An attorney for Rose Fairchild came to visit us, Mr. Justice. Mr. Brofsky's bills are covered for as long as he needs to stay with us."

"Are you sure there's not some mistake?"

She scanned the computer screen again.

"No mistake. It's all right here. The bills are to be sent directly to Mrs. Fairchild's attorney."

I managed a smile.

"How thoughtful of Mrs. Fairchild."

I asked if it was possible to see Harry. The woman walked to the doorway and pointed toward the back of the building where glass doors opened into a garden courtyard. Roses bloomed in containers and water spouted up and splashed in a central fountain. I made my way past elderly people with walkers or in wheelchairs, hearing some Yiddish along the way. I'd never thought of Harry Brofsky as Jewish, but of course he was; he'd just never talked about it much that I could remember. There had been a lot Harry and I had never talked about.

He sat alone in the shade of a patio umbrella, propped up on pillows in a wheelchair, wearing yellow pajamas, a pale blue bathrobe, and white terrycloth slippers. I pulled up a chair, sat down beside him, and straightened his robe before retying it at his waist. His eyes moved in my direction, and settled slowly on mine, but that was all the response he made.

"You know what, Harry? They were right. Turning forty's a bitch."

I took his limp hand and held it. I'd never held Harry's hand like that, and I hoped he wouldn't mind. The longer I sat there, and the more I thought about it, I didn't think he would.